USA TODAY bestselling, RITA®-nominated and critically acclaimed author **Caitlin Crews** has written more than one hundred books and counting. She has a Master's and a PhD in English Literature, thinks everyone should read more category romance, and is always available to discuss her beloved alpha heroes. Just ask! She lives in the Pacific Northwest with her comic book artist husband, she is always planning her next trip, and she will never, ever, read all the books in her 'to-be-read' pile. Thank goodness.

New York Times and *USA TODAY* bestselling author **Jane Porter** has written forty romances and eleven women's fiction novels since her first sale to Mills & Boon in 2000. A five-time RITA® Award finalist, Jane is known for her passionate, emotional and sensual novels, and loves nothing more than alpha heroes, exotic locations and happy-ever-afters. Today Jane lives in sunny San Clemente, California, with her surfer husband and three sons. Visit janeporter.com.

A BILLION-DOLLAR HEIR FOR CHRISTMAS

CAITLIN CREWS

THE CONVENIENT COSENTINO WIFE

JANE PORTER

MILLS & BOON

First published in Great Britain 2023
by Mills & Boon, an imprint of HarperCollins*Publishers* Ltd,
1 London Bridge Street, London, SE1 9GF

www.harpercollins.co.uk

HarperCollins*Publishers*, Macken House, 39/40 Mayor Street Upper, Dublin 1, D01 C9W8, Ireland

A Billion-Dollar Heir for Christmas © 2023 Caitlin Crews

The Convenient Cosentino Wife © 2023 Jane Porter

ISBN: 978-0-263-30701-6

11/23

A BILLION-DOLLAR
HEIR FOR CHRISTMAS

CAITLIN CREWS

MILLS & BOON

CHAPTER ONE

LILLIE MERTON ALMOST missed the fateful newscast entirely.

She'd been faffing about in the kitchen of the shared house she'd lived in since university, washing the usual mess of dishes left in the sink no matter how many times she asked her housemates to tidy up after themselves, cleaning the surfaces because no one else could manage it—apparently—and fixing herself a bit of beans on toast as if that might take away the deep chill of a November in Aberdeen, Scotland. And once her meal was ready, she hadn't intended to go and eat it in the shared lounge, because the reality was that she hadn't been the least bit comfortable with her housemates since her pregnancy had started to show.

There had been house meetings without her and then house meetings with her, but in the end, everyone had agreed. Regretfully, or so they claimed, but the house was comprised of merry singletons. They were all much younger than Lillie, who had moved in here with her best mates from uni and had watched each and every one of them move out again as the years passed. To better jobs elsewhere, partners, marriages, madcap adventures abroad, and so on. Only Lillie remained, the decrepit thirty-year-old spinster who the newer housemates increasingly viewed as the de facto house mother.

Or had done until it was clear she was *actually* going to be a mother.

It was decided that the house was for young professionals who worked hard by day and liked a bit of a laugh by night. It was certainly no place for a baby. That was the verdict that had been delivered to her at the last house meeting with great solemnity, as if Lillie hadn't personally accepted each and every one of them into the house in the first place since hers was the name that had been on the lease the longest.

It wasn't as if she'd imagined she'd stay here in a house share with a wee bairn, thank you very much. She had as little desire to bung a cot and a changing table into her tiny bedroom as they did for her to parade an infant about through one of their Friday night drinking sessions before they went out to the city center bars and clubs. The same drinking sessions she always ended up cleaning up after even though *she* hadn't drunk herself legless in ages.

But no one liked to be *told* to leave, did they? Much less given an eviction date, and not very subtle threats that she would be chucked out if she didn't vacate on time—mostly because the ringleader of the younger set was dead set on having *her* best mate move in at the new year.

Needless to say, relationships had cooled all around.

Lillie was no longer cooking family-style meals for the lot of them or providing endless cups of tea and a sympathetic ear as needed. She rather thought they all regretted it. She'd seen more than one of the housemates mooning about, making big eyes in her direction while she—by far the best cook in the house, not that it was a distinction to be unduly proud of with this lot—made herself food for one and left them to their ready meals and boil-in-the-bag curries.

True, she was lonelier than she cared to admit, but at least she knew it was only going to be that way for a few more months. Then she would have a child to care for. She liked to tell herself living in this house with all these grown children was excellent preparation.

But that didn't make sitting in her bedroom and worrying over her fast-approaching future feel any better.

She didn't know why she stopped in the door of the lounge with her plate in hand, all that being the case. She *meant* to go straight on back to her room while it was still hers and settle in to watch videos on her mobile, while having a bit of the usual fret about her options.

Because she had options. It was just that Lillie wasn't sure she could face moving home with her parents in their quiet village. Lovely as they were, it had always been hard to live in the shadow of their grand, life-long love story—and she expected it would be doubly hard now that she'd gone and made it clear *she* would not be enjoying the same great passion as a single mum. She knew there was an extra room with her name on it in her cousin's place down in Glasgow, but she was trying to get her head around what it might be like not only to live with her very particular cousin Catriona, but what her child's life would be like under such a regime. In Glasgow, which was, according to everyone, including Lillie, far more metropolitan than home. Catriona called weekly to remind her the room was on offer, with babysitting on tap, and Lillie had always adored her persnickety cousin. That wasn't the issue. The issue was that this wasn't quite how Lillie had seen her life going.

Shouldn't have gone and gotten yourself up the duff then, auld lassie, she told herself stoutly.

And by that point she'd accidentally roamed far enough into the lounge that she could see the news program playing on the telly. Her housemate Martin fancied himself a man of the world when he was all of two and twenty, and his primary way of showing this was watching a bit of news every evening when no one else bothered.

Maybe later she would think about the series of tiny events and happenstance that led her to be standing there—beans and toast in hand, a little bit flushed of cheek from both the heat of the kitchen and her own enduring indignation at her ungrateful housemates—at the precise right moment to see the next segment as it began. A little bit of chatter from the anchor, and then there he was.

And even though he was on the screen of the communal telly in the same old house in Aberdeen where Lillie had lived for some eight years now, not even in person, it was the same as it had been five months ago in Spain.

She felt…transfixed. Rooted straight to the spot, but not by concrete or the like. It was as if electricity coursed through her, connecting her to the ground below, the sky above, and yet centering like one ongoing lightning strike inside her.

Lillie forgot to breathe. She forgot to do anything at

all but stare—though at least this time he wasn't watching her do it.

There was only fresh-faced Martin as witness, turning around from his place on the sofa to frown at her.

"Why are you lurking about?" he asked crossly, because he had always been fond of Lillie and was covering his embarrassment at her visible pregnancy with bluster. It didn't help that she knew *why*. It was still a lot of blustering. "You know it does my head in to have people stood about behind me."

As if the path from the front hall to the kitchen wasn't directly behind the sofa he liked to sit in.

"Wouldn't want to do your head in, Martin," Lillie had the presence of mind to reply, dryly enough so that she felt slightly less despairing of herself when she turned and left the room with no explanation.

She had no memory of moving through the house, hefting her pregnant bulk up the narrow stairs to her room and then locking herself in. So that she could stand there, back to the door, for far too long. Panting less from the exertion than her emotional response to *seeing him* after all this time.

When she had given up on the notion that she might ever see him again.

And then, plunking her little plate down on her desk and then forgetting all about it, she snatched up her mobile to look up the name she'd seen flashed across the screen.

Tiago Villela.

She might have stopped to think. She might have paused to *breathe*, even, but she didn't have that option because typing his name auto-populated her screen without her even having to hit the search button.

It was like her *bones* shifted inside her. And everything else along with them.

Her eyes had not been deceiving her, there in the lounge.

It was him. It was really and truly *him*.

And he was not, as she'd come to tell herself over time, a pool boy who'd wandered into that particular part of the resort and found her there by the pool bar. Credulous and overwhelmed enough at a glance to take him at face value when he'd said there was no need to exchange anything more than the attraction they both felt so keenly.

She had tried to get the resort to help her once she'd faced the truth about the odd stomach issues and malaise she'd been battling as summer turned to fall, but all she could tell them was that he was dark and tall, almost supernaturally compelling, and had swept her off her feet.

"I am afraid you have described approximately ninety-seven percent of the gentlemen in Spain, madam," the resort's front desk had replied at last. Sniffily.

They had even gone back to her room, not his, so she didn't even have any potential context clues to go on. She'd had to face the fact that she possessed no possible way of identifying him, much less dutifully informing him that he was the father of the baby she was carrying.

He'd been gone before she'd woken up that next morning and Lillie might not have done anything like that before in her life, but she'd told herself she was delighted that he wasn't there for any awkward conversations that might make him seem as human as anyone.

That way it had felt as if he was simply part and parcel of the Spanish adventure she'd never expected to have. She'd assured herself that she was *thrilled* that it was her happy little secret to keep.

She'd intended to keep it forever. Hoard it and hide it away, so she could enjoy all those blazing hot memories in the cold of Scotland that waited for her.

Alas.

Five months ago, she'd been set to have her usual chilly summer holiday. She normally spent a few days with her parents, wishing she could find that kind of love and life's purpose, then visited Catriona in Glasgow for a taste of the high life for a day or two. But as she'd been beginning to make her actual plans instead of daydreaming about, say, a flash holiday to New York City or the like that she would never *really* do, her longtime supervisor, the sleek and ferocious Patricia, had called her in all of a sudden one Tuesday morning.

Lillie had obviously assumed she was being summarily sacked.

Instead, Patricia had informed her that the company retreat had been moved at the last minute and Patricia had sadly already booked a week's holiday in Spain for the very same span of days. Lillie had then assumed that she'd be sent down to the dreary so-called retreat in Swindon in her boss's place because she couldn't imagine Patricia—shaped like a gazelle's front leg and sporting that jet black, always perfectly sleek hair—going without one of her precious weeks in the sun. Because Lillie had been Patricia's assistant for going on four years now and she'd shown up in her place before, if not at the same high executive level.

But that day Patricia had sighed and said that, sadly, her actual presence was required at Swindon and her assistant would not be able to fill in for her. She'd asked. What she wondered, she'd said then, was if Lillie might like to take her place in the pre-booked accommodation that Patricia would simply lose if she didn't use it?

"I would love to," Lillie had said frankly, "but I can't possibly pay for it."

Patricia had smiled in her usual way, a bit of a quirk of a closed mouth, nothing more. Her head had inclined slightly.

"You can consider it a bonus for your dedication these last years," she said. "One of us might as well have fun."

In the months since, Lillie had wondered what her boss's life—so seemingly glamorous from the outside—was actually like if her assistant was the only one she could think of to offer such a gift. Then again, the friends she knew of that Patricia had were as sharp and brittle as she was. She could see all too easily how Patricia might not wish to offer any of the lot of them any kind of gift of all.

For her part, Lillie didn't need to be asked twice. That was how she found herself in a flash resort in Spain for the most outrageous week of her life.

She hadn't *meant* to assume Patricia's identity. It was only that when she'd checked in, the staff had made that mistake and she hadn't corrected them. And then it had seemed as if pretending to be Patricia made everything that much more magical. Because while Lillie might not have gone ahead and taken part in the various activities offered of her own volition, she reckoned Patricia certainly would have.

So she did.

There were daytime excursions to Spanish sites, pools to visit, and boats to set sail on. There was dancing with strangers beneath the stars. There were yoga classes and massages, and Lillie indulged in them all. Because she was certain Patricia would have if she'd been there.

That was how she found herself slinking about in a bikini and a sarong on her last night there, as if she was the sort of person who wore such things, with her usually wild and unmanageable curly hair in a state of epic disarray that she'd decided was *a statement*. It had been one final and glorious evening in paradise. She'd gone to a cocktail hour gathering at the adults-only resort's prettiest poolside bar, so she could sip on the resort sangria that had helped keep her delightfully happy the whole week through.

One last night of glory, she'd told herself.

And that was where she'd met him.

Tiago Villela, who hadn't given her his name.

She stopped this little trip down memory lane, thanks to all the pictures of him on her mobile screen, because she needed a bit of reminding that she was still there in her same old bedroom in the same shared house in Aberdeen. Not in Spain again. Not sunburnt everywhere with freckles she'd never seen in the weak Scottish sun, her hair a mess of snarls and salt, more drunk on the sea air and soft breezes than the all-inclusive drinks.

Lillie wasn't surprised to find herself breathing a bit too quickly, her head going a little funny. That was how she'd felt then, too.

She went and sank down on her bed. And because she was alone, locked away from prying eyes and not required to make the best of anything, she let the full scope of the emotions that buffeted her take hold.

Because she'd pretended all this time that it had all been a bit of fun. Once she'd gotten the test results and had fully accepted that they were real, she'd understood at once that she would be keeping the baby. She had never considered any other path.

People would think whatever they would think, she'd told herself. And mostly it turned out that they thought she was seizing the only chance she'd ever have to be a mother—which was insulting—but then, so was the clear speculation on the part of every person she knew that she might have ditched the Spanish holiday altogether and got herself a turkey baster baby at a clinic. So impossible was it, her meanest housemate informed her, to imagine Lillie actually naked and having it off with a man.

"You're not really the sort, are you?" she'd asked pityingly, as if Lillie was making up stories. "It's horrible to think of it."

"Then perhaps don't strain yourself thinking about it," Lillie had replied, half laughing at the *affront* of it all from this girl whose hair she'd held back while she was sick after too many Saturday nights out to count. "If it's so *horrible*. Heaven forfend."

But she alone knew that her desire to be a mother had nothing to do with the spinsterhood that seemed top of mind to all and sundry. It was that it was *his* baby.

That they had made the child together on the most magical night of Lillie's life.

And once she understood that there would be no locating him, as if he been some kind of phantom she'd made up as the last, best part of her Spanish daydream, the baby she carried became that much more precious to her.

Because it was all she had left of him. All she would ever have.

She hoarded the truth to her like the treasure it was.

What did it matter to her if everyone thought she'd gone and got paralytic one night abroad to end up this way? Or that she'd forgone the notion of finding a man entirely and had visited a doctor's office to get herself pregnant, something her younger housemates clearly thought was shameful. She knew better.

Oh, how she knew better.

And when she was alone, she liked to go over the facts of that night. One moment after the next, committing each and every one of them to memory. Because every single second she'd spent with that man was like spun gold, each moment its own bright coin, and all of it was hers now to do with what she liked.

Mine, she thought, with a protective hand over her swollen belly.

"Mine and yours," she said out loud to the bairn within, because this was where she could be honest about Spain. Here in the safety of her room, though, she'd be giving even that up soon for the false smiles and forced laughter about her supposed behavior at her parents' or her cousin's.

Though she knew she was lucky to have choices, and hated neither one of them, she still wanted to hold on to *these* moments as long as she could. When it was just her and her memories and the baby they'd made tucked up safe and sound inside her. Healthy as could be, according to the doctor.

The truth was, Lillie had never made it to the bar that night because the moment she'd laid eyes on *him*, alcohol would have been superfluous at best.

He had been far more intoxicating, even at a glance.

And this was the truth that she could never tell a soul. Because no one would believe her. They would think her a sad cow, at best. They would imagine she was telling tales to preserve her pride, or some such thing. She could see it in her mind's eye, the way they would pity her. And it wasn't that she would have minded that too much, really, because she wasn't so dim that she didn't realize that far too many people in her life already pitied her.

It was more that what had happened that night felt sacred.

Because it was as simple and as complicated as this: she had looked up, and he had been there before her. There had been one split second before he saw her, when she had very nearly formed the dazed sort of thought that he was *astonishing*—

That rumpled, too-long dark hair. Those eyes, not green and yet not blue, like a sea too pretty to name. That *face* of his, an angel gone dark, with the fierce blade of a nose like some kind of ancient gladiator, God help her—

But then he had clapped his startled gaze to hers and it was as if everything that followed had been inevitable.

More than that, *magical*.

Lillie could no more have stopped it than she could flown over the moon with her own two arms as wings, and anyway, she didn't regret a bit of it.

She'd almost rather that everyone she knew dismissed

the whole thing as a drunken shag with some stranger, as tawdry and shameful and uncharacteristic as they could imagine. Better that than attempt to explain to them the unvarnished truth.

The weight of what had flared there between them had been almost too much to bear.

It still felt like that now.

Too much.

Too big.

Too intense.

It had exploded in that single glance, so suddenly, that she knew without a shred of doubt that both of their lives had changed forever in that moment. And more, that both of them had known that, right then, in the same flashing instant.

As if the world was divided into *before* and *after*.

Here in her bedroom, she replayed it in her mind the way she always did, as if it were new. As if it were happening all over again.

"Who are you?" he'd demanded, coming to her side and looking at her with an impassioned sort of *vividness* that had shaken her. She could feel it inside her now, as much a part of her as her own blood. Even then, when it was new, it had felt *right*. That he should frown down at her as if she was an apparition. As if he had found something he hadn't known he had been searching for. And as he came to stand before her, his closeness had felt like a gift.

Because he was there at last and though she had only seen him for the first time a moment ago, she felt as if he was still not close enough when she had waited *forever* for him.

"Who are *you*?" she had asked in return.

But neither one of them had answered that question.

They'd stood there, frozen in place, while people moved all around them. They stood there, rapt and amazed, breathing the same air that smelled of flowers and sweet salt.

Together at last, Lillie had thought, though that made no sense.

Lillie had known even then that she would never be able to explain the thing that bloomed between them, that feeling that her whole life had led her to this moment where they finally clapped eyes on each other. As if it had all been preordained. As if they'd been born for this, to find each other and hold on tight.

If she'd been swept up by the breeze itself and lost high above in the Spanish skies, forever, she would not have been at all surprised.

And in a way, that was precisely what had happened.

They didn't speak. They didn't laugh and get to know each other, flirt and dance and take part in the usual rituals of such evenings, according to every book she'd ever read and television show she'd ever watched. All of that would have made sense.

But nothing about that man made any sense.

It had been as if they had both been struck by the same lightning and had to stand there at the side of the pool in that resort, staring at each other in wonder, fascination, and a kind of panic, as they each tried to make sense of the way they burned.

Lillie could have stood there for lifetimes on end. It was possible she did, but didn't notice, because all she could see was him.

Until finally he had reached over, as if he did not quite trust his own hand, and had fit it gently to her cheek.

And then they'd both made the same sort of sound, a kind of sharp inhalation, and yet another bolt of that same electricity had shot through them both.

"I think," he said quietly, that voice of his dark and deep and tinged with flavors she could not identify, "we should take this somewhere private, *benzinho*. Yes?"

"Yes," Lillie had breathed.

And she had said that again and again and again that night. *Yes.*

Yes, yes, yes.

And now, lying on her bed, she felt a great sob work its way through her, though it wasn't quite grief. Or a darker sort of joy. It wasn't even sorrow. It was all of those things and none of them, because she knew his name now.

She knew his name.

The next day at work, she put together the latest presentation so that Patricia could take charge of her noon meeting with her usual ferocious competence that made the men she managed call her *the dragon lady*, not quite behind her back.

And while Patricia held court in the boardroom, Lillie did a bit of a deep dive on Tiago Villela.

Last night it had been enough to look at pictures of him, confirm that she had not been drunk on sangria, and get a general sense of the man. That he was no pool boy. He was powerful. He was enormously, almost absurdly wealthy. She had believed those things on the night, but as time passed and he had been unidentifiable, she'd tried to convince herself that she'd made it all up.

If anything, she had underestimated exactly how wealthy and powerful he really was.

But she wasn't interested in his net worth. She was far more interested in his location.

Because, she told herself piously, he deserved to know that he had a child on the way.

It had nothing at all to do with the fact that she wanted—desperately—to see him again.

Or so she tried to convince herself as she sat at her desk, pretending to be thinking only of her unborn child.

It took a little digging and a few carefully placed phone calls, once again pretending to be people she was not—namely, the secretary of a specific, higher-placed woman in her organization, because she doubted very much that a man like Tiago Villela could be found by anyone socially if he didn't wish it.

And that was how, in the space of an hour and a half, she discovered not only that Tiago Villela was currently at his London headquarters but that he would remain there for the remainder of the week.

Once she knew that, it wasn't terribly hard to ring down to London and manage to set an informational meeting with him—and the woman she was not—to take place the following afternoon. Because Tiago Villela was apparently well known for taking meetings that would normally go to his underlings. He liked to hear some cold calls and pitches himself—but only on select Wednesday afternoons when he was in the office and had no raging fires to put out elsewhere. That had been the point of the news segment on him. His surprising *accessibility*.

And once she'd secured the meeting, she found herself looking, almost regretfully, for the next cheap flight south because the sleeper train would take far too long.

"I beg your pardon?" Patricia asked in astonishment when Lillie informed her of this upon her return from the meeting. "You're leaving in the morning? Are you mad?"

"Not *mad* as such," Lillie replied. "Though I am pregnant."

And maybe there was something wrong with her that she found it amusing, the way Patricia let her gaze travel down the length of her body to her bump, then back up.

"I just thought you'd gotten fat," Patricia said, with her usual directness that Lillie had come to find refreshing. It was such a pleasant change from her housemates' typical passive-aggressiveness.

"I have," Lillie agreed, tapping her round belly with a laugh. "But not from too many sweets, I'm afraid." But there was no time to laugh. She had a plane to catch in the morning.

Because it was the right thing to do, as she kept telling herself. That was all.

"I finally tracked down the father, you see. And this is my chance to let him know. So he can be involved in his child's life, if he wishes."

Patricia had eyed her for a moment, looking almost wise—and far kinder than usual. It put a lump in Lillie's throat.

"I certainly hope he's someone you can stomach having in your life, then," Patricia said, almost gently. "And the child's life, for that matter. I've personally never met a man who would be worth the bother. You could also…not trouble yourself with a bloke at all, surely? In this day and age?"

"It's the right thing to do," Lillie said.

Virtuously.

Patricia only looked at her, for a moment that stretched on far too long. "Right. Well. Better you than me, my girl."

Lillie thought about that a lot as she boarded the plane, with only a measly carry-on bag she still had to pay extra for. She thought about that when she landed in Heathrow Airport, heaving with people, and had to work out how to get herself where she needed to go on the legendary Tube.

It was all a bit much for someone who had taken precisely one school trip to London, long ago.

She turned it all this way and that inside of her, the way she'd been doing for months, as she walked down gray, cold streets and got turned around, then had to retrace her steps. And when she finally reached the right building and went inside, it wasn't much better.

Because this was a different sort of before-and-after moment, she knew. She explained to the security guards that she had been sent to step into a meeting for her boss at the last moment, showed her work identification, and was directed to the gold-edged lift that offered only one stop—the very top floor.

As the elevator rose, taking her closer and closer to a lightning strike once again—or, maybe, no lightning at all, and she could admit she wasn't sure how she'd handle *that* if it happened—she slid her hand down over her belly, held on tight, and tried to get her pulse to settle.

"I think this is the best thing," she said aloud, and

pretended she was talking to the baby inside her instead of to herself. "I really do. It's the right thing to do no matter what happens now."

And when the lift doors slid open, she walked out into a marble lobby and felt nothing short of dizzy at all the understated—and not so understated—opulence.

It took every scrap of willpower she had not to turn around and leg it back to Aberdeen as fast as she could. She didn't belong here. She didn't know what to do with all this obvious wealth beaming down from chandeliers better suited to castles, by her reckoning, marble for miles, and everything gilt-edged and gleaming.

But she was to be a mother soon enough and so it didn't matter if she, personally, was brave. She couldn't let that matter. What mattered was what she did to make her child think he or she could be, too, and it started here.

So she took a deep breath, fixed a smile on her face as she announced herself to reception, and prepared herself for another lightning storm.

One way or another.

CHAPTER TWO

WHEN HIS OFFICE door opened, Tiago Villela glanced up from a typical afternoon of paperwork between meetings and froze.

"Impossible," he bit out.

He was rising, then, without thought. His gaze was fixed on the face of the woman who stood just inside his office, as if she was a ghost.

Was she a ghost?

But her eyes were too big and too blue, just as he remembered. Just as he'd replayed in his head so many times since. He had seen them hot with need and bright with laughter, but he knew them even now, far more cool and solemn, and yet too filled with life to be anything like *spectral*.

He would know her face anywhere. A narrow oval, no longer bright with too much sun or sprinkled with freckles on either side of her nose, each and every one of which he had tasted and committed to memory. Today she looked pale, and paler still as she stood there and regarded him with such determination. But most of all, he recognized that hair. Her riot of dark blond and brown spirals was far more subdued today than he remembered them, but still clearly *hers*. For he could still feel the soft coils against his palms, having held her tight with his fingers sunk deep in her curls while he'd driven into her again and again and again—

God, the ways this woman had *haunted* him, ghost or memory, did not bear thinking of in the light of day.

"Your name is not Patricia MacDonald," he grated out. "Your room was in her name."

And he was Tiago Villela. He had inherited fortunes from both sides of his family and made his own to match. His name was whispered in corridors of power and invoked in corporate boardrooms from London to Hong Kong, then back again. He had no need to waste his talents playing games like poker, no matter how sweet the pot—not when there were corporate negotiations with far higher stakes that he could win.

And did.

All that and yet he—praised far and wide as a man who might as well have been a glacier, with whole winters running through his veins—had given away his obsession with this woman without even being prompted.

He expected her to look triumphant, as people in his world so rarely did in his presence, but she floored him by smiling instead.

As if he was still deep inside her.

"At least you had a name to go on," she replied, and it was that voice again. *Her* voice. Slightly husky and shaping words in a way that sounded like music to his ears. That same voice that seemed equal parts sex and laughter, like a punch in the gut. And a much harder sucker punch lower still. "I thought you were the pool boy."

Tiago was certain that every member back down

along his ancestral lines, Spanish and Portuguese alike, had a bit of a communal roll in their assorted mausoleums at that.

But he couldn't seem to muster up the appropriate level of outrage.

Not when he could feel his heartbeat inside his chest like it was fighting to get out and more, had a decent chance of winning. The whole of his body had gone taut and wild, as if he was still in that appalling hotel in the part of Spain he usually tried to avoid—overrun as it was by entirely too many tourists—after concluding a wholly unsatisfactory business meeting. He could still remember it entirely too well. One moment he had been annoyed beyond reason at the waste of his time and the next he'd been captivated by her face. That impossibly compelling *face* that he had spent a great deal of energy since convincing himself could not possibly have been real.

Because he had not been able to find her, and that was an unacceptable outcome, so it had been much preferable to imagine he'd perhaps allowed himself to be overserved in the hotel bar that night. He, who never allowed that kind of loss of control. He, who had never had trouble maintaining a grip on reality in all his days.

Still. These were the things he had attempted to convince himself, and staring at her now, *right here in his office*, he understood why.

If anything, she was even more compelling than he'd allowed himself to recall.

"I looked for you," he told her, his voice darker now. Almost as if he was straying into the realms of temper, when he did not typically allow himself such indulgences. It was that *face* of hers. He could not imagine how she lived a whole life somewhere, walking around just…*looking* like that, without a warning label. It was unconscionable. "It was apparent at once that you did not use your own name."

"You can't have looked too hard, then, can you," she replied, cheerfully enough, as if that changed the fact that she was insulting him. "Since I work with the real Patricia MacDonald. It was her holiday, you see. She pre-booked. And who was I to argue when everyone kept calling me by her name?"

"I looked for you," he said again, and this time it felt like a relief to feel the stirring of what he assumed was temper, somewhere deep within him. Because that felt right in these unprecedented circumstances. It felt more like him, at any rate. Because he was not a man who ever *felt* much of anything around women. They came and went like hours in the day, and he thought as much of them when they were gone.

For his had always been a life of duty and accomplishments, not dissolution and selfishness. The Villelas were not raised to rest on their laurels. No idle sons of wealth cluttered up *his* family tree. While there might have been a questionable cousin or status-obsessed great-uncle on his mother's more easygoing side, the Villelas had produced generation upon generation of heirs who knew full well that their role upon this planet was to act as steward of what had come before as well as the legacy and nobility of the Villela name. And more, that the power that name wielded should only and ever be used for good.

It was true that some of his forebears had looked

for some wiggle room in that last directive, but Tiago wasn't one of them. He had always taken his responsibilities seriously.

And in all that time, this woman was the only thing that had ever worked its way beneath his skin, like a sharp bit of wood that wouldn't come out. He had not forgotten her. He had not spent a single night since meeting her without wondering where she was.

She had made him do things he would have sworn he would never, ever do, or even conceive of doing— like send one of his men to a dreary oil-industry-adjacent conference in Swindon to intercept a woman who didn't exist.

"Right name, wrong face," he'd growled when they'd sent him a shot of the wrong woman.

And had not liked how difficult that was for him to accept when he had not exactly furnished her with his contact details that night.

He realized that he was staring at her—at that impossible face of hers that he had imagined, and taken apart, and imagined anew too many times to count in the months since the night they'd shared.

"How did you find me?" he asked in the same dark manner, because she didn't need to know anything about what had happened since that night. Only that they hadn't exchanged names. But as she looked back at him, he knew the answer. "That news program."

He said it with something near enough to disgust, though that wasn't his prevailing feeling in this moment. It was only that this was too unsettling, after so long. It was too much. He had too many memories as it was and he didn't want them.

Or maybe it was that he had given up on this particular wish and yet here it was, granted all the same.

It made him feel…unsteady.

And Tiago was a Villela. He was made to be a mountain, as solid as sheer rock with high, proud peaks. He was bright with impassable snow.

He was not *unsteady*.

And yet.

"The news, yes," she agreed. And was that the faintest hint of color on her cheeks? "I caught the program quite by accident."

"But I am meant to be meeting with a representative of…" He trailed off, because he hadn't committed the name to memory. He would now, however, assuming… "Is that your real name? Whatever name you used to make this appointment?"

Her cheeks took on a bit more color. "Julieta Braithwaite really is a vice president in the company, but I'm not her."

"So these are more games. You hunted me down off a news program to turn up and continue the pretense." Tiago reminded himself that despite the night they'd shared and the fact that it had felt more like a reunion than a first meeting, he didn't know this woman at all. Why should he think less of her for these games? Why should he have any opinion about her at all? Still, he kept going. "Why?"

And for the first time, either that night or today, he thought she looked uneasy. "That's a bit of delicate matter."

It was only then, as her hands went to the wide collar of the great, shawl-like thing she wore as a coat, that he actually stopped staring at the face that had haunted his fondest dreams for so long. And took a look at the rest of her.

Even before she'd finished opening up her coat, he could see that there were changes in her body. Her breasts were so full now he felt certain they would overflow his large palms. And below, the soft belly he recalled so perfectly looked hard, high, and round.

Very much as if she was…

He became aware of harsh breathing, but he could not tell if it was hers or his. Letting his eyes move over the clear evidence he could see before him, it was clear that his mind wished to reject what he saw. To assert that he could not have been so reckless. To tell himself that he must have made certain this could not occur.

But she was wearing a soft dress that clung to her body as he had, once, and there could be no mistaking it.

The woman was pregnant.

The repercussions of that seemed to fall through him like all that hard, snow-covered stone he had only just been thinking about.

"Right," she said with forced brightness. "I see you've guessed my happy news. Well. I was prepared to make a go of it on my own. I think that's important for you to know. But I also thought that it was the moral thing to inform the father either way. I called the hotel and tried to give them some sort of description that would lead to your name, but they couldn't help me."

"I was not a guest of the hotel," he said, prosaically. "I was there for a meeting."

Because nothing at all made sense, and he could only keep staring. As if waiting to laugh at whatever joke this was that she was pulling here, even though something in him knew full well that was not likely to happen.

"Ah," was all she said.

And he was aware of her in that same overwhelming, impossible way he had been in Spain. He could see her pulse beat in her throat. He could see how each breath she took made her breasts move. In the whole of his life, he had never found a woman ripe with child to be anything but an object of distant interest, unrelated to him in any way, but this woman was something else. He could feel his sex stir as he looked at her. At all that *roundness*. At the changes her body had undergone already. Everything about her fascinated him and made his hands itch to discover how each and every bit of newness stood up to his memories.

As if she was his when she was not.

When he did not want any woman to be *his*, not like that, with all that need and longing and the sort of mad passion that ruined men entirely.

"I was weighing up my options," she told him, speaking into that loud, ringing silence between them. "But I really do think the best course of action is to take the spare room in my cousin's flat in Glasgow. She likes bit of company, mine in particular, though she can be a fussy, *fykie* sort. And she's quite committed to staying single as well, so between the two of us I reckon we can make our own family." She swallowed, as if this was hard for her when it didn't sound as if it was. Just as she had that night, she talked to him as if he was a regular man. As if they were already in the middle of a conversation and could pick it up and put it down as they chose. But he did not wish to be charmed by her.

Not now. "Still, when I saw you on the telly I knew that regardless of any plans I might or might not have made, I had to do the right thing."

He moved closer then, and though what he longed to do was run his hands over that tempting bump of hers, he refrained. That felt too intimate. As if it would be straying too far into the realm of something he couldn't take back. Some terrible longing he did not wish to face.

As if this mattered in ways he did not wish to acknowledge. Already.

Still, something in him corrected.

He ignored it, reaching over and taking her chin in his hand. And he could feel the sharp little breath she took, as if she could feel that touch the same way he did. All of that instant heat, like a flash that illuminated them both.

"Your name," he commanded her, in a voice that sounded nothing at all like his. "Tell me your name."

"Lillie," she whispered back, her eyes like the sky in the lands he was from and nearly as wide. "Lillie Elizabeth Merton. Lately of Aberdeen, Scotland."

Many things surged in him then. Memories of that night when Tiago had acted so unlike himself that it had haunted him ever since.

Though he could admit, now, that he had also allowed himself a measure of relief that it really had been as if he'd created her in his own mind. As if he'd dreamed the whole thing, after all.

Only now did he understand what a gift that had been.

Because he had no place in his life for this. For *her*. For that unquenchable fire that had swept over both of them on that poolside terrace in Spain and had been firing sparks at him from his own, treacherous memory ever since.

He made himself let go of her chin, because the touch of her skin radiated through him, making him question everything he'd ever thought about what he would and would not accept. Who he would and would not allow himself to become.

What he was even capable of feeling.

"Lillie," he said, as if tasting the name.

And he set aside all of the things he should have told her then. About who he was. About what his family had always expected of him. What the weight of his legacy meant and what he did to manage it.

These things that could not change, that would not change as long as he lived, and yet all he could seem to do was repeat her name.

Like some kind of prayer of deliverance.

When he knew better.

Villelas cannot be men of passion, his quietly stern father had told him many years ago. *It is not who we are. It is not what is expected of us. We must hold ourselves to a higher level. We must exhort ourselves to become a credit to our bloodline. Your mother is my bride because her family is like ours and thus she understands the traditions that shape and guide us. Because of this basic understanding, there is nothing in our relationship that could ever threaten our dual legacy. Do you understand?*

Tiago had not been raised to entertain the sort of feelings that felled so many of his peers. The only person he had ever loved, and who had loved him back, was the grandmother he'd lost when he was young—and he had quickly learned what a liability that was. What a terrible carnage grief was, on the inside.

And so he comprehended what his father had been telling him all too well now.

Lust. Passion. Greed. These were things that led venal men to murder and great men to stumble, but he would not allow any of them to do such things to *him*. He had always handled his body's needs with women who understood there was nothing more to be had from him than the fleeting pleasure they shared. He took pains to never, ever let greed dictate his decisions. He treated the power in his name like a kind of volatile poison that could kill him as easily as it could gain him anything, and there was only one night in his entire life he had ever risked any of it.

He would not do it again.

Tiago did not trouble himself with emotion, passion, or any of the things that made humans act so contrary to their own interests. He did not need to learn his lessons more than once.

He should not have required the reminder.

And so even though it felt a bit too little, too late, he stepped back then. He looked at Lillie for a long moment, then reached around her to open up his office door.

"Caroline, if you please," he said to his secretary in the next room, "have the plane waiting for me. And cancel the rest of my day."

That was unusual, but the unflappable Caroline had been with him for over a decade, and she did not so much as blink. "Right away, Mr. Villela."

"You could have sent a letter," he said to Lillie when he closed the door again, and he told himself it was only right that he let his gaze go cool and assessing. Not only was it right, but it also felt far more rational that he could trust himself to take one look at her without the whole world getting knocked back on its axis, for a change. "Instead, you chose to come in person. To my place of business, under an assumed name. In a pretty dress, no less."

She blinked, and looked down at her dress. "It seemed like the sort of thing people wear in giddy London." She ran her hands down the dress as if she'd only just seen it for the first time, then looked back at him, her eyes sparkling. "Is it not? I wouldn't want to seem a Scottish country mouse. Not while informing a man that he's the father of my baby. That would be a tragedy, I'm sure."

And he really, truly could have done without the reminder that she was this charming. That she alone seemed so capable of charming *him*, when no one else had ever seemed to possess the faintest shred of the ability.

"We are going to have to come to terms, you and I," he told her, channeling his father's deliberate sternness.

Her eyes did not dim, precisely. But she did hitch her chin up a notch or two, so in the end, perhaps it was the same thing. "I don't know what sort of terms you mean."

"There will have to be tests. I mean no disrespect, but I'm sure you understand that we must both be certain."

That time, there was no question that she looked dimmer, and it was shocking to him that he disliked it. Intensely. "Do you mean a paternity test?"

"*Benzinho*, you know who I am now," Tiago said. Kindly, he thought. "You cannot imagine that a man in my position can simply take it on faith when told he is unexpectedly a father, can you?"

But he could see by her crestfallen expression that she had imagined exactly that. And he held back from letting himself get cold and cutting with her, as he knew he could. It would be easy enough to make it abundantly clear that he had earned every bit of his glacial reputation, but this woman was different.

Because as much as he wanted to imagine that she was a scheming, naive fool to come here and think he would simply believe her, he knew better. That long night they'd shared and the connection between them was something he still couldn't begin to puzzle out.

But he did not need to tell her that, either.

Tiago waited until her shoulders seemed to deflate, and then nodded. "I will call my personal physician from the car."

He thought she might argue then, but all she did was look at him as if he was coming into focus—but slowly—until he felt something in him lose its place.

A sensation he could not say he cared for in the least.

"Take all the tests you like," she said after a moment, her voice huskier than before. Quieter. "But I shouldn't like to miss my return flight to Aberdeen, if at all possible."

And Tiago had not become the man he was, in this position he enjoyed, by engaging in unnecessary arguments. Even before the tests came back, he had made up his mind.

He did not share that, either. He knew it made no sense, and that in all other areas he was seen as the soul of prudence and circumspection. The world was filled with scheming people, men and women alike, forever running their little cons to better their positions. To change their lives. To get a little more and leave others with a little less. He'd seen it all in his day—and there had always been various attempts to wrap him up in such webs, too. It came with the territory.

But he was not at all surprised when the paternity test came back with the indisputable proof he hadn't needed, because he already knew that he intended to keep her.

That was the troubling thing about Lillie.

If he'd had his way, even five months ago when he hadn't been looking for anything but a car to take him away from that loud, garish resort, he wouldn't have left her.

Lillie. Her name lilted inside him like a melody. It was both not at all the name he would have chosen for her and at the same time, perfect. Even the way she spelled it at the doctor's office—not quite a flower, but something else. Something *her*.

"I hope you are not too distressed by the news," she said in that arch, Scottish way of hers when they were back in his car and his driver was making his way through the typical snarls of London traffic.

He should have expected the question. He wasn't sure why he hadn't. "*Distressed* is not the word I would choose."

"This is slightly disappointing," Lillie confided in him, once more as if they were the best of casual friends. "I expected at least a few accusations of whoring myself about before the results came in. Some thundering on, at the least. You seem to be accepting this rather easily. I thought men in your tax bracket were forever ranting on about bloodlines and legacies and all the rest of it. *The shores of Pemberley polluted* and so on."

And he remembered this, too. That in places where other people, and specifically other woman, might cower—Lillie had done the opposite. She got very dry. And amused. And there was something about both of those things that he found entertaining, when he had been told a thousand times by business associates and romantic assignations alike that he was bereft of even the faintest nod toward any kind of sense of humor. Something he had always chosen to wear as a badge of honor, because he was a Villela. He had things of import to accomplish in this life. Laughter was the province of the weak. He couldn't recall ever seeing his father or mother do more than offer a genteel smile.

It was one more thing that was different with this woman.

Maybe it was in that moment that the decision he'd already made firmed into certainty.

"Until now you have perhaps not had a particularly good overview of my character, I think," he told her then. "As you imagined me some kind of pool boy Lothario, of all things. But I hope I have never been the sort of man to deny reality when it is right there before me."

She looked as if she wanted to say something to that, but didn't. Her blue eyes found his, then dropped, and he found himself transfixed by the way she moved her hands over the rounded swell of her belly.

Tiago had never wanted to touch anything as much as he wanted to touch her, then. It was as if wanting his hands on her was some kind of ache within him. And he was forced to face the fact that he was not used to wanting things he could not have. For all he liked to think of himself as a man who was somehow not out of touch with the real world, despite his wealth and power, perhaps he had been fooling himself about that all along.

But he remembered too well what it had been like to lie with this woman on that bed in Spain. To explore every part of her, and let her do the same in return, and lose himself somehow in a communion that should never have affected him the way that it did.

He had not felt out of touch that night. He had felt, for the first and only time in his life, not like a Villela at all—but like a man. A regular, red-blooded man, who wanted her.

Only her, in every possible way the two of them could imagine.

But he forced himself to thrust those memories aside.

He did not reach over and touch her, though the more he yearned to do it, the more stern he was forced to get with himself. Because the way forward was clear, as he had discovered long ago. It would require self-control on his part, but that had never been something he had struggled with before—self-control was how he'd survived his childhood after his grandmother had died. His self-control was the only part of him that his parents had ever praised, and therefore he had made certain he exerted it over all aspects of his life.

A bit of deprivation was good for a man's character. Tiago was living proof.

Surely all that was needed with Lillie was a bit of exposure therapy to weaken this hold she had on him, that was all. All he needed was to banish the ghost of her and focus on the real, live woman instead.

Because it was her memory that had haunted him.

The reality of her would not—he knew this, because no real woman ever had.

And once he vanquished this *pull* she exerted on him, he would be himself again. Perfectly capable of what was necessary.

That was what he wanted. Not those haunting memories that kept him up in the night, dreaming of things that could never be.

He did not touch her, but he turned so that he could face her, there in the back of the car. "It must have been difficult to get used to this notion that you are to become a mother, I imagine."

"There was a bit of denial at first," she agreed, with that astonishing frankness that he hadn't the slightest idea what to do with. "But I've come round."

He was not sure that he had ever seen anything quite as remarkable as this woman who he thought he'd lost forever smiling at him the way she did then, her hands folded gently over the mound of the child she carried.

His child.

His child.

But that, too, was neither here nor there.

"All I ask is that you allow me the chance to *come round* to it as well."

She inclined her head then, as if she was royalty. He should have found her gauche and presumptuous, he who had squired princesses on his arm. But he did not.

He really did not.

"You have a fair few more months," she said, her eyes gleaming. "I expect you'll catch up."

He wanted to laugh, but he was not that sort of man, so he frowned instead. The very soul of the exacting

Villela code of conduct that his parents had modeled for him from the start. He was just as happy neither one of them was here now to see how he'd fallen short.

"I will need this time to get to know you as well, Lillie," he told her. Reprovingly. "As something more than a bit of pleasure." And he knew, when he saw the flash of emotion in her gaze, that she didn't like to call what had happened between them something so dismissive. And more, that he had called it that for precisely this reason. "For you are now the mother of the Villela heir, like it or not. And both of us will have to come to terms with that."

CHAPTER THREE

LILLIE HAD NEVER been to Portugal before.

But then, Lillie had never really been *anywhere* before, not really, aside from London that one time. She'd otherwise remained in Scotland for the most part, with only the occasional trip down to Whitby with her parents to spend a few cold summer beach days in that holiday caravan park they liked so well.

Her trip to Spain had been the start of a glorious new international *jet-set* kind of a life. That was what she'd told herself all the way home, still sunburnt and buzzing and half-wild from her night with Tiago. Spain was the *beginning*, she'd told herself as the plane landed in drizzly, bleak Aberdeen. The future was going to feel just as magic as that long, lush night had done.

She'd meant it. She really had. But thus far her glorious jet-setting had been confined to daydreams and bright, happy travel documentaries. Then she'd discovered she was pregnant and such things seemed even more out of reach than they'd been before. Because all it took was one positive pregnancy test to start thinking a lot more seriously about the reality of…well, everything. Such as the things she'd put off thinking about for ages, like why she was still living in a house better suited to new university graduates. Or what she really and truly wanted to do with her life, which she was pretty sure wasn't making PowerPoint presentations.

The trouble was, all of that felt like a fight and Lillie had never been much for fighting. That seemed part and parcel of the sort of passion her parents enjoyed, but had missed *her* little life entirely.

Sometimes she even told herself that a small, comfortable life was a virtue.

But nothing about this day was small or comfortable.

And Lillie was not at all prepared to be swept out of Tiago's car on a rainy, blustery tarmac somewhere outside of London, then ushered up the steps to the private jet that waited there like it was the most ordinary thing in the world when it certainly was no such thing.

It was all she could do not to gape about her like the overset, overawed country lass she most assuredly was.

And it had not been a long flight, but it had certainly been eye-opening.

Just like his office, the plane was a pageant of gleaming marble mixed in with the liberal application of rich, dark woods and lashings of plush, inviting leather besides. There were *couches* littered about the place like it was a high-class lounge in the sort of desperately posh and unaffordable flats Lillie only looked at in magazines. And in case anyone was feeling peckish there was a full cream tea service with plate after plate of clever little sandwiches cut *just so*, airy crumpets with pots of butter and jam, and scones drowning in clotted cream that tasted of dreams come true.

Lillie had three, just to be certain.

It was all a far cry indeed from the tiny packet of

overly dry pretzels she'd had to pay for on her desperately uncomfortable flights to and from Spain and down from Aberdeen this morning. Bargain airfare, after all, was about efficiency, not comfort.

Tiago's jet was nicer than any home Lillie had lived in.

It was nicer than any home she'd ever *been in*, for that matter.

Tiago had left her to her tea, retreating to what one of the stewards called "the office suite," to be distinguished from "the staterooms," to handle some of his business. Leaving Lillie to scoff scones and tea and darling little *petits fours* and reflect upon the fact that she hadn't objected when he'd suggested she not go back to Aberdeen at all.

"Not when there is so much to sort out between the two of us," he had said in that way of his that made everything inside her feel light and shivery. Especially when he had looked at her bump, in a way she wanted to call almost...possessive. It had made her heart flip inside her chest. "Excuse me, I mean the three of us."

The man was a menace.

But apparently she didn't think he was *too much* of a menace, because there she was. Lounging about on an achingly lovely leather couch on a plane she reckoned was nicer than some of those old medieval castles with all the dungeons and drafts. Having a bit of a high tea all on her own while she was being flown off to sunny Portugal at a moment's notice, *thank you very much*.

She had texted Patricia, though she knew that was unlikely to make her boss happy.

It looks like this might take longer than expected. Not sure when I'll be back, to be honest.

The reply had been surprising.

You take as long as you need. And don't be afraid to hold his feet to the fire, either. Bloody men.

Lillie had wanted to send back something suitably rousing and woman powery in solidarity, but the truth of it was that no fires held to feet seemed to be necessary. She wasn't sure what to make of it. Her stomach had been in knots all the way to his office, certain that he would be horrible to her. Or that his battalions of staff would bar her from even laying eyes on him.

She'd expected a fight, was the thing, and this didn't seem like anything of the kind.

Though, somehow, she couldn't quite let herself be lulled into any sort of sense of security. Not quite yet.

They landed in Portugal some while later, the sea in the distance as they flew in over rolling vineyards and stretches of green that looked like golf courses. Lillie felt she ought to ask questions about where they were going, but she was much too sated and drowsy from the lovely tea she'd consumed. Added to the fact that her pregnancy made her a whole lot sleepier than she'd ever been before.

Still, she followed Tiago out into a glorious bit of sunshine happily enough, pleased and yet, now, unsurprised to see yet another vehicle waiting for them. No scrabbling about looking for Tube stations or taxis for Tiago Villela. The SUV that waited near the airfield looked suitably rugged, given that they were out in a bit of countryside, and she wondered if they might be in for a spot of off-roading. Maybe there was something wrong with her that she found that exciting when, by rights, she should have been a bit more put off by this man who'd swept her off to a foreign country without blinking an eye.

Wasn't *he* lucky that she carried her passport as a matter of course when she got on a plane, on the off chance she might be seized with the urge—and blessed with the funds—to fly to the Maldives.

Lillie assured herself now that she was *well ready* to get stern with him if necessary, should any of this suddenly seem less glamorous and more, well, anything else—

But instead she found herself gazing out the window beside her, the lovely, bright afternoon sunshine making her want to sigh with the pleasure of it. It was so dark and cold in Scotland this time of year. This past weekend had been the annual Christmas lights switch-on parade in Aberdeen. Lillie loved the holiday season. She loved the parade with Santas on scooters and all the choirs singing and the lights coming on, bright as you like, to make at least a small dent in the thick fall darkness.

Yet the lights over Union Street had nothing on the Portuguese sun.

Tiago sat beside her in the back of the SUV, looking up now and again from the mobile where he was typing rapidly—just in case she'd forgotten for even a moment that he was a very important and busy man. Not the pool boy at all. And so, not to be outdone, she pulled out her own mobile and fired off a few texts of her own—mostly to her housemates, reminding them that there were garbage bins to take out and rent money to start getting together for the first of December, and it felt better than she'd ever thought it would to remind them that she would not be taking responsibility for such things moving forward.

Might be a good idea to elect one of your lot to take over these duties, or see to that cleaning rota chart I suggested last summer.

She attached a smiley face, because that was how they liked to communicate unpleasant things to her, like the fact they wanted her out by Hogmanay so the new, age-appropriate housemate could move in by the time the new year had been adequately celebrated on the second of January.

And then she felt better still when the responses started coming in, most seeming *deeply shocked* that they could hold meetings to make her move out and then expect her to carry on playing the part of house mum all the same.

When she stuck her phone back in the pocket of her coat, she found Tiago studying her from across the car's back seat that had, until that moment, seemed spacious indeed.

Now it felt…close. And much hotter than it should have been, with the cold air from the vents blowing on her suddenly too-warm face.

"You look pleased with yourself," he observed, as if he'd been studying her, a notion that did not make her feel any cooler.

"Have you lived with a great many housemates? In shared accommodation?" They were following a long, narrow drive between high walls. There were olive trees hanging overhead, moss and vines creeping this way and that, and the walls' ancient granite caught the sun. It looked magical. It looked as if they might drive straight on into Narnia, and if they did, Lillie would not have been at all surprised. "I'm guessing not."

"When I was at university I lived in a house with some friends," he said after a moment, as if he would have preferred not to share that. As if it was a deeply personal bit of information to tell her that he had once shared a home with anyone. Or maybe the personal part was that he'd once had friends and, presumably, still did. Like a regular man instead of a *world-famous billionaire* who had *private jets* and the like. "I much preferred that to living in halls."

"Then you know they can take a bit of managing." She smiled, because dispensing with a role she'd outgrown long since felt *so good* that she was forced to wonder why on earth she'd taken this long to do it. Maybe this unexpected trip to the closest thing she'd ever seen to Narnia was, at last, the proper start to the new life she'd promised herself five months back. Maybe this was her chance to step straight in instead of *waffling* about it and carrying on the same as ever. Because one way or another, everything was changing. What if this was her chance to *choose* a few of those changes? Lillie made her smile a bit wider. "I've resigned as manager, effective immediately. And while they were happy enough to rid themselves of the pregnant woman making things awkward in the house, by existing apparently, they really didn't think through the fact that now someone else will have to step in and see to the managing. Is it wrong that I'm enjoying it?"

It wasn't that she'd forgotten his eyes, because she hadn't forgotten a single thing about him. She doubted she could or ever would. The trouble with them was that they were not quite blue, not quite green. And that looking at them felt like falling from a great height, or possibly flying, and somehow bracing for it didn't make it any better.

But she would be lying if she tried to tell herself she didn't like that soaring sensation.

He gazed at her for a long moment, as if shocked she'd asked him to weigh in on her prosaic concerns. She wasn't sure why she had, but she didn't take it back. "I do not think it is ever wrong to allow others to marinate in the consequences of their actions," he told her, as if measuring each word. Then he inclined his head. "Nor to enjoy it when they do, if only privately."

"Thank you." Lillie smiled wider, that soaring feeling getting even more intense when she did. "That's vindicating."

The steep walls gave way, opening up over views of tidy vineyards and whitewashed buildings with red-tiled roofs. At first she thought they'd come to some kind of village. Then she realized that no, all the buildings had the same crest on their walls. The crest she'd seen behind Tiago in the news program, and all over his offices. This must all be his.

She felt something inside her shift, hard, as she stared out at the sun and the vineyards and the trees in the distance. How far did it go, this land of his? Was it possible he truly owned…everything?

Lillie couldn't quite get her head around it.

They were back to the narrow lane with high walls again, rounding a tight curve that had her closing her eyes for fear they'd crash head-on into oncoming traffic—but when there was no screeching of brakes or the like, she opened up her eyes again.

The SUV shot out of the shadows into another dazzling bit of light, and that was when the house came into view.

Once again, she had no idea how she managed to keep her jaw from dropping.

Because it wasn't a proper *house* at all. It wasn't a tidy semidetached in a quiet village like the one she'd grown up in. It wasn't Catriona's flat on the top floor of a converted row of terraces. It wasn't even one of those tarted-up houses out in Bielside, where all the flash oil and gas men lived and various royal personages were said to have once visited.

The place went on and on, terraces and balconies, pools and gardens, all arranged around a magnificent multileveled home that commanded the hillside it stood upon and looked out at the surrounding area like a conquering hero. It was like a private palace, and Tiago wasn't even looking at it. He wasn't sat there, poised for her reaction—that was how commonplace it all was to him, she realized.

This was when it began to really hit home how wealthy the man really was.

"How did you find this place?" she asked, because it was that or succumb to the wild buzzing in her ears. And because it sounded like the right sort of thing to ask.

Appropriately neutral, she thought.

He looked at her, too much blue and green. "Portugal?"

Lillie could hear from that carefully blank undercurrent in his voice that it was a stupid question after all. But all she did was gaze back at him, as if daring him to say so.

And she thought she saw the hint of a smile move over his face, after a moment or two, when there'd been very little of that since she'd tracked him down. But it was only a flash, so quick she wasn't sure that it was real. It was far more likely that she *wanted* to see him smile and that she'd made it up because it made her feel better to think he might.

That he might be as captivated with her now as he'd been that night.

Don't be foolish, she lectured herself. *This is about the baby, not you.*

And if she was a decent person and had the faintest hope of being a good mother, she wouldn't need it to be about anything more than that, would she?

"My mother's family are Portuguese," he was saying, once again in that careful, deliberate way of his. As if words were a precious resource and he intended to cultivate each and every one of them. "This land has been in her family some generations. The Villelas, as perhaps you know, maintain our ancestral presence in Spain."

"Fascinating," Lillie said, wrinkling up her nose. "The Mertons have maintained our ancestral presence in Scotland as well, though the thatched huts of us peasants don't stand up to the test of time nearly as well as ye olde family pile."

And once again, he looked startled. As if she'd surprised him.

But not, she thought after a moment, in a *bad* way. Necessarily.

Because once again, she thought she saw the hint of a smile on that marvelously rock-hard jaw of his. And it was clear to her that she was becoming a little too enamored of that. By this notion that she could actually burrow down beneath his skin in some way. *Disrupt* him, even.

Hadn't that been what had happened that night? She wouldn't have put it into those words. She hadn't. But that was what he had said himself in that hotel room in Spain. Again and again. *What have you done to me? What sort of sorceress are you?*

She'd thought it no more than a bit of flowery language—or anyway, she'd told herself it was, in retrospect. While ordering herself to forget about him.

But now she had to wonder if this man really went about living out his life with no one to tease him a bit. She thought that was sad. Lillie was fully aware that she'd let her own life get a bit sad, these last few years. It was just that she hadn't felt that overarching need to change things the way all her friends had, one after the next. She hadn't felt pulled to anything the way they had.

That was what happened when a person was raised in the shadow of a great love story. It made all else pale in comparison. Lillie had been conditioned to seek out her passions—but she hadn't exactly tripped over loads of passions lying about in the course of her life, had she?

While they'd all lived in the house, everything had

been a grand old laugh, and that had seemed quite grand enough, for a time. Even now, though the lot of them were rarely able to get together as a group any longer, any time she visited one or the other of them it was always the same. The old jokes, the endless laughter, the sheer delight in poking at each other. It was one of the things that made life worth living, as far she could tell, whether there were passions aplenty or not.

Yet unless she was mistaken, it was all new to Tiago.

Because apparently the personal palace and endless vineyards and *private jets* weren't quite the laugh they seemed from afar.

"You came with no luggage," he said as the car pulled up to a stop in front of the grand entry. Or perhaps it was the servants' back entrance. How was Lillie meant to know the difference on such a grand scale? "I've taken the liberty of instructing my staff to provide you with a wardrobe during your stay. I hope that is not too impertinent."

"How do you know what size I wear?" she asked without thinking.

His blue-green gaze changed, then. It went dark like a sudden storm and her breath stopped.

She knew she shouldn't have asked that. Because Lillie knew exactly how he knew her proportions. She knew that he had taken her measure, inch by glorious inch. That it was likely he was the only person alive who knew her body better than she did.

Of course, now she also knew that he remembered that night in at least as much detail as she did.

"When in doubt," he said quietly into the thunder that rumbled—waiting just out of reach—between them,

"I told them to err on the side of accommodating the changes your body has gone through since last I saw you."

That was such an innocuous sort of thing to say, wasn't it? There was no reason at all that her throat should go dry. That she could feel her breasts press insistently against the fabric of her dress. There was no reason at all that it should all feel like a sensual assault, leaving her breathless and doing her level best to ignore the slickness and heat between her legs.

Worse, she felt certain he knew exactly what she was trying to ignore.

Down to the slightest, faintest sensation. He knew.

For a moment, she thought that the storm hovering *right there* would blow her away. That they would be caught up, once more. That all of that lightning and longing would crash over them and light them up the way it had in Spain—

But instead, his gaze shuttered. He looked away.

And in the next moment, the doors of the car were opening and she had no choice but to get out after him and try her best to hide her reaction.

Out there in all that bright, revealing sunshine.

"This is my family's long-term housekeeper, Leonor," Tiago announced with some formality there by the side of the SUV. He beckoned an older woman closer and Lillie realized with a start that she hadn't paid the slightest bit of attention to anything but him. She hadn't even noticed the staff who waited for them, arranged in lines before a set of great doors that were flung wide open, presumably to receive the master of the house.

She ordered herself to get her body back under control before she made a complete fool of herself, because surely all this sunshine meant that everyone staring at her could *see* her reaction to this man. Surely they could feel that same storm approaching, the same as she could, and could track it *on her*.

But it was hard to keep her mind on such horrors, because she was hot. The sun was glaring down, her body was still reacting to the way he'd looked at her inside the car, and it was all too much. She found herself shrugging out of her favorite big coat that doubled as a cozy blanket in a pinch, only stopping when she heard a murmur of reaction from the waiting staff.

Tiago looked at them, then looked at her and the obvious bump that was her belly, and was that…dismay she saw move through his gaze? Pride in all that distracting blue and green?

But she couldn't tell, for it, too, was gone too quickly.

"I leave you in Leonor's capable hands," Tiago said, when there were so many other things he could have said. So many other things she wished he would have said. Then he did something with his head that put Lillie in mind of a bow.

It was quick, and then he turned and marched toward the grand doors, all of his staff trailing behind him after a few rapid commands in what she assumed was Portuguese.

What she noticed most of all was that he didn't look back.

"If you will come with me, madam," Leonor said, though Lillie was not fooled by her overtly polite tone. Not when she could see the glint of steel in the old woman's eyes.

Lillie aimed a big smile her way, and tried her best to look sheepish, or docile. Or whatever it was that would be expected of her, since Tiago hadn't seen fit to offer her any instructions.

The old woman's brows arched up, but she said nothing. She only did a version of that head-only bow herself, then led the way into the waiting house.

Unsurprisingly, it was a dazzling affair. Airy, open rooms that let the sunlight in on every side. White walls, exposed beams, tiles and mosaics everywhere. There was even a wide, center courtyard that was its own lush garden.

"This is beautiful," Lillie breathed, staring at the flower—*flowers!*—that were blooming right there before her this close to December.

"Senhor Villela's grandmother loved nothing more than her plants," the housekeeper told her, with what sounded like pride. "In her later years, she became obsessed with orchids and grew them here in our mild climate. She could often be found here, chatting with the bees and the birds, and singing to her flowers. We like to think that sometimes, she can still be felt here. Or heard singing on the breeze."

"What a lovely notion," Lillie said quietly, drinking in the bright colors and so much green.

And she wasn't sure she understood the assessing way the other woman looked at her then, so she pretended not to see it.

Instead she followed Leonor through the rest of the sprawling house, crossing through the courtyard and then heading out into the wing that waited on the far side. Lillie didn't know where to look. At the stunning furnishings, clearly placed just so, that very clearly utilized interior design elements that she'd only ever read about in magazines. Every room had its own specific character, she thought, yet was clearly a part of the whole—and each one was inviting. There were windows everywhere and skylights, too. The walls were filled with art, and though she couldn't identify any of the paintings, it seemed clear that each and every one of them had been chosen as much for the mastery of the artist as a particular enjoyment of what had been painted.

"Your rooms will have everything you need, I'm sure," Leonor said with a certain serene confidence as they walked down yet another hallway. "You are welcome to enjoy the rest of the guest wing as well. It has its own small library and a media room, should the private one in your rooms prove insufficient. Down at that end—" she nodded off toward what looked like nothing but a great wash of light down the length of the hall "—there is a patio that leads to a small pool that you may use exclusively while you are here. There is also a well-equipped gym, if that is your preference. If you wish to ride, you need only ring the stables to let them know you're coming, so that they might be prepared for you. And, naturally, you are welcome to walk wherever you please on the property."

Lillie could hardly take all that in. So she simply nodded, as if she spent every day of her life being offered such luxuries so offhandedly and stopped when the older woman did, just outside the first room along the hall.

Leonor flung open the doors and strode inside, leaving Lillie to trail after her. She saw quickly that she hadn't misheard. The housekeeper had said *rooms*, plural. There was a vast yet comfortable lounge with enough seating to fit an army, then what looked like a bit of an office space, complete with a computer and some other corporate-looking appliances. Another sort of sitting room a bit farther along opened up into a whole walk-in closet *complex* comprising three separate rooms, a sprawling en suite bathroom with a separate area for a bath with a view, and then, at the very end, the bedroom.

Which was, not to put too fine a point on it, much bigger than the entire ground floor of her house in Aberdeen, complete with the shared lounge and kitchen.

The room had a fireplace on one end, its own sitting area, and the most over-the-top four-poster bed she'd ever seen.

"I hope this will suffice," Leonor intoned.

"Yes," Lillie said, somehow managing not to laugh out loud at the notion there might be anyone alive who would find this *insufficient*. She tried to look posh. "It should do."

And when the other woman left her there, saying something about leaving her to settle in, Lillie finally broke. She burst into a helpless sort of laughter. She laughed and laughed, clinging to the nearest post at the foot of the bed until she felt weak and tears were streaming down her face. Then, gingerly—a bit as if she expected armed guards to burst in and carry her away—she crawled up onto the bed, and began laughing all over again. Because the mattress was soft as a feather and she had never felt anything like it. It was tempting to believe they slept on *actual clouds* here.

It was *so* soft, and so clearly elegant, and smelled ever so faintly like lavender and far fancier herbs besides, that Lillie doubted very much that she'd be able to actually drift off to sleep surrounded by such class—

And so was surprised to find herself blinking awake some time later.

The position of the light and shadows in the room suggested she'd slept a good while. She pushed herself up onto her elbows, frowning and cranky, the way she always was after a nap. Her cheeks felt flushed too hot and she had to shove her damp curls back out of her face, quite certain that she'd slept hard the way she always did. As if felled by a huntsman's ax.

She heard faint sounds from somewhere outside this room and everything inside her leaped a bit, with his name inside her like its own dancing bit of flame.

Tiago.

And as she swung her feet off the side of the bed, not at all surprised to find she'd slept with her boots still on, the rest of the day came flooding back to her. Tiago himself. Seeing him again in his office in London. That ridiculously fancy plane. This house that was its own city, it was so large.

The way everything had sparked between them again in the car—though Lillie wasn't sure how she felt about that. She was happy that she hadn't made the whole thing up, the way she'd tried so hard to convince herself she had all these months. Or if it actually only hurt more, because now she knew it was real.

But she also *knew that it was real.* Without question.

And she also knew where he was.

Though as she got to her feet, rubbing her palms over

her face and heading toward that soft noise she'd heard, she had to question that, too. *Did* she know where he was? This was a very large house in what appeared to be its very own countryside, for one thing. Not to mention, he also had his own plane. He could be anywhere.

But she found she couldn't follow that up the way she wanted to, because when she emerged into that sitting room she'd seen when she first walked into her rooms, Leonor was standing there overseeing the staff as they laid out a meal for her.

And it turned out that she was ravenously hungry.

"I hope you enjoy what the cook has prepared," the housekeeper said, standing to the side of the table near the window, looking…assessing, yet again. "Some local delicacies have been prepared alongside what we consider more typical fare for you."

"A bit of haggis, then?" Lillie asked with a laugh and then regretted it, because the other woman only gazed back at her.

"Please make yourself at home in this wing," she said in that excessively calm manner of hers. "Relax however you see fit, refresh yourself after your journey, and I will come to you in the morning."

It was not until after Lillie had polished off enough food to feed a football team or two that she realized that Leonor had obliquely suggested that she stay put. That she confine herself to this wing, in fact.

But Lillie…had not agreed to that, had she?

She went and availed herself of that glorious bathroom, rinsing off the travel and the nap and her feast. Unable to help herself, she went and peeked into the wardrobe, and found that Tiago—or his staff, it was almost certainly his *staff*—really had thought of everything. And more, that every single item of clothing that hung in all three rooms of that walk-in closet *complex* was exactly the sort of thing that Lillie would have chosen for herself.

If, that was, she had ever had unlimited funds at her disposal.

And though she had considered herself practical and frugal the whole of her life, it turned out that all it took was two good meals and a well-stocked closet and Lillie was nothing but a silly little madam after all, more than happy to play dress-up.

But when she finished with that, and was wearing the kind of outfit that once would have made her laugh because it was so out of her usual reach, she set off out of her rooms. Plural. She looked down the hall toward the bit that led to all the parts of the great, big house that weren't a part of the guest wing, and decided that what she really wanted to do on her first night in Portugal was a spot of exploring.

"It has nothing to do with Tiago," she told herself virtuously. And loud enough to bounce back at her from the quiet, likely reproachful walls. "I just want to get a sense of the place."

And she kept right on lying to herself as she set off, *absolutely not* looking for him at all.

CHAPTER FOUR

TIAGO DID NOT come to the house in Portugal as much as he had as a child, when he had spent a great many school holidays here with his grandmother. And then, after both she and his mother were gone, his father had switched off and on between this estate and the Villela land in Spain so he would be familiar with them both.

Yet these days he spent more time in London than anywhere else, so he could be closer to the office.

But he still knew every single sound that the old house could possibly make. The rattle of the breeze against the windows. The rustle of the trees outside. The way the wind moved in the courtyard that a fanciful person might imagine was an old woman, still murmuring to the flowers she'd loved to tend.

Not that Tiago allowed himself any such flights of fancy.

On this late November night, Tiago had repaired to the office that had once belonged to his grandfather and still smelled faintly of cigars and port. He sat in the old leather armchair where the old man had napped away his later years and found himself brooding in the general direction of his grandfather's bookcase. It was packed tight with well-worn volumes of books that Tiago had been fascinated with when he was young. He'd thought the world of his grandfather. And he'd imagined that all he needed to do was read this particular selection of books and he would somehow find himself the same sort of man.

It was as close as he allowed himself to get to the memories of his grandparents he'd buried long ago, then packed down tight beneath the cool practicality that he'd been expected to embody. The composure that they had prized far above any leftover sentimentality that, these days, lived on only in the flowers out there in the courtyard.

Flowers he told himself he barely noticed some years.

But he had read all the books in this study, years ago now, and still the man *he* was had ignored every single lesson he'd ever been taught.

In so doing, he had failed to adequately protect both Lillie—and he still couldn't get enough of thinking that name, her *actual name* when she had been nameless in his head for far too long—and his own family legacy. The very thing he had sworn to protect, always.

Now she was pregnant with his child, his heir. The future of his family was hanging in the balance. There were things he needed to do, and soon, in the wake of the knowledge she'd dropped on him today. There was no time for *brooding*.

But all he could think about was the night they'd shared in Spain. About the things that they could do stretched out across a bed, with nothing but their bodies moving together in the dark.

The things their bodies called out in each other, God help him.

He knew better than this. Those flowers remained not as a love letter to a grandmother long gone, but to remind him of what it had been like to give himself over to his jangling, discordant grief. He had sobbed, out in that courtyard in the rain, and his parents had left him there.

They had decamped to Spain for the rest of that season, leaving him to sort himself out—or, Leonor had told him with her usual serene demeanor despite the unusual gleam in her gaze, they would wash their hands of him.

And he had been just a boy. He had barely been able to process the loss of his favorite person, how could he lose his parents, too?

He had taught himself how to…put those things away.

To hide them as if they did not, could not, exist.

Until sometimes he believed they never had.

And thus tonight all he could do—all he would allow himself to do—was stay where he was, frowning across the room at a bookcase that had been carefully filled by a far better man, listening to the sounds of the old house as the hour grew late around him.

He could hear the wind outside, coming in from the sea. There were the usual sounds of the old house settling into another night, the groundskeeper doing his rounds in his rattly old jeep, the staff opening and closing doors in the distance.

And yet when he heard footfalls in the hall outside the study, he told himself he was imagining it. At first.

Or he wanted to be imagining it, because no staff member moved like that. He knew that without question. They all moved swiftly and almost entirely silently.

Not those meandering, hesitating steps down the length of the hall that led to this office, where everyone here knew he did not like to be disturbed.

Everyone except his guest, that was.

His guest. His Lillie.

Tiago still could not understand how this was happening. Not the mechanics. He remembered those all too well, and happily.

But he had never felt such things before. Even before today, she had consumed his thoughts and he had *felt things*. It was an outrage.

He had told himself for months now that was all a function of the fact that he could not have her. That if she'd been there in front of him, he would have been as disinterested as he normally was after enjoying a woman. He would have politely disengaged and never thought of her again.

At the moment, Tiago could barely imagine maintaining a polite veneer in front of Lillie, much less *disengaging* with her. Hell, he'd brought her here, to the one place on earth he considered some kind of sanctuary, where no one who was family or someone hired by the family had set foot in ages.

Perhaps he had been lying to himself all this time.

He scowled at the books, seeing not a single one of the old, cracked, much-loved spines. He was thinking instead of Lillie moving over him in that bed in Spain, rocking her hips against his in that maddeningly lush rhythm that had undone him. He was remembering her back arched in a perfect bow, her head thrown back, and all those glorious curls moving with her.

And when he shifted his gaze to the door once more, she was there.

Quite as if he had summoned her—though Tiago already knew too well that despite his best efforts, that never worked.

It never had before.

"Oh." She looked as startled as she sounded, but he drank her in as if she was a dose of clear, sweet water and he had been wandering for five some months in a barren desert. He felt as if that was no more than the simple truth. "Tiago."

Her hair was haphazardly pinned up on the top of her head, as if she'd tossed it up and forgotten all about it. And he was a sophisticated man. He attended formal black-tie events as a matter of course, ate at the finest restaurants, and normally dated women who were renowned for their beauty and elegance above all else.

Yet this was the one who seemed to have taken up all the space inside his chest. With that wild hair and her siren's eyes, too much like the sea.

She had changed into soft-looking lounging pants, obviously made of the finest cashmere with what looked like a touch of merino wool for structure, and the sort of T-shirt that looked defiantly simple yet was cut by artisans to make her curves into a song.

And there was no denying what he had already noticed—that he had found her astounding before, in Spain, but this new ripeness of hers might very well be his undoing.

When he was not a man who could be *undone*. Everything in his life forbade it.

"I'm sorry if I'm intruding," she was saying, though

she did not appear particularly apologetic, to his eye. "I was exploring."

"I feel certain I made it clear that you were to be kept to your wing of the house," he said, softly enough. And perhaps she could hear the menace in his tone. Or perhaps she had no experience with such things and couldn't identify it when she heard it.

Whatever it was, she seemed unfazed. He was unused to...*not* eliciting reactions wherever he happened to find himself.

"What a lovely house," she said instead. "I can't wait to walk around tomorrow and pay more attention to the view. It must be epic."

"Lillie." And he meant to cut her off. To cut her down to size while he was at it. But instead, just as it had in Spain, his gaze...got caught. On her.

And he couldn't seem to do a thing about it.

Because nothing in his life before or since had prepared him for the sight of her, like a sledgehammer, as he'd walked through that crowded pool area, and had seen her there.

He still wasn't prepared.

Tiago found himself on his feet and moving toward her. When he knew that what he wanted to do was stay put. Keep his distance. That was what he *needed* to do. At the very least, it would be wise to avoid these interactions with her until ground rules were set out, contracts signed, and the way forward carefully plotted out and wholly understood by both parties.

What he could not understand was why this woman was the one thing on the whole of the earth that made him reckless.

And maybe she was reckless too, because surely a wise creature would take one look at him in this current, dangerous mood he was in, turn, and run.

But Lillie, *his Lillie*, stayed where she was. She leaned against one side of the open doorway, doing nothing at all but gazing back at him as he prowled toward her.

Tiago wished that she would say something. Point out that he should not think that he could so easily hide her away here. Fight with him. Yell at him. Hold him to account for getting her pregnant in the first place, and leaving her no possible way of finding him again.

Why didn't she do any of these things?

But as he came to a stop before her, he knew.

He had never asked for this ability to read her, this strange woman he still barely knew. But he could.

Just as he had once before.

And so he knew that it wasn't that she didn't feel all of those things. She did. It was that she felt other things far more.

Damn her.

But even as he thought that, he was moving again. Closer. Much closer.

This time to do the very thing he shouldn't, but he seemed to have no ability whatever to stop.

His hand slipped under the hem of her T-shirt, then smoothed its way over that high, round ball of her belly, finding her skin satiny and hot. And then, as he kept his hands there, he felt her shiver, too.

"You are carrying my child," he said, his voice a mere scrape across the space between them.

Her eyes were wide, her lips slightly parted, and for once she did not laugh. "I am."

"I want to be furious," he told her, or perhaps he was confessing to the bump he held between his palms. "I want to rage, throw things, break whatever I get my hands upon."

"I know," she whispered. "I wanted to be angry. Ashamed. But instead… Tiago…"

Something inside him felt as if it was cracking. Falling apart, crumbling—

And he knew he didn't want her to finish that sentence. He didn't know why he'd started it.

So instead of continuing down this dangerous road that could not lead them anywhere good, he dropped his head and fit his mouth to hers.

And that, too, would have knocked him back if he hadn't been holding on to her.

Because it turned out that he hadn't been telling himself fairy stories about what it was like to kiss this woman.

She tasted like every dream he'd had about her since, and better yet.

Because she kissed him as if she'd been waiting her whole life to do nothing else. She kissed him as if they'd been crafted for this, hewn from flesh and blood precisely to drive each other mad.

And so, for those sweet, breathless moments, that was what they did.

She licked into his mouth. He angled his jaw, one hand going to slide along the side of her face, to hold her where he wanted her. To keep it hot like this. Wild and perfect and wholly theirs.

It was as if no time had passed. As if this was that morning after that they had been denied in Spain.

As if nothing had ever or could ever keep them apart.

He made a low noise in the back of his throat and moved closer, so that his body was pressed to hers again. *At last.* And Tiago exulted in the parts of her that would change even more, the parts that were already pressed up flush against him.

The changes that *he* had made in her.

Both of his hands moved to cup her face, his fingers spearing into her hair, exulting in those curls that clung to him as every strand wanted him as badly as he wanted her. And as he took the kiss deeper, more carnal, he found nothing but magic in her taste.

Just as he remembered it. As he remembered *her*.

She kissed him back the same way, her hands sneaking up to lace around his neck, and this was how it had started last summer. This was how it had ended up here, with the proud jut of the baby they'd made between them even now.

One kiss, and then everything had bloomed into brilliant golds and fiery reds, and he hadn't had another coherent thought since.

Not where she was concerned.

And yet that, ironically enough, was what got through to him.

He tore his lips from hers, though everything in him resisted such violence. And for a moment, because he could not make himself step back the way he should have, he rested his head against hers.

Sharing her air. Exulting in the way she breathed. Taking pleasure in the way her breasts shuddered against his chest.

It took him far longer than it should have to disengage entirely and move back.

"That cannot happen again," he told her. Severely.

"It seems likely to happen again and again and again," she replied after a moment, her voice husky. Roughened in a way that made him want nothing more than to lay her out before the fire crackling in his grate, follow her down to the ground, and see if it was even possible to indulge in her enough that this hunger might somehow be sated. "Otherwise, I don't see why you transported me all the way to this lovely, remote estate where no one could possibly hope to find me."

"I am afraid you have the wrong idea."

And he heard the way he said that. So stiff, so unyielding, that he might as well have been made of stone. He sounded like every lecture his father had ever given him. All that talk of duty, legacy. Responsibility. Until tonight, he had always thought those things were stamped deep on his bones. That he would not need to think of them, for he simply *was* them.

In every possible respect, it seemed, except where she was concerned.

Tiago expected her to react badly to what he said. To look hurt, at the very least. He braced himself for it, not sure that he would be able to handle it the way he needed to, but already lecturing himself on why it was necessary that things be done in the way he had decided earlier.

But Lillie laughed. "You think I've got the wrong idea, do you?" Her laughter was not helpful. It was like a bright song, filling the room and pouring through him, like the melody a wish might make as it was granted.

"Do you reckon? I'm nearly five months pregnant. What *wrong idea* do you imagine I might have?"

"I intended to have a discussion with you tomorrow," he said, even more stiffly than before, as if he was an awkward man. As if there had ever been a situation that he could not master.

This was the first. He disliked it, intensely.

Her brows arched as she studied him. And though she laughed again, it seemed less an expression of pure amusement—not with that new edge to it. She crossed her arms, her siren eyes looking narrower than before.

He didn't like that either.

"I've ruined everything by not staying locked up in my room like a naughty child, clearly," she said, and then she even rolled her eyes. As if that was something people could just...*do* at him. "You really don't seem to like it much when things don't go according to your plan, do you? I expect that's all the money. It makes a person imagine that everything they think and do is more important. And that if others don't fall in line, that it's necessary to maneuver them into whatever it is you think they should do. No one likes to be maneuvered, Tiago. Maybe you don't know that, having grown up like this. I accept that it's possible no one has told you. Likely because they work for you and are too scared to tell you much of anything, if you want my opinion."

"I do not," he grated out. "And as it happens, Lillie, you are the only thing that has ever failed to go according to plan."

She didn't ask him if he meant tonight, or five months ago. But then, he knew she didn't need to. Because he knew that she possessed the same confounding skill that he did, but in reverse. He knew this woman was perhaps the only person alive who could read him with a glance.

He didn't care for that, either. But he comforted himself that at least he wasn't meeting her in a delicate contract negotiation where his ability to bluff his way into a better position would be at risk.

"I hope you don't think I'm going to apologize for that," she said, after spending too long looking for God only knew what on his face. "Besides, this is all you playing catch-up. I can assure you, falling pregnant after one night on a Spanish vacation was not in my plans, either. And until yesterday, I assumed that was a responsibility I'd be taking on all alone."

"That obviously won't be necessary." He could *taste* her, was the thing. That made it feel like nothing short of an indignity that he could not go to her, strip her naked, and taste her everywhere else, too. But he didn't do it. Somehow. He moved, though his body felt as if it was fighting him every step of the way, and located himself behind the desk over against one wall. So he could at least attempt to feel more in control. "I'm a man of limitless resources. There is no need for you to struggle ever again, and indeed, I intend to see to it that you do not."

But she did not look even remotely relieved. Or grateful. She scowled at him. "I didn't seek you out for a payday."

Tiago raised a brow. "Did you not? Then you would be the first."

"I sought you out," she said, very primly, "because it was *the right thing to do*."

"And the fact that I am a wealthy man by any standard played no part in your decision to turn up in my office, I am certain."

She stared at him for a moment, and he realized that she wasn't coming back at him with a knee-jerk response. It looked as if she was considering what he'd said. "No, you're right. I thought you were the pool boy, after all. It was a pleasant surprise to find that if you chose to take responsibility, this baby would be well looked after."

And that was what he wanted her to say, surely. It was what he'd expected her to say from the start. But now that she'd said it, he found it rang false. It sat in him wrong, and he had long considered himself a finely tuned instrument when it came to other people's veracity. It was part of what made him such an excellent businessman, capable of keeping his fingers in a great many pies at once, secure in the knowledge that it was a very difficult thing indeed for anyone to fool him.

He could not say that what he felt at the moment was *secure*.

"There is obviously a great deal of chemistry between us," he said baldly, because he was always good at that, too. Never one for messing about with thinly veiled this and implications of that, not when he could aim straight at it instead. He saw her eyes widen and could not have said if the sensation that seemed to punch through him was delight that he had gained ground, or a strange regret. "But that is not something I choose to indulge in when it comes to matters of business."

"Matters of business?" she echoed, sounding as if she *wanted* to laugh but couldn't quite get there. "Are you referring to your child as part of your…business?"

"The child will not simply be a baby, Lillie." He sounded forbidding, he knew, but he leaned into it. Because she needed to hear this. She needed to fully take the reality of the situation on board. "This child will be the heir to two great dynasties. Both come with their own august legacies and considerable mythologies, which would be burden enough. But both also come with significant fortunes attached, and that, like it or not, is business. For if it is not, it will soon be a moot point. It will all disappear. The work of generations, that easily."

There was something in her gaze then, making all that bright blue turn dark. "What exactly are you trying to say to me?"

Tiago sighed, as if she was being dense. And he hated himself for that, too, when she stiffened. "This cannot be an affair, Lillie. No matter what happened between us in Spain. Do you not understand? I will have to marry you."

Her eyes went wide. Her face paled, and not, his ego could not help but note, in the transformative joy a man in his position might have expected to see after a proposal. "Marry me? Marry *you*? Are you mad? On the strength of one night?"

"On the strength of your pregnancy. Because the Villela heir must be legitimate." He looked at her as if he had never seen her before and would never see her again, or maybe it was simply that he did not wish to say the thing he knew he must. But that was life, was it not? Forever forcing himself to do what was necessary, what was right. Never what he wanted. So he took a deep breath. "We will marry. Quickly. And once that happens, I will never touch you again."

He didn't know what he expected her to do. Cry, perhaps. Look torn apart by such declaration.

Make it clear that she thought that was as much of an injustice as he did.

But instead she straightened against the doorjamb. Then she glared at him as if she was the one in charge here. As if she had the power.

"Good," she said, her eyes flashing. "Let's hurry up and marry, then."

CHAPTER FIVE

THE WEDDING TOOK place three days later.

And if Lillie was discomfited by the speed of it, and how clearly it had all been planned before they'd come to Portugal in the first place, that seemed to be the least of her worries. Primary among her actual concerns was…what had become of her.

In Scotland she'd been…diffident. Forgiving. She'd let all those idiots in her house condescend to her for ages. She'd let them get away with all that passive aggressiveness while she'd spent the last few years of her life adrift, because all of her actual friends had gone ahead and got lives while she hadn't had the slightest idea what to do with hers.

She had been asleep for years, perhaps, but she was wide awake now.

And she had to stay awake, because while *she* might have been worryingly happy to remain drifting to and fro in the tiny little tides of her little life, that was not the sort of life she wished to model for a child.

Once she started thinking like that, the stakes seemed even higher.

What sort of mother did her baby deserve?

Not the sort who let a scrum of housemates treat her ill, that was certain. And not the sort to bow down to the man who'd fathered her baby, either. She might have been spirited away to Tiago Villela's Portuguese retreat. She was pregnant with his child and set to marry him, fair enough.

That hadn't exactly been the proposal of her dreams, but *she* wasn't backing down, because being Tiago's— legally—was no more than *her* baby deserved, and Lillie had discovered to her delight that there were some things, it turned out, she was perfectly happy to fight about.

The life her child could and would have topped that list.

Leonor, who was clearly more family than house-keeper, assured her that everything was well in hand. All Lillie had been asked to do over the past few days was rest, eat, and entertain herself. All of which she had done, to excess.

A lot like she was trying to prove something to Tiago. How comfortable she was. How at her ease with his dictates.

Only when she was all alone, late at night, did she admit that the fact it was so easy for him to ignore the passion that still scorched her, just thinking of it, hurt her more than it should.

It was only there in her bed of clouds, covers over her head, could she let herself shake with all the pent-up *nerves* she dared not show to a man she'd thought was made of molten heat who, apparently, could *decide* to make himself an ice sculpture at will.

But when she woke up each morning, she allowed none of her bewilderment to show.

He didn't want to touch her? *Marvelous.* She could entertain herself without him forever. She found out quickly that most of the books in the house were languages she didn't speak. Portuguese, of course, but also Spanish, French, and what she thought was German. It was only in the guest wing that the books were in English. But because she had a stubborn streak, she liked to take books she could actually read and settle down to read them…in other parts of the house.

Because if no one was going to admit that Tiago wanted her to remain confined to quarters so he need not gaze upon her unless he expressly wished it, she was going to pretend she had no idea that she was supposed to stay put.

She swam in the pool that Leonor had pointed out to her that first night. Even though it was the waning days of November, the pool was warm, the sun was bright, and it was all much more delightful than it should have been.

Ice sculptures be damned.

They brought her a decadent high tea each day at four on the dot. Besides that, there were all the meals she could possibly want, the food so good it would have made her eyes roll back in her head in sheer delight…

But she was too busy pretending not to be affected by any of it. And all that pretending was a lot of work. It made her hungry.

It made her shake in her bed, night after night, when no one could see her.

Today, however, was her wedding day and she was finding it difficult to keep up the same stubborn front.

She felt fluttery and odd, she acknowledged, as she sat in the sitting room in her guest quarters to take her breakfast that morning. More fluttery by the moment.

"Maybe it's jitters," she told herself as she sipped at her tea.

Jitters were normal. They had to be, or there wouldn't be a name for them, would there? Though she'd never felt anything quite like them before. And she needed to talk herself out of them, or slap herself into shape, because she had no intention of appearing anything but calm and in control today.

Lillie was just starting the process with a sound internal lecture, when the door swung open and Tiago walked in.

"I'm sure I've heard that it's bad luck to see a bride before the wedding ceremony," she said, hoping it sounded as unwelcoming and self-contained as she wanted it to.

But even if it did, it was a wasted effort, because all Tiago did was help himself to one of the seats in the room. He settled into the comfortable couch across from her that he made seem entirely too small, and then fixed her with that mesmerizing gaze of his.

"There are a few things we must go over," he told her, as coldly as if they had never kissed. Much less spent a night naked and sweating, with him so deep inside of her she could still feel him now.

The flutters in her belly increased.

"Wonderful," she said, spearing a piece of sliced ham with more force than was perhaps warranted. Or perhaps not, she thought when she saw that he'd brought a whole sheaf of papers with him. "It's the romance for me."

He ignored that, but in a manner that suggested she was *gauche* for even mentioning *romance*. "In the coming months, we will pay far more attention to the intricacies of your role, but this is what I must impress upon you now. The Villelas do not and will not divorce. But that does not mean that there will be the sort of scandals that inevitably spill out into the pages of tawdry newspapers. You and I must never become fodder for tabloids, Lillie."

"No worries," she said blandly. "I've managed to avoid appearing in all the tabloids so far."

She got another cold look from Tiago, that was all. "My expectation is that this will function like any other business arrangement. We will both state our needs. We will negotiate until we reach an agreement. And we will abide by the conclusions we reach together. Do you understand?"

"You seem to be under the impression that I work for you," Lillie said, pleasantly enough. Conversationally, even. "I'm the woman you knocked up, Tiago. I don't actually owe you anything. The only reason I haven't run screaming from this house is because of the baby. The only thing that interests me is what might be good for this child. If that means the front page of every tabloid in the universe, I'll sign right up. Do *you* understand?"

And for a dizzying moment, she saw the Tiago she knew. The man with all that passion and wonder in his gaze, even if, this morning, it was less wonder and more indignation. Whatever it was, it wasn't *cold*.

She knew, then, that there was something in her that would do anything to bring them back here. Anything at all. No matter what it took.

Though in the next moment, she dismissed that. It was childish. It didn't matter what was going on *in his eyes*, for God's sake. What mattered was what she'd just told him mattered.

The baby, beginning and end.

"A Villela marriage is a business arrangement," he told her. Very much as if she hadn't said a word. "They are run to work in the mutual best interests of both parties, as agreed from the start."

"How charming."

"Things are different when there's so much money involved, Lillie." His tone was repressive then, but Lillie did not wish to be repressed. "I do not expect you to understand that, of course, but if your true interest is in the child, then it must be clear to you that making certain he or she is capable of assuming my position one day with as little scandal as possible can only be a good thing."

"I'm not signing anything," she told him.

She didn't know she was going to say that, but when she did, it felt a lot like shaking up a bottle of bubbly, popping the cork, and letting it spray all around. A mad sort of joy, in other words. So when he frowned at her, she lifted her chin and shrugged nonchalantly, as if this had been her plan all along.

"I must insist," Tiago said.

"It's not in my best interest," she replied, with a wave of her hand. The one holding the fork, so it looked like nothing so much as a scepter. "Whatever those papers

are, they're not for me, are they? They're for you. So
I'll have to decline. If you feel that we need to get married to protect this baby, that's fine. I'll do it. And not
because I agree with the way you framed the whole
thing. But because, obviously, having this baby born
as your legitimate heir can only be good. For the baby."

"And, of course, for you."

"Are there benefits to being the wife of one of the
richest men in the world?" she asked facetiously. "I
guess we'll see. But if you were so worried about me
getting my hands on all your wealth and consequence,
you shouldn't have offered in the first place."

He sighed. "I think there's been a misunderstanding."

"The only misunderstanding is how you managed to
act as if you were fully human while we were in Spain,"
she retorted, with enough heat that she surprised herself.
"And now it turns out that you're nothing of the kind.
You're not a man, you're…a *corporation*."

That gaze of his went glacial. "I beg your pardon?"

And for some reason that she couldn't have put into
words, Lillie found that she was suddenly enjoying
herself. "I mean, think about it from my perspective.
I have a blisteringly hot night with a mysterious man
on a Spanish holiday. And then, months later, accidentally see his face on the nightly news. As I happen to be
pregnant with his child, I make an appointment to see
him. Partly it was to see that he knew about the baby,
as is only right. But the other part, naturally, was to see
if that night was real. If I'd made it all up in my head.
And behold. It appears I did."

"Lillie."

And for a moment, she felt exhilarated. As if she'd

somehow managed to goad him into…some kind of explosion that would bring back the Tiago she liked.

And, possibly, lead to more kissing.

Because she'd thought of little else since that night in his study.

But instead, he leaned forward, resting his elbows on his knees and letting his hands dangle. It made him look entirely too much like the man she'd just accused him of not being. "I can see that I've gone about this the wrong way."

And he sounded so reasonable, so relatable. It took her a moment to remember that this was literally his job. Making people believe him so that he could make even more money.

If the searches she'd done on him since she'd arrived here were true, he had a gift. He was that good at it.

You need to steel yourself against this man, lass, she told herself grimly.

But he was looking at her square. And there was nothing cold or arrogant on his face, which she told herself was yet another tell. He was putting on an act, surely. He had to be.

"The truth is that I'm just as concerned about the baby as you are," he told her and more, sounded as if he meant it. *Part of the act*, she assured herself. "I want to make sure that our child has all the protection that I can offer him, or her, and as quickly as possible. I think you're taking all this talk of marital business the wrong way. It isn't as if we won't have a good working relationship within the marriage, it's just that when it comes to what I have to offer you and the child, I think it's better to focus on the big-ticket items first. And also the realities."

Listening to him talk like this was dangerous. She found herself wanting to nod along and talk more about this *good working relationship*. To stand up from a little table and go to him, so she could sit beside him on the couch and perhaps put her hand on his, to make sure he knew that she was listening. Carefully. With her whole body—

You need to sort yourself right out, she told herself sternly.

"And I don't mean that these realities are a bad thing," he continued in the same seemingly earnest tone. "You and I barely know each other. We were together for one night, and I think we can both agree that it was…out of the ordinary. It can only make sense to hammer out an agreement that protects us both. Don't you think?"

"I do," Lillie shot back at him, with enough ferocity that he blinked. But she didn't walk it back. He was doing a job, but *she* was fighting for something. For her baby, for herself. She was *taking charge of her life*, for once. "But you can't imagine it makes sense that all that hammering out is being done by your attorneys. Who's looking out for me? And don't say you." She made herself smile, despite the quick clatter of her pulse. Especially when he looked as if it troubled him that she would make such an accusation, when she hadn't even properly made it yet. "Even if you're the kindest, most self-sacrificing person in the world, it would make sense for me to verify that, wouldn't it? Not simply trust you blindly."

"Lillie," he said in that quiet, intense way of his. "I want you to marry me. Today."

And she knew, at once, that she was lying to herself. That for all her noble intentions of doing this, that, or the other *thing for the child*, what it all came down to was this.

The way her heart beat even faster when he said that. The way she reacted when she was near him. Her nipples stood at attention. Between her legs, she could feel his voice the way she'd once felt his tongue, licking into her.

The truth of the matter, whether she wished to admit it to herself or not, was that she was a right fool where this man was concerned.

Or she would have sent him a letter, as he'd said. An email. She could have called. She wouldn't have turned up in his office, kitted out in a nice dress and her best boots, would she?

"I want you to marry me," he told her again, his blue-green gaze even more intense. "But I also need it. Tell me what I have to do to get you to sign this agreement. Name your terms and I will make them happen. That's how important it is to me that we secure our child's future. Today."

She thought about the phone call she'd had with her parents the day after he'd announced they would marry and how overjoyed they'd been that she was attempting to work things out with the father of the baby.

Is he a good sort? her father had asked, obviously doubtful from the get-go, given the last they'd talked.

He's not a bad *sort, if that's what you mean*, she'd replied. *Though it's early days.*

Women have been handling the fathers of their un-expected babies since the dawn of time, her mother had said with a laugh. *All it takes is as much honey as vin-egar, darling. And a little bit of backbone while you're at it.*

Lillie did not ask her mother how she knew that, since she and Lillie's dad had met in primary school and had been inseparable ever since. *It was always a matter of when, not if, we'd have you, love*, they'd told her.

But the important thing about her parents' marriage was that it was a very, very good one. It was clear to any-one who encountered them that they doted on each other. That they were fond of each other, day in and day out. They had always laughed more than her friends' par-ents did. They held hands, still. Her father brought her mother cups of tea every morning. She cooked him his favorite meals every night. They sat at the kitchen table and talked well into the night at least once a week. They locked their bedroom door when they were in it, still.

They would have been embarrassed to call what they had *a great love*, but Lillie knew that was what it was. She had felt it. She was *part* of it.

Maybe it didn't matter how a thing started. Maybe what mattered was how it went along.

Or maybe, Lillie countered herself in her head, *you're just delusional enough to imagine that no matter what this man thinks he feels, you can change it.*

But when she looked at him across from her, she won-dered about that, too.

Maybe she wasn't delusional at all. Because Tiago could talk all he liked about business this and no touching that, and all the rest of it besides, but he hadn't kissed her as if he cared about any of those things.

And at the end of the day, what was her alternative? Her cousin's spare room when her child could be the heir to all of this? For the sake of her pride?

How could she think she could call herself a good mother if she did something like that?

So she tilted her head a little bit to one side, though she couldn't quite manage to be as flippant as she wanted.

"Well," she said, and had to swallow, hard. "Since you asked so nicely, I will. I'll marry you."

And because he smiled at her, she even signed his papers, too.

Because what she wanted was a father for her child. She wasn't a gold digger. She hadn't had the slightest idea there was any gold to dig. That being the case, she didn't see any reason why she *shouldn't* sign. How silly would it be to turn around and make some claim to this land, this house, this grand legacy for herself?

For her child, now—that was a different story.

So she signed the papers. And she stood in his study with the celebrant from the local registrar, the notary, the unreadable Leonor, and several other officials who might actually have been his attorneys, and she married him.

"That was not exactly the culmination of love's young dream," she said not long after, when the official-looking men had all been ushered out by the housekeeper and only she and Tiago remained. "But I suppose it got the job done."

Because she was trying to sound supportive.

He glanced over at her, this man who was her *husband*—a word that felt silly to even *think*—and Lillie told herself it was just as well that they'd done it this way. There was no big white dress. No crowds of family or friends. No flowers, no attempt at emotional vows, no deeply embarrassing yet always entertaining wedding disco.

He was wearing what she supposed was a more casual version of his usual clothing. The usual dark suit, but the collar of his crisp white shirt was open. Wide enough that she could see not only the strong column of his throat, but the hint of the dark hair she knew was sprinkled over his chest—seeming to exist purely to emphasize the marvelous shape of him. Those hard planes of muscle, the intriguing ridges of his abdomen.

Though it was better not to think of such things right now, she warned herself. She looked down at her own outfit instead, a simple dress from her suddenly expansive wardrobe. Deceptively simple, that was. She knew perfectly well that it made her look somehow delicate and elegant at once, when she felt more awkward and misshapen by the day.

And instead of being bridal in any regard, it was a serviceable navy.

Yet they were married all the same.

Tiago kept looking at her intently far too long. And then he beckoned for her to follow him as he opened up the floor-to-ceiling windows that were everywhere in this house, all of them doubling as doors that let out to the various tiers of terraces and balconies and patios aplenty. In this case, the red-tiled patio was set beneath an arbor, trailing vines that might not have been flowering in the first flush of spring, but were pretty all the same.

Though all Lillie could think of was how pretty they would look if she accentuated them with some Christmas lights. Out here, in all this winter sunshine, it seemed entirely too easy to forget what day it was. What month. She supposed that if she didn't have a baby growing inside her to mark the time it would be the easiest thing in the world to simply drift off into a daydream of some eternal Portuguese summer and lose touch with herself entirely. It was already difficult to imagine that there was any scenario that would lead her to return to all that cold hard rock in Aberdeen.

Tiago ushered her to a seat at the table that had been set up there, waiting for them.

"How lovely to have a bit of a meal after a wedding," Lillie said brightly. "Almost makes it seem real, doesn't it?"

Tiago's brows knitted together as he stared at her. "I assure you, our marriage is very real. Did you imagine there was some pretense in the proceedings?"

"It was more a figure of speech."

"I would never play games with something so critical," Tiago told her darkly.

"Because you're known for otherwise playing a great many games, of course," she said with a laugh.

And Lillie was not surprised that he did not laugh with her. She wasn't sure why she was laughing herself, except she thought she was a bit more nervous than she wanted to let on. Because it was one thing to think about nights in Spain, and to make the best of things as she had been doing since, which had perhaps not been the hardship some people liked to think.

There was a part of her that mourned the loss of her solitary nights in her little room in Aberdeen, with the baby inside her and memories of Spain to keep her warm.

Because now the man in those memories was her *husband*, just as he would shortly become the *father* of their child—who she would no longer carry inside her—and maybe she wasn't quite as resigned to all of this change as she pretended.

This was all a little more disruption than she'd had planned when she'd taken Patricia's place at that resort.

It had certainly never occurred to her that if she did somehow find her mystery man one of these days, he would be so *stern*. So uncompromising, even though she was sure she could see little hints of that fearless, fiery lover she'd met that first night. But she supposed there was no crying over spilt milk. Not now.

She concentrated on the food instead, because she knew by now that it would be stellar, but as she was walking over to the table to take her seat, she stopped short. Her hands moved over her belly and she frowned.

Tiago was at her side in a moment, his hand on her elbow, his frown now an expression of concern. "Is something the matter?"

"I don't know…" Lillie murmured, because that fluttering sensation she'd felt off and on all day was back. But now it was more intense. And it didn't feel like a *jitter*, whatever that was.

Then it happened again, and she knew.

She looked up at him and did nothing at all to stop

the delighted smile that moved over her face. She even laughed a little as the strangest feeling washed over her. A kind of relief, but far stronger than that, a kind of *marvel*.

That this was real, too. She was well and truly going to be a mother. She had made a baby who would grow up to be a *person*.

With this man beside her, who looked at her now as if he would tear apart the sky itself to keep her safe, if she only said the word.

It was like a different storm, brighter by far than any she'd known.

Lillie felt her smile becoming sappy at the edges, but she couldn't mind. She reached over and took his free hand and pulled it to her belly, holding it beneath hers so his palm was flush against her roundness.

And it came again, that fluttering.

"Is that…?" His voice sounded like she felt. The disbelief. The delight.

The wonder.

"It's the baby," she whispered, her eyes welling up a little. "The baby's kicking."

When he looked up at her again, she could see the emotion in those green-and-blue eyes, making them gleam like silver and gold besides.

"Our baby," he said thickly.

They were married. They were having this baby, together. *Ours*, he'd said.

Ours, she thought, like another vow.

"Yes," she said out loud, though her throat was tight. "Ours."

And Lillie understood for the first time just how much

trouble she was in here. With Tiago, who looked at her in amazed wonder, his hands warm against the mound of her belly.

Because he would keep her safe, that she knew beyond any doubt.

But she wasn't sure she could say the same about her heart.

CHAPTER SIX

BY THE TIME the last month of this strange year began, Tiago felt certain he had everything in place. He had married Lillie and made certain she signed enough documents to keep his lawyers happy. He had secured his heir.

He had fixed the mistake he had made that heedless night in Spain, and he had made certain that kind of irresponsible recklessness would not be repeated.

"This is all irregular," the head of his legal team had tutted at him. "Normally we would never—"

"The Villela heir cannot be born out of wedlock," Tiago had replied, simply enough. "It simply is not done."

But he had carried that word like an indictment.

Because the man was not wrong. This was all highly irregular. And Tiago was not used to the sensation of finding himself in such a position. He had always done his duty. He had always made certain to handle each and every one of his responsibilities.

He did not make mistakes.

Lillie had been an anomaly from the start.

"I assume you roamed about Europe, hither and yon,

conducting mad, passionate affairs wherever you went," she said one night at dinner.

Tiago had insisted on the same nightly meal that his parents had engaged in every single night of his childhood. When he had told them that his friends from boarding school did not spend their time eating with their families, his mother had scoffed.

Then they must not have much of a sense of their families, she had said. *But that will never be your fate,* meu filho.

Tonight, he questioned—not for the first time since he had brought Lillie home with him—what precisely he was thinking. He had spent the day in London, as he did often. It would have been easy enough to stay there, but then, it was not precisely a hardship to fly back to Portugal in the evening. He told himself that he was getting used to this routine, because he intended to be a presence in his child's life. He already knew how important that was.

But every time he thought about all the things he needed to put into place to raise a son or daughter the way he had been raised, he seemed to forget that Lillie was always a wildcard.

She wasn't even in her cups, as anyone else he knew would have had to be to carry on in such an indelicate manner, asking such impolitic questions.

By now he understood that this was simply Lillie.

"I beg your pardon," he said coolly. "I don't know what makes you think that I, Tiago Villela, would ever be so indiscriminate."

"Yes, what could possibly make me think that?" And

in case he missed that she was being facetious, she let out that laugh of hers again. Speaking of indelicate things that he should probably attempt to curb, her laugh was a marvel of a thing. Husky and filled with light and merriment. There was something almost bawdy about it, and he told himself that it was more evidence that she was completely inappropriate in every possible way.

And yet, inappropriate or not, she was his wife.

"Is this your way of telling me that you have had many such nights yourself?" he asked, and was then appalled at himself. Men of gentility and breeding did not ask such questions. And he, personally, did not wish to know the answer. And more, did not wish to examine why he wished to protect himself from that knowledge.

"Certainly not." She wasn't looking at him. She was tucking into the local delicacies before her, with her usual deep and obvious relish for every bite. The spicy *franga da guia*, and *javali*, the wild boar that his people hunted on his own lands. And his favorite, *conquilhas à algarvia*, a mess of clams and garlic and coriander, cooked with savory Portuguese sausage and fried onions. He had not realized until Lillie how many meals he'd sat through with women who did not like food. Or feared it. Women who had elaborate rituals and a great many rules.

Lillie simply ate her fill, and it was one of the most sensual things he had ever beheld.

"No?" he asked, perhaps too intently as he studied her. As if that might show him the fingerprints of her history all over her skin, little as he wished to see it.

She smiled at him in that guileless way she had that he could not understand. She was as free with a laugh as she was with a smile, and he couldn't make any sense of it. Tiago told himself he resented it, but that did not explain the hunger he felt for her, for her very presence, for the delight he took in what she would do or say next—

No, he corrected himself. *Delight* was not the right word. *Dismay* was much better. He was *dismayed* by her, obviously, because she was completely different from the sort of polished wife his parents had wanted for him.

The sort he had wanted for himself—someday far in the future.

Now he had to do his best to make *her* appropriate, because it was that or fight off this terrible *delight* that made him imagine he could be a different man. The kind of man he had been taught so clearly he could never, ever become.

Villelas were called to be better than that.

He had beaten back everything in him that was different to make sure he not only heeded that call, but exemplified it.

It did not matter if he liked it. This was who he was.

But she was talking in that artless, appealing way of hers. "It might shock you to learn that I did not, in fact, indulge myself with a stable of European love interests to sustain me through the long Scottish winters."

"That resort has a reputation," he found himself saying, without meaning to. As if, in her presence, he was no longer the careful and considered man he was everywhere else. He could not account for it. "It is well known for fostering romantic interactions amongst the clientele."

"That would explain why my supervisor has always loved it so much," Lillie said. "She's told me many a time that she quite likes a drink and a shag of an evening." Her smile only deepened when she saw the frozen, appalled expression he could feel like a mask on his face. "I like to tell folks that I'm a bit of an acquired taste. By which I mean, I've always been cursed with standards."

"Standards are not a curse."

"Many of my housemates would disagree." Lillie picked up her glass and swirled the sparkling water she preferred at dinner around in it, her smile dimming—but only slightly. "I had a boyfriend my first two years of uni. He betrayed me, I'm afraid, and quite shockingly. There were scenes. It was ugly."

Once again, Tiago felt frozen, but for a much different reason. "What does that mean?"

"I caught him in the act," Lillie said simply, and while she wasn't smiling as she had before, she did not look devastated by the story she was telling. Was it time, he wondered? Had it dulled the sting? Or was it that it had been less devastating than dramatic even then? He couldn't know, but he could feel himself…thaw, slightly. "It was quite a palaver. I will admit that I was torn up at how *public* it all was for ages. Even though I knew that *of course* I was better off without the sort of person who would do such a thing, it took a long while for that to really sink in. And when it did, I found I was much less interested in being chatted up, or really having anything to do with a bloke on the pull. And then, somehow, years passed, and I didn't mind, but then I met a mysterious man who was not a pool boy in a Spanish resort."

She reached out and plucked up a plump shrimp from the platter that sat between them. With her fingers, which should have appalled him. He told himself that it did. That everything about her appalled him because it should have but instead, he found he was watching the way she popped the shrimp in her mouth, her lips closing over her own fingers—

He needed to stop.

"I'm sure your dating history is much more sophisticated and elegant," Lillie said. "Princesses and debutantes and endless galas, one can only assume."

"I have dated," he said, carefully. Even though *she* looked perfectly cheerful, as if unaware that this was a minefield. Because *he* certainly had not wished to hear about the uni boyfriend. The one he now felt the distinct urge to seek out, so he might mete out some overdue justice on Lillie's behalf. "But there is a very specific set of qualifications and attributes my future wife was meant to have, and I saw no need to get serious with anyone until I was ready to find the woman who exemplified that list."

"Oh, dear," Lillie said, those blue eyes of hers sparkly again. "I don't think I've ever *exemplified* a thing. Your poor list."

And when he thought about that later—after he'd left her there before dessert arrived, muttering something about a business call he did not have to make—what he remembered was how unconcerned she seemed. As if she truly did not care one way or the other about any list of attributes the wife of a Villela should have possessed.

She hadn't even asked what they were.

Tiago found himself brooding about them instead. And as the days passed, he cataloged Lillie's many flaws as he observed them, matching them against that list of spotlessness and sophistication in his head.

Especially when he was tempted to tell himself he didn't care about the discrepancy.

"You're doing it again," she said another night. This time, he had insisted they dress and eat in the elegant dining room. She sat to his right, and he expected that she would be overwhelmed by all the different plates and utensils that made up the sort of overly formal dinner he felt certain she had never indulged in before. But this was Lillie. She looked *entertained*, not overwhelmed. She even smiled at him now, her eyes dancing. "Looking at me and finding me wanting, at a guess."

That she could read him when no one else could made his skin feel too tight on his own body. "It is only that we will have to make certain that you receive the instruction you need," he told her stiffly. "There are certain expectations surrounding my name. I would hate for you to be out in the world and seen as a representative of this family without possessing the necessary skills, that's all."

"You are all heart, Tiago."

She said that serenely and then, holding his gaze in a manner he could only call challenging, she picked up the fork he had just been at pains to tell her was the wrong one, and used it anyway.

And later on, once again barricaded in his office—because he needed to leave her after these dinners where she sat about in pretty dresses, laughing and sparkling too brightly when the only thing that was meant to *sparkle* were the chandeliers—he thought about that list again. And more, about the way his parents had raised him.

They had made it perfectly clear what was expected of him.

Our family has too much wealth and power for you to expect that you should spend your life seeking happiness, his father had told him when he was a teenager. *You will hear many things as you grow, about how you must seek your truth. About how what truly matters is your own personal happiness. But the people who say these things are not Villelas.*

Yes, Pai, Tiago had replied when his father had leveled that familiar glare on him.

Villelas cannot be selfish. A Villela is more than welcome to seek contentment, Tiago, but happiness? His father had shaken his head. *It is better by far to strive for usefulness. You are a steward, not a star. This is what you must remember.*

Tiago had never forgotten.

Just as he never forgot being left when he'd dared *grieve* where they could see him.

Over time, there were more things he did not question. The way his parents always looked taken aback to see him, as if they'd forgotten all about him while he was off at school. The many holidays he and Leonor had been left to their own devices in one house or another, because his parents did not see any reason to curtail their schedules to see him.

The year that became two that he did not see them at all, because they had important things to see to elsewhere.

He had been ten, then eleven, and he had known better than to mention it when he saw them again.

Just as he knew, deep down, that all of this had made him stronger. More capable of doing what was necessary. More, that he needed it.

Because now he understood that he had a gift that most men of his wealth and consequence did not: he did not expect that he was the center of anyone's thoughts. He did not expect to be thought of at all.

It made him less arrogant—and more successful—than his peers.

He had never questioned what his parents had taught him, because he could see in everything he did that they had given him innumerable gifts. And he told himself he was not going to start questioning them now.

What he did question was how he was ever going to raise his own child with a woman who did not herself understand—or even *try* to understand—the realities of life as a Villela.

His parents had not loved each other. They would have recoiled at the very idea that they might. There were far more important things to concern themselves with, as they always made sure to tell him. They had always liked to say, quite proudly, that the vagaries of emotion were beneath them.

And his grandmother might have been a counterpoint

to that in her time, but Tiago had only known her as a small boy. Small boys wanted to believe in all manner of impossible things. He felt grateful indeed that he had outgrown it.

He did not know why he did not tell Lillie these things.

Instead, he attempted to model his parents' relationship and modify Lillie's behavior as he went. Like the nightly dinners where he would ask her coolly what she did with her day, and, when she remembered to ask him the same, give her the concise and emotionless breakdown that he expected in return.

But though he realized this was how he expected colleagues to behave in business scenarios too, his wife did not seem to get the message.

"What exactly is the plan?" she asked one night.

He had spent the first part of their meal staring at her hair. She had caught the heavy mess of it up in the top of her head so there were riotous curls spilling out from what looked like a makeshift bun she had done herself. When he knew full well there was staff for such things, as he had hired them himself. She was a Villela wife now, and really, he ought to make it clear to her that she needed to think more elegance and less efficiency.

Yet somehow, he was too busy imagining wrapping his fingers in those curls to say anything about how she'd styled them tonight. "At the moment, the plan is to have a quiet, congenial dinner and an early night, as my presence is required in London in the morning."

"I mean for me," she said. "I can't say I minded being on a bit of a holiday from the real world, but surely I'll need to *do* something. I can't drift about the house all day long, can I?" She sighed. "I need a job, Tiago."

He blinked at that, letting the sheer temerity of it settle. A bit. "Villela wives do not work."

Lillie propped her chin on one hand. "What did your mother do with her days?"

Tiago sat back in his chair. "She had a great many interests. Her family had once been deeply involved in the cork industry here, and she was instrumental in the founding of a local museum that explores the impact of cork not only on this region, but on Portugal as a whole. Her other charitable interests included literacy, medical conditions that were dear to her heart for any number of sad reasons, and she also bred her hounds. Podengos."

"None of that sounds like a job."

"Lillie." He shook his head, taken back. "You cannot *work*, of course."

"You make that sound dirty. *Working*. When you do it yourself."

"Villela wives do not," he replied. And he sighed when she stared back at him in a kind of amazement. "It isn't done. I understand that you came into this accidentally, Lillie. That can't be helped. I'm willing to make allowances."

She laughed, but somehow, it was less merry than usual. "Allowances?"

"The ideal wife for a man in my position would have been trained from birth to assume this role. Part of the training would include being an heiress of great rank and fortune herself. She would have been educated in the finest schools and would have involved herself in only the most worthy charities afterward. There would never be any question of her *working* in some menial job."

"It is a terrible pity, then, you could not have married this paragon." Lillie gazed at him as if she pitied him. But also, if he wasn't mistaken, as if she wanted to take the fork she held and throw it at him. "What a shame it is that you have been saddled with the likes of me, a peasant straight through. Why, I don't know how you can hold your head up."

"I didn't offer any moral judgments," he said, and it was distressing to find that he had to work to keep his voice steady. Calm. To remain the man he had worked so hard to become, and not give in to the strange urges this woman brought out in him.

"Didn't you?" she asked. She pushed back at the table and stood up too quickly, and he shot to his feet, too. Without knowing he meant to move.

"Villelas do not make scenes in the middle of a meal," he told her, a bit more darkly than was wise. He knew it even as he said it. "Or at all."

Lillie glared at him. "Villelas can do whatever they like, with my blessing, but I am a grown woman who will continue to do as she likes. What I'm trying to tell you, Tiago, is that I'm bored."

"Bored." He repeated the word as if it was a curse. Because, to him, it always had been. His parents had made sure of that.

"Bored silly," she shot right back at him. "I've taken a thousand walks. I've read stacks and stacks of books. I've entertained myself by asking your staff for outrageous things to see if they can provide them on a moment's notice, and guess what? They can. If this is the life of the rich and famous, I'm sorry to tell you it's tedious in the extreme."

"There are many people who would kill to have these advantages you consider so boring."

"It's not the advantages that I don't like," she fired back. "It's that I need a purpose. Surely you understand that. You seem to have such an ingrained idea of what your life is meant to be. You know your purpose here. But what's mine? Given that I'm not this perfect, effortlessly aristocratic Villela wife of myth and legend. I need to do *something* or I'll go mad."

"You are my wife. You will be the mother of my child." He very nearly laughed, not that he found this amusing. "It seems to me that should be enough to occupy your thoughts instead of all these unnecessary concerns about some outside purpose."

"Oh," Lillie said sweetly, "you are my husband and will be the father of this child. Does it consume *your* thoughts?"

He thought he might actually have growled. "I think of little else."

She blew out a breath. "The baby is going to come one way or another. And like it or not, I will have to figure out how to be a mother then." She shook her head. "In the meantime, I'm a wife, but I don't even know what that means. And I don't think you do, either."

"I know exactly what a Villela wife must be," he retorted. "As I have been at pains to tell you. My mother was remarkably good at it. After she died, my father told anyone who would listen that there is no point in him remarrying, because no one else could possibly do it as well as she did."

"Do what?" Lillie asked, very distinctly, as if he was the one being obtuse.

"She supported him in all things. Everything she did, everything she said, brought honor to our name."

"But what about their marriage?" Lillie demanded. "Did they laugh? Did they play games? You never say what they were *like*. Did they kick off their shoes and dance around this table? Did they fight, have private jokes, and hold hands on their afternoon walks?"

Tiago stared at her in astonishment. "I don't have the slightest idea what you're talking about. They worked well together. They were an excellent team."

"Did they *like* each other?" Lillie asked, throwing her hands wide.

"Do yours?" And it was exactly the sort of ill-measured, ill-considered retort that he knew better than to make. What was it that this woman did to him?

She crossed her arms then and tipped up her chin, glowering at him as if this was some kind of altercation. When Tiago did not have altercations. "They do all of those things. My parents met when they were children. They grew up in the same village. They were each other's first…everything. They've been wildly in love with each other and the very best of friends as long as either one of them can remember."

Tiago could not have said why he felt so…unnerved by this revelation. And almost embarrassed, as if this was not the sort of thing that ought to be discussed in polite company.

"That's very nice for them, I'm sure."

"It's not always nice at all," Lillie shot back. "They love me, don't get me wrong, but they love each other more. Sometimes, growing up, I felt a bit like a third wheel. I always suspected the real reason they didn't have more children is because they preferred not to divert much more of their attention from each other. And then there was the impossibility of living up to a love like that. I suspect that half the reason I felt so wrecked by my university boyfriend's behavior was that I had to tell my parents that I wasn't like them after all."

"My parents never pretended to be in love," Tiago said, and he could not understand why he felt on the defensive. "They would have been horrified if anyone suggested that they should succumb to such mawkishness."

And he had closed the distance between them again, when he knew better. When he knew, in fact, that it was the last thing he should allow. Yet there he was, so close that if he'd wanted, he could have reached out and touched her—but he didn't.

Lillie's eyes were too big, too blue. "That's one of the saddest things I've ever heard."

"You don't understand." He wanted to rake his hands through his hair, but he did not *fidget* like a child. Tiago blew out a breath. "That's my fault, not yours. I clearly have not adequately explained to you the weight of the responsibilities that both of my parents carried, and that you and I must carry as well. There is no space for any of these things that you've been talking about here. There is only duty. Responsibility. And the contentment that those things can bring."

"That," Lillie said, very distinctly, with what could only be called the light of battle in her blue eyes, "sounds like a terribly sad life, Tiago."

He leaned closer, just slightly. Just to make his point. "You don't know what you're talking about."

"What I know is that what you're describing sounds like a long, slow, frigid death," she shot back, something like passion—or fear—in her voice. He didn't like either. "I want no part of that. I've been close enough to it myself and I don't want to go back. I don't want all that numbness and banging on about *responsibilities*. Responsibilities are there no matter what, aren't they? I want to feel *alive*."

And then, as if that wasn't outrageous enough, she closed the distance between them, shot up on her toes, and kissed him.

CHAPTER SEVEN

LILLIE WISHED SHE'D thought to kiss him sooner, rather than daintily waiting for *him* to kiss *her*.

That was the only thought that worked its way through her as she stood there, her mouth on his at last, no longer quite so concerned with boredom. Or purpose. Or long, slow slides into a walking death, all in the name of the family honor. Whatever *that* was when it was at home.

This had been the answer all along.

This was what she should have done the moment she'd walked into his office, to remind them both that this lightning bolt was what had brought them together and everything else was secondary to that.

This felt as right tonight as it had that night in Spain.

And what she felt, first and foremost, was relief.

He was still *him*. They were still *them*.

This was still real.

So she just kept right on kissing him.

Lillie kissed him until he made a low sound, like a growl, in the back of his throat. She kissed him until his hands came to her face, then traveled over the rest of her. He trailed fire and need down her back, her upper thighs. He found her breasts, moved over her belly, and then his palms gripped her bottom.

And still the kiss went on and on.

Though there was nothing the slightest bit *frigid* about it.

"What are you doing to me?" he grated out, tearing his lips from hers for the barest second.

"Doing something," she whispered back, "about this terrible boredom."

And then she laughed, because he swept her up into his arms. It shouldn't have worked. He should have staggered under the weight of her, because she was big and round these days and she had never been an airy little thing in the first place.

But Tiago did not seem to notice. He hoisted her high against his chest, and gazed down at her in a way that made her shiver.

Because she knew this look. She knew this man. She even knew why he carried her like this, the way he had back in Spain that night because he did not want to part with her for even as long as it would take for her to walk from one part of her room to the other.

Like then, he kept stopping so he could kiss her again. Deeper. Hotter.

With all those storms she could see in his eyes.

And she knew that this had been building for too long. Since Spain, maybe. And ever since the wedding, she had been waiting for him to do something about it, but that was foolish. Left to his own devices, Tiago would sit about in stiff-looking suits, droning on about duty and honor until she wanted to start throwing the crockery about, just to make *something* happen.

Note to self, she thought as he carried her down one hallway, then up a set of stairs, not seeming to even breathe heavily while he did it. *Kiss the man. As often as possible. So he is not tempted to forget that this is how we got into this mess in the first place.*

It was one thing to ponder that particular mess while sitting on her own, yet again, in her guest suite. It was one thing to brood on it as she walked out into the vineyards, alone.

Revisiting that mess, with all the heat and wonder that had caused it in the first place… Well. That was something else.

Lillie pulled him down with her when he laid her out so carefully on a big, wide bed in what she took to be his bedchamber.

And later she might think more about the fact that it seemed so stark in here, so austere, that it reminded her of a monastery. More like a hotel suite than a man's personal bedchamber, but she couldn't care about that. Not now.

Not when he was finally stretched out beside her once again.

Lillie accepted, in that moment, that she'd thought this would never happen again. She'd thought it and she would have said that she'd come to terms with it, too. Because what choice did she have? She had first tried to find him, but had been forced to give up on it. And woven into all the ways she'd thought about the fact that she was set to become a single mother had been that secret bit of sadness she hadn't known how to share. Not with herself. Not with anyone.

She'd missed him. She'd missed this.

And there was no possible way to explain that to anyone.

Because it was only one night. That was all they'd shared. It shouldn't have meant anything.

But that had always been the trouble with Tiago.

She knew, and she thought he knew too, that everything had changed when they'd laid eyes on each other. That kind of thing was supposed to be a myth. It wasn't supposed to be possible. If asked, she would have told anyone who would listen to her that love at first sight wasn't real. Even her own parents, still in love to this day, hadn't had that. Theirs was a love that had grown deeper and richer over time, as they liked to tell anyone who would listen.

But that didn't change the fact that Lillie had looked up, seen Tiago, and everything after that had felt…inevitable.

It still did.

He was muttering words she didn't understand now, pressing them into her skin as he moved over her, kissing her as he went.

And there was no time for this. There was no *time* because there had been nothing but time and she couldn't bear it. Lillie couldn't keep her hands to herself. She pulled at his clothes, pushing his hands away when he got in her way. She was in a kind of panic, so desperate to get her hands on his bare skin. To get her mouth into the crook of his neck. To rediscover that astonishing V carved above his hips.

To learn him all over again, like this was new.

But before she came anywhere near getting her fill, he was rolling her over again. He put her on her back so he could peel her dress from her body, make short work of her undergarments, and then settle there beside her so he could finally learn this new shape of her.

And he dedicated himself to the task.

He ordered her to lie still when she wanted to fight him, because she wanted to rise up and wrap herself around him. She wanted to reacquaint herself with him, too. She wanted to feel him everywhere, real skin to real skin, not the dreams she'd been surviving on all this time.

"My poor, greedy *benzinho*," he murmured, that current of laughter back in his voice.

At last.

It wasn't there when he told her what Villelas did and didn't do, as if he couldn't decide to change it if he liked. It wasn't there when he lectured her on duty and told her about the perfect wife he hadn't married.

It was only here, with his mouth against her skin and his hands moving from her tender breasts down the length of her body. Here where he lingered over her bump, then found his way to the oversensitized furrow where she longed for him most. It was only here, she thought, that he was truly himself.

That he was actually alive.

But she knew better than to say it.

"Why aren't you inside me?" she demanded instead.

Because she wanted him there, but also because she wanted the dark velvet of his laugh. The rumble of it, whisking over her skin and then into her, too, even before he pressed his long, strong fingers deep into her soft heat.

Even before he made her sigh, then moan.

As she rose, pressing her hips up to meet him, he began to move his fingers in and out of her, so slowly she didn't know if she wanted to scream or cry.

So instead of making such impossible choices, Lillie did both at the same time.

And it seemed as if an eternity crept by with her strung out there, stretched between the two, lost in the sheer perfection of his touch. Lost in how well he seemed to understand each and every one of her body's responses. He anticipated them. He worked her toward them, then through them.

Over and over again.

It seemed as if there was nothing to do but surrender to such mastery, so that was what she did.

And Tiago, gentleman that he was, gave her a great many opportunities to get it right.

Then, when she was reduced to nothing but a shivering, shuddering mess of sensation and need and desire, he rolled her over to settle her astride him.

He slid his hands to her hips. And his gaze was a storm, deep blues and complicated greens.

"I do not know how different this will be for you," he said, his voice gruff and low.

A warning, maybe. Or a statement of intent. Either way, the shiver that moved over her was made entirely of delight.

Even though Lillie thought that there ought to be something wrong with this. In kneeling there as she was, her knees spread wide on either side of him and that great, thick length of him standing up between them. Standing up and rubbing gently against the swell of her belly. Where their baby grew, even now.

She thought it shouldn't be sensual, but it was. Because he and she had come together just like this to make this baby in the first place. They had done all of this together, just like this.

And that they were together again, naked and wild-eyed and filled once more with all this heat and light, felt like magic. Like a miracle.

Lillie thought this was the season for it, anyway.

And then shuddered again when he smoothed his hands over her bump, as if he felt it, too. The sweet joy that they were married. The particular glory of the fact that the wildfire, astonishing connection between them had made a person. A person that they would meet in a couple of months.

The wonder of all of this—of everything that had come from their gazes clashing together in Spain. Of all that would come, stretching on far into the future.

She thought she ought to have felt dizzy, but that wasn't it. Not quite.

"I have no idea how it will feel," she told Tiago.

And then watched as a smile moved over his face.

Because this was the only way Tiago Villela smiled, as far as she knew. Naked and in bed—and wickedly.

"We will discover it together, you and I," he promised her.

And then his hands moved to her hips. It occurred to her that she had essentially told him that she'd been with no one since him, and even though that was no more than the truth, she couldn't help but think that put her at some kind of disadvantage—

But then there was no point thinking about advantages or disadvantages, because there was only feeling.

There was only this.

There was only him.

Because his hard hands moved her until she was kneeling up, then moving so she could press down on that thick, hard length of him.

And it was…different. He felt bigger, harder. She was so sensitive, so new.

Or maybe it was because he lay there beneath her, watching her closely with those glorious eyes gleaming darkly, and once he had her positioned the way he wanted, he…took his time.

First he played a bit at her entrance, and then, when she shook and sobbed and cursed his name, he laughed. Then he eased himself inside, only slightly. Only a little, then pulled back out.

Then he did it again.

And again.

Then, with that iron clasp on her hips that prevented her from doing anything but giving herself over into his hands, he eased in just the faintest little bit more, then back out.

And he seemed perfectly content to continue doing exactly that. Moving into her a little more each time, but only in the tiniest increments.

But so slowly.

So terribly, wonderfully slowly and with such perfect control that it made Lillie almost embarrassingly aware of how out of control she was. Outside herself, turned inside out.

At points she tried to fight, but it was no use. He would not let her simply sink down and take all of him. He would not let her control a thing.

Instead, he murmured words of encouragement in several languages. He made that low, growling sort of noise that seemed to set each and every one of her nerve endings on fire.

His voice was a kind of husky croon, its own sensual bombardment.

Lillie found herself with her head thrown back, her hair everywhere, her back arched so intensely it should have hurt.

And it was possible it took whole lifetimes before he finally lowered her all the way down, so that he was embedded inside her as deep as he could go.

Once he did, she could do nothing but pant as she opened her eyes and stared down at him. Not sure if she wanted to kiss him or kill him as she trembled, still held fast in between his hands.

Again, that smile of his moved over his stern face. He lifted her up and she almost cried, thinking he was starting the whole process over again—

But instead, Tiago thrust up into her and brought her down hard to meet him, and it was like everything before was thunder, but this—

This was the lightning.

It hit her, she ignited, and then she splintered into too many pieces to ever fully recover.

She shook and shook. She rocked against him, sobbing out the white-hot, overwhelming pleasure of this. Of him.

Tiago moved beneath her, but only enough to keep her going and going, dancing in the flames, shaking and sobbing.

Until finally she was limp and dazed, and so he sat

up. Staying deep inside her, he pulled her against his chest and began to move her that way.

And once again, every thrust was a revelation.

Lillie was oversensitive, or maybe it was just him, but all she could seem to do was burst into flames. Again and again, one time barreling straight into the next. He wrapped his arms around her back, so that all she had to do was meet his thrusts as best she could—

Because it was all too much. And it was nowhere near enough. It felt brand-new and as if she'd finally come home.

She lost count of the times she shivered and sobbed her way over that cliff. Each time was infused with that lightning and as much of a glorious shock as the first. He made her fall apart with her hands sunk deep in his hair, and his in hers, that tiny stinging, making it better. Different.

Another time, she was kissing him hungrily, deeply. So that he was inside her in two places, her nipples rubbing against his chest, so she simply imploded there, unable to do anything at all but let it happen.

Again and again she caught fire and each and every time, he caught her as she came down and threw her straight back up again.

Demonstrating all the while that iron control that she'd thought about far too many times over the past months. And thinking about it now, while experiencing it again, had predictable results. Because the harder he was inside her, the more the intensity of the way he held himself back made his eyes dark and gleaming, the softer she was. The hotter she was.

And the wilder it was when she broke apart.

Until finally his whole body tightened, and he grew stiffer inside her. He reached up to put his hands on her face, so they were gazing at each other once more, both of them flushed. Both of them chiseled bare at the overwhelming magic of this thing between them.

Raw, she thought. *Mine.*

"Hold on," Tiago ordered her darkly.

"I always do," she whispered back.

Maybe what she meant was, *I always will*. Maybe that was what he heard.

Because he bared his teeth, those maddeningly steady thrusts inside her grew wild and erratic, and this time, it was the scalding heat of him inside her as he roared out his release that sent her over the edge, chasing after him, tumbling over and over and into the stars beside him.

And it seemed as if a great many years had passed by the time she woke up again to find herself curled up at his side. Though he had clearly gotten up in the meantime. The fire danced in the grate, warming the room. And he had pulled a throw over her, as she rested her head upon him like a pillow.

He was his own furnace. She remembered that, too. And she was a Scottish girl, always cold. A man who burned like Tiago did made her feel nothing but safe, warm, and cared for.

Even though she felt as if she was moving through a fog just now, she knew better than to say that. She smiled sleepily at him, finding his gaze in the firelight.

Tiago looked…brooding, if anything. But he did not speak. He reached over and dragged his thumb over her lips, then ran his palm over whatever shape her curls had made.

"Tiago," she began.

"I sent for food," he told her curtly. "As I expect you will be hungry."

And she hadn't been a moment ago, but the minute he said it, food was all she could think about. He rolled to the edge of the bed and she followed him, accepting the whisper-soft wrapper he handed her, like a caress against her bare skin.

Then she sat with him in front of the fire, only too happy to tuck into the platters of food that waited there. Cheeses and meats, warm breads and pots of sweet butter. She was thirsty too, and drank deep, and it was only when she sat back and sighed a little that Tiago made that low, growling noise again that made her shiver all over again.

And then she forgot all about the food, because he was moving over her. He shifted her into place beneath him on a soft leather couch, then shouldered her thighs apart, settling himself there between her legs so he could eat her up, like dessert.

After he got her screaming and falling apart all over again, he lifted her up and carried her with him into a bathroom suite even more impressive than hers. He took her into what seemed to be a large tiled room, but turned out to be as big a shower as she'd ever seen, with sprays of water coming from all sides.

Tiago had her again there, holding her up against the warm walls and letting the water pound down all around them until they both burned too bright to bear.

And it reminded her so much of Spain. It had been like this then, too.

Every touch seemed endless. Every spark a whole bonfire.

It had been an eternity, that night. Maybe only one night had passed outside her hotel room, but inside it, there had been this. A deep knowing she never could have explained to anyone. A recognition.

An eternity.

And now it was threaded through with so many more layers. The baby. Their wedding, however businesslike.

The lifetime she'd felt with him that night, stretching out in front of them.

And she slept so deeply beside him that she shouldn't have been able to wake, but she did—to find his mouth wicked temptation, teasing her back into that wicked dance again and again all night, as if all of this was new.

As if none of it could last, just like before.

But this time, she told herself dreamily, she would not wake alone. This time, she knew his name. She would not spend months without him.

She could see the smudge of a new day's light outside his windows when she woke for the last time that night. And this time it was slow.

An inexorable unraveling, not a bright lightning strike.

And maybe all the more unsettling because of it.

Lillie felt undone, unspooled. She shuddered against him. His head tipped into the crook of her neck, and they shook together, there in what was left of the dark.

Leaving them raw.

Bare.

Seen, she thought as she drifted off to sleep once more.

When she woke the next time, the sun was pouring in from outside and she was alone in his bed.

Lillie didn't really like how that felt, but this wasn't Spain. For one thing, she was already pregnant.

As she swung out of the bed, she told herself all the rest of the ways this was different. She knew his name. She supposed she'd taken his name, though for all his talk of *Villela wives*, she hadn't given any particular thought to keeping her name or taking his. Still, she was in his bedroom, not some random hotel room.

"This isn't the same thing at all," she told herself briskly.

She went to use his shower, though she was half-afraid of drowning herself in all those different sprays. When she came out, there were new clothes waiting for her on the bed she'd left a mess that was already made.

They were like ghosts, these servants of his, and she wasn't sure she would ever get used to it. But she still pulled on the outfit someone else had picked out for her. And like all the clothes that had been provided for her here, it was a lesson in simplicity. Another one of those shockingly comfortable T-shirts that bore no resemblance to any T-shirts she had ever worn in her life. A pair of jeans that were softer still, but the stretchy waistband that not only fit her belly, it made her feel supported. Not simply bloated and round, but a woman with a figure.

She pulled on the sweater they'd left for her, too, a simple crewneck thing, except it, too, felt like soft, sweet dreams as it fell into place against her body. And when she glanced in the nearest mirror, she laughed, because she looked well classy in a way she never had before.

Who knew that all it took was posh clothes, well cut.

Something about that made her laugh again, though

it didn't quite take away from that clutching sense of uncertainty deep inside.

And Lillie didn't like that at all, so she set out to find him, only realizing as her toes got cold that she'd neglected to stamp her feet into the boots they'd left next to the bed. Meaning she was padding around the gaspingly fancy house in her bare feet, which she did not have to consult Tiago to know was not how a Villela wife was meant to comport herself.

She chose to take that as a good sign. Because the last thing she wanted was to live her life in that kind of coma. Everything he'd ever said about his parents made her stomach hurt.

Lillie went to his study first, but he wasn't there. She had thought that study of his was his office, but it was only in exploring the house in her bare feet and morning-after hair that she came across him in a modernized office space tucked away on the floor below his bedroom. When she peered in, he was on a video chat of some kind, nodding with ill-concealed impatience as people spoke to him rapidly in different languages.

When he replied, it was as calm and stern as ever, and Lillie couldn't tell if her reaction was a sweet joy or a kind of deep consternation—but either way, it made her flush.

When the call ended, he turned from the desk where he'd been standing, arms folded, frowning into the screen on the far wall.

She'd been uneasy since she woke up. A little dismayed, even, that he'd repeated his original disappearing act. But the whole time, she'd told herself it was a hangover from Spain. That everything was different now.

She'd counted all the ways.

But all it took was one look now, and Lillie knew she been right to worry.

Because her husband looked straight through her, long and slow and frigid, as if she was a stranger.

CHAPTER EIGHT

THE DECEMBER DAYS rolled along and it was as if Lillie had somehow found herself married to two husbands instead of one.

It would have been panic-inducing, if she let it.

Every night was a mad, intense exploration of each other. Just like Spain had been. Only this wasn't one night in Spain followed by five months of longing. This was better, because it was deeper.

Because they knew each other now. They knew each other better every day. And every night their bodies sang out in recognition of that ongoing intimacy. What had struck them both like lightning at that resort became hotter because it was deeper now. Because of the things they shared. The baby they were expecting. The house they lived in. The interactions they had that brought them inexorably closer, like it or not, and then set them alight in the dark.

Every night was better than the night before. Every night seemed longer, more shattering. They turned to each other in that bed again and again, but no matter how endless and devastatingly *good* it all was, one thing held true.

Every morning Tiago would wake up and act as if none of that had ever happened.

As if he had actually kept his promise that he would never touch her again.

He became that stranger, and Lillie had to fight to keep her panic to herself, because she wanted the man she knew. The man she had clapped eyes on back in Spain and had longed for ever since.

Not this ice sculpture who made her worry that she was slowly freezing over herself.

Daytime Tiago was all business and frigid straight through, and while he did not look at her as if she was a *stranger* necessarily, he maintained a certain chilly distance.

"I cannot countenance boredom," he told her that first morning, when she'd gone to find him in her bare feet and had found him as shut down as she'd ever seen him. "So I've taken the liberty of making sure that tedium does not overtake you while, at the same time, directing your considerable energy in a more appropriate direction."

"That sounds a bit boring, actually," she replied, mostly to see him glower, but also to cover up the panicked catapulting of her pulse at the sight of him like this. "Who fancies being *directed* anywhere, much less somewhere *appropriate*?"

But the Tiago she was married to by day did not react the way she knew he would at night. He did not even sigh, though his expression suggested that he might. Internally. And what Lillie learned that day was that when Tiago *took the liberty*, as he put it, what he was actually doing was laying down the law. Arranging his world in the manner he saw fit. Whether it was providing her with a wardrobe that matched his sensibilities or filling her days with lessons.

Lillie was tempted to complain, but the truth was, she'd always loved school. Private tutoring was even better, as it allowed her to go at her own pace without having to slow down for anyone else. Tiago started her off with Portuguese and Spanish lessons in language and history, because, he told her, the child would certainly speak both fluently.

"You can be sure the bairn will speak English as well as Scots, then, too," Lillie replied when he made one of his decrees about their child's future fluency, as if he was handing down stone tablets from on high. "Shall I get you a tutor? *Chan eil aon chànan gu leòr.*"

But it was daytime Tiago she was telling that one language was not enough, so all he did was gaze at her in that way of his. It suggested the imminent possibility of disappointment and more forbearance than ought to be required.

Tiago by day was a frustration in male form, Lillie often thought in the weeks that followed. Panic lurked in their every interaction, because how could she stay married to a man so cold? How could she let him raise her child?

She couldn't answer that to her satisfaction. But she wasn't the slightest bit bored.

In addition to her language and history classes, she received lessons in comportment so that her sometimes-elegant appearance could be matched by a host of elegant actions. Or in any case, that was what the tiny woman dressed in an ever-changing array of chic scarves worn with notable aplomb informed her.

With enough hauteur that made it clear that *her* elegance was innate, not taught.

"I don't quite see the point polishing up this particular sow's ear into any kind of silk purse," Lillie said chattily at one of the stiff dinners Tiago insisted upon, this one after a day of lessons on cutlery. "What does it matter?"

"It only matters if you plan to go out in polite company at some point," Tiago said in that *I am the Villela heir* voice of his, all steel and certainty. "I assumed you would not wish to embarrass your own child, who, make no mistake, will be raised with all the manners incumbent upon his or her station."

Lillie poked at the salted cod before her. It appeared in some form or another at every meal, because it was the national dish of Portugal, according to Leonor. And Lillie was a proper Scottish woman who might prefer haddock from her local chippy, but she had never met a piece of fish she didn't like. The infinite variations of *bacalhau* pleased her immensely.

But tonight what she liked most was stabbing at it. "This is a very special talent you have, Tiago. To already be using our child as a bargaining chip when it hasn't even been born yet."

"I will never *use* our child," he replied in a low voice, with an intensity that made her sit a little straighter, so much did it remind her of the man she met only in their bed when the moon was high, almost like he wished he was still nothing more than a dream she had. "What I will do is protect that child, just as I will protect you, even if what I must protect you both from is you."

He delivered that last bit in faintly ringing tones. Lillie stopped abusing the poor meal before her. She sat back in her seat and eyed him for a moment. "And who will protect you?" she asked.

She didn't add, *from yourself.*

But he didn't answer anyway.

Because he insisted that they spend the whole of the evening meal in the very stiff and formal manner he felt was appropriate. That was how his parents had raised him, and he made it clear each night that he thought they'd had the right of it.

And she wanted to flip the table when the panic got into her bones, but she didn't. She went along with it, because she knew that after dinner there were drinks. Because that was also what civilized people did, apparently. They very theatrically rose from the table and moved to a drawing room or study—likely because they had houses with so many rooms and needed to use them all. Once in the chosen second location, they sat and had further conversations, though more casually, and it was only then that the Tiago she preferred emerged.

Every evening, when he came back to her, the relief just about bowled her over.

Lillie would have been happy if the nights went on forever. It was the endless days that made her wonder if she was going mad. Or if she'd stumbled into one of her favorite torrid novels where a woman found herself married off to a grim man in some castle somewhere, only to discover the passionate lover he only became in the dark was his disgraced twin. Or a vampire, she wasn't picky.

She wasn't picky about Tiago by night, either. She

tried to enjoy him as fully as she could, and warm herself in all that fire of his, because she knew it would be chilly again come morning.

But there was less time to puzzle over the mysteries of the two sides of Tiago when he added to her lessons halfway through December. This time, it wasn't more attempts to make up for her lack of a debutante ball, it was classes on finance. Business. Wealth management and estate planning.

"Dare I hope that it's your intention to add me to your company roster?" she asked one afternoon as they were coming up fast on the bleak midwinter. Not, of course, that there was anything particularly bleak about the Algarve at this time of year, though the locals complained about the cooler weather and the clouds. Facetiously, to her mind. All Lillie saw was the light.

Nighttime Tiago might laugh a little when she said things like that, and scrape his teeth along the line of her neck as punctuation, en route to driving them both wild. The daytime version only gazed at her, making a bit of a show of that faint frown between his eyes.

"I was unaware that you wish to interview for a position in my company," he replied, with that coolness that she believed was *meant* to make her wither where she stood. Which was only one of the reasons she did not. "Competition is fierce and the process is considered grueling."

"I assumed that was why you added all those new classes," she said, fighting the panic within at the slap of chilliness from him. She tried her best to meet it with a certain…languid unconcern, whether she felt it or not. She'd taken to invading his office for a cup of tea in the afternoon, as that was what *she* considered behavior appropriate to her people. And tried to act as she meant to go on. As if he was the husband she wanted, not the one he played by day. As if she could make him see, somehow, that it was better when he was. As if this might all work out, somehow, instead of stranding her and her baby on this relentless glacier he liked so much. It was more of an effort every day. "I'm becoming quite an expert on financial matters and the business affairs of the landed gentry. I thought perhaps you were planning to make me your new chief financial officer or the like."

Lillie thought nothing of the kind, but it was amusing to claim otherwise. Because he would draw himself up in all his offended dignity and try to invoke a blizzard or two with his freezing tones, and she would smile innocently back at him and wait for sundown, when he usually readdressed the outrageous things she'd done in the light. Deliciously.

That part of this game she liked.

It was better than driving herself mad with the increasing fear that she was going to be stuck here, and not with the man she wanted. And how would she keep her child from withering in this terrible, endless winter?

Lillie tried her best not to think of it, and, therefore, thought of very little else.

"In a manner of speaking," Tiago said. And when he looked at her then, he was expressionless, but there was something about that dark gleam in his gaze that made her sit straighter in the chair. Usually she preferred to lounge about in complete defiance of everything her tiny dictator demanded she do in her comportment classes. "You are my wife now."

"In more ways than one," she agreed, and then beamed at him when his gaze narrowed. Because he did not like to be reminded that he was not maintaining the boundaries he'd set down long since.

Tiago had been perfectly clear about that in those first few days, when it became clear that he could not stay away from her at night and more, that he hated himself for it in the morning. At first Lillie felt almost complimented. She had never been the sort of woman who inspired such strong reactions in anyone. Certainly not in men.

But she felt significantly less complimented as time went on. And had got a bit salty about it in turn.

Because the salt covered up what she knew—that this couldn't last. That at least one of them would break, and she was horribly worried it was going to be her.

If I could control myself, benzinho, *I would*, he had growled at her, backing her across the length of the small study that second evening, after such a long, cold day. Because it was dark outside, and as she was about to discover, he was his very own kind of werewolf. *If I could keep my hands off you, I would. And believe me, the day will come when I will make certain that we behave appropriately. The way we should have been doing all along.*

What does appropriate *even mean between us?* she had dared ask him. *Everything that happened has been anything but.*

But we are both Villelas now, he had growled, coming to a stop there before the bookcase once he had backed her as far as she could go. He had placed a hand on either side of her and leaned in so she could see the blaze of fire in him. The intoxicating heat, just there, shimmering in all that blue and green. *And Villelas have standards.*

As it happens, she'd whispered, lifting her chin, *I haven't decided whether or not I'm taking your name.*

Though she had certainly called it out a lot that night, both there in the study and upstairs in his bed, until the dawn turned him to ice again.

But she did not think that was what he was thinking about as he stared at her now, forbiddingly, across the expanse of his very important desk.

"You are my wife," he said the way he often did, making sure she could see how he had to call upon his patience. "And it is entirely possible that I might die before you. I would hate to imagine you adrift after I'm gone, a target for disreputable people. It would be far better if you were capable of stepping in and controlling my estate yourself. It's only rational."

But there was something about the way he tacked that last part on, she thought. As if it had only occurred to him just then that he could use that as an excuse.

And as she stared back at him, that gaze of his changed. It became…less cool.

Lillie did not pretend that she didn't know that no matter what he said, or how he dressed it up and tried to make it matter-of-fact, he was giving her a compliment. More than that.

Because his responsibilities, his duties, were the most important thing in the world to him. And if it was her opinion that he clung to them like a drowning man, desperately reaching out for any bits of floating debris to call a life preserver, she wisely kept that to herself.

At least by day.

"If it's up to me," she said, aware that her voice was hushed, then, "I'd prefer it if you lived."

And she knew she wasn't wrong about the way he looked back at her, hushed himself, as if all of this was a sacred moment. And more, that he might not have intended it that way. That he might have convinced himself that it was, indeed, only a purely rational move that had to do with the estate, not her.

But their eyes locked in that way that had always been almost too honest to bear. And Lillie knew, the way she always knew, that they both knew the truth.

She also knew he didn't like it.

"Time is not granted to us," he gritted out after a long moment. "If it was, my parents would have lived forever. They might not have loved each other, not in the way you insist your parents do. But they loved what they built. They loved the history of their great families and the legacies that made them who they were. If it was up to them, they never would have left those things behind."

"And what of you, Tiago?" she dared ask, though her ribs seemed to clamp down hard against her heart. "Surely they loved you?"

He looked almost stricken for a moment. Then he looked down and she saw his mouth curve, though it was no smile.

"As I said," and it took him a moment to raise his gaze to hers again, she thought, and a moment more to keep his gaze so clear, so fiercely steady, "they were both deeply enamored of their legacies."

She slid a hand over her belly and pressed her fingers

in to meet tiny kicks that greeted her. And silently she vowed, *I will never be* enamored *of you, my wee sweet bairn. I will love you madly all the days of my life.*

But Tiago continued to look at her in that almost-stricken manner from behind his desk, and she felt a sharp stab of pain—for him. For the man who had been left to stand here behind an uncaring desk, talking of legacies when what he patently needed was love.

And she knew he would never ask for something he wanted. She doubted he knew how. So she held his gaze, and kept hers solemn. Befitting the solemnity of this occasion, even though she knew he would deny it was happening even now. Even though he would argue to the death that it made sense, that was all.

"Thank you," she said. Very carefully. Very deliberately. "It will be an honor, though I hope I'm never called upon to do it."

And that night, he was like a man unleashed and untamed, raw and wild.

As if both of them were more naked than ever before, more connected and more *real*. Yet come the morning, he reverted right back to form.

Later that same day, when her lessons were done, Lillie found herself out of sorts. She took herself off for a wander out in the tidy rows of the wintering vines, letting the relative warmth of the Algarve sun fall all over her though she felt as dark as if she was back in Aberdeen, with a gloomy sun that started sinking near enough to three in the afternoon this time of year.

When she was not normally given to brooding.

"We need to decorate the house for Christmas," she

announced when she returned, tracking dirt into his office and slouching down as far she could go in that chair.

She chose not to notice that he was obviously trying to ignore her.

"If you don't mind," he said in glacial tones, and oh, wasn't he at his most cutting today. That was how she would have known that last night was something different. Something that had stripped them both bare down to the bones, even if she hadn't already felt that way herself. "Much as I enjoy your interruptions, I do have a significant amount of work to get done."

"This can't work, you know," she said. She hadn't meant to. But the words came out anyway and she was glad of it when he didn't even do her the scan courtesy of *glancing up*.

"I'm not in the mood for histrionics today," he replied with that same frigid disinterest. "And in any case, as I have told you more than once already, there are no divorces in my family. It is not who we are."

"I'd like to know exactly who you think *we* are, actually," she threw back at him, a different kind of lightning firing up her blood. "I hear a lot about *us*. But you only ever seem to be speaking about yourself."

Tiago did look up then, though he took his time with it. Lillie thought he had a lot of nerve to bring up *histrionics* when he made such a meal out of a mere glance. "There will be no divorce, Lillie."

"I wasn't asking for one, though I'll be sure to keep in mind that you've decreed it can't occur when the time comes." She shook her head at him, as if she despaired of him. When he was like this, it was possible she did. "I mean *this* can't work. You acting distant and remote by the light of day and then, at night, behaving as if we are lovers in the midst of a mad, passionate affair."

"This is not the time or place for this discussion."

"Isn't it? I'm so sorry. What would be the correct time and place?" He wasn't the only one who could throw a little pageant while doing an ordinary task. Lillie quite theatrically pulled out her mobile, swiped it over to the calendar, and then waited there, poised to type in the appointment time of his choice.

She had never seen the man grind his teeth, but she thought he was close just then. "I told you. There are certain boundaries that need to be observed and it is a point of deep self-recrimination that I cannot seem to hold myself to these standards with you."

Lillie dropped her mobile to her lap. "I have an alternate idea. You could stop trying to live your life, and certainly stop trying to run your marriage, according to the whims of people who aren't even here, and didn't like each other when they were."

Maybe she shouldn't have said that. But she couldn't bring herself to take it back.

"They liked each other fine," he replied, and she wondered if it cost him to sound so emotionless. So cold, straight through. "One of the reasons they held each other in the utmost respect for all of their days is because they adhered to very simple rules. They did not attempt intimacy. It was not expected or desired. Not once I was born."

And she had already opened her mouth to argue about that. To point out to him that, fair enough, it seemed that his parents had made the best of the kind of dynastic marriage that was likely never entered into with any hope of love or true intimacy or even friendship. Liking each other, respecting each other, must seem like a triumph. A victory for the ages. She could concede that much, even if she and Tiago were something else entirely—

But instead, she stopped dead at that last thing he said.

"Is that how you're getting around it?" she asked softly. "You can excuse all these nights away because the baby isn't born yet? You can beat yourself up, but not too hard, because you haven't broken *all* the rules. Not really. But once the baby is born, that's it, I'm cut off. Is that what you're doing, Tiago?"

And she watched, fascinated, as a muscle clenched in his marvelously chiseled jaw. On another man, it would have been the same as a fist through a wall. A table overturned.

She had to repress a shudder, as if he'd done both.

"You came here to ask me about Christmas," he said, the coldest she'd ever seen him. But she knew better. She could feel the emotions he did not wish to show her, too big and too raw, crowding out the breath inside her body. "Portugal is not like your northern countries. We celebrate on Christmas Eve, but not in the manner you might be expecting. It is quiet. Restrained. Traditional. We prefer to err on the side of quiet sophistication rather than too much gaudy noise and decoration."

Every word an icicle, designed to stab her straight through the heart.

"Tiago…" she began. She tried to keep going, but her throat felt tight. Almost too tight to bear.

"If you will excuse me," he said, in that same way, whole winters in his voice, "there are calls I must make."

He did not look up again, dismissing her that easily. That completely. And Lillie staggered a bit as she left his office, from the weight of all that raw pain of his.

It was inside her now, whether she liked it or not.

And it sat heavy on all the fear and panic she'd been fighting off for too long now. Because she could see the future now, and it was the one she'd been afraid of all the while.

She kept going until she was in that central courtyard, where flowers still bloomed even now. Birds sang as if no one had told them it was December. If she closed her eyes it might as well have been the height of summer, green and lush.

"Almost as if your grandmother never agreed to forgo of all the gaudy light and color you think is so beneath you," she muttered under her breath, but out loud the same. Scowling down fiercely at bright purple and pink and orange flowers, but seeing only Tiago's frozen expression. Hearing only his frigid words.

Feeling those icicles like knives, cutting deep.

Leaving her reeling. Bleeding. Carved into chilly little pieces.

She sat down heavily on one of the stone benches near a small fountain that burbled and sang. If she closed her eyes, she could imagine it was her very own Christmas carol.

And Lillie always had loved a good Christmas carol.

When she opened her eyes again, the sun was on her face, and it couldn't have been less Christmassy if it tried.

And Lillie thought, at last, that it was high time she fought.

That she harnessed all those passions she'd been looking for all her life, and dived straight into them, for a change.

Because nothing good had come to her from waiting. Or wondering.

Or hoping he might see the light all around him.

It was high time she showed him.

As Tiago kept informing her, and not only when he was being fierce and cold from behind a desk, she was a Villela.

And if she was tracking all of her lessons, one thing was clear in all the stories they told her. All the history on both sides of his family. Not to mention her own proud Scottish heritage.

When in doubt, they all did exactly as they pleased and sorted out reactions later. It might as well be the family motto. She reckoned she might have it sewn up and put on a fancy bit of tartan while she was at it.

Lillie took a deep breath, then blew it out, hoping any leftover icicles went with it.

But then she got up and marched back into the house to find Leonor.

Because she intended to fight with everything she had to the future she imagined, not the one he was threatening her with.

And she was going to start by having the Christmas she wanted, whether Tiago liked it or not.

CHAPTER NINE

THE FIRST HINT Tiago had that things had gone horribly awry in this home that was meant to be his sanctuary was when he left his office late a few days later, then stopped dead in the hall outside.

Because he could hear singing.

And for a tense moment he actually wondered if he was hearing ghosts, after all—

But with the next breath, reality returned, and he was more concerned that he was having some kind of a medical event, because ghosts weren't real. Not even his.

Still, the singing continued.

Tiago followed the sound from his wing of the house into the main section, not sure if he was relieved or more irritated when it became clear that he was not, in fact, imagining things. There were choirs singing.

And what they were singing was Christmas carols.

But that was not the worst of it, he discovered as he stopped dead in his front hall and stared around in amazement. The house—*his* house, the ancestral home of his mother's people—had been transformed.

And while he had not exactly locked himself away in his office, Tiago knew he had been less available these last few days. While it was true that he had a lot of work to do, as ever, it was also true that he'd found himself a bit more keen to do it than usual.

Even after he'd realized that he was waiting for her to turn up for her afternoon tea break, which had infuriated him. What had infuriated him even more was that she hadn't, as if he'd finally succeeded in chasing her away.

This is what you want, he'd told himself sternly. *You can take this opportunity to create more space between the two of you, as you know you must.*

But he had gone to her that night anyway.

And since she'd skipped dinner, he'd had to go looking for her. He had found her back in her guest suite, which had outraged him. He had expressed that outrage by crawling into the guest room bed with her, using the four posters to great advantage as he exercised his opinion on his wife's skipping of meals and sleeping alone.

I had no idea you felt so strongly about it, she'd said, her smile sleepy and her blue eyes full of heat and laughter. *I had no idea you were* allowed *to feel strongly about anything, in fact.*

He had ignored that. Virtuously. Though he had expressed the feelings he most certainly did not have in other, more creative ways.

But the next night, when he had to hunt her down again, he carried her across the house to his quarters because she was his wife and she should be in his bed.

A point he made certain to belabor until the dawn.

And that was the order he had given this very morning, to move all of her things into his rooms, where she belonged.

He had thought that settled it.

But instead, Lillie had turned his house into a Christmas card.

A very particular sort of Christmas card, traditional and certainly not Portuguese.

There were evergreen trees everywhere, strung with lights. And where there weren't trees, there were even more lights. There was mistletoe. There were seeming truckloads of ornaments. There was the usual nativity scene his grandmother had put up every year, mercifully left alone, but everything else was red and green, as if Santa Claus had come and exploded everywhere.

Even his grandmother's garden was not spared. There were lights strung from the surrounding rooftops, covering the courtyard in a latticework of gleaming white lights that sparkled as he glared at them.

He stood there for much too long, something simmering in him that he could not identify, but it was big. Unwieldy.

And he was not at all sure what to do with it.

Tiago turned and saw the housekeeper standing there, looking as self-contained as ever.

"Where is she?" he gritted out.

But Leonor had never been cowed by a member of his family, which was why she had stayed here so long. "If you mean Senhora Villela, she is waiting for you to join her." She did not raise her brows at him. She would not dare. All the same, the suggestion that she might remained. "I assume that is where you were headed."

"I know my way around my own house, I think," he bit out, cold. Frigid, even.

The older woman did not appear to notice the chill. "The *senhora* has prepared something special." And this time, she actually did indulge in something a little too close to a lift of her brow. "It is Christmas Eve, after all."

She did not wait for him to respond to her, because she was impertinent. And clearly did not fear that he might fire her, which, naturally, he would never do.

And in any case, he followed her. Unwillingly, or so he told himself. But he also knew that Lillie was waiting wherever it was his housekeeper was taking him, so there was no possibility, ever, that he wouldn't go.

That realization only made him…icier.

And his mood did not improve as Leonor led him outside onto one of the far patios. Where he did not find the seating areas he expected, usually quietly arranged to take in views across the vineyards that ended where the sky met the sea far off in the distance. Tonight the patio itself was transformed.

Into what he could only call…a full-on Christmas assault.

Complete with an avenue of evergreen trees, bristling with silver bells and lights, down which he was compelled to walk until he found himself in what might once have been a tastefully done seating area with braziers for a touch of heat. Now it, too, was unrecognizable and was…

"It's a Christmas grotto," came Lillie's voice, full of that deep amusement that still drove him mad. Maybe even more so today. "Isn't it magical?"

"A 'Christmas grotto'?" he repeated, as if she'd cast aspersions on his family name with that term. In truth, it felt as if she had done more than that.

"More properly, it would be Santa's grotto." She said that as if she hadn't heard his tone. As if she couldn't see—with her very own eyes that were as blue as the sky and never before the slightest bit blind—how he stood here before her, clearly in no way transported by these shenanigans.

He ordered himself to keep that steadily growing sense of unease at bay. That growing unwieldiness that seemed to make the very ground beneath his feet buckle and shift when he knew full well that everything on these lands had been built to withstand the march of generations.

But he also took the opportunity to take a good, hard look at his wife.

The wife of Tiago Villela, mother of the future Villela heir, was dressed in bright red and green as if she imagined herself a holiday elf. Instead of what she actually was—one of the wealthiest women in the world.

He made a mental note to restrict both colors from her wardrobe in future.

The dress she wore looked like velvet and was therefore completely inappropriate for the Portuguese climate, even on a night like tonight when the weather was relatively cool. As if that was not enough, she wore a pair of knee-high boots in an overbright red leather. He supposed the heels on those boots added length to her already well-formed legs, and no doubt to her height as well. He estimated that would put her red-slicked mouth in a fascinating place before his, but he could only imagine it because she was not standing before him.

She was *lounging*. On what looked like one of those ghastly peppermint candy canes that were festooned about everywhere Christmas was not contained, when the rational part of his mind understood that she had simply transformed a settee with red and white fabric.

Tiago was opposed to holidays of any sort and liked Christmas least of all, because it had once been his grandmother's favorite. He didn't like to think about how much she had loved it, and how he had, too, while she'd been alive. It was far better to simply hate it, ignore it, and move on. But it was hard not to think that he might as well rethink his historic dislike of the season if the packaging was like this. Making his ripe, lovely wife look like a Christmas sweet herself.

She had made the whole of this part of the long, wide patio into a Christmas scene, lifted from a climate far north of here. All those evergreens festooned with lights. Some kind of cottony fluff strewn about to replicate snow. Tiago had never personally experienced such a Christmas, but he had seen it. Like everyone else alive, he had been subjected to cold-weather Christmas images the whole of his life.

But tonight it was simply one step too far.

"This is unacceptable," he told her grimly.

Lillie shifted position on her candy-striped settee, but only slightly. As she did, the dress moved and he found himself distracted by the way the hemline rose, showing him the creamy expanse of one thigh.

He gritted his teeth.

"Merry Christmas Eve to you, too," she said, sounding lazy and merry at once.

"First of all," he said, not sure why he felt half-drunk when he hadn't touched alcohol. Not tonight. Though he thought a shot or two of the hard stuff would not go amiss as he faced down this outrageous temptation.

"You are in Portugal. Everything you've done to this house seems to suggest that you are confused. Geographically."

"What I am," Lillie replied, a quiet note in her voice that was at odds with all the surrounding commotion, "is married to a man who does not communicate with me. If you are opposed to Christmas, you should have said so."

He did not like the way she said that. *Opposed to Christmas.* As if *he* was the issue here. "I'm not opposed to Christmas. What I am opposed to is my family's ancestral home being turned upside down with all these tawdry and tasteless decorations."

"Why don't you like Christmas?" she asked, calmly, as if he hadn't just questioned her taste, the infernal woman.

"I don't like Christmas or dislike Christmas," he told her impatiently, though he was aware this was not as true as it could have been. Still, it was what he wished to believe. What he'd long assured himself he believed. "I never believed in fat men in red suits tallying up my misdeeds to see whether or not I might receive a gift. My parents held the typical *consoada* on Christmas Eve, as is tradition. We went to church because that's what one does. On Christmas we ate turkey, lamb, and goat when I was small. But after my grandmother died, the rest of us merely ignored the holiday entirely. She was the one who insisted on a proper Christmas meal. We were just as happy to forgo that once she was gone."

He wasn't sure what he expected after that simple statement of fact, but it wasn't the way Lillie looked at him then, her blue eyes suddenly too bright for his liking. "Tiago. That's terribly sad. You do know that, don't you?"

That massive *thing* inside him shifted again, making him doubt he could trust himself to stand and he could not allow that. He would not.

"I understand that you have an emotional connection to the holiday," he said stiffly. "But that does not mean everyone must. Perhaps I should have foreseen that you would react in this way, as you are so far away from your home and no doubt experiencing a great many physical and—"

But he stopped when Lillie laughed. In that airy, entertaining manner that he wished he hated. That would make it easier. He ought to find her embarrassing, surely, but he didn't. That was the trouble. She was like clear, sweet air and he wanted to inhale her and—

Focus, he ordered himself.

"If you're about to comment on my hormones, there's no need. I've always loved Christmas. I've always decorated for it, too." She shifted on the settee, somehow drawing that hem up even higher, yet still *barely* preserving any shred of modesty, and he felt himself come perilously close to breaking out in a sweat. He rather thought she knew it. "And for all the lessons you seem determined that I should take on board, here's one for you. It's only a few decorations. Perhaps on a grand scale to match the house we're in. But Tiago. I promise you that it's not going to hurt you any to ignore them, if you must."

And she stayed where she was, *lounging* at him and too delectable by half, and how was he supposed to handle her when she was so outside the boundaries of everything he knew, everything he'd been taught?

Tiago didn't know what to do with her. That was the trouble.

He gazed down at her, and as ever, there were too many warring impulses fighting for purchase inside him.

Did he want to go to her? Sprawl there beside her? Get his hands on that lush body of hers and put his mouth where he wanted it most?

Or did he think that it was far better to indulge only the reality of this, which was that he knew how their marriage ought to be run. He knew exactly what needed to be done to make certain that his family legacy was preserved.

He could not understand—and had not been able to understand, at all, since the moment he had laid eyes on this woman—why it was that she seemed to muddy waters he'd long believed were crystal clear, all the way down.

When he knew where that mud took him. Back to grieving in the dirt and cut off for his trouble.

Tiago had vowed he would never let him drown like that again.

"I think there are some things that need to be clarified between us," he said, aware that his voice was harsh.

But even as his words hung there in the air, his staff began to flood in, bearing platter after platter and piling them high onto the table that waited on one side of the red and green and snowy seating area. The table, too, was gleaming with gold and silvers, bright glossy reds and exuberant greens.

Lillie rose to her feet for the food, clapping her hands together before her like a child. Except she was no child, he recognized. She was unbearably earnest, and she had never been taught to hide her enthusiasm for any reason, and there was nothing in the whole of him, his entire personality and experience, that had the slightest idea what to do with that.

Or with her.

As he had demonstrated since she'd walked into his office in London.

Though he found he liked the idea that she was even less guarded than she'd been then. That she'd been honest, but wary. And he wasn't sure he knew exactly when she'd decided to be this open, this gloriously transparent.

Only that it had happened here, with him.

And that he had come to hunger for it.

"I worked with the kitchens on the menu," Lillie told him, clearly delighted with all of this. "It's a proper Scottish Christmas dinner. Roast turkey and all the trimmings. Cranachan, clootie dumpling, Dundee cake, and proper mince pies for sweets. We have Christmas carols playing, fake snow on the ground, and finally, a little Christmas cheer round here."

She smiled at the servants as they passed her on their way out of the little evergreen cave she'd made them, then turned that meltingly bright smile on him, so vivid that it outdid all the lights she'd strung up.

And she made him ache, that was the thing. She pierced him straight through the heart, when he had gone out of his way to make sure that organ held no sway over him. Ever.

Because the only purpose of the heart, as far as he could tell, was to hurt.

Tiago had no time for such things.

He let the heel of his palm press against the offending spot on his chest, hard, and then he glowered at the woman who had caused this in the first place. With all that infernal *brightness*. Those blue eyes that would be the undoing of any man. And that laughter that he worried would haunt him through the rest of his days.

"I don't want any of this," he said, his voice so dark that there was a part of him that was shocked it didn't put out all her twinkling lights.

Her smile dimmed as she straightened where she stood. "I'm sorry to hear that."

"If I wanted a British Christmas, I would go back to London. I don't need it foisted upon me here."

He thought she looked at him too long, then. And he was afraid she saw too much.

As she had from the beginning.

"But you see, I will need my child not only to be fluent in your languages and able to eat with the proper utensils when called, but to be familiar with the things that are important to me, too," she said. "I think that's what making a family is all about, isn't it?"

And there was something about how calm she sounded that only pricked at him more. Because why should she be calm? How *dared* she? Tiago was known for his glacial composure and unshakeable calm with everyone on the planet, save her.

Why should he be the one to feel as if the earth was shaking beneath him when she looked as if she could stand just as she was, forever?

That ungainly thing inside him seemed to grow with every breath, crowding out everything else. Making him wonder if he had never really known the true contours of who he was at all.

And that, too, he had to lay squarely at her feet.

"If I am permitted a moment of honesty, Lillie," he growled out then, as dark and as harsh as he liked. "The unvarnished truth is that you are entirely inappropriate."

"Inappropriate?"

He had expected her to flinch at that, and hated himself that he wanted this to happen, but it couldn't be helped. Surely the truth was what was important here. It needed to be said at last, and he had never before worried about being the one unafraid to voice even the most unpleasant of truths.

Though it didn't seem as if she'd truly heard him, because all she did was raise a careless sort of brow.

"I went to a meeting in Spain and it somehow ended up ruining my life," he continued, darker and harsher. "I don't know how it happened."

"Don't you?" She sounded…bland. Much too bland. "I remember exactly how it happened. And I'm not sure I believe that you can't."

"Never in my life have I taken leave of my senses the way I did that night." He shook his head as if it was a horror, the memories that came at him. When the only horror was that those memories claimed as much of him as they did. Even now, when he should have had his fill of her by now. He should have moved on and he hadn't. He couldn't. He didn't understand why. "All this time later, I still can't make the slightest bit of sense of it."

"It's a terrible mystery," she said, as if she was agreeing.

But the way she folded her arms above her round belly indicated that she was not agreeing with him at all.

"I have spent my entire life being raised for one

thing," he told her, perhaps too intensely. "My destiny has never been in doubt. There is no argument to be had, no wiggle room. I was brought into this world to carry on my family's legacy and to uphold to the best of my ability all the duties and responsibilities that are part of that." When she started to open her mouth, he shook his head to stop her. "Part of what has always been expected of me is an excellent marriage. It was expected—*demanded*—that I would find an heiress to an exceptional line. A woman of spotless lineage, whose family legacy would complement my own."

"It sounds a bit like you're discussing breeding a horse."

"Because, in a way, I am." He knew he was not making his case in the cool, considered manner he preferred. But he needed her to understand him, at last. He more than needed it. He thought that if she didn't, he would have to begin to consider unthinkable options. Like the divorces Villelas did not indulge in.

Because they didn't have to, he understood now. Because none of his ancestors had made such a terrible choice in a wife.

"You're comparing this to horse breeding?" she asked, but that laugh of hers raked over him as if she had taken a razor to his skin.

"We do not come from the same place," he said, severely. "That is simply a statement of fact. It was never my intention to marry for any reason at all save the perpetuation of my family line. From the time I was very young, I knew full well that I was never to allow chemistry or emotion to be my guide. And do you not see why? Do you not see the trouble we are already in?"

"If we're in trouble," she said, and he didn't like the way she was looking at him. Too carefully, to his mind. As if she was trying to figure out how best to *manage* him. As if he *required management*. "And I'm not saying that I think we are. But Tiago—if we are, don't you think that has rather more to do with the fact that you can't seem to decide who you are?"

She could not have said anything to offend him more. To strike more deeply into the places he held most sacred inside him.

For a moment he felt winded.

But then a kind of storm rushed in, a fury all its own. "I know exactly who I am. There has never been a moment I drew breath where I was not keenly aware of my *precise* position in this world."

"In the world, perhaps. But not in this house." And she pressed her lips together for a moment, though he couldn't have said if it was to keep words in or simply because her frustration was that great. *Her* frustration. "You are one man when the sun goes down, Tiago. Raw. Passionate. A man who smiles and sometimes even laughs. Most of all you're fully present. And then, every morning, the sun rises and that man disappears. And in his place is a creature of stone and distance, like some kind of gargoyle."

"You have that backward," he grated out, too far gone even to take offense at being compared to hideous statues. "This gargoyle you speak of? He is who I really am. It is the other man who is the aberration. And it will stop now. I should never have let this happen in the first place."

"But you did let it happen." She took a step toward

him, shimmering red and green and her hair curling wildly around her head. "You let it happen, when, as you have been at great pains to tell me, you have been the master of the universe, or at least *your* universe, since the day you were born. Surely the fact that you did not stop it the way you said you were going to—that you, in fact, clearly enjoy our nights together as much as I do—suggests that you've got this wrong."

"The only thing I have gotten wrong," he told her, his voice like steel slicing through wood, "is in imagining that I could take such a lump of clay and fashion it into a proper Villela wife. It is a Herculean task and it turns out, even I am no demigod after all."

She blinked at that, but once more, she didn't quail.

Instead, Lillie raised her chin again, and the sheer bravery of that gesture made something in him...howl. Despite his efforts to shut it down, it kept on and on, like too much grief to bear.

"I may not be the perfectly sourced work of art you were expecting to marry," she said after a moment in a voice he couldn't read, her gaze darker than before. "But who wants to live out their lives with an actual oil painting? I prefer a real, live, often deeply flawed person."

"I'm not trying to insult you," he growled at her, though that *deeply flawed* cut at him. "I am only taking heed of the unchangeable facts of the situation."

"You mean...that I'm pregnant with your child? Or that you're the one who insisted on marrying me in the first place?"

He slashed his hand through the air and focused on the facts. Because if anything could save him, it was facts. Facts did not roar and carry on inside him. Facts did not drape lights everywhere and talk of *being present*. Facts were cold and unemotional, just as he was supposed to be.

"You have no lineage worth mentioning," he pointed out, as if ticking off items on that list he'd mentioned long ago. "You have no fortune—in fact, I believe you have precious little money at all. Nor were you a properly raised, untouched virgin when we met, raised to give herself over to her husband and his bloodline for all eternity."

"You, of course, were as pure as the driven snow." She said that dryly. And again, he couldn't see any hint of hurt, or awareness, or any of the things he would have expected her to feel. She looked neither wounded nor shamed nor remotely impressed with her own unsuitability.

He hated himself for laying it all out so baldly, so rudely, but this was reality, wasn't it? And he was tired deep into his bones of being the only one who seemed to be even remotely aware of it.

"The sad truth is that the only thing we have in common is a troubling physical connection that in and of itself should have excluded you from consideration in the first place," he said, forcing himself to finish this when he should have had this very conversation that day in London. Before he'd found that memories of her were pale imitations of the real thing. "It is nothing but the wildest, most unhinged folly to imagine that we will ever find common ground. This Christmas scene you have created only underscores these facts."

"I don't know what makes you think that just because you have all the money in the world you get to control your heart, Tiago," Lillie said softly. "No one else can."

"I can," he threw back at her. He felt something raw surge inside of him, sharp-edged and engulfing, like desperation. But he was a Villela. And Villelas did not do *raw* or *desperate*. They did not. "I have to, Lillie. This is not a negotiation."

"Fair enough," she said. "That's quite a list. It's no wonder you don't have a queue wrapping round the place."

And then, far from bursting into tears, running off, or any of the responses he might have expected from her, she only shrugged.

As if…she didn't care?

Why did that make all those raw places in him… worse?

But in the next moment she made it even more precarious by smiling. And not that bright, earnest, Christmas light of a smile she'd aimed at him already tonight.

This smile he recognized.

Because he usually saw it when they were in bed, and she was astride him, rocking herself against him, hard, for the express purpose of tearing him into pieces.

It was that wicked. It was that knowing.

Keeping her eyes fastened to his, she reached down and took the edge of her dress in her fingers, then began to tug it up.

Tiago meant to tell her to stop. He meant to insist that she cease and desist right this very moment. But he couldn't seem to get the words out of his mouth.

And so, as he stood there as if frozen into place by forces outside his control—which was exactly how everything had felt with this woman from the start—she pulled her dress over her head and tossed it aside.

Leaving him dry-mouthed and too taut, everywhere, at the discovery that she wore nothing at all beneath it.

Lillie was standing there wearing nothing at all but those bright red boots, that riot of curly dark blond hair, and their baby.

She looked ripe and perfect.

And he might not have cared much for Christmas, but there was no denying that the way the lights danced over her skin was a kind of blessing. She looked rosy, bright.

Lit from within.

Tiago couldn't seem to do anything but stand there, as incapable of movement as if someone had come and struck him on the head, and then she made it worse by smiling at him all over again because she was wicked to the core.

Because she had been a sorceress from the start.

"I meant what I said," he managed to get out.

"And I heard you." But that smile only deepened, and there was pure fire in the blue of her siren's eyes. "Pity you can't resist me, isn't it?"

CHAPTER TEN

LILLIE HAD NEVER seen a man…break apart while standing still.

And she never would have imagined that Tiago could—that he would allow that loss of control.

But as she stood there, wearing nothing but her boots and the conviction she carried deep in her bones that she knew what was happening here even if he didn't, she watched him…crumble.

A look very much like anguish made his face twist. And for a moment she thought she'd miscalculated and made a terrible mistake. That this was something else entirely from what she'd assumed it was—

But even as that thought formed in her head, he was moving toward her. He was reaching out with those clever hands of his and that anguished look in his blue-green eyes turned instead to a storm she knew well.

She not only knew it. She longed for it.

Tiago lifted her up and swung her into his arms, as he did so often. And he held her there for a long moment, so intense that she felt suspended somewhere between the lights in the trees and the storm in his gaze. She was aware of the way his chest moved, harsh with every breath, as if somewhere, somehow, he was running flat out when she could see he was standing still.

"You are a sorceress," he growled with his head bent to hers. In a voice nearly too dark to bear, with all that thunder laced through it.

She lifted her hand and put it to the side of his face, where she could feel that muscle clench, once and then again.

"It's not my magic," she whispered. "It's ours. The only difference is, I'm not afraid of it."

The sound Tiago made then, raw and wild, thrilled her. So too did that sudden blaze of something not quite fury in his gaze.

And then everything went white hot and molten.

He took her down onto that chaise she had made into its own ornament. And he came with her, his hands frantic on his clothes, until he could press against her, skin to skin.

At last, she thought, as if it had been an eternity since last they'd touched instead of a matter of hours.

Then Lillie stopped thinking altogether.

Because it really was magic, this thing between them. It was an enduring glory, what he could make her feel with a single touch. And she was nothing but wildly, deeply, eternally thankful that he did so much more than simply touch her.

And better yet, that she could practice that same magic right back at him.

So that if there was a sorcery, shimmering there between them on this Christmas Eve, it belonged to them both.

It was the way he took her breasts in his hands, as if

they were precious, making her nipples sing and the rest of her clench on a wave of that delirious pleasure. It was the way she crawled over him and then down the length of his body, so she could kneel between his legs and take that satiny length of him, hot and heavy, in her fist.

Then, better still, bend her head to taste him.

If it was magic, then spell after spell, they made it better. Deeper. More perfectly theirs.

They spun it out into the sweet sea breeze and the smell of pine, chasing that storm as it spiraled deep inside each of them and then bloomed hot and sweet.

Once, then again.

Because once was never enough.

And when they were finished, when they both lay there, panting and limp with the beauty of it all, there were so many things that Lillie wanted to say to him. The words crowded on her tongue.

But before she could get even one of them out, he moved. Not far.

Tiago rolled so he sat at the edge of the candy cane settee. He propped his elbows on his knees, and put his head in his hands. She sat up, too, not liking the look of that for this proud, beautiful man—

In the next breath, he straightened, raking his hair back from his face.

But he still did not look at her, and Lillie thought she knew why. Because there was not a hint of that iceman who had stood before her earlier, sharing that list of all her deficiencies. Enumerating all the ways she would never live up to whatever ideal he had in his head of who his wife should be.

And therefore how he would never live up to the people who'd put those ideals there in the first place.

"You want me to be nothing more than a husk of a man, broken beyond repair," he said, in a low voice she hardly recognized as his. "And I do not understand why."

Lillie had the urge to laugh at that, but she didn't. And was glad she didn't in the next moment, because there was no way he would take to that lightly. It didn't matter what she thought was happening here. What mattered was that he was experiencing it as brokenness.

And she believed that he felt that way. It was just that she suspected that the thing that bothered him was the *feeling* part. Not what might or what not be broken in him because of those feelings.

She reached over and carefully, gently, smoothed a hand down his back. He reacted instantly. He stiffened, then sighed.

And still did not look at her, almost as if he didn't dare.

"I don't want you broken, Tiago," she said quietly. She pulled in a breath, then let it go, and since this was a night for the telling of truths, decided it was time she told him the only truth that could matter. "Don't you know? I love you. And what I want is you *alive*. In every possible way."

But she knew even before the words were all out that she'd gone too far. Because he was moving then. Tiago stood, that graceful, athletically masculine body somehow jerky tonight. As if he was stiff with some particular arthritis that only all these Christmas lights and unsanctioned *feelings* could give him.

And when he turned to look down at her, he looked betrayed.

"What did you say to me?"

"That I want you fully alive," she replied at once. "Not simply going through the motions. Not ticking off boxes on a list that someone long dead made up to make sense of their own unhappiness. That's not living. That's simply existing, and I—"

"You love me?" he interrupted her to demand, still looking and sounding as if she'd stabbed him through the heart.

This time, she did let out a laugh, mostly because she was startled.

"Of course I love you," she said, baffled. "How could you imagine otherwise?" Now it was her turn to rub a hand over her face. "You're not the only one who doesn't normally trot off with a stranger at a Spanish resort. I've certainly never done anything like that before, and didn't intend to do it again even before I found out I was pregnant. I didn't believe in love at first sight before you, but I certainly do now." She shrugged helplessly. "Obviously."

And she had not intended to say all of that, she supposed. She might have had the odd fight with phantom versions of Tiago in a mirror or two, but she wasn't unaware of the state of her relationship with this man. It was one thing in the night. But that was *only* in the night.

There was daytime Tiago to contend with and she didn't need a primer on the fact he wouldn't be receptive.

Though it was possible, she could admit as he stared

at her in an amazement that she found a touch insulting, that it was sheer stubbornness that made her say it now.

And also because it was true. She didn't see why she should pretend not to know the truth of things just because that truth might upset him. It wasn't as if he'd held himself back from sharing his thoughts on how she fell short.

"No," Tiago said, what felt like several lifetimes later, all of it caught in that gaze of his the way she always was.

And he did not elaborate.

He simply said the one word, flatly. Coolly. As devoid of emotion as if he was discussing bloody office supplies, she rather thought.

Lillie blinked, but he only stared back at her. No longer did he have that look of betrayal on his face. No hint of that anguish from before. It was as if he was wearing a solid stone mask of Tiago Villela. As if he was one of the statues that littered his grounds.

She understood at once that this was what he wanted. This was exactly who he was trained to be. And this was what he had been telling her all along—that this was all he ever wanted to offer anyone.

But she refused to accept that.

"It wasn't a yes-or-no question," she said, keeping her voice as careful and quiet as she could though her heart was pounding wildly in her chest. "It was a statement of fact."

Tiago's eyes gleamed, but darkly. "What it was, Lillie, was the last straw."

And the way her pulse was careening about began to seem like more of an alarm, but she found that she was frozen in place. She could do nothing but watch him as if through a glass wall as he moved around the candy-cane-colored settee, gathering up his things. He hauled his trousers up over his hips. He threw his shirt on, but did not button it.

"These delusions cannot be indulged," he said when he'd accomplished those things, in that same flat way. "It is already a disaster. What we must do is perform the necessary triage, now."

"I'm sorry, I'm not following. What are the delusions?"

But he ignored her. Then she watched as this man who reacted so little raked his hand through his hair again, seemingly unaware that he was doing it. He made a noise that she rather thought would have been a full shout from another man, but from him was little more than a growl. "It's not your fault. It's mine. I should have followed my instincts and known that there was no possible way that you could understand."

"I am many things," Lillie said, feeling a spark of her temper ignite—something that came as a relief after all the raw emotion and biting back the things she wanted to shout at him like the fishmonger's wife he clearly thought she was. "A grubby peasant cluttering up the hallowed halls of the Villela family, clearly. Unworthy of the great honor of having been knocked up by you, anonymously. Message received. But I've never been an idiot, Tiago. I understand with perfect clarity what's happening between us."

"Evidently you do not."

She went still because she had never heard him raise

his voice before. It made her heart knock hard against her ribs, and not because she was afraid.

And he continued, getting louder as he went. "Clearly you have no comprehension of what you've done. I told you. I keep trying to tell you. What you're talking about is the antithesis of everything I have done and everything I have left to do. I don't believe in love, Lillie. I can't. I won't."

She cleared her throat because it felt tight. "None of those are the same thing," she pointed out.

He moved then and a sudden, wild surge of joy rippled through her, because she thought he was going to put his hands on her again—

But he did not.

Sadly enough, all he did was scoop her dress up off the ground and thrust it toward her.

Lillie took it and held it to her, though she did not put it on.

"The duties and responsibilities that are mine to handle cannot be clouded by emotion," he ranted at her. His eyes blazed. His mouth was twisted, and he slashed his hand through the air again, and harder this time. "There is no possibility that any good can come of pretending otherwise. It was a mistake from the start to allow this—to let our physical connection take hold. I blame myself."

"As far as I can tell, you blame yourself for everything," Lillie said as blandly as she could when her heart had moved to her throat. "Even when no blame is required."

"Because you don't understand what's at stake," he threw at her. "How could you?"

"Here's a news flash, Tiago. There's more to the world than spreadsheets, bank balances, and endless talk of family legacies."

"You make light of the situation because you're not suited to it," he bit out. "This is why, I understand now, my parents were so determined that I understand how crucial it was to marry within my class."

And Lillie might have been offended by that—maybe she ought to have been—but she wasn't. Mostly because she knew exactly who she was and where she came from, and she wasn't the slightest bit ashamed of it.

But she also didn't think he was *trying* to offend her. The man was simply stating the facts as he knew them.

So she swung her legs over the side of her candy cane couch, and stood. And she did not pull her dress on over her body as he obviously wished she would, because she wasn't a saint here. She was no more and no less than a woman in love, fighting for something she'd never expected to find in the first place.

She was, at last, the woman her parents had raised her to be.

Finally, she had found something worth fighting for.

And she was stubborn, wasn't she, because she did not intend to let go of it.

Whether he believed in it or not.

"Your mother and father sound like miserable people to me," she said, careful to keep any emotion from her voice, then, because otherwise she reckoned he would hear only the feelings, not the words. "It seems as if they married in cold blood and barely tolerated each other, then decided that those things were virtues. And who am I to question what works for someone else? But you're not them, Tiago."

"I know I'm not," he threw back at her, still loud in ways the glacial Villela heir never was. Ever. "Because if I was either one of them, I never would have allowed this to happen. I never would have let it get so bad."

"And if you hadn't," she threw right back at him, "we wouldn't be expecting this baby. And I can't regret the fact that we are. Even if I'd never found you again, I have every intention of loving this child for as long as I live. I already do."

"You can love whatever you like," he thundered at her then, his face in the grip of all those things he didn't believe in. "But I will thank you to leave me out of it. I will be the appropriate father to my heir. I will teach this child what is expected. What is necessary. I will not traffic in these childish notions of yours. Christmas grottos. Santa Claus. *Love.*"

He spat those things out as if saying them might take him out at the knees, especially that last.

"Believing in magic doesn't make you weak," Lillie said softly, with her whole heart, because he had all the wealth and consequence in the world, but she had that. And she'd bet on her heart any day. "It isn't something that's inflicted upon you—it's a gift. It's only people who can't believe in themselves who struggle with it. Because what is magic but another word for love, Tiago? And it isn't weak people who love. It's the strong. The brave." When he looked as if he might argue, she shook her head. "You already know this. Because every night, we strip each other bare. Until we are both raw, vulnerable, naked in every sense of the word. If it wasn't hard, if it wasn't *terrifying*, you wouldn't have to hide from it in the light of day."

He didn't like that. She saw him reject it, even as a different sort of storm worked over him. "I'm not hiding from anything. I'm trying to break the spell I should never have allowed to take hold of me in the first place. Because there are certain responsibilities that need to be met, Lillie. Like it or not. And if you can't concentrate on those responsibilities, we will have to make certain that we find you an environment where you can focus on what's actually important."

She didn't like the sound of that, but she didn't let herself pay attention to the way her stomach dropped, or the worry that swept over her. She didn't let herself tip over into the fear of what she thought he was threatening. Because he wasn't talking about only her when he talked like this.

And she couldn't bring her child into the family he kept describing. She wouldn't.

Lillie stepped forward then, heedless of her nudity, and pointed a finger in his face. And she could see by the arrogant astonishment in the way he reared back that no one had ever done anything like it before.

"Let me tell you what my responsibilities are," she threw at him, no longer caring if he heard her voice shake. "They do not involve worrying over much about a family name. They have nothing to do with your houses. Or chilly dinners where we act as if selecting the correct fork is the only thing that stands between us and a barbarian horde at the gate."

"You have no idea—" he began.

But she only jabbed that finger at him again, as if she

might thump him in the next moment, and she was as surprised as he looked that he fell silent.

"My responsibilities are to love the man that I married, as best as I'm able, and cherish this baby we made together. No more and no less." She pulled in a breath. "And you are not the only person on the planet who takes his responsibilities seriously."

And for a long moment, they both stood there, bathed in twinkling Christmas lights. Christmas carols swept all around them from the strategically placed speakers, all sounding like choirs of mourning to her now. Perfectly harmonized grief, only highlighting and underscoring how unhinged the both of them were while they belted these things at each other that smarter people might know better than to say.

She could see it in him, in the way his hair was disheveled for the first time since she'd met him, his eyes so dark, and his chest like a bellows.

Lillie didn't think she was in any better state.

He stared back at her, once again looking as if she'd delivered him a mortal wound. He took a step back. And another, and stopped only when it looked as if he might crash straight into a Christmas tree.

"Tiago…" she whispered.

"No, *benzinho*," he said, a gruff sound of anguish this time. *"No."*

Then he turned and pushed his way through the trees, setting off in the direction of the vineyards. Out into that rolling, lovely land that stretched out from this house and reached to the sea. All of it his.

All of it a prison.

And Lillie wanted to run after him. She wanted to

fight. She wanted to *do something*, whatever she could and however she could.

But she couldn't make him love her if he didn't.

Maybe, she thought, just maybe—she'd been horribly wrong about all of this from the start.

Lillie pulled her dress on over her head then. It fell into place and she pushed her curls back out of her face.

And there, surrounded by the bright glare of the Christmas lights while choirs sang softly of days merry and bright, she wrapped her arms around herself, and cried.

Because for the first time since she'd found out that she was pregnant with Tiago's baby, Lillie felt truly alone.

CHAPTER ELEVEN

TIAGO STAGGERED FROM the patio, down the stairs, and didn't realize he had neglected to put his shoes on until his bare feet hit the earth.

He couldn't remember the last time he had allowed himself to go barefoot, and certainly not here in the dirt. Not here on this land of his, of his family, that had defined him for the whole of his life—both here and in Spain, where the Villela stronghold was far less pastoral.

A true steward of the land would indulge in it more, he thought. And he had the sudden memory of his grandmother kneeling in her garden, looking at him with her wise green eyes.

Dirt is medicine and water is magic, and a wise man knows how to use them both in their time, meu dengo, she had told him.

He hadn't permitted himself such memories since he was small. And tonight, he felt neither medicine nor magic. What he felt instead was the coldness of the earth beneath his feet. Not frozen, for this was still the south of Portugal. Not frigid or too hard.

But certainly it felt dark and cold here, so far away from the woman who smiled at him, pointed fingers at him, and wrecked him by asking him to do the one thing could not.

He could not. He would not.

Tiago started forward, his usually cool and rational brain whirling around in a haze.

It wasn't only that he felt like a stranger to himself, loud and unruly and unsteady on his own feet, but now the world seemed to feel strange around him. When whatever else he had felt, he had always been certain that he belonged right where he was.

He accepted that it was possible, as only Lillie had ever dared say, that his parents might have been miserable people. But that hadn't mattered, not when what they had in common was this.

The family. The legacy.

These lands and what they meant, throughout time.

He didn't know how he was meant to lose that, too— that connection to history and the future that had sustained him all his life—and his first reaction was a bright-hot fury at Lillie for holding up a mirror he never wanted to look into.

Tiago, who had always prized his own steadiness, staggered on a while longer, but then stopped again. Because suddenly the cold dirt beneath his feet, the careless stars overhead—it all seemed futile.

Because where could he go?

If there was a place on this earth where Lillie would not haunt him, wouldn't he have found it by now?

Despite himself, despite all the promises he kept making to himself, he found himself turning back.

And then he was looking back at the house. He saw all the light, beaming out into the dark like beacons. The lights he expected to see and all the Christmas fervor Lillie had brought to this place.

All that bright and unapologetic light, and all of it reminded him of her.

The way her blue eyes lit up when she saw him. The way she smiled, heedless and wide open. That laugh of hers, infectious and bawdy and so necessary to him now that Tiago could not comprehend how he truly believed there was any way to survive without it.

No matter how he tried to castigate himself for his weakness, it remained. As stubborn as she was. As rowdy as those irrepressible curls of hers.

He let his gaze find that patio she'd taken over with that silly grotto of hers, all red and green and foolish.

It wasn't as if his opinion on it changed, but it looked different from out here in the dark. It looked like a bright and happy bit of folly, a touch of the frozen north here, where it never snowed—except perhaps in the mountains at Monchique.

And for the first time, he wondered if it was possible that Lillie was a little bit homesick for all that cold, damp, and all-day gray.

He found himself raking his hands through his hair once more and as he did, his gaze kept moving—

Until he found her.

And his heart seemed to seize inside his chest.

Because in all the time he had known her, Tiago had seen this woman in a thousand intimate ways. In bed and out. When his doctors visited to check on the baby. At her lessons, at the table—she inhabited all the roles he threw in her with that same laugh and her careless ease, because no matter her pedigree, she possessed the confidence of a queen.

But tonight she stood on the edge of the patio, looking out into the dark.

Tiago doubted she could see him, but he could see her. Far too clearly. Because he could see the way she slumped a bit as she stood. How she wiped at her cheeks, then hugged herself again.

Because Lillie, *his Lillie*, was crying.

And he had told her that he was broken before. But he knew now that he hadn't even started.

Because watching her cry was the end of him.

Everything he'd said to her, everything Tiago had believed the whole of his life—none of that held a candle to what rushed through him at the sight of this woman in pain. Weeping, because of him.

What he said. Who he was. Because of everything, perhaps.

He found himself moving again as if she'd called him to her.

And there was a part of him that wished she had, because he could have ignored it, then. He could have used it as more evidence that everything about her was wrong—that everything he'd said to her was true.

For a moment there, he tried to convince himself—

Instead, she wiped at her cheeks again and her face crumpled, and everything in him simply…ended.

And then began again.

With the breath that moved him toward her. With each step that brought him near, because the land that owned him was useless if all he could do when he stood upon it was hurt her.

Tiago took the stairs two at a time and finally found himself walking toward her, his hands already outstretched, to touch her. To hold her. To simply be near her.

As if she had been the candle in the window all along.

"Why are you crying?" he demanded, and that wasn't what he meant to say at all. Not so harshly. So gruffly.

Lillie offered him a tremulous smile, so unlike the one he was used to, and he reached out to wipe another tear away.

"I was waiting for you," she said, her voice thick. "I didn't want you to get lost."

"*Benzinho*, how can I get lost?" He did not drop his hand from her face, though his voice was urgent and gruff and he was sure he would not recognize himself if he looked for a reflection. "I grew up here. I know every inch of this land, backwards and forwards."

"It's not the land I'm worried about," she said quietly. "It's your poor heart, Tiago."

He kept breaking. He kept breaking and breaking when he should have been too broken to crack apart any further.

For a moment he did not know if he could speak again, but then he did. "My grandmother did not only tend flowers," he told her, keeping his gaze on her face. On her overbright blue eyes that showed him the only version of himself he needed to see. "She also took care with me, her only grandchild, because she said she did not like how stiff my parents were. Her Christmases were filled with light, like yours. She sang songs every day on the way to the Epiphany, and there were sweets to make the singing better. *Bolo Rei* and *Bolo Rainha* cakes to tempt anyone. Every kind of fried, breaded thing you can imagine. And always at least one *lampreia de ovos*. She was a disciplined woman in her way, but not when it came to Christmas."

"Because Christmas is no time for discipline, Tiago," Lillie said with mock severity. "Magic requires comfort food. Everyone knows that."

There was no reason his throat should feel as tight as it did then. "When she died, my mother wasted no time in ridding the house of all the things that brought my grandmother, and me, that joy. She told me it was childish. That she, too, had enjoyed such things as a foolish child, but she had grown up." He watched her intently, desperate for her to understand. Or maybe it was that he wished to understand himself, with every word he said. "Over time, I began to see even the hint of happiness as the same kind of thing. Childish. Embarrassing, because joy and light were for fools. And one thing I could never be, with all the responsibilities that waited for me, was a fool."

"Tiago," she began, but her voice cracked, so he did, too.

"I never saw you coming," he blurted out, the words too gruff to keep to himself. "I'm ashamed to say I would have run from you if I had. I never wanted this, Lillie. I wanted to stay as I was, wrapped up tight in the armor I've worn almost all my life, secure in the knowledge that nothing and no one could ever affect me. I learned, year after frigid year, how to make sure I loved nothing. My parents taught me well. They did not love each other or anything else. They did not love me. I told myself I had no need of such nonsense. That it had been the immature longings of a child that I had ever imagined otherwise, and I had outgrown it. I had come to think myself invulnerable. And then there you were."

"I don't know," she whispered, her lips curving again. "Maybe it was the sangria after all."

"I kept making boundaries and then breaking them myself," Tiago said in that same rough way, as if this kind of honesty hurt, so raw and real. No ice involved. "I thought if I pushed you away by day, it could erase what happened in the night. But it never did."

"Nothing could erase you," she said softly. "Nothing ever did."

"And despite all the things I did to you, so desperate to keep you at a distance, to make you pay for the things I did not wish to feel, here you are." He shook his head, all those cracks inside him filling, then, with wonder. With her. Siren blue eyes and all that bright light, even in the dark. "Standing before me, worrying about the state of my heart."

"The thing about hearts," Lillie said with as much sternness as she could muster, "is that they beat whether you want them to or not. And they keep on beating no matter how sternly you tell them to stop. And I'm afraid that that's what love is like as well, Tiago. It doesn't give you choices. It just allows you opportunities. If you dare."

Tiago did the only thing that felt right, then. He swept her up in his arms and held her there, his face close to hers. He looked deep into her fathomless gaze, losing and finding himself there the way he had since that very first moment.

He saw her tears, her fierce determination, so much of her light—and saw, too, her hope.

So much hope, and nothing could have humbled him more.

He shifted her, setting her down so that she leaned back against the balustrade. Then he stood there before her, letting his hands frame her lovely face. Then tracing patterns down her sweet neck, along her arms wrapped in soft velvet.

He smoothed his palms over that firm, round belly where his child grew.

"I'm not sure I believe that I have a heart," he told her in a low voice, a confession he would make to her only. "But I have no need of it. Because our baby's heart beats right here." He leaned down and pressed his lips to her belly, feeling more than hearing the little sob she let out. Then he straightened, settling his hand in that sweet space between her breasts. "And your heart beats here. And I have to believe that I will learn enough to find my own, in time. If you let me try."

"I love you," she whispered. "And I already know where your heart is, Tiago. I always have."

"I would have told you that I could never love." But he gathered her close, and she melted into his arms. "Yet since the moment I laid eyes on you, I have never been without you. In those five months when you were lost to me, I carried you inside me. And just like now, every night, you wanted me. While I was asleep. While I was awake. Every night, I woke with your taste on my lips. Back then I wished I knew your name. Now I do, and it is like a song in me."

"I love you too," she said, and as he watched—

though her cheeks were still damp and her eyes were too bright—she gifted him with that smile.

That big, beautiful, wide smile that felt like laughter inside him and made him feel that he belonged in a way that land never could.

He understood, now. All he had to do was love her, and he would always fit. All he needed was her, the family they made, and he would never be cold again.

For a man who had always believed himself impervious to the vagaries of weather, Tiago understood then that all he'd wanted, all his life, was warmth.

Light. Joy.

All those things he had locked away.

As if all along, he'd been waiting for the key.

For a woman with a siren's eyes and chaotic hair to upend all his preconceptions and bring him home.

"You will have to teach me, *minha vida*," he said.

My life, he'd called her, and she was. He leaned down to kiss her on the forehead, the tip of her nose so that she laughed, and then, finally on her mouth. Like a vow.

"I want to live like you do. So brave. So open. I want to learn how to love as you do, beyond all reason."

She tipped her head back and slid her hands up along his chest, making him realize he had been walking around with his shirt wide open, which was something he would never have dreamed of doing before. And now he couldn't imagine why.

He was Tiago Villela, was he not? He could do as he pleased. And he thought it was about time he started.

Especially when he watched his wife, his Lillie, light up there before him, and then laugh as if she'd known how this would be all along. The two of them like this, their baby on the way, and nothing but choirs singing in between them.

"I'll tell you right now," Lillie told him when the laughter danced away into the pine trees standing tall around them this Christmas Eve. "It's as easy and as hard as this. All you do is look for the light and the joy no matter how it scares you. And hold on to me, just like this." She reached down and took his hands in hers, lacing their fingers together. "And then we'll do it together."

And they did.

Starting right then and there, bright all the way through.

CHAPTER TWELVE

FIVE YEARS LATER, Lillie spent Christmas Eve morning dressing herself in a beautiful white gown. She had her mother at her side, tearing up at the slightest provocation and fussing with all the flowers the staff had cut from the courtyard garden.

And when it was time, she gripped her father's arm as he walked her down the aisle they'd made that led to the fountain in the center of the garden, where even on the twenty-fourth day of December, the sun shone down like a blessing.

Today of all days, Lillie thought, that's exactly what it was.

"We're so proud of you, my darling girl," her father said roughly as they walked. And Lillie grinned up at him, so hard it made her face hurt.

All of her friends from university sat waiting for her and across the aisle, the friends Tiago really did have sat with matching smiles. Because Lillie and Tiago had spent these years strengthening their bonds in all kinds of relationships, not only with each other. Even Patricia, her old boss, was here, happily sporting her latest Spanish tan and a lover to go with it.

Tiago had flown with her to Aberdeen before the new

year began. And Lillie had taken far more pleasure than she should have when she'd brought him into that shared house that had been her home for so long, that he had reacted to as if it was an actual prison cell she'd only narrowly escaped.

She packed up her things and then left without looking back.

Because, finally, she knew her purpose. Her life had meaning because she loved, was loved in turn, and had a child on the way. Those three simple facts changed everything. Infused everything. Made sense of everything.

Tiago and her parents circled each other a bit warily at first. But when it became clear that everyone involved loved Lillie to distraction, they found their way to a friendship that was grudging at first, and then bloomed into its own kind of beauty.

Lillie moved down the aisle, happy that once she'd left Aberdeen behind, she'd found her way back to herself. To the woman who fought for what she wanted, wasn't afraid to stand up for herself, and let herself get vulnerable. She and Tiago had spent a lot of time learning how to love each other, something that only worked when they both let themselves love fully and wholly.

Once it had been clear that Lillie also had a head for finance and business, Tiago had wasted no time giving her access to the company too, so that she couldn't have been bored if she tried.

Though every now and again she claimed she was, just to see what her ferociously inventive husband would do.

Her father stopped at the head of the aisle and kissed

her on the cheek, then solemnly handed her over to the best man.

The best little man there ever could be, Lillie thought as she gazed down at sturdy little four-year-old João with eyes like a stormy sea, and a mess of dark curls.

"Come, *Mãe*," the Villela heir, who was normally a mischievous bolt of light and energy, told her sternly. "It's time to get married."

Lillie looked over at Leonor, who held one-year-old Carolina in her lap, named for the great-grandmother whose gardens bloomed around them even now. The baby gurgled happily and waved her chubby fists.

And Lillie let her son lead her forward, to where Tiago waited for her.

Tiago, who had dedicated himself to the task of learning how to love with all of his considerable strength and power.

And now the man known as a glacier left his iciness at the office.

At home, he laughed and sometimes, like the night when Carolina had come too fast into this world and they had thought they might lose her, he cried.

But he never let go of Lillie's hand. He never stopped searching out that light, that joy.

And he never stopped relying on the heart that Lillie had found in him when he'd thought he'd somehow lived his whole life without one.

"Lillie," he said now, "*você é tudo para mim*. You are everything to me. Light of my life, at last."

The night before he had made her sign papers all over again, though she had laughed at him and told him he was being silly. Something he could not have heard five years ago, but found entertaining these days. These papers, to the horror of his entire legal team, invalidated all that had gone before.

"You're in for it now," she told him when she signed. "I can divorce you at any time and take you for everything you're worth."

"You do that every night, my love," he replied.

And they had practiced, there in the study, to be sure.

Now, his hand wrapped around hers and he pulled her to him. To stand there with him so they might renew their vows and have the wedding they'd hurried through the first time around.

Though they knew, even if no one else did, that the truth of the matter is that their fate had been sealed by the side of a pool in Spain. At a resort that Lillie insisted they visit at least once a year, even though she now knew how little Tiago cared for the place.

What does it matter? she always teased him. *You like the bed just fine.*

I like you, he always replied. *It doesn't matter where.*

Though he was still aristocratic enough to complain, every time.

They stood there in the courtyard where his grandmother had taught him how to love, long before his parents had encased him in ice. And finally, they said all of those things out loud that had always been there between them.

Right from that very first glance that had knocked them both sideways.

With the weight of all the things they were to each other, immediately, even when they were strangers.

They spoke of love, and light. Of the children who

were little terrors, and utter joys, and who would be welcoming another sibling in the spring.

They spoke of trust, of medicine and magic.

And when it was time to kiss his bride again, Tiago swept Lillie up into his arms, kissed her thoroughly, and then carried her down the aisle.

Later that evening, they celebrated Christmas Eve in the Portuguese style, there in that rambling old house where her children believed in the possibility of Santa Claus, and their four-year-old could barely sleep among all those Christmas trees and candy cane settees, and the lights on all the trees seemed brighter every year.

"But I know the truth," Tiago said as he moved in her long after midnight, while their children and their guests slept. "The magic is in Christmas, *minha vida*. It's you. It's always been you."

"It's love," she whispered back. "And it's ours."

"Forever," Tiago agreed.

And as they lost themselves in this lightning-bolt dance of theirs, old and familiar and new every time, Lillie found herself laughing.

Because she knew that forever was only the beginning.

Love was like that.

And true love was even better.

* * * * *

THE CONVENIENT
COSENTINO WIFE

JANE PORTER

MILLS & BOON

PROLOGUE

THE FUNERAL WAS held the same weekend the wedding had been supposed to take place, although Rocco scheduled the private burial service for the day after the wedding, so as not to draw too many comparisons.

The funeral was very small as Rocco Cosentino wasn't interested in a drama-filled service for Marius, his younger brother, and only member of his family. Marius had been everything. His world, his responsibility, his hopes, his dreams. But then daring, fun-loving, big-hearted Marius died after being thrown from a horse, doing what Marius loved—and knew—best. Polo had been Marius's passion, and so Rocco grieved, but it was his private grief, and he refused to have others there to witness his pain and loss. He'd raised his brother since Marius was six, and now Marius was gone.

Unfathomable. The aristocratic Cosentino bloodline ended with Rocco then, as Rocco would never marry, not again.

Rocco had politely, but firmly, told all that it was a private funeral, only family would be in attendance. But Rocco couldn't refuse Clare Redmond's attendance as the twenty-four-year-old American had been Marius's fiancée.

If Marius hadn't broken his neck, Clare would have been Marius's wife by now.

One could say, if only Marius hadn't played that final match on Wednesday, Clare would have been his sister-in-law, but it was too late for that. Accidents happened, and a most tragic accident had happened, and Marius, the little boy who'd become a brilliant, generous man, was forever gone.

Rocco stood next to the young American woman who'd arrived for the service shrouded in black, head to toe, wearing even a veil as if she'd stepped from a Gothic novel. He couldn't see her face, but he didn't need to—he could hear her weeping during the brief service, making Rocco wish the service was over.

It was said that funerals were for the living, not the dead, but Rocco had attended far too many in his life, and never once had he been glad to be there. Never once, had he thought ah, thank goodness for this archaic service filled with prayers and scripture that mean nothing to me. He'd never found comfort in the priest's words, not when he'd stood in the family plot for his father's funeral, his mother's funeral, his young bride's funeral, and now his brother's funeral.

The fact that he was the last of the Cosentino line meant nothing to him. He viewed his family as cursed, which in of itself was problematic, so perhaps it was a good thing there were no more of them. He was the last, and he would remain the last, and there would be no more to grieve. No more funerals to attend. No more good people to be missed. No more guilt for being the sole survivor.

Once today was over, he'd shut the Cosentino ancestral

home, sell off Marius's Argentinean estates and move to one of his smaller estates, far from Rome. Far from everyone. He was done with death, done with grief, done with caring for anyone.

Clare had cried so much the past few days she didn't think she could shed another tear, but somehow during the service, listening to the lovely eulogy for her beloved Marius, the tears started again. Tears because Marius was truly one of the best people she'd ever known—strong, kind, honest, loving. She never knew how he'd grown up to be just so loving when he'd been raised by his stern older brother, who she found nothing short of cold and disapproving, but Marius always defended Rocco, saying Rocco might not appear affectionate, but he was fiercely proud and protective of him, and would die for him if need be.

Those words, *die for him*, came to her now, and Clare cried fresh tears because it would have been better if Rocco had died and not Marius. Marius was so full of light and love whereas Rocco barely interacted with the world, living like a hermit in his monstrously big house, a house he'd inherited as a sixteen-year-old when his parents died just weeks apart from an infectious disease they'd picked up on their travels. Clare hated visiting the big dark house, but Marius would drag her there every six months for either Christmas or New Year's, and then again late July for big brother Rocco's birthday.

Rocco was never friendly on those occasions, barely speaking two words to her. When Marius proposed, her first thought was yes, yes, because she loved him desperately, but later, when she'd gone to bed that night, her new ring so wonderful and strange on her finger, it crossed her mind that now Rocco would be her family, too.

And that thought hadn't been pleasant.

In fact, that thought had kept her awake far too late.

Now she stood next to the man who'd never be her brother waiting for the service to conclude. She would be leaving as soon as they returned to the house. She had a car already arranged to pick her up and take her back to the airport. No point remaining in Rome longer than necessary. It's not as if she was wanted or needed here. Rocco didn't need comforting, at least not from her. Marius didn't have a will. The estate in Spain was all in his name. There was nothing else to be done but for her to return home and figure out how to continue without her heart, as that had been buried with Marius.

From where Rocco stood in the drawing room he could see outside to the manicured circular drive where a big black Mercedes waited for Clare.

He admired the young woman's foresight, appreciating her desire to not prolong today's events. Any mourning Rocco would do, he'd do in private. He suspected Clare felt the same.

"I see your car has arrived," he said, hands clasped behind his back.

She still wore that heavy black lace veil, but he could see the haunting lavender blue of her eyes as she looked at him. "Yes." She hadn't sat down, either. The two of them were standing still in the formal room. "I hate to leave you like this—"

"But you don't," he said, cutting her short, raw pain

in his deep, gravelly voice. "We're not close. We have no desire to grieve together."

She lifted her head, and again he could see that lavender of her eyes beneath the lace. "Will you grieve for him?"

"He is all I had left." The moment the words left his mouth, Rocco felt foolish. Exposed. It was easier if others believed he didn't care or feel. Easier to let strangers believe he was as hard as he appeared. He gestured toward the tall ornate doors. "I have no wish to keep you. You mustn't miss your flight."

Her head inclined, once, and then she folded the lace veil back, exposing her golden hair and her pale face with the deep violet shadows beneath her unusual lavender eyes. "I probably won't see you again," she said, "but maybe it will help for you to know just how much Marius loved you. He said you were the best brother, father and mother a boy could have." Then she dropped the veil and giving him another faint nod, walked out of the house to the car.

That should have been the last time Rocco saw her. In any other situation it would have been, because he had no desire to be reminded of Marius, or the others he'd lost, but when the envelope finally reached him, catching up to him in Argentina where he was supervising a harvest on his late brother's estate in Mendoza, Rocco had set it aside, and then it had been covered by other papers and mail, and when he went to open it, the envelope had gone missing. He'd searched everywhere and then feared it had been thrown out. Instead it had simply been misplaced, gathered with an expense report and filed for end of the year taxes.

When he'd finally discovered the envelope amongst his tax paperwork, eleven months had passed. Opening the envelope Rocco discovered he wasn't the last of his family.

Beautiful American Clare Redmond had delivered a healthy baby boy two years ago.

CHAPTER ONE

THE DISTINCTIVE ROAR of helicopter blades caught Clare's attention, and her hands paused over the keyboard of her laptop as she listened to the jarring hum and vibration.

The shuddering noise grew closer.

Clare listened for another long moment before pushing away from her desk to walk to the window of her villa's office and look up. The helicopter hovered now directly overhead. It wasn't high, either, but low, far too low to just be passing over. They were either looking for someone or something as the helicopter dropped lower, no longer above the sixteenth-century Renaissance villa, but appearing to prepare to land. Then it did descend, right onto the great lawn behind the villa.

Helicopters had landed at the seaside villa before with VIP guests, presidents and prime ministers, celebrities wanting a quick arrival and departure, but she always knew in advance. Her team would be alerted, security would be alerted and there would be staffing to manage the arrival and to keep other guests back for safety. But there had been nothing shared and the arrival of this helicopter made her uneasy. Why she felt uneasy, she didn't know, but her instincts were usually correct, honed by grief and work. Clare left her office and quickly descended the wide marble staircase to step out the front door.

Gio Orsini, her head of security, appeared next to her. "You know about this?" he asked, his polished bald head tipping, his gaze riveted on the helicopter filling the expansive lawn, huge blades still spinning.

She shook her head, aware that whatever it was, whoever it was, she'd meet the problem head-on. If there was anything she'd learned from her tumultuous life it was that fear couldn't be given power. Adrenaline was fine. Weakness was not.

Clare followed Gio onto the villa's broad front steps. Six months ago the villa had still been an exclusive luxury hotel, one she'd owned as part of her luxury property portfolio, but she'd discovered she was happiest at Villa Conchetti, and closed the hotel so she could make it her family home. "Is it a charter helicopter, or privately owned?" she asked.

"Privately owned I believe." Gio glanced at her. "Adriano is still asleep?" he asked.

She nodded, picturing her son napping in his nursery with his nanny in attendance.

"I will secure the nursery wing," Gio added. "But I'd be more comfortable if you returned to the house until we know who is here and why."

Gio had protected her and her young son for the past two and a half years, a constant in her life from the moment she'd left the hospital as a grieving single mom. "Give me a moment," she said. "I have a feeling I know who this is."

"*Chi, allora*?" he asked. *Who, then?*

"I'm hoping I'm wrong," she said instead. Praying she was wrong.

Gio's eyes narrowed, but he said nothing else, and she didn't, either. Seconds later the pilot climbed out, but before he could open the passenger door, it opened and a tall man with black hair and a pale olive complexion stepped out, carrying a small leather duffle bag. He was so tall he had to stoop to avoid the whirring blades and even though Clare couldn't see his face, she knew immediately who it was.

Rocco.

Her stomach fell, a sharp plummet that made her feel sick. She'd expected him so long ago. She'd written to him more than eighteen months ago but when he'd never responded, she'd finally given up on hearing from him. Instead he was here, at her villa, in person.

Clare's skin prickled with unease, and her mouth dried as her pulse raced.

"What do you want me to do?" Gio asked quietly, as they both knew Rocco Cosentino was a threat.

"Nothing for now," she said. "Just have staff remain vigilant."

"Of course."

She held her position on the front step and outwardly she looked calm, but the wild thudding of her heart made her hands tremble. Just a month ago, in late July, she'd given up thinking Rocco would reach out. It had been so long since she'd written to him about Adriano, over a year and a half ago, she'd stopped worrying, stopping imagining an unpleasant reunion, but just when she'd relaxed and her defenses had come down, he was here, quickly approaching the entrance to her home.

"I've been looking for you," Rocco said, reaching her side. His deep voice was deeper than she remembered, but every bit as grim. His hard, chiseled features were without expression and his icy silver gaze swept her from head to toe. There was no smile in his eyes, no warmth in his greeting.

Apparently nothing had changed. "For over a year and a half, really?" She tipped her head, met his eyes, such an unusual shade of gray, more like pewter than mist. "And to think I have been so close, just twenty-four kilometers from Rome."

"You waited a year to tell me about my nephew."

"And you waited over a year to reach out." Her chin lifted, and she lifted a finger in Gio's direction and he silently retreated, not far, but giving them space. "But then, you are busy."

Rocco stepped up, joining her on the top stair. "Once I knew about the child, I hired detectives as you were not easy to find. But I think you know that." The corner of his mouth lifted, but it wasn't a smile. "Perhaps next time you'll add a return address to your correspondence?"

It was on the tip of her tongue to say there wouldn't be a next time and then she thought better of it. There was no reason to provoke Marius's older brother. She and Rocco weren't close, but as this was the first time they'd seen each other since the funeral, she didn't want to create unnecessary friction. She wanted to leave the bad blood in the past. It was her hope they could be cordial in the future.

"The birth announcement took some time to find me," Rocco said. "I was in Mendoza when it finally reached me. But before I could read the contents, the envelope was caught up in paperwork. I only found it when I was gathering my files for taxes in May."

"Have you moved to Argentina?" she asked, surprised.

"No. I spent a few months there last year trying to sort out some issues at Marius's winery. There were problems with the management, and I was tired of excuses."

"I would have thought you'd have sold it by now."

"I've sold nothing of my brother's."

"Why not? The two of you have very different approaches to your finances." Her lips curved faintly. "He liked to spend money and you don't. I can't imagine the winery is earning a significant return on the investment."

"It's not, but it makes good wines, and with proper management, it could be far more profitable." Rocco's gaze met hers and held. "But I haven't come to discuss my investment strategy with you."

She broke free from his magnetic gaze, her attention dropping, skimming his scarred left cheek, thinking it both strange and shocking seeing him here. Rocco was so like Marius in coloring…a quick glance revealed the family resemblance, but Rocco was taller and considerably broader through the shoulders and chest. Their features would have been similar if it weren't for the thick scar and burn mark on Rocco's cheek, creeping into the hairline. Even without the scars, Rocco's eyes were so different from his brother's. Marius had lovely brown eyes, warm, smiling. She didn't think she'd ever seen Rocco smile, his silver irises perpetually flinty. Frosty. But then, everything about Rocco was imposing and cold, and no one she wanted near her, or in her home or around her son.

But he'd come because of her son and she couldn't very well leave Rocco on her front steps forever.

"Let's go to the terrace," she said. "It will be more private there."

She led the way through the house's airy entrance hall to the glass doors that opened onto a secluded terrace overlooking the sea. The terrace had numerous small sitting areas, as well as a table she and Adriano enjoyed when they ate an early dinner outside. Potted citrus trees dotted the long terrace, while the doorway was fragrant with climbing roses.

"I'll have refreshments brought to us," Clare said, choosing one of the small sitting areas in the shade and sitting down in a wrought iron chair with pale pink cushions. "Would you care for juice, a spritzer or an espresso?"

"What will you have?" Rocco asked, taking the chair across from hers.

"A spritzer," she said. "It's a warm day."

"I'll have the same," he answered.

Clare glanced at Roberto, her *maggiordomo*, standing in the doorway, awaiting instructions. "Two wine spritzers," she instructed, "and perhaps something light to eat."

Roberto disappeared, but Clare knew she wasn't without her staff. Gio was just inside the doorway, standing in the shadows. Other security were on the perimeter of the property. She took no chances with her son's safety. He was her heart and her world and everything she did was for him now.

Clare carefully crossed one leg over the other, high on her knee, the hem of her dress just touching her knees, revealing her slim calves. She felt Rocco's gaze rest on her legs, and saw a flicker of something in his eyes. She wasn't sure, but she wished she was wearing trousers and a long-sleeve tunic now, but in the warm months she preferred dresses as they were cooler and more comfortable.

"It's been quite some time," she said, voice crisp. "I'd begun to think I'd never see you again."

Rocco shrugged. "If it weren't for the birth announcement you wouldn't have."

Neither said anything for a long moment. Clare was content to leave the ball in Rocco's court. After all, he was the one who'd traveled here today. Let him say what he'd come to say.

Rocco had opened his mouth to speak when Roberto appeared with a silver tray. Rocco's mouth closed and they waited as Roberto positioned the wineglasses and little plates in front of them—nuts, crostini, a small charcuterie board.

"Help yourself, please," she said as Roberto disappeared.

Instead Rocco sipped his wine spritzer and then frowned.

"Too much bubbly water and not enough wine?" she asked.

"No. What wine is this? It's not Italian, is it."

"It's a California Chardonnay, from Paso Robles, near the Central Coast." She hesitated. "I've bought a vineyard there. Have put in some olive orchards, too. It was a good opportunity so I took it."

"You always surprise me."

"Because I'm not the silly society girl you thought I was?"

He opened his mouth to protest but then closed it without saying anything as they both knew he'd disapproved of her from the start and his opinion of her had only worsened during the time she and Marius were together. "Did the birth announcement really get lost in the shuffle?"

"I was incredibly embarrassed to discover I was the one who'd 'lost' the envelope. For the longest time I thought Marius's staff was careless, thinking it was maybe thrown out in a cleaning."

"And what did you think when you finally opened it?"

"Shock. Disbelief." He hesitated, expression grim. "It still seems impossible, especially as no one seemed to know of this...development. None of Marius's circle. None of yours, either."

"I didn't send out birth announcements. In fact, I told no one other than you, and it wasn't an announcement as much as a very brief note, because yes, he is your nephew."

"I've brought him gifts."

"That's very kind of you."

"Not kind. Essential. I am determined to make amends, as well as make up for lost time. To think I've had a nephew for years and am only meeting him today." Rocco's brilliant gaze looked at her, most intently. "When can I meet him? Is he here?"

"He is here. I never leave him. But he's napping at the moment. I still insist on an afternoon nap, otherwise he becomes a little bear, cranky and unreasonable."

"That doesn't sound like Marius."

"No? Perhaps he's inherited those traits from me." She smiled thinly as it crossed her mind they were no longer united in grief. Adriano had given her a purpose for living. His birth had centered her, strengthened her. He depended on her and she wasn't going to let anything—or anyone—harm her child.

Rocco set his flute down. "Want to fill me in on the parts I've missed?"

His voice was so gentle it made the hair on her nape rise. She didn't trust his tone, didn't trust him. Rocco was not a man to be trifled with. Fortunately, she was a woman not easily intimidated. "Which part?" she asked, crossing her legs.

"The part where my dead brother fathers a child."

Her gaze met his and held. So that's what this was about. Rocco didn't believe her. Interesting. But honestly, she didn't care. She didn't need him, or his money or his acceptance. She didn't need a damn thing from him. "It seems I conceived before Marius died."

His brow lifted. "It was possible."

Clare bit her tongue hard, holding back her indignation. She couldn't let him know how much he upset her. She wouldn't give him the satisfaction. After a moment she smiled. "Is that a question, or a statement? Can't tell from your tone."

"I just find it ironic."

"Maybe we should switch to Italian as I'm concerned about your word choices in English. It's not ironic, it's tragic." Her chin lifted, and her eyes blazed. "It's tragic that I have a beautiful little boy who will never know his father. Tragic because Marius was the one anxious for children and I was in no hurry as I just wanted to enjoy being a newlywed. Marius's bride." Her throat threatened to close but she fought hard to keep her emotions in check. "But God had different plans for me and so here we are, a mother and a son."

"And an uncle," Rocco added.

She lifted an eyebrow. "It doesn't sound as if you want to be an uncle."

"I don't want to be played, that's all."

"And why would I do that, Rocco? What would I get out of it?"

He ignored her questions and asked another of his own. "You've had a DNA test? For confirmation?"

Clare held her breath and briefly closed her eyes. She would not curse Rocco Cosentino. She would not spit at him. She would not spew a stream of livid, hostile remarks at him, no matter how arrogant he should be.

She opened her eyes and looked at him directly, her gaze locking with his. "I don't need one. I was a virgin when we met. There had been no one else in my life. Marius was my first, my only, and most likely my last. I have no desire to replace him, ever."

Rocco just looked at her, intently. But she found his silence insulting, nearly as insulting as her need to discuss her private life. "Besides, it doesn't matter what you think. Adriano is my baby, my son. I don't need to prove anything to you." Clare was so angry she was trembling, but so far she'd kept her voice even. "I think you should go."

"I've come a long way to meet him."

"*So*?" She laughed, simultaneously amused and livid. "Am I supposed to feel badly for you?"

"This isn't about me."

"No?" Clare set her glass down and rose. "You could have fooled me." She looked to the doorway where Gio stood in the shadows and nodded once.

Rocco noted her nod and growled with displeasure. "You're throwing me out?"

"We have nothing to say to each other after all."

"I want to see my nephew."

"No, you don't. You came to shame me and I won't be shamed. Yes, Adriano was born out of wedlock, but that's because his father died two days before the wedding." Her lips quivered and she could feel the hot sting of tears in her eyes, but she smiled fiercely to keep the tears from falling. "Marius always defended you, saying that you couldn't help the way you were, that you'd been hit with too much too soon, but that's not my problem. It's not Adriano's problem, either. So, no, I don't want you to meet my baby. Not today, and maybe not ever."

Clare walked away from Rocco, through the open French door to the cool interior of the villa even as Gio stepped out to deal with the guest.

Roberto shut the door behind her, standing in front of it, another sentry on guard, all here to protect Adriano, a child vulnerable to those with malicious intentions. She didn't yet know Rocco's intentions but her guard was up, and her temper was high.

Clare walked swiftly down the marble entry into one of the elegant salons she'd turned into the music room with the high frescoed ceiling with the gleaming pink and gold marble floor. She paced the room, past the grand piano, oblivious to the priceless oil paintings on the wall, and the beauty and history of a home hundreds of years old. Her heart pounded and emotion surged through her—confusion, frustration and anger. Anger that Rocco had finally appeared, but so many months after she'd expected him, more than a year after thinking he'd care. But now he was here and instead of arriving with warmth or genuine feeling, he was infuriating her all over again.

He'd always infuriated her.

She had wanted so badly to have a happy family, and share Marius's love of his brother, but Clare never could be comfortable when Rocco was around. He was hard and ruthless, like the walls of the ruined medieval fortress just down the beach from her villa. Tourists lined up to visit the ruined fortress, but she had no interest in ruins, not when she was working so hard to create a safe world for her son, giving him the stability and love she'd never known, but this focus wasn't about the past, but the future. Adriano's future. Her future. A future with hope and happiness.

"*Mi scusi*," the housemaid said from the doorway.

Clare turned at the far end of the room, pausing in front of the ornate marble fireplace surround. "Yes?"

"Ava wanted you to know that your son is awake."

Clare pictured Rocco outside, aware that he was probably still on the terrace, aware that he was thinking she would return, because really, how was the conversation over? How had they settled anything?

"Have Ava bring him downstairs to me after he's had a snack. I will be on the terrace with our guest." Clare's voice firmed. "I'd like Ava to remain close, in the event that Adriano isn't comfortable."

The maid nodded and disappeared. Clare drew a deep breath and squared her shoulders preparing for battle, because that's exactly what this was with Rocco Cosentino. He wasn't her friend. He was a foe and they both knew it.

CHAPTER TWO

ROCCO EXHALED AS Clare disappeared into the villa. He
hadn't anticipated a warm welcome, and he hadn't helped
things by asking about a DNA test, but he needed to ask.
He needed to know, but he wasn't going to pursue that
conversation further especially as there were other ways
to verify Adriano's ancestry. He just needed time to get
the verification. He needed time, period. Now that he was
here, it was hard to imagine just walking away from her.
To be honest, he'd never walked away from her. She'd
been the one to leave the Cosentino villa in Rome after
the funeral. She'd called for a car, and yes, he'd put her
into it, but it was the right thing to do.

Seeing her again was painful, though. Just looking into
her eyes stirred up intensely conflicted feelings. Their last
visit had been the day of the funeral. It had been such a
dark, dark day, the grief numbing. He'd been numb for
months after.

But Rocco was determined to block out the memories, and just as determined to keep a tight rein on his
emotions. He couldn't allow himself to feel anything. He
couldn't allow himself to be drawn into the past, with
all its guilt and regret. Rocco had hated himself the day
of the funeral. He'd hated himself so much that he just

wanted to be buried with his brother, be over it, be done with it once and for all. Too many funerals, too much death, too much remorse, too much grief. Unfortunately, in typical Rocco Cosentino fashion, he survived the day, and said his goodbyes to Clare, and moved forward with this life, managing both his estates and his brother's, in Spain, Italy and Argentina, the Argentina property left to him by his mother.

He still remembered the moment he found the file with the birth announcement tucked inside of it.

Marius had fathered a child? There was an heir? Another generation of Cosentinos?

Could he trust Clare to tell the truth?

But why would she lie? She was an heiress herself. The two families had billions between them, a shocking amount of wealth, but that wealth hadn't protected them from loss or loneliness. The birth of a child, a Cosentino, was huge, but the fact that it was Clare's child…that was incredibly problematic.

So first Rocco needed facts. The truth. And then, if Adriano was a Cosentino, Rocco needed to remain close.

Rocco glanced now at the bodyguard who had remained on the terrace with him. The man's head was shaved smooth, his gaze shielded by a pair of dark sunglasses.

Rocco knew that the moment Clare decided Rocco was to be shown off the property he would be, but so far that hadn't happened, which gave Rocco hope that he and Clare could still have a conversation, a civil conversation.

That would require Rocco keeping his temper in check. His temper wasn't usually an issue, but from the beginning, from that very first meet, Clare had brought out the worst in him.

She made him feel, and he hated that.

She made him think—not of business, not of family, not of loyalty—but of lives not lived, emotions not experienced.

The only way he'd ever known how to function around Clare was to hide who he was, containing himself so that she didn't know him. Couldn't know him.

But that hard exterior was a sham, the walls erected to keep Clare away, distant, so that he could be detached and keep his head.

She was that much of a temptation. Still.

The French doors opened and Clare appeared on the threshold.

"Still here?" she asked, perfectly framed by the pale stone walls covered with the lush bloom of late summer roses. The pink roses perfumed the air, creating a softness around Clare that was at odds with her fierceness. She hadn't been fierce when Marius was alive. She'd been anything but fierce, leaning on Marius for his love, drinking in his devotion as if a flower deprived of sunlight.

She didn't lean now. Although petite, she stood tall, her chin up, her eyes flashing at him. Her new toughness wasn't the only change, though. Her hair was darker, the light golden strands now a rich cocoa. Her face had some color, as if she'd spent hours on the sunny terrace, or perhaps down on the sand. It would be impossible to avoid the sun when living here at the sea.

"I ask your forgiveness," Rocco said formally in English before switching to Italian, and repeating it. "It was not my intention to make us enemies. We are family—"

"We've never been family," she interrupted, walking toward him. "You never wanted me as family," she added, voice dropping. "Remember?"

The bodyguard had stepped back into the shadows and Clare now stood in front of Rocco, hands on her hips, her dark head thrown back, revealing her stunning violet-colored eyes.

She was right. He did not want Marius to marry her. He did not want her as a sister-in-law, but to admit it now was adding insult to injury. He said nothing rather than make things worse.

Her full mouth curved, a faint dimple appeared in her cheek, but there was fire in her eyes. She was not happy with him, not happy to see him. He sensed that she would have preferred to never see him again.

"You've never really talked to me," she said. "But maybe it's time we were honest. We should be truthful. We both know you never liked me." Clare held his gaze, daring him to contradict her. "Can you at least admit that?"

"How will this help anything?"

"I can't trust you if I don't know you. I can't know you if you don't have a real conversation with me. I think we both owe Marius that much. A conversation, and maybe a chance to come to an understanding."

She barely reached the middle of his chest. Her dark hair fell below her shoulders. Motherhood hadn't aged her. She was still exquisite, and still oblivious of her beauty. "These truths might make things worse," he answered.

"They will if we're wanting to wound. I do not wish to hurt you, and to be honest, I've no desire to be hurt by you. I just want to understand why…" her voice faded and she sighed, shadows in her violet eyes. "Why you tried to keep Marius and me apart."

"I didn't think you were a person of substance, and thus, I didn't think you were right for my brother," Rocco answered bluntly.

"But *why*?"

"It's difficult to articulate. The only way I can explain it is a gut instinct."

"A gut instinct?" she repeated, color deepening in her cheeks. "That's it? No proof? Nothing to substantiate this?"

"It was my job to look after my brother, and in my mind, you weren't the right one for him." Rocco's voice dropped, deepened. "I told him as much."

"You had no right."

"I had every right. I was his older brother, as well as the only father figure he remembered. I had to represent the entire family—"

She laughed, interrupting him. "That's so ridiculous," she said, walking away, leaving him to go stand against the balustrade. For a long moment she didn't speak and Rocco watched her, studying her, taking in the white dress with the dark purple trim, it was such a simple sundress, but it flattered her.

Clare turned to look at him. "Your brother was also an adult, a man, capable of making his own decisions."

"And yet he looked to me for reassurance," Rocco said.

"Because you exerted too much influence. He felt as if he had to constantly please you, but that shouldn't have been necessary. No younger brother should ever have to grow up fearing his older brother's censure—"

"That's not how it was between us, not at all."

"Then how was it?" she asked, leaning against the railing, head tipped, expression somewhat mocking.

He slowly crossed the distance between them until he was just a foot away, blocking the sun, and able to clearly see her light eyes with the lavender irises, so stunning, so unusual. Like her. He'd never met anyone like her, which was both good and bad. "Marius was my family, my world—he was very loved."

"He was also *my* world, *my* family and his death broke my heart. I will never love anyone the way I loved him, which is why I'm so careful with Adriano. He is so young, so innocent. He is to be protected, not pulled between us."

"I would never do that."

"No?" she challenged.

"No," he replied firmly. "I swear to you as a Cosentino, and on my family honor, to do what is best for Marius's son always."

She considered this and then nodded. "Good, because he will be coming down soon, and you shall have the chance to meet him." Clare gestured to the grouping of chairs where they'd been sitting earlier. "Shall we sit, and try this again?"

He followed her to the sitting area and waited for her to sit down before he sat. He waited a moment to give her a chance to take charge of the conversation but she just looked at him, waiting.

That was fine with him. He had countless questions. "I thought you were blonde," he said. "Or was that just color?"

She almost smiled. "I'm a natural blonde. When I was young I had silver blond hair, but it darkened to the gold

shade in my twenties. I dyed it black after Marius's funeral. I couldn't stand looking into the mirror and seeing myself. I didn't want to be me anymore, especially as
seeing my hair, reminded me of Marius. He'd loved my
hair, the pale gold color, and so every time I saw myself,
I felt angry. Cheated. I covered it up. Looking back, it
was my way of mourning."

"Did it help?"

"It did. I felt different. Strange to myself which helped
me cope with all the grief."

"Are you still grieving?" he asked.

"I will always grieve his loss, but the fire that used
to consume me is gone. The rage and pain have become
acceptance…reluctant acceptance."

"I understand."

"Do you?" And then in the next moment she shook
her head. "Forgive me. Of course you do. I can see it in
your face, in your eyes. You're still wearing your grief,
but you've lost so many people that I'm not surprised."

"And you have your son which gives you purpose."

She hesitated and then nodded. "Yes, it does. And
hopefully when you meet Adriano, you will feel some
of the hope I feel."

Hope. Such a strange concept, Rocco though, suddenly
unable to remain seated. He rose and walked the width
of the terrace, briefly glancing out past the garden to the
rocky cliff and the dark blue sea beyond. "Tell me about
my nephew," he said, walking back toward Clare. "Is he
much like my brother?"

"He's a toddler, almost of preschool age, but in other
ways, very much a baby still. It's hard to say who he's
like, but he has your brother's coloring, and his smile."

Her expression softened. The tension in her job easing. "Just as Marius's smile lit up the room, Adriano's does that, too. His nanny adores him. Those that know him love him. I know I'm biased as I'm his mother, but I do think he's special. I look forward to hearing what you think."

"But he's happy?" Rocco persisted.

"Very. He laughs a lot. He smiles a great deal. He brings tremendous joy to my life, and those around him." The light in her eyes dimmed, shadows returning. "I don't think I would have survived the last few years without him."

Rocco forced himself to sit, trying to contain his energy. Everything within him felt stirred—restless—and he didn't like it. He took a sip of his drink. It was no longer cold and he set it down, knowing he wouldn't try it again. "And his intelligence? Is he bright? Marius was always very smart, very curious."

"He is speaking three languages, or more accurately, he can understand three languages. I speak several languages, but only speak to him right now in English and Italian. His nanny speaks to him mostly in Spanish, which I thought important, seeing as his father loved the family home in Argentina. I thought Adriano should know the language should he ever visit."

"Thank you," Rocco said simply. "In case there's any doubt, let me reassure you, that I have no wish to take him from you. He is your son. That is not a point of contention. I am merely here to meet the son of my beloved brother."

As if on cue, a young woman appeared in the doorway and spoke to Clare, addressing her in Spanish. Clare answered the young woman in Spanish. It sounded as if the child had finished his snack and was ready to join them. Clare instructed the nanny to bring Adriano out, along with a few of his toys, and maybe the green ball he liked so much.

Ava stepped back into the house and Clare focused her attention on Rocco. "He's coming now."

It was just a minute later when a childish laugh came from within the house and then a boy burst through the door, at a run, heading straight for Clare.

He was small but sturdy, and he flung himself at Clare. "Mama," he cried, climbing onto her lap.

Her arms wrapped around him and she pressed a half dozen kisses to his cheeks, forehead and then finally the tip of his nose. "Hello, my baby, my beautiful boy. Did you have a good nap?" she said in English.

"*Sì*," Adriano said firmly, answering her English with Italian.

Rocco checked his smile, remembering how Marius used to do the same thing as a young child. He understood everything, but chose to answer in whichever language he felt like answering in.

Clare turned the toddler around on her lap, so Adriano was facing out. "We have a guest," she said, tone cheerful. "Adriano, this is your papa's brother. This is your uncle, Zio Rocco. He has come to meet you. Isn't that exciting?"

Rocco watched Adriano's expression shift, his friendly smile growing slightly more guarded, his pale brow creasing. He had long thick lashes, a firm chin, a firm press to his lips and a dark but focused gaze.

"Adriano, it is true. I am your papa's brother. I was the big brother. I loved your papa very much."

Silence stretched. Adriano processed this, expression still guarded, no emotion evident.

Rocco noticed that Clare allowed the boy to respond when and how he wanted. She didn't hurry him, or tell him how to respond. Rocco approved.

After several long moments Adriano wiggled off Clare's lap and stood on his own two feet. His expression revealed curiosity and after another moment of scrutinizing the guest, the child crossed to Rocco with the same athletic grace he'd shown when running onto the terrace. Now he stood quite still before his uncle, scrutinizing him from head to toe. "*Zio* not *tio*?" Adriano asked.

Rocco glanced at Clare and she smiled at him, clearly proud of Adriano's perceptiveness.

Rocco was impressed, as well. "Zio," Rocco looked back at the child. "*Italiano*," he confirmed.

Adriano extended his hand. "*Mi chiamo Adriano.*" *My name is Adriano.*

Rocco felt a stab of pain thinking how much his brother would have loved this child. But with Marius gone, Rocco would do everything he could to protect the boy. He took the child's small chubby hand in his, and gave it a formal shake. "It's nice to meet you, Adriano."

Adriano gave a firm shake back, but he wasn't smiling. He looked serious, his brows pulling in concentration. Marius, for his part, was rarely serious, always quick to smile and laugh. Marius loved a joke, and although bright, found it difficult to focus on academics, excelling instead in sports. And friends. He'd had countless friends. He was a true friend, and loyal, and of course, handsome, charming and generous to a fault.

Rocco's lips twisted.

Clare spoke, suggesting Adriano show his uncle how good he was playing *calcio*, or soccer. Adriano glanced at Rocco, checking his interest. Rocco nodded at him. "*Mi piace molto il calcio*," he assured him.

Adriano seemed to approve as he finally gave Rocco a smile and with a dash he was running to pick up his ball. He threw it down the terrace, and then chased after the ball, intercepting it before it could bounce downstairs. He kicked the ball right, and then left, as if showing off his footwork. As if he himself was in a game.

Rocco couldn't help smiling, touched, and amused, because there, in the fancy footwork, in the intense concentration was Marius. "*Lui e bello*," Rocco said quietly. *He's beautiful.*

Clare nodded, sudden tears in her eyes. "He is," she agreed.

They applauded Adriano as he raced up and then down the terrace, and then finally Adriano came to his mother's side, and leaned against her legs. His face was flushed and he had a sheen of perspiration on his brow. "*Com'e stato?*" he asked his mother.

"Wonderful. You won the game, didn't you?" she answered in English.

Adriano laughed. "There was no game, Mama. It was just the warm-up."

"Aren't you tired now?" she asked, giving him a little hug.

"No." Adriano flexed his arm, showing a nonexistent bicep. "I am very strong."

"You are. But maybe perhaps you'd like a little gelato, just because you've worked so hard?"

Adriano jumped and clapped. "*Sì!*"

"Then go find Ava and tell her I said you could have one scoop of gelato. Just one, though, as we don't want to spoil your appetite for dinner. Understand?"

"*Sì*, Mama." He pressed a kiss to her cheek and then with a wave at Rocco he ran into the house, the door closing silently behind him.

Rocco hadn't even realized he'd been holding his breath until the door had closed, and then he exhaled, pain splintering in his heart. Adriano was very much like Marius in some ways, handsome and athletic, but he'd also inherited Clare's keen intellect.

With Adriano back in the house, Clare should have felt better, safer, but instead her nerves were wound tight, her shoulders tense, her insides knotted.

She was waiting for whatever would come next.

What *would* come next?

Now that Rocco had seen his nephew, would he be satisfied? Would he summon his helicopter back and leave, curiosity answered? Somehow she doubted it. Somehow she knew this was just the beginning. But of what? That was the question. This wasn't a chance meeting. Rocco had been searching for them and clearly he'd been intrigued by Marius's son…so what would Rocco want now?

Rocco left his chair and passed behind her and she found herself stiffening, as aware of him as if he'd reached out and touched her. Her skin prickled everywhere, the hair on her nape rose and a shiver raced through her.

Her stomach, already in knots, lurched and she drew a slow breath, trying to ignore the wave of unease rushing through her. There was no reason she should be anxious. He had no power over her. He couldn't hurt her. He wasn't a man who hurt people—words from Marius's lips more than once. Rocco might look scarred and fierce, but he wasn't dangerous. Not to her, or to Adriano.

And yet, she wanted Rocco gone. Soon. Now.

But she said nothing, letting him prowl about, once again inspecting the terrace, the view, the ocean brilliant beneath the September sun.

"Thank you," Rocco finally said, breaking the silence. He'd walked halfway down the terrace before returning.

"For?" she asked, trying to gather her calm.

"Loving him so well. He's obviously very happy and healthy. I'm not surprised, but I am impressed. Marius would be pleased."

"I do everything for Marius."

"In that case, may I remain for a few days? I'd like to get to know my nephew better. Obviously, I have no desire to impose. The last thing I wish to do is make you uncomfortable."

Clare didn't know how to answer because Rocco did make her uncomfortable, but not for the reasons she would have expected.

Ever since she'd returned from the music room Rocco had been unfailingly polite. He'd been gentle with Adriano. There was nothing that should make her uneasy and yet she was unsettled. Her skin felt too sensitive, and her pulse wasn't quite steady. Clare didn't know why she couldn't find her center. Rocco had knocked her off balance.

And yet, how could she refuse his request?

This was Adriano's only blood relation on his father's side. Rocco could be—perhaps should be—an important figure in her son's life. "I have no objection," she said at length. "Do you intend to leave and return, or…?"

"I'll have my bag dropped off later."

"Another helicopter landing?" she said, lips curving faintly.

Creases fanned from the corners of his eyes, amusement flashing briefly in the silver depths. "I think my bag could travel by car, if that's all right with you."

It wasn't a smile, she thought, but it came close. For some reason this pleased her and her smile deepened, a hint of warmth offsetting some of the ice and fear filling her chest. "A car is perfectly acceptable," she replied, rising. "In the meantime, the staff will prepare your room. It should only take a few minutes. Would you like to wait here, or perhaps in one of the indoor salons?"

"Anywhere I won't be in the way."

"You're not in the way. I'm going to return to my office as I have a number of emails to answer before the workday ends. My staff—my company's management team—are waiting for me to respond to some questions from this morning's meeting. You don't mind me escaping for a bit, do you?"

"Of course not. I'm good to wait here. Don't worry about me."

"Gio will keep you company," she said, glancing at her head of security, suppressing a smile. "He's not very talkative, but he'll keep you safe."

"Am I in danger?" he asked, a teasing glint in his eyes.

For a moment Clare couldn't think, her mind going

blank, caught off guard by this very different Rocco, a Rocco who smiled at her, a Rocco with laugh lines, a Rocco who made her feel as if she was part of the conversation instead of excluded. Her chest felt strange, tight and tender at the same time. She wasn't sure how to manage this Rocco. It was easier to dislike him, easier keeping him at arm's length.

"You're not in danger," she said, deciding truth was the best policy now. "The security is for Adriano."

Rocco's smile faded. "Has there been an issue with safety?"

In the past she wouldn't have shared anything, but she needed an ally, and Rocco could be a powerful one. She swallowed and chose her words carefully. "My father isn't well, and when he goes, his estate will pass to Adriano. Children are vulnerable, let alone children worth billions."

Rocco's expression didn't change, but his voice dropped, deepening. "You live very quietly. You don't publicize your wealth. I found it almost impossible to find you."

Her head tipped. Her smile was strained. "And yet you did. It just took you time." She turned at the door. "So you see, I must be on guard. Not trying to be dramatic, just realistic."

In her upstairs office suite which sprawled over two rooms, each giving her a different view, one of the garden, and one of the sea, Clare sat down at her desk but couldn't bring herself to even touch her computer keyboard.

She wasn't exaggerating when she'd expressed her commitment to keeping Adriano safe—and out of the limelight. Clare's childhood had been so very different. She'd been raised in the upper echelon of American society, which meant her family spent considerable time abroad, socializing with the upper echelon of European society. When you were the only child of one of the wealthiest men in America, you had access to everyone and every event.

But Clare had never cared about money. Wealth didn't make one happy. Just look at her father—he'd been married countless times and each divorce left him more bitter than the last. He always said that the smartest thing he did was to have an ironclad prenup—his wives would get whatever jewelry and property he bought them during the marriage—but that was it. He also made sure there would be no more children as he'd hated the horrendous custody battle that had occurred when Clare was young. He'd ended up having to share custody with Clare's mother, and the deep resentment on both her parents' parts would have continued throughout Clare's life if her mother hadn't died when Clare was twelve, succumbing to a heart defect that none of them had even known about.

It was only after Clare's mother was gone that her father claimed Clare's late mother was a virtual saint, and that there were no woman who could compare to her. Thus his procession of new, and ever younger, brides. Slimmer. Sleeker. More ambitious than the last.

Clare was delighted to be sent to Europe for high school and then university. Far better to live away from her father's parade of wives, women who were determined to get pregnant and remove Clare's status as Daddy's beloved little girl.

Clare enjoyed Europe, and gradually it became home. She used some of her pocket money to buy a small Paris flat, and then later she invested in a little island off the coast of Italy. It had once been inhabited but vines and drought had killed off many of the old olive trees and orchards, but Clare liked the idea of having a place of her own, and had hired a couple, and then several workers, to make the crumbling stone house habitable. She periodically sent money, and paid bills, but she didn't visit as she'd also purchased other properties that had more commercial value.

It was the weekend of her twenty-second birthday and she was on a yacht anchored off Cádiz celebrating with friends when introduced to Marius. She hadn't thought love at first sight was possible—after all, that was her father's favorite line—but she'd taken one look at him and felt as if she'd known him forever, or, perhaps, she wanted to know him forever.

They had two and a half years together, and were planning a lifetime together, when he died just days before their wedding.

The only comfort she could take in the following weeks, and then months, was that she was pregnant and at least she'd have his child. Clare hadn't wanted to know the gender of the baby, and the nurse practitioner she saw for monthly checkups kept insisting it was a girl, so it had been a shock when she went into labor and twelve hours later delivered a boy.

The baby had dark hair and deep blue eyes and a hint of a dimple in its fat cheek, the dimple almost identical to the one Marius had, that Clare cried as she held her son, missing her Marius.

The nurse had gently removed the baby from Clare's arms, saying it wasn't good for the baby to hear such grief so soon after his birth, and Clare had continued crying without him. The first six weeks were filled with tears, but gradually she recovered from her bleak depression even as her body healed. She named the infant Adriano Marius Jonathan Cosentino, after her son's father and both grandfathers, and had him baptized at six months. It was some months after the baptism that she wrote to Rocco, letting him know she'd given birth to a son and he was doing well. She'd been tempted to add, that they were both doing well, but stopped herself knowing Rocco wouldn't care.

Had she been wrong, though?

Clare shifted in her desk chair, sitting forward as she pictured Rocco arriving in the helicopter, as well as their first tense conversation following his arrival. He'd been searching for them, Clare and Adriano, and once he'd met Adriano, Rocco had clearly been entranced. But it was easy to adore Adriano; he was the best of all of them.

But that didn't mean she was going to drop her guard. If anything, Rocco's arrival, and request to remain for a day or two, had made her even more conflicted. She had to remain vigilant. Rocco was brilliant and still not to be trusted.

Her watch buzzed. She glanced down at the text from Gio. Her guest wanted to know what time dinner would be served.

Clare arched an eyebrow. She hadn't thought that far in advance. To be honest, she hadn't wanted to think about dinner, or having to entertain. She usually had an early dinner with Adriano and then returned to her office after he was in bed. She couldn't imagine Rocco eating dinner at five thirty, though.

She texted Gio back.

Where is Rocco now?

Gio responded.

In the blue suite.

The blue suite was on the third floor in a different wing from the family's wing, which allowed security to keep visitors from the nursery and Clare's rooms. Clare rarely had visitors, but when a university girlfriend stayed three months ago, Clare had her in the guest wing, as well.

She texted Gio.

I will go to him.

CHAPTER THREE

ROBERTO, CLARE'S BUTLER, had shown Rocco to his suite of rooms on the third floor, but Gio lingered just outside the door, as if uncomfortable leaving Rocco unattended.

Rocco was more amused than offended and recognized that he'd handled things with Clare badly when he'd first arrived, but hopefully they were past that now. He went to the doorway and faced the bodyguard. "I have not come to cause trouble," he said to Gio. "But I was tactless. I should have reassured her first that I have only come to pledge my loyalty and protection."

The bodyguard's expression was impassive, his gaze briefly landing on Rocco and then away.

"Well, it was a good talk. I'll leave you to do your job." Rocco nodded at Gio and then closed the door, shutting Gio out.

Rocco inspected his rooms, a very luxurious suite with a living room, elegant spacious bedroom and an opulent bath, all with views of the sea. The decor of blue and white, reflecting the ocean view, the furniture antiques mixed with a few modern pieces for ultimate comfort.

He opened the bedroom doors onto the balcony and stepped outside, hands resting on the wrought iron railing, eyes narrowed against the sun. He knew that until a year ago this had been a much in demand hotel, one of those exclusive word-of-mouth resorts that charged upward of one thousand a night for a small room. This suite would have been ten times that. He was curious why Clare had turned the former hotel into a family home when it'd been a hotel for several decades now. He'd have to ask her at dinner, which reminded him, when was dinner?

He crossed through his suite and opened the door to the hall, and yes, there was his good man Gio still standing sentry. "Do you know what time I'm expected for dinner?"

"I will find out," the bodyguard answered.

"Thank you." Rocco didn't bother closing the door this time and was still wandering around the living room of the suite, studying the artwork, when he heard footsteps behind him.

"Will these rooms work for you?" Clare asked.

He turned, surprised she'd come. "I'm sorry to have disturbed you. I know you had work to do."

She shrugged. "I wasn't getting anything done. Too much on my mind." She looked up at him, her stunning eyes searching his. "This is…unsettling…having you here."

Rocco realized he liked her hair dark, the rich brunette shade made her eyes look like violets. She was even more beautiful now than before, if that was possible. "How can I make it more comfortable for you?"

She went to the pair of French doors that matched the pair in the bedroom, and opened them, letting the late afternoon breeze sweep into the room, providing warmth and the perfume of the roses below. "It's not your problem," she said after a taut silence, glancing at him over her shoulder. "It's my problem, and I'll figure it out. I'm surprisingly good at handling problems."

"And I'm a problem?" he asked softly.

She visibly stiffened. "It wasn't my intention to imply such a thing. It's that...you know...we had a complicated relationship, and even though we want the best for Adriano, we're still virtually strangers. We knew of each other, but we didn't know each other, if that makes sense."

"It does."

He joined her on the small balcony and glanced over the railing to the terrace below. His suite of rooms in this wing faced the ocean, but below were gardens, extensive gardens from the look of it. Immediately below was a tidy ornamental garden with fountains and gravel paths, marked with boxwoods in fanciful shapes. There were other gardens beyond, paths curving around the villa walls, leading to secret gardens and a cluster of gnarled olive trees in the distance. "The gardens are so impressive," he said, "I thought I'd go for a walk, but wasn't sure what time you serve dinner here."

"There really isn't a set dinner hour. With Adriano, I tend to be informal. He eats very early and in summer we've been eating outside, alfresco, or if he's tired, in his nursery. It's a gorgeous suite of rooms—possibly my favorite in the house."

"So we'll eat with him tonight?" Rocco asked.

She hesitated. "Probably not tonight. But you'll see him in the morning at breakfast, if you're an early riser, as he is."

"Why not tonight?"

"He's in bed usually by seven. He eats at five thirty,

has a bath and stories. It's five now. If you'd like to eat soon I could make arrangements—"

"That is indeed early," he interrupted with a grimace. "Breakfast would be better."

He could tell she was fighting a smile. "So what time would you like to eat? Eight, nine, later?"

"What is best for you?"

"I'd prefer eight, as I'll probably return to my office after dinner."

"Do you work every night?"

Her eyes narrowed and she looked at him, as if trying to understand if there was an ulterior reason for the question. "Once Adriano is in bed, I will read, or work. I like to keep my mind busy, and I find work very satisfying. But then, I imagine you feel the same way. The Cosentino family has an extensive portfolio of investments."

"And I am the only Cosentino left. Well, until now."

"That must be a relief," she said.

She had no idea. Adriano changed everything, in more ways than one. "Dinner at eight," he said, content to leave it at that.

"I will alert the kitchen," Clare answered. "Oh, and dinner will be informal. I suggest you wear something comfortable, that is, if your bag has arrived."

"It should be here within the hour," he said.

"Perfect."

He walked her to the door, and as she joined Gio in the hallway, she paused and glanced back at Rocco, her gaze meeting his. For a long moment she just looked at him, truly looked at him, before turning and walking away.

What had that long look meant?

What had she been trying to see?

Rocco slowly closed the door, but he could still see her lovely face with those lovely lips and haunting violet eyes.

Her eyes did haunt him, as did the memory of the past. She was right when she'd said they had a complicated past. Their history wasn't pleasant, and he was the one who'd made it impossible, he was the one who'd made it difficult and she didn't even know why. He knew, but he could never tell her. He wouldn't. But that didn't mean he wasn't aware of the truth, tormented by guilt.

But with her gone, and the heavy door closed, he felt trapped, and angry. He didn't even know why he was angry only that he suddenly wanted to hit something, break something, even though he never physically lashed out. He always held emotions in. He always bottled them up, reducing those emotions until they could be ignored, forgotten.

But the emotions were bubbling up, just as the past wasn't sleeping, either. Everything seemed to have broken free, history mocking him for being an ass. Selfish. Destructive.

Rocco paced the length of the room again, as caged as a big cat in a small zoo enclosure. He couldn't do this, be here in Clare's home, pretending. Pretending he wasn't responsible for the rift between them. Pretending she was the problem, or had been the problem. Clare hadn't been anything but Clare...polite, curious, reserved and hopelessly beautiful.

He stopped pacing and drew a slow breath, trying to get a handle on the anger. He needed fresh air and perspective. He could get both, but he had to walk, move, clear his head.

This luxurious suite with its priceless antiques and dazzling view of the sea was nothing more than a gilded box.

Returning to the door, Rocco opened it, relieved to discover the bodyguard gone. Quickly he retraced his earlier steps along the long corridor to the formal marble staircase, down the stairs to the ground floor where he exited onto the terrace, and then from the terrace into the gardens. The winding gravel path appealed, and Rocco walked quickly, as if the devil was chasing, and maybe the devil was, because that beast, that monster wasn't behind him, it was in him. He was the monster and there was nothing he could do about it now.

His shoes crunched the pea gravel as he skirted the rose garden for the small orchard, and once he'd entered the orchard, he slowed, appreciating the shade.

Earlier Clare had asked about his animosity, asking him for the truth, wanting him to confirm what they both knew—that he didn't like her. She'd wanted an explanation and he'd done his best to deflect the question, not at all prepared to tell her the truth. Because he could never tell her the truth.

There was no reason for him to dislike her so much. His dislike had been immature, illogical, which only made his interactions with her more complicated.

Until Clare entered the picture, Rocco had prided himself on his self-control. His self-control had gotten him through so many difficult times, helping him manage pain and disappointment, but he wasn't in control with regard to Clare, and he hadn't been kind to her, or supportive of Marius and Clare's engagement.

It had taken him a long time to understand his animosity to Clare. But it was not something he could explain to Clare. He could barely admit the truth to himself, but he'd been hard on her because she'd elicited such a strong response within him.

He'd been drawn to her immediately, and in a way he hadn't been drawn to any other woman. Ever.

She had made him feel. She had made him want. She made him crave.

It was maddening, infuriating. How could he be so physically attracted to her, this American woman who wasn't even his?

How could his body betray him, tightening every time she was near, stirring his senses, arousing his hunger. Testing his control.

And she, beautiful violet-eyed Clare, was his brother's. His brother's girlfriend, and then his brother's fiancée, and soon to be his brother's wife. And throughout it all, Rocco battled himself, horrified that he wanted his brother's woman.

What kind of brother was he to desire someone that didn't belong to him? Someone that meant so much to Marius, the brother he adored?

How could he justify fantasizing about taking Clare's mouth, her body, filling her, owning her, making her shiver and shudder in his arms.

And yet he did.

His dreams were filled with her, his thoughts so primal and carnal he felt out of control. The fact that she elicited such strong feelings in him frustrated him, and he snapped hard on those feelings, embarrassed by the attraction. The only way he could cope when around her was to detach himself, becoming distant, even cold, but it was necessary. By freezing his emotions he could block her out, pretend she wasn't there, pretend that she didn't exist.

Marius had asked him several times why Rocco was so cold to Clare, especially as Clare had done nothing to warrant such frosty behavior, and Rocco had always simply replied that there was something about her he didn't trust, that there was something he couldn't respect, when the truth was, he couldn't trust *himself*, not when close to her.

Rocco had been married in his twenties. After his wife died, he took a mistress in Rome, but those relationships didn't prepare him for lust, for hot, raw, desire. All-consuming desire. A need that kept him awake at night, his humming thoughts burning as he imagined all the things he'd do to Clare, with Clare, if only he could.

Indecent things with his shaft and hands, his lips and tongue and teeth.

During those long nights he'd palm himself, bringing himself to frustrated climax, but the orgasms didn't ease the need. Or the pictures in his head. Clare made him feel animalistic. Untamed. Like a man who'd been starved because in his heart of hearts he thought she should be his.

In his heart of hearts he didn't believe his brother deserved her.

Every time he saw Marius and Clare together, he felt a surge of frustration, frustration that grew into anger, anger that bighearted, good-natured, easygoing Marius had won Clare's heart.

Did his brother even understand how lucky he was?

Did his brother know that there weren't many women like Clare? In fact, there was only her, the one, and she loved Marius.

Rocco couldn't let his brother know his feelings. Worse, they were feelings that confounded Rocco, feelings that tied him in knots, and so he did his best to avoid Clare, with or without Marius.

In all fairness, when Rocco handed Clare into the limousine after Marius's funeral, it had been a relief. He'd never see her again. He wouldn't feel this awful temptation, or the impossible desire, again. He'd hated feeling like such a bad brother to Marius, hated the conflicted desire—so tragic and Shakespearean, as well as plain ridiculous—so saying goodbye to Clare had been a relief. He'd have his life back. Not life as he wanted it, because God only knew that Rocco would give everything to have his brother still with him, but at least he didn't have to struggle with guilt and remorse, and the needling voice in his head that constantly whispered that he was a terrible man. Because a good man, a man of integrity and honor, wouldn't have coveted his brother's soon-to-be wife, but Rocco had.

Clare dressed for dinner with care, showering and then once dry, slipping on a long feminine kaftan in a green malachite pattern, a deep purple sash tied at the waist. As she blow-dried her hair, the soft silk fabric brushed her bare legs and slid across her shoulders. She couldn't have worn these intense colors as a blonde, but they worked with her dark hair, and the soft purple tie at her waist made her happy. It was playful and youthful and with Rocco Cosentino here, she could use the confidence booster because she found him so very intimidating.

She didn't even know what it was about him that unsettled her, but when near him her pulse tended to race and she felt vulnerable and sensitive, which was why the long kaftan appealed for dinner—it covered her, from her shoulders to her ankles. Even the sleeves extended past her elbows, fluttering on her forearm.

Clare put on a little mascara and lip gloss, and after adding a pair of gold dangly earrings with bits of amethyst, and slipping her feet into wedge sandals, she was ready to go downstairs and entertain her guest. This was her house, she reminded herself firmly. She was the host and she wasn't going to be dictated to by Rocco. She wasn't going to be used by him, either.

She understood the way of the world and how powerful men had run society and civilization for thousands of years. She'd been raised by such a man which gave her a unique perspective, as well as a position of strength. Clare had money and power of her own. She didn't need to fear Rocco, or fear anything he had to say. His opinion was simply his opinion. She was every bit as wealthy as he, every bit as educated, every bit as confident. She didn't need his approval or his permission. In fact, she didn't need him at all.

But her cool resolve faltered as she paused outside the dining room, surprised by the dimmed chandelier, and the flickering candles on the table and in the pairs of delicate Venetian sconces.

Rocco was already there, admiring one of the seventeenth-century Baroque gilt wood floor lamps flanking the doorway. "Did all of this come with the house?" he asked, turning to greet her, dressed in a black suit, white shirt and black silk tie. "Or are these acquisitions you've made?"

It was hard to focus on his question when her heart was beating fast. She'd told him that dinner was informal, and yet Rocco looked dashing—elegant—in a stunning, sophisticated twill suit made from an incredibly fine wool. One of her newest ventures was the purchase of an Italian fashion house specializing in menswear, high-end menswear, and she was curious to know more about Rocco's suit but didn't feel it appropriate to ask.

She forced her gaze from his chiseled jaw to his strong aquiline nose, to his silver gaze beneath black eyebrows. "A combination," she said, trying not to feel like a gauche schoolgirl. She wasn't a girl, but a woman, and she wasn't a virgin, but a mother. Just because Marius had been sunshine and laughter, didn't mean she had to be cowed by Rocco's brooding intensity. "When I first purchased the villa, it was fully furnished, but as it was a hotel, I refurbished tired rooms and began to collect pieces that would fit the different rooms and decor."

"I think that's what made finding you so difficult. I was looking for a private residence, not a hotel, and I'd been under the impression this was still a hotel."

"It was until a year ago Christmas. We always closed for January and February, reopening in March, but when it came to reopen, I realized I'd rather live here full-time, and so we never reopened, and little by little I converted the hotel into what it had originally been—a private home. A family home."

"But it's so big for just two people."

Clare laughed. "I employ a small army, and most live on the property, so as you can imagine, the space comes in handy."

The chef appeared in the doorway, letting Clare know the first course was ready, if she was ready to sit down.

Clare gestured for Rocco to join her at the table. Again she noted the candles and the dimmed overhead lighting.

"I'm surprised by the candles," she told him as he held her chair for her. "This isn't something Adriano and I do."

"I asked for them," Rocco answered, sitting to her right, instead of at the far end of the table. "I thought after a long day it'd be more restful."

But as the first course was served, Clare struggled to eat with Rocco so close and her pulse continuing to drum, making her feel strangely breathless. Ideally Rocco should have been seated across the table from her, instead of on her right. He was left-handed and she was right and there were moments their hands brushed and each light touch made her even more light-headed.

It had been a long day, though, and she was unaccustomed to entertaining, never mind Marius's brother who'd always been so brusque with her. She knew he didn't think she was good enough for Marius, and she'd decided that hostility would get them nowhere, but it was hard to forget the tension, hard to not resent him for making those last few months leading up to the wedding so stressful.

She and Marius could have had a wedding anywhere. They could have had a huge wedding, something lavish, even ostentatious, but that wasn't Marius's style. Despite his background, he preferred to be casual, and he'd wanted their wedding to be relaxed, fun, something his closest friends would enjoy. Since most played polo, or were sponsors of the sport, they scheduled the wedding for late August to coincide with the end of the polo season in Spain, and just before everyone shifted to Argentina for the fall. The wedding would be held at Marius's sprawling villa in Sotogrande, ten minutes from the breathtaking beaches of Cádiz, and thirty minutes from the Gibraltar airport.

The Spanish villa's gardens were expansive, as well as tropical and lush, and they'd planned to have tents erected to cover the broad lawns, while the reception would feature colorful flowers and the best music for dancing, as well as truly great food. The wedding reflected Marius's personality. He was color and passion personified.

It was there at the Santa María Polo Club in Sotogrande that Marius died, a freak accident just days before the wedding, an accident that no one could have seen coming. Everyone knew that polo could be a dangerous sport. Risks were an inherent part of sports, but for Marius to be thrown? Unthinkable.

The funeral was a blur. She traveled to her main property then, a small private island off the coast of Italy, and it was there she realized she was pregnant. She'd known in September she'd missed a period but with grief it hadn't surprised her. Her shock had almost incapacitated her. She'd stopped eating, drinking, sleeping. How could something have happened like this…to Marius of all people? He was the ultimate horseman. The horse whisperer, his friends teased him. No one knew or loved horses like Marius.

It wasn't until late October that Clare realized she'd missed a second period, and her body felt different. Her emotions felt different. She'd ordered a pregnancy test kit to be delivered to her secluded home. When the results flashed positive, she traveled to the nearest medical clinic, consulted a doctor, had a blood test done, along with an ultrasound, confirming the pregnancy, and how far along she was. She'd probably conceived the day Marius died, or the day before. They'd made love all week, but they'd been a little reckless near the end, knowing the wedding was just days away.

The baby arrived as scheduled on May the nineteenth. She'd named him after Marius's Argentine grandfather, a famous polo player just like Marius. She'd added middle names to include her father, and Marius, of course. It was a long name for an infant but Clare knew he'd grow into it, and he was.

One of the staff approached the table, quickly removing one course to return with the second. Although Clare usually loved seafood, tonight the plated fish made her stomach heave a little. She was finding it so hard to relax. Maybe sharing memories of Marius would help. Maybe it would comfort them both. "Do you remember Marius as a baby?" she asked Rocco, who didn't seem to have a problem with the Acqua Pazza.

"Of course. I was ten when he was born. It was exciting. Everybody was happy, and from the beginning Marius was easy, a very cheerful baby."

Clare smiled wistfully. Adriano had been more challenging as a baby, but Marius would have been patient with him, and wonderful. "I always assumed due to the age difference between you and your brother, Marius was an oops baby, but maybe that isn't true, maybe your parents—"

"Our mothers were different. The age gap was due to the fact that our father took his time remarrying after my mother died. But I'm glad he remarried. He married two good women. He was lucky in love."

"I had no idea Marius was your half brother?"

Rocco's eyes narrowed. "There is no half anything. He was my brother, period. My family, my world."

Clare flushed, embarrassed. "I didn't mean to imply that the relationship was less then—"

"And yet you said *half*."

"I was surprised, that is all. He never mentioned it."

"Why should he? It wasn't important, certainly nothing to discuss with an outsider."

"I was his fiancée, not a stranger."

"Family is family. There are no lines drawn, no division based on genetics. My mother died when I was about Adriano's age. I have no memory of her. The only mother I knew was Marius's, and she was wonderful. I was her son." Rocco fell silent a moment. "Children need parents. I needed a mother. It weighs on me that Adriano has no father."

"But he does have me," Clare said firmly. "He is my first priority, my only real priority. The rest is just—" She snapped her fingers. "Stuff."

"But you yourself implied you must juggle motherhood and work—"

"I wasn't complaining. I like being busy."

"But if you didn't work, you could be with your son more—"

"I am with him for breakfast, lunch and dinner, plus bath time, bedtime, and playtime after his afternoon nap. On weekends there is no nanny. It's just us." She lifted her chin, fighting anger. Who was he to judge? And if he wasn't judging, but thinking he was being helpful, he was wrong. "I'm a better mother for working five hours during the day, and it's good for him to have others to love him. No one can ever have too much love."

"But does your staff love him, or are they just paid to act loving?"

Clare bit down, jaw clamped, as she counted to five and then to ten. "Your input isn't wanted or needed, not if it's going to be so critical."

"That isn't my intent. I'm playing devil's advocate."

"Well then, please don't. It's the last thing I need. As a single parent I'm aware of the challenges, but work gives me pleasure, and it's not something I need to give up—not for you, not for anyone."

"Even though you don't need the money?"

"You work and you don't need the money," she countered, thinking that would finally silence him.

It didn't. He shrugged. "I have no family. I have nothing in my life but the family estates and portfolio. It's all I have."

"You could remarry and have a family."

He grew still, his expression almost haunted. "I couldn't," he said after a long tense moment. "It wouldn't be right."

Clare's heart suddenly ached for him. The fact that Rocco still grieved for his wife moved her profoundly. He understood love, and loss, and honored his commitments. She wasn't sure she liked him, but at least she was beginning to get to know him. "But you have thought about it?" she asked gently, searching his shadowed eyes.

He shifted uncomfortably. "And dismissed the idea."

"Why?"

He looked away, his gaze skimming the room with the flickering sconces and the soft candlelight reflecting off the table. "It's complicated."

Still she said nothing and he glanced at her, lips twisting. "You should let it go. Suffice it to say, I don't take marriage vows lightly. Marriage is for life."

Staff returned to take their plates, removing the second course. "Dessert?" she asked Rocco. "Cheese and fruit, or something a little more decadent? I think chef has made *marizotto* for you, but there's no pressure."

"I'm actually fine without anything. Maybe just a coffee."

She looked to the server. "Just the one coffee, but we'll have it in on the little terrace." Clare pushed back from her chair and lifted her wine. "Shall we go outside? It's lovely this time of night outside."

The little terrace was her favorite place to be at night. Strands of white lights were strung across the pretty little patio garden, illuminating a fountain built against the stucco wall on one side and a wall of purple bougainvillea on the other. The patio's floor was covered in creamy travertine tiles and the furniture was comfortable—sumptuous ivory lounge chairs each with its own lavender blanket.

Clare settled onto one of the lounge chairs and covered her legs with the soft pastel blanket. "Too feminine for you?" she asked, curious as to what he'd think of her secret patio garden with the tinkling fountain and the crashing waves in the distance.

"Not at all. It's beautiful, and very peaceful. I can see why you like to come here at night." He sat down carefully on the other chair, but he didn't stretch out.

Clare studied his profile, his broad shoulders, lean muscular torso and long powerful legs. Marius had been lithe and athletic, but Rocco was powerful, with the look of a prizefighter. Strong, physical, tough. For a little bit neither said anything, but Clare was acutely aware of Rocco not far from her side, aware of the size of him, and his physicality so different from Marius.

"You're not who I thought you were," he said gruffly.

She arched a brow. "How so?"

"I assumed you were a trust fund baby. Indulged. Entitled."

"I am a trust fund baby. I've never had a real job—"

"You have a real job."

"Yes, but in high school and college I didn't have to flip hamburgers or wait tables or be a barista like other young women my age. I have always had financial security, which allowed me to be make different choices, enabling me to be successful sooner, younger."

One of the kitchen staff appeared with an espresso and a glass of sparkling water and after moving a small table closer to Rocco's chair, positioned the water and espresso at Rocco's elbow.

Rocco drank some of his water and then sipped the espresso. "*Va bene.*" *It's good.*

"You sounds surprised."

"I'm picky about my espresso."

"I know. Marius told me."

Rocco laughed, a low husky sound that made her pulse jump, and her insides did a strange tumble. In the soft nighttime lighting, Rocco's hard features looked sculptural, all carved planes and hollows. He fascinated her tonight. He wasn't who she'd thought he was, either, and even though she wasn't relaxed, she wasn't ready to go to her room and be alone.

"And Marius once told me you were not close with your father," Rocco said.

"It's true. My father was never abusive, just…disinterested. Perhaps if I'd been a son he might have been more invested, but I even question that. My father loves himself." She looked at Rocco, eyebrows lifting. "And money, of course."

"So he didn't advise you on investing?"

"No. Never. That would be a waste of his time. In my father's eyes, women were decorative objects, pretty to look at and nice to hold, but not to be taken seriously. I wasn't to bother him, so I didn't." She smiled mischievously. "So I didn't, and I used my allowance during my university years to buy my first property, and from that early foray into real estate I discovered I liked investing, and creating a portfolio of my own. I was not your typical university student. I didn't enjoy parties, I didn't like beer, I don't drink hard liquor and, thanks to my cautious nature, I still rarely drink more than one glass of wine. I had to do something with my free time."

"I would have thought studying took up a lot of time."

"When you're reading Kierkegaard's recollection and repetition of dichotomy and the infinite qualitative distinction looking at photos of pretty properties is pure pleasure."

"Did your father mind that you were using your allowance in a different way than anticipated?"

She shrugged. "He didn't know, and I'm sure he didn't care. My father didn't want a family, but someone had to inherit, because heaven forbid the government take it all when he died, and he is not altruistic, so he isn't going to donate it to charities who could use the money. So, as the heir, I'm to stay alive, fulfilling my responsibility to him." Her lips curved but her voice cracked. "I will be donating most of his money to charity. After he's gone. I don't want it, or need it. He could have helped so many people but..." her voice faded and she didn't try to finish the sentence.

Rocco was sitting forward, forearms resting on his thighs. "And there is just you? No other siblings?"

"No siblings. Not a chance. He had a vasectomy after I was born and made it clear to his various wives that they were not to get pregnant. He didn't like the look of a pregnant woman, and he wasn't interested in having a broodmare in his bed." She reached for her wine, suddenly needing the wine to ease the lump in her throat. "You can see why Marius was so very dear to me. He was the first person that truly loved me, and not because I could do something for them, or open doors for them, but just because I was...me."

"I think there are many who will love you, for you."

She shook her head. "Not interested, not giving anyone a chance." She cleared her throat. "So, do you mind me asking how you found out about my different companies? What do you know?"

"In looking for you, I discovered your LLC, in which you are the sole owner. The corporation includes six hotels and resorts, all luxury properties catering to the wealthiest, most discriminating clients. More recently you've bought into a company that provides private jets, allowing your discriminating clients to book a private flight to their luxurious private property. And there are other companies, too, from high-tech security to farms and orchards, allowing you to diversify your investments, offset losses, better protecting your wealth."

She'd sipped the wine as he rattled off the facts. "You are quite the sleuth."

"You are the CEO. You're not just a figurehead. You actively manage your companies."

"Who knew that a girl with a degree in classical studies would have a head for business?"

He didn't smile. He just looked at her, silver gaze penetrating. "Is it hard juggling the businesses with raising a child on your own?"

"But I'm not on my own." She gestured about her, indicating the house and all within it. "I employ a virtual army to help me. Cooks, maids, gardeners, nannies, security—" She smiled. "Which you know all about because no one can do it 'all' on their own. Even if Marius lived, I would have needed help."

"Would you have worked if he'd lived?"

"I worked while he was alive." Her brow creased, perplexed. "But you knew that."

"I don't know that I did."

"What did you think I did all day?"

He shook his head. "I don't know, and it doesn't matter. My brother died a little over three years ago. It feels like a lifetime ago."

"I'm not surprised. You were such a good brother to him—"

"But I wasn't," Rocco interrupted, voice flinty.

"That's not what he said. He had so much love and respect for you."

"Don't, please." Rocco's firm mouth compressed, his expression grim. "Marius deserves the respect, not me." He looked at her then, his silver gaze meeting hers. "I live with guilt that I wasn't a better brother. I had hoped that by now the guilt would have eased, but it hasn't. It's grown stronger, heavier."

"Because you're alive, and he's not." She reached across to where he sat, and put her hand on his, but that was a mistake. The moment her palm and fingers touched the back of Rocco's hand she shuddered, shocked by an invisible current of energy that passed from his skin into hers. She quickly removed her hand, but her fingertips tingled, her palm hot, the nerve endings feeling burned. She curled her hand into a fist, pressing the sensitive skin to soothe it.

The heat wasn't her imagination, either. She could tell from Rocco's expression he'd felt the electric charge. His silver irises glowed and his heat emanated from him in waves.

Her gaze dropped from his magnetic eyes to his firm lips which had escaped the burn.

She knew he'd been burned when Marius was just a boy. Rocco, in his early twenties, had been at the wheel and there had been an accident—not their fault. If it hadn't been for Rocco's quick reflexes Marius would have been killed. Instead Rocco turned the steering wheel hard, spinning the car enough that he, on the driver's side, took the brunt of the impact. Rocco was crushed in the accident, pinned beneath the steering wheel and driver's door, and before they could free him, the engine exploded, the car quickly engulfed in fire. Marius escaped with just a few cuts and bruises, but Rocco suffered life-threatening injuries.

Marius had told Clare that Rocco never once lamented the choice he made, instead saying quietly, firmly that burns were nothing. Scars didn't matter. How could they, when Marius meant everything?

Marius said that was just who Rocco was—the ultimate protector, the perfect big brother.

Looking at Rocco now, perched on the lounge chair, a wave of dark hair falling forward on his brow, half his face chiseled with strong lines, the other half thickened with scars, she could only imagine how awful these past three years had been for Rocco.

"You've always been Marius's champion," she said, feeling remorseful. "I regret you didn't find out about Adriano sooner. I regret that I hadn't included contact details. That was wrong of me. I'm sorry. And I'm sorry for my part in the past, because I know I came between you and your brother, and that was wrong—"

"*Cara*, you did nothing wrong, and it's not your fault that Marius and I had words regarding your engagement. All I can say is that I was too controlling and it wasn't fair, not to either of you."

Inexplicable tears rushed to her eyes and Clare blinked hard. "It seems neither of us knew each other, but Adriano has brought us together, and Marius, if he's watching, he must be happy. It's what he always wanted…us to be a family."

Rocco made a rough sound in the back of his throat.

Alarmed, Clare's gaze lifted, her eyes meeting his. "Was that presumptuous of me? If so, I'm sorry—"

"Stop apologizing. It wasn't presumptuous. You are exactly right. Marius hated the conflict between us. He'd be pleased that we're coming together—" he broke off, swallowed, expression impossible to read. "For Adriano's sake."

"But not just Adriano's," she said, tears filling her eyes. "Yours, too. You've been alone, and I am sure you've been in a very dark place. I'm hopeful we can move forward now…truly brother and sister."

CHAPTER FOUR

ROCCO FOUND IT impossible to sleep.

Brother and sister? Is that what she saw…what she imagined?

His gut churned. He felt nauseated. He did not view Clare as a sister. He did not think of her as anything but…his. The source of his torment, the constant nagging guilt, the unattainable dream. He wanted her. He could picture the future with Clare. Making a life together, having a family with her. Not just Adriano but children of their own.

Rocco threw the light feather duvet back and left his bed, going into the adjoining marble bath to splash cold water on his face. He looked up at himself in the mirror, expression grim, determined.

He would have her. He would win her. There was no way he could lose her, after losing everyone else.

Rocco dried his face with a plush white hand towel and then turned out the bathroom light and returned to bed. But in bed, sleep still evaded him.

After Marius died Rocco was in a very dark place. For the first six months he'd been numb, in absolute shock and denial, and then he felt so much emptiness and grief that he questioned the point in living. But when he despaired, he pictured Clare, and it was her face, her full soft mouth, her wide lavender-blue eyes that gave him strength. And hope. Not that he deserved it.

But now he'd found her again and he wanted to protect her the same way he'd always protected his brother. Was it so terrible wanting her?

He'd never touched her when Marius was alive. He'd never said anything inappropriate to her. He'd just struggled with the desire, so intense and consuming, but he'd kept it all in, kept the love and need to himself.

Could he continue to contain the desire, suppressing his love and need for her? Not if he stayed here. But how in God's name was he going to leave?

Rocco finally fell asleep sometime in the middle of the night and was still deep asleep when a knocking—pounding?—sounded on the door in the living room. Groggy, he rolled out of bed, couldn't find his shirt, and just tugged the waistband of his sweatpants higher on his hip bones before going to the door.

He opened it expecting Gio or Roberto or another member of the staff. Instead, it was Clare and Adriano, and Adriano was smiling cautiously up at him.

"We've come to ask you to join us for breakfast," Clare said crisply, when Adriano buried his face against her skirt, suddenly overcome by shyness. "We've been waiting on our breakfast, hoping to see you, but we're getting hungry." Her hand went to the top of her son's head and she lightly ruffled his hair. "If you wouldn't mind company this morning."

He saw her gaze drop to his bare chest, and lower, to where the sweatpants he wore in bed hung precariously low on his torso. He carried a lot of muscle, lean muscle, but scars covered much of his chest, up half of his neck, and most of an arm. He was so used to the thickened skin that he forgot others might feel uncomfortable, but Clare didn't look uncomfortable, curious more than anything.

"I should have put on a shirt," he said gruffly as Adriano turned to look at him again, the child's smile not quite steady.

"Who hurt you?" Adriano asked in English.

Clare shushed Adriano, but Rocco didn't mind. "I was in a car accident," Rocco answered. "There was a fire."

The little boy was staring at the burns, examining them. "Did you cry?"

"A little bit," Rocco admitted.

Adriano nodded, clearly thinking. "Did the doctor give you a shot?"

"Several."

"I don't like shots," Adriano said.

"I don't, either."

Clare cleared her throat. "I take it we woke you up."

"Yes. I had trouble sleeping last night, but give me five minutes and I'll meet you for breakfast. Dining room?"

Adriano turned to his mom. "*Possiamo mangiare fuori*?" he asked. *Can we eat outside?*

"*Sì*." She smiled at him and then looked up at Rocco. "I think we'll have breakfast on the terrace. It's where you first met Adriano yesterday."

"I remember."

"We'll see you soon then." She steered Adriano away and they walked down the hall hand in hand and Rocco watched them for a moment, before closing the door.

Something was different about Clare this morning but he didn't know what it was, at least not yet.

***

It was a beautiful morning, the sun warm and bright, the sky a vivid blue with not a cloud in sight. September was Clare's favorite month in Italy. The temperatures were warm but not humid or hot, and the garden was in full bloom, all the flowers a riot of scent and color.

Clare sat at the table on the terrace with Adriano on one side of her and Rocco on the other. The breakfast dishes had been cleared, but they were lingering in the glorious sunshine unwilling to break up the party yet. Adriano, who tended to be shy with strangers, had decided Rocco was someone he liked, and chattered away to his uncle in a mix of Spanish and Italian with a little English thrown in. Rocco, to his credit, understood everything and usually answered in Italian, but sometimes would switch languages, too.

"Mama," Adriano said, turning to look at her. "Do you have to work today?"

She hesitated. "I should."

"Could we go to the *castello* today?" he asked, eyebrows lifting, expression hopeful. "*Zio* would like it."

She checked her smile but it was difficult to resist Adriano when he looked at her with that sweet face. He had a serious side, but he also could be terribly charming, as he was now. "But maybe your uncle doesn't like castles," she said.

Adriano looked at Rocco. "Do you like castles? We have a big one near here."

"Have you seen it before?" Rocco asked him.

"One time. But maybe we can go today and then it's this many," Adriano said, holding up two fingers.

Rocco glanced at Clare, amusement in his eyes. "Should we make it two times?"

She thought of the work waiting for her, and yesterday's unanswered emails. The hotel manager in Galway that had threatened to quit. The decisions needing to be made after the staff management meeting yesterday morning. But then there was this beautiful son of hers who deserved all the happiness in the world. It was difficult sometimes juggling everything, but her son always came first. Every single time. "Yes," she said, then laughed as Adriano jumped out of his chair and cheered. "But I need a half hour. Can we do that? Adriano, you need to go to Ava and brush your teeth and put on walking shoes. And Rocco—" she broke off, flushed.

"Yes?"

Clare shook her head, embarrassed, realizing she didn't know what she was going to say to him, only that she'd wanted to include him. "Nothing. I'll see you in thirty minutes."

The massive castle was just two kilometers from the villa. It dated back to the sixteenth century, but before that, there was another fortification on the same spot, a fortress from the Middle Ages. The castle's foundation rose high from the rocks, and the castle walls and buildings stood tall, pale gold stone outlined against the brilliant blue sky. Unlike some *castellos* this was intact, the heavy walls, smooth round towers and narrow windows beautifully preserved. As it was early and midweek there were very few tourists. Gio had accompanied them to the castle and he kept pace with Adriano as the child burst into a run as they entered through the front entrance.

Clare watched Adriano stop and examine a tall wood door, the door studded with iron. Clare and Rocco caught up to Adriano and then together they went through the door to the stairs that curved inside the tower. The stone steps were narrow and high and Rocco offered his hand to Adriano who happily took it. Together they climbed to the fourth floor where the stairwell opened onto a walkway leading to the next tower.

Rocco was explaining features of the castle to Adriano, and Adriano nodded, eyes wide. She'd brought him here a year ago but he'd grown so much since then, and his understanding of things was greater and he asked Rocco questions which Rocco answered.

Gio was now at her side and she thought it was interesting how Gio had been in their lives since Adriano was born, but Gio rarely spoke and only interacted with Adriano as security, not family, and Adriano even at two and a half, could tell the difference.

They climbed stairs and peeked at things, exploring for an hour and a half before Clare could see that Adriano was growing tired and it was getting close to his lunch. She suggested they return to the villa and all readily agreed, but Adriano looked happy as he'd learned new things today, and the castle had been dramatic and full of possibilities, especially for a young child with energy and a vivid imagination.

Back at the villa, Clare, Adriano and Rocco had a picnic lunch down on the villa's private beach, and as Adriano had brought his green ball down with him, Rocco and Adriano kicked the ball up and down the sand until Adriano drooped with exhaustion. Ava, who'd been waiting at the house, was summoned and she came down to take a yawning Adriano up to the nursery for his afternoon nap while Clare and Rocco remained on the blankets on the sand.

"He'll sleep well," Clare said, her lips curving as she watched Ava lead Adriano up the stairs. She couldn't look away, her heart so full. Adriano was changing daily. It was exciting to watch him grow up, thrilling being his mom.

"You're a good mother," Rocco said quietly.

She turned to look at Rocco and there was something in his expression that made her breath catch, air bottling in her chest. She felt a shaft of sharp emotion, emotion she didn't understand, but it made her realize how alone she'd been these past few years. Yes, there was staff, but they were all on payroll. She had no family, no friends; it was her and Adriano against the world.

And now Rocco, which just made her chest ache all the more.

"I do love that little boy," she said after a moment, voice hoarse.

"He knows it," Rocco said, "and love is the most important thing at this age. Love creates stability and confidence."

Clare's eyes burned and she blinked. "You should have been a father."

"I got to be father and brother to Marius."

He glanced away, giving her his profile, the one without the burns and it was so hard and masculine—the cheekbone, the jaw, the flat black eyebrow over his silver eyes—and she felt a little shiver of appreciation race through her. In a different life she might have been drawn to him. In this life she…

Clare swallowed, stopping herself, unwilling to continue the thought. There was no point. It was too unsettling. Just thinking about a different life made her feel scared. Unsettled. She couldn't be attracted to him, or anyone. It wasn't her future. She and Adriano were tight. They were a team.

"It was a good morning," Rocco said, shifting the conversation to a neutral topic.

She nodded. "A wonderful morning," she agreed. "It felt so good to be out enjoying the day." Clare slipped her hand beneath the edge of the blanket, digging her fingers into the sand. "I sometimes forget that we're right here on the beach. We should get out more."

"Why don't you get out more?" he asked, leaning back on his hands, legs stretched in front of him. "Is it because of your workload?"

She shook her head, her gaze traveling up his legs, which were long and muscular, even in the dark denim which hugged his powerful thighs.

Blushing Clare glanced away. "I think I fall into a routine and forget how much I enjoy—and Adriano enjoys—excursions. Sometimes it seems easiest to remain at the villa. It's spacious and safe. There's a big lawn for Adriano to play on. We have this private beach. There is also a pool, but that is indoors, which is nice in winter but unused this time of year."

"Can Adriano swim yet?"

"Yes, but that's because he had lessons since he was one. It was something I insisted on as we live so close to the sea."

"You are always thinking of the dangers," Rocco said, his voice low.

She looked at him, feeling raw, and shy, as if she'd just been caught changing, revealing more of herself than she should. "Because the world is full of dangers."

"Would you feel this way if Marius was still alive?"

Hot tears pricked her eyes and she drew a deep shuddering breath. "But he's not." She blinked and a tear fell, sliding down her cheek.

Rocco leaned toward her and wiped the tear away. "So what is your plan? You and the child alone together, forever?"

She felt the swipe of his thumb all the way through her, his touch so tender that it made her long for a life not yet lived. "I will never love again," she said huskily. "Marius was my soul mate. He was my love, my best friend, all I ever wanted. I will never replace him. I will never even try."

Rocco's expression was sympathetic and kind. "Your lovely Adriano should have more. A father. Brothers and sisters—"

"I've thought of that. I've thought a great deal about him being an only child. I was an only child, and I hated it. I was lonely, but I do have options, should I want to give him a sibling. I can use a sperm donor. Many women have children without being married or in a significant relationship. There's no reason I can't."

"True. You could do that, and it would give you control. You wouldn't have to share the children with anyone, and you wouldn't have to compromise, but what if you were sick, or there was an accident...what would happen to the children? Do you have a backup plan?"

Clare didn't answer. She'd thought of that, but also dismissed it. She was young, and healthy. In her mind, she was indestructible. But perhaps that was dangerous thinking. She, who planned everything, should be planning for the worst-case scenario as well, worst case being that she also died. Her insides knotted thinking of her own mortality. Obviously, accidents happened—she only had to think about Marius—but she wasn't going to go through life afraid. "I don't play extreme sports. I'm a good driver. I'm quite healthy. I don't plan on getting sick."

"Does anyone plan on getting sick?" he retorted, but his silver gaze was warm, his expression intent, but there was no mockery in his expression, just concern.

She looked at him and then couldn't look away. His silver eyes captivated her, the deep timber of his voice mesmerizing. She didn't know this Rocco Cosentino. He'd never shown this side of himself to her. Marius had always said he was protective. Genuine. But all she'd experienced was coldness, brusqueness. Obviously here was the Rocco Marius had adored.

She was beginning to understand why Marius had loved his brother so. But why had Rocco hidden his kindness from her?

"You mean to remain here always?" Rocco asked lifting a handful of sand and squeezing it in his palm. Living apart from society in your own walled fortress?"

"It's not a fortress, it's a villa—"

"You know what I mean."

She laughed incredulously. "This isn't a prison, Rocco, it's rather like heaven with the orchards, and gardens, the ocean and extensive lawn perfect for games of football."

"But who does he play football with? His security details? Come on, a child needs friends. Companions. Tell me you will at least send him to the local school."

Her shoulder rose and fell. "I plan on hiring tutors for him. In America many children are taught at home."

"And you think that will be a happy life for him?"

Heat suddenly swept through her, making her speak

sharply. "What do you know of a happy life? Marius said you had experienced so much pain—"

"I have lost too many people, and after my brother died, I wasn't sure I could take anymore, but I am still here. I am still trying to live."

"And love?" Her eyebrows lifted. "You could have more, you know. You don't have to live in isolation."

"Touché. If you don't approve of isolation, why raise Adriano apart from the world? He shouldn't be alienated from society. He should grow up surrounded by family, friends."

"But I have no family. Just my father in Florida and he's not long for the world—"

"Has he met Adriano?"

She bit down into her bottom lip, pain sweeping through her. She could only shake her head, unable to speak. Her father's indifference toward his own grandson had crushed her.

"Your father wouldn't meet him?" Rocco guessed.

"No." She held her breath a moment, pushing away the sting and the rejection. She'd vowed she'd never let her son know just how unfeeling his grandfather was. "You are the only family he has other than me."

"Then it's good I've come," Rocco said rising.

She watched him step off the blanket and walk to the edge of the water, his gaze out on the horizon where the blue sky met the darker blue-green sea.

After a moment she got to her feet and crossed the sand, joining him. He was like a magnet, she thought, pulling her to him. But maybe it was because she wanted to be near him. She liked the company. Liked *his* company. She couldn't say he made her feel safe, but it did make her feel, and it was…something she didn't understand, but it was strong, almost electric, much like the jolt she'd felt when she'd touched his hand last night.

"I will give him friends," she said after the silence had stretched too long. "When he's older."

"Why not now?"

"He's still very young, not yet three."

"Children benefit from friends at all ages."

She nodded out at the sea, and then glanced to the right and left, which was all her property. "Where would these playmates come from? The village is four kilometers away, but it wouldn't be comfortable having strangers here."

"I agree. But Adriano is very bright. If he can speak three languages now, he's ready for playmates. The bonds of friends and family are important to emotional growth and well-being."

Clare had grown up very alone, and her loneliness had been like a wound, festering, aching, and it wasn't until she'd been sent to a boarding school in Europe that she finally met girls her age, and made her first friends, and with time those friends became a makeshift family. "I don't disagree. But as a single mother it's not easy, especially as I've no interest in dating let alone remarrying."

"But you were never married," Rocco said softly.

Clare flinched, going hot then cold. "Semantics," she choked. "And you know what I meant."

"I do." Rocco walked a little way down the beach, his back to her as he stared out at the ocean, hands thrust into the front pockets of his jeans. His shoulders were wide. His posture was erect. He reminded her of a Roman general surveying his troops.

"I have tried to give him everything," she said, raising her voice to be sure he could hear. "Adriano is not deprived of anything."

"But a father," Rocco replied, turning to face her.

She inhaled sharply, eyes widening. "That's cruel," she said, "even for you."

He held her gaze, expression inscrutable. "Am I cruel?"

"You can be, and you were, putting so much pressure on Marius, trying to break us up—"

"I didn't," he gritted.

"You did. Maybe you never said to him, 'she's not good enough for you,' but you implied it in a dozen different ways. I still don't know why you objected to me, but let's not pretend now that you supported our marriage."

Rocco's faint smile faded, his silver gaze disturbingly intense. "You're right. I did not."

"Why?"

"I wanted—"

Whatever he was about to say was interrupted by Gio's shout. She couldn't hear what he was saying but she glanced at her phone which was buzzing on her wrist. Urgent, read the text. A call from the States.

"I'm needed in the house," she said looking at Rocco, meeting his silver gaze and holding it. "But this conversation isn't finished."

Rocco watched as Clare hurried across the sand, the breeze picking up tendrils of her dark hair, the full skirt of her pale blue sundress with the tiny embroidered daisies swishing around her legs as she rapidly climbed the stairs to the villa's terraced garden. He'd come so close to telling her the truth, to saying *I wanted you for myself.*

He wanted her to know how strongly he felt about her,

but it'd blow up in his face. It'd be a disaster. She wouldn't be comfortable with the truth, or him. No, some things were best left unspoken.

But that didn't change how he felt, and it didn't change his desire. The years apart had only made the want and need stronger.

There would never be another for him now. It was Clare or no one. That's all there was to it.

Two hours later he was in the spacious library on the first floor reviewing financials when he received what could only be called a summons to meet Clare in her office. In Rocco's world no one summoned him so it intrigued him to be at Clare's beck and call. She was comfortable in her villa. She felt safe here. He wondered, though, what it would be like to have her feel a little less controlled, a little bit out of control, her mind and body overwhelmed by pleasure.

Her office was on the second floor in the wing opposite where his rooms were. A bodyguard was positioned at the top of the stairs and he escorted Rocco to Clare. When she opened the door, afternoon sunlight poured in through the tall windows, creating a halo of light around her. She'd changed into trousers and a black knit top, her long hair pulled back in a sleek ponytail. She looked businesslike and no-nonsense and even more beautiful.

She stepped back to let him enter the room before closing the office door behind him. "Thank you for not keeping me waiting," she said crisply, returning to her desk and sitting down. She gestured at a chair on the opposite side of her desk. "Please."

He sat, trying not to feel like a schoolboy called before the headmistress.

"I shouldn't have called you cruel," she said, not wasting time getting to the point. "You've spent your life devoted to your family, and you were an exceptional brother to Marius. He would be so happy you're here now, spending time with Adriano. He would love to see you and Adriano playing football, and just talking about things. I'm grateful, because as you say, Adriano doesn't have a father, and I don't want to deprive him of anything—"

"So don't," Rocco said quietly, interrupting her. "Give him a father."

"And where do I find such a man?"

"You could marry me."

Clare's lavender eyes grew huge. She blinked and stared at him, lips parted in shock. "But…you don't want to be married. You've made that abundantly clear."

"I don't wish to date, and I don't wish to start over. But you're not a stranger, and you have a son that needs a father, that could benefit from a family. From me."

Rocco hadn't come here expecting to say any of this, not today, and certainly not now, but the moment seemed right and he seized the opportunity. "I understand this would not be a love marriage. This is about being practical, and proactive. We can give Adriano a family—the structure and safety—as well as the heritage and traditions that are part of his Cosentino legacy. Culture and heritage are the very heart of my family, and I am confident it is what Marius would want for his son."

Just hearing him say Marius's name made her heart ache. "We live together…but as strangers?"

"Not strangers. Family, and partners, raising Adriano together."

Her jaw worked. Fear darkened her eyes. "You want him."

"I want to be part of his life. He's the only family I have. Is it so strange to think he is important to me?"

"I worry you'll take over his life."

"Did I do that to Marius?"

She chewed on her lower lip and Rocco waited, wanting to give her time, knowing that if he came on strong and exerted too much pressure she'd feel threatened and reject his suggestion out of hand.

A minute ticked by, and then another. Finally Clare spoke. "Forgive me for being blunt, but I don't see what I get from this? I like my life with my son. I like how it is now. We're content—"

"For now. But what about later, when he is older? Have you thought about that? Children without fathers are vulnerable. Boys can be ruthless."

"Not just boys." Her gaze met his, her expression somber. "Girls can be equally ruthless. If not more so."

"Then protect him from that. Give him two parents who can love him and protect him."

"But I can't replace Marius."

"You needn't replace him," Rocco said quietly. "It would be impossible to replace him. But you could at least give his son the appearance of family."

"Exactly what are you proposing?" she asked, her voice equally low.

She had not said no. She had not shown him to the door, or demanded her security drag him out. "Marry me." Rocco's gaze met hers. "Take my name. It is already Adriano's last name. No one will think twice about his parentage. It will be assumed—"

"That you are his father?" Her voice rose, not high, but it was sharp, and brittle. "But you are not his father. And I will not have him thinking you are his father—"

"I would never presume."

"You presume now."

"I'm talking with you. We're brainstorming, discussing different possibilities for Adriano and his future. Having raised a little boy before I believe now is an ideal time to make changes, should you want to make changes. But if you don't…" He shrugged and left it at that.

She started to rise and then sat down again. Clare had gone white, and her naturally pink lips and lavender eyes were the only color in her pale face. "You've caught me off guard. I don't know what to say. This isn't something I expected, or even wanted to happen." Her eyes briefly met his before looking away, guilt suffusing her because time was passing and change was needed, but it was so hard to let Marius go. "I will always love Marius."

"I will, too, but here is the terrible, awful, painful truth. Marius is gone. Adriano will never know him. He will never know Marius's laugh or his big hugs. He will not be taught how to ride by one of the greatest polo players in the world. He will not have the memories we do. But Adriano can have different memories. You don't have to deprive him of a father figure. I can be there for him, just as I was for Marius."

She reached for her glass of water, hand trembling. She took a drink and then another before setting the glass back down. Her expression was stricken. Clare used her knuckle to wipe beneath her eyes, knocking away the moisture. "Wouldn't he be so confused? That he goes from knowing no one in his family to I'm suddenly married to his uncle? Isn't it rather appalling? It's like a Shakespearean play and the very suggestion makes my skin crawl."

Three years ago he'd thought something similar, but Marius was gone now, and Rocco desired Clare more than ever. "I have no desire to confuse Adriano. That is not my intention. We can marry and take things slowly so that everyone can adjust. There is no need to traumatize anyone—you or him."

"A marriage of convenience?" she asked, words clipped.

"Eventually I'd like Adriano to have brothers and sisters." Rocco hesitated, taking his time, wanting her to be able to process it all…as much as she could. "I loved being a big brother," he added. "It's a privilege, and a responsibility, one that would benefit Adriano, even if he feels a little jealousy at first. It is normal, you know."

Her mouth opened, closed. Rocco now knew she'd been an only child and she'd hated it. She wouldn't want Adriano to grow up alone. But Rocco wasn't going to push now. Now was the time to ease back and let her think. Her mind had to be reeling.

"I need time," she said, no longer pale, but rather flushed, her cheeks filled with hot pink color. "I have to think."

"Of course."

He hesitated and then rose. "Was there anything else you wished to discuss with me?"

She looked up at him, expression stricken, confusion evident in her eyes. "No," she whispered.

He nodded and walked out.

CHAPTER FIVE

CLARE HEARD THE door close behind Rocco but didn't see as she'd put her head down on her arms on her desk, hiding.

She felt sick, heartsick, her body heavy and leaden. How could he suggest such a thing? How could he come here and after just one day propose to her?

How dare he?

And how could she even consider it because, God help her, she was.

Otherwise she would have shot him down on the spot. She would have laughed in his face. She would have told him to leave—and stay away. But she hadn't done any of those things.

If she married Rocco it would be for Adriano. It wouldn't be for her. It'd be to, as Rocco said so succinctly, protect Adriano and to raise him as a true Cosentino, something she couldn't do on her own. She wasn't a Cosentino. She wasn't Italian. She wasn't aristocratic.

But Rocco was nothing like Marius…and it had been easy to love Marius. Marius had been light and laughter, humor, warmth, security. She hadn't had a lot of that growing up and meeting him had been a revelation. He'd added so much to her life in so many ways. She couldn't imagine ever replacing him. She hadn't wanted to replace him, and to contemplate replacing him with his older brother? A man that didn't make her feel safe…a man that made her feel, but it wasn't a brotherly emotion, or a brotherly attraction. She shouldn't be attracted to Rocco, and yet there was this curiosity humming through her, an awareness that made her feel alive again.

But desire…she didn't trust it.

Perhaps if the marriage was just a marriage in name only it wouldn't be so overwhelming, but Rocco thought Adriano should have siblings. And Rocco was a physical man and she couldn't imagine him being okay with a platonic arrangement.

She couldn't imagine either of them surviving such an arrangement.

But to make love to him? To become Rocco's?

Clare suppressed a little shiver, sensation rushing down her spine, making everything in her feel tingly.

To be fair, she and Rocco didn't have to get intimate to make a baby. They could go the IVF route, use fertility doctors and all, specialists who'd put the sperm and egg together, saving them from becoming physical with each other. The thought calmed her.

There were options. She didn't have to panic, and brothers and sisters for Adriano would be wonderful. Built-in friends—lifelong playmates—and a bond that would be stronger than anything else in the world. Clare did like the sound of that. She liked the idea that Adriano would have someone else in his life, someone who would be both friend and family, someone close to his age who would be in his life even when his parents were gone.

Her phone pinged, the alert reminding her she had a

conference call in five minutes. Clare left her desk, refreshed her sparkling water and sat back down trying to mentally ready herself for the call, but all she could really think about was Rocco's proposal.

Forty-five minutes later, Clare left her office and exited the house to cross the long stone terrace and take the stairs down into the garden. She smelled jasmine and the heady fragrance of the late summer roses, and she inhaled and exhaled the perfume trying to clear her head, hoping to find a little bit of peace and calm.

She shouldn't have agreed to let Rocco stay. He hadn't done anything wrong, but she no longer felt easy with him here. They'd had a wonderful morning, breakfast together, and then the visit to the *castello*, followed by a picnic on the beach…but now her heart was racing and she felt panicked.

She couldn't lose her son, not to Rocco—not to anyone. If she were completely honest, that was her biggest fear. Having been so alone and lonely as a child she'd always wanted family, her own family, one that she could cherish and shower with love, attention and affection. She would raise her children differently than she'd been raised. She'd make sure they knew they were the most important thing in the world, and nothing, and no one would come between her and them.

Would Rocco truly sneak Adriano away? No. But she couldn't help worrying—what if her son ended up loving Rocco more than her? What if Adriano preferred Rocco over her?

It was childish of her, but Clare had never felt safe, and loved, until Marius entered her life, and then after a few wonderful years, he'd been taken from her and she'd felt abandoned all over again.

Miracle of miracles she was pregnant…and Adriano came into the world like the angel he was, helping heal her broken heart, helping give her purpose. And laughter. And love.

Because of Adriano, she loved and was loved.

But what if…what if something did happen to her? What would happen to Adriano? She couldn't leave him orphaned. She couldn't leave him without family. Parents.

Heart aching, Clare walked through the elegant boxwood garden and sat down on a bench facing the elegant eighteenth-century fountain with its marble Poseidon in the center, and reclining maidens in different pools.

Rocco.

Marius.

What was she to do?

If only her anxiety would ease. She needed to calm down and slow her racing pulse. There was no reason to feel frantic. Nothing bad had happened, and no one was forcing her to do anything. Rocco wasn't pressuring her, and he wouldn't hurt her. He wasn't a threat.

So why was she afraid?

Why was she so full of adrenaline and emotion?

Was it because he reminded her of Marius? Or was it because he had suggested change—life-altering change?

Or was it because Rocco was unlike anyone she'd ever met…intensely masculine, so masculine that she couldn't ignore his physical energy?

When he'd come to the door this morning he'd been shirtless, and yes there had been scars, but the scars weren't what held her attention. It was the musculature, the powerful chest, the narrow waist, the hard ripple of abs disappearing into the waistband of his pajamas, which barely clung to his lean hips.

Then on the beach, she'd been so aware of his hips and his thighs, and how the denim shaped to his quadriceps and she'd glanced up higher, to the zipper and how he'd filled his jeans there. He was a man, fit and virile, and she didn't want to think of sex, but he made her feel sexual. He made her wonder what it would be like to make love again, to be touched, and kissed, and not just by anyone but *him*.

This was why her heart raced with adrenaline and emotion. Because the more time she spent with Rocco, the less she thought of Marius. They were two very different men, and she felt very different with Rocco than she'd felt with Marius. Marius made her feel safe, and snug. Loved and wanted. Rocco made her feel naked. Vulnerable.

Being around him rattled her. Sitting at the same table, or on the same blanket, made her hands shake, and her pulse thump and her stomach do crazy flip-flops. She wasn't afraid of Rocco, so why was she so affected by his proximity? Why did her mouth dry, and her heart race and her skin prickle as if it had become painfully sensitive?

Because...

And she knew the answer but couldn't admit it.

Wouldn't admit it.

Clare jumped up off the bench and circled the fountain before passing beneath the rose arbor arch to enter the formal rose garden laid out in intricate shapes with hedges and roses and delicate purple and white ground cover.

Suddenly Clare wasn't alone in her garden. She knew by the tingling sensation at the back of her neck, fine hair rising at her nape. She glanced over her shoulder, and there Rocco was, in the garden behind her.

"Did you follow me here?" she asked.

"No. I've been out walking and am on my way back to the villa. Don't mind me," he said. "I'll just continue on."

"No, it's okay. I was thinking of you." She blushed. "Well, your suggestion anyway."

"But if you want to be alone," he said.

"I've been alone," Clare answered. "Now I'm just restless. And thinking. My brain is spinning."

"I can only imagine."

"When do you need an answer?" she asked.

His broad shoulders shifted. "Whatever makes most sense. In my mind, the sooner the better, at least for Adriano. He'll benefit from the change, in every way possible. But for you, this is all such a shock. You need time."

"But give me too much time and I'll pack us up and run away!" she joked.

He smiled faintly. "Many a truth was said in jest."

"Yes," she agreed. "I'm rather overwhelmed."

"Then let's not discuss it anymore. Let's take the proposal off the table and focus on other things, like what could we do with Adriano tomorrow? He certainly seemed to enjoy himself today."

"He did," she agreed.

Rocco was silent a moment. "When Marius was a boy, he loved the zoo, which makes me wonder if Adriano has been to the Bioparco di Roma lately?"

Clare shook her head. "He's never been to Rome's zoo."

"It's in the Villa Borghese gardens and is the best zoo in Italy."

"Adriano would love it," she said.

"Good. Why don't we do that tomorrow and keep things light…no pressure, no decisions, nothing but creating some happy memories for Adriano."

"I think that's a wonderful idea."

Clare couldn't remember ever going to the zoo herself. She hadn't wanted to confess such a thing to Rocco, but the next day as Gio parked—he'd insisted he'd go, and drive, but promised to follow at a discreet distance— Clare felt a surge of eagerness and excitement. She felt almost as happy as Adriano who skipped between her and Rocco as Rocco handed over the tickets and the four of them entered the zoo grounds to be met by one of the zoologists overseeing Rome's zoological garden.

The zoologist turned out to be an old friend of the Cosentino family, having gone to primary school with Marius, with an older sibling that had known Rocco. Marilena was delighted to give them a private tour, including behind the scenes where some of the new zoo babies were being zealously observed and nurtured.

They learned that the zoo was over one hundred years old, designed by Carl Hagenbeck who believed animals should have open spaces and moats instead of small cages, a novel idea in 1911. Over time Rome's zoo became one of the leading zoos in Europe, surpassing even Paris's and Berlin's which still had the old system of cages. But the war put the zoo into decline and many thought it wouldn't survive, but in the nineteen-nineties the zoo was reimagined as a zoological garden, a place of education and conservation, not just entertainment.

At the primate exhibit Marilena let them into a small glassed-in area behind the public space where they could observe one of the chimps holding her new baby. They watched the new mother with the tiny infant for a long time, and Adriano stood, hands pressed to the glass, awed.

"The baby is just a week old," Marilena said, "and since the mama is a first-time mother, we wanted to give her lots of privacy."

"But can't she see us here?" Clare asked, voice low.

"It's an observation mirror," the zoologist answered, looking down at Adriano since she noticed he was listening closely. "It's a special glass that lets us see in, but none of the primates can see us."

With the tour over and Adriano wilting a little, they were invited to join Marilena for a special lunch on the lawn by the lake in the Villa Borghese grounds. Pizza was provided and Adriano happily chomped on his pizza while Marilena and Rocco visited. The sun made Clare sleepy and she closed her eyes for a moment, only to feel a tap-tap on her arm. She opened her eyes to find Adriano smiling into her face, a smear of red sauce on his cheek.

"Wake up, Mama," he said.

She yawned and glanced around, feeling guilty she'd been a bad guest, but Rocco and Marilena were gone, and it was just Gio, Clare and Adriano.

"Signor Cosentino walked the *signorina* back to the zoo office," Gio said.

"Was I asleep long?" Clare asked, running her fingers through her hair, still sleepy and trying to wake up.

"A long time," Adriano said.

Gio checked his smile. "Just a few minutes."

Rocco returned ten minutes later with gelato for all, even Gio, and Adriano sat cross-legged on the blanket eating his gelato with great relish. Clare exchanged small smiles with Rocco, aware that Adriano's face and shirt revealed his lunch, but the little boy was so happy there was no point trying to tidy him up when he was still licking the ice cream cone.

Finally it was time to head back to the villa and as they returned to the car, Clare felt a warmth in her chest that was new, the warmth a mix of hope and a fizzy sort of happiness that was so very different than the usual oppressive weight she carried within her—grief, and worry, and exhausting responsibility.

It felt good to share life with someone. It felt good to know that there was another who cared about Adriano's well-being.

"Thank you for organizing the private tour," Clare said as they settled into the back of the Mercedes SUV. "That was really special."

"I'm sure Adriano's been to many zoos—"

"He hasn't," Clare interrupted, taking a baby wipe from her purse and cleaning off Adriano's face and hands. "This was his first zoo trip." She glanced at Rocco and added shyly, "Mine, too."

Rocco looked stunned, but she returned her attention to Adriano's hands, making sure they were no longer sticky, before belting him into his car seat.

Gio drove them back with quiet efficiency, Adriano in

the car seat in the middle of her and Rocco. Adriano had taken Rocco's hand and fell asleep holding it.

Rocco didn't pull his hand free, not even once Adriano slept, mouth open, long lashes resting on his sun-kissed cheeks.

Clare felt a pang as she glanced at the two of them. Seeing Adriano and Rocco together made her realize just how much Adriano had craved a father figure in his life. Not because she wasn't enough, but moms were different than dads, and Adriano was definitely all boy.

Back at the villa, Rocco carried the still sleeping Adriano up the stairs to the nursery where Ava waited for him. Clare took a quick shower and changed into a fresh sundress, drawing her hair back in a loose ponytail. She went downstairs to find Rocco and he was there on the terrace studying the sea. "Would you like an *aperitivo*?" she asked him.

He turned to face her. "No, thank you."

She could tell something was on his mind. His jaw was set and his gaze shuttered. Had there been an incident when he carried Adriano to the nursery?

"Did something happen?" she asked, going to stand next to him at the terrace railing. "I can tell something has upset you."

"Not upset," he answered, voice deep. "I just feel… grateful."

"Grateful?" she repeated.

He glanced down at her, his brows pulling. "I didn't think I'd ever have this feeling of family again. I didn't think I'd ever be part of a family and it's wonderful but also bittersweet."

She searched the hard planes of his face, the scars almost invisible to her now. "Why bittersweet?" she persisted, thinking she knew the answer but wanting to hear it from him.

"Because you are not mine, and Adriano isn't my child to care for. This all could be gone tomorrow."

A lump filled her throat. Her eyes felt hot and gritty. Rocco was alone, very alone, and she was lucky to have her son. "Even if we didn't marry, you'd still be in our lives. You'd still be his *zio*."

"True," he said.

Clare heard a note of pain in Rocco's voice that made her chest tighten and her heart ache. This was becoming increasingly complicated. She didn't know what to do anymore, didn't know what was right, or best. "I haven't decided," she said honestly. "I didn't even think about your suggestion today. Instead I just focused on us, at the zoo. It was lovely, all of it, from start to finish."

"It was a good day."

"A very good day. Adriano was the happiest I've ever seen him. His joy gave me joy." She reached out and lightly touched Rocco's arm. "I am considering your suggestion. I just need time. I don't want to give you a rushed answer and have it be the wrong answer. I want to consider what's best for all of us."

His dark head inclined. "Me being here will only create unnecessary pressure. I should go and give you space. Take as much time as you need to make the decision that is best for you and Adriano—"

"And you," she interrupted softly. "I want what's best for you, too."

The shadows were back in his eyes. "Then that is easy. You and Adriano are best for me. Having a family to love would be my choice, but I don't want my needs to influence you. This isn't about me. Take time. I'm in no rush."

"What if I need days?"

"Fine."

"Weeks?"

"Fine."

"And what if I don't?"

He laughed, the sound low and surprisingly warm, the husky timbre sending a shiver down her spine. "Then you don't." He leaned toward her and pressed a kiss to her forehead. "I'll leave my contact details in my room. Let me know when you want me to know…whatever it is."

He walked away from her, his long legs making short work of the terrace. Clare watched him disappear into the house, her heart in her mouth, baffled by the alternating waves of relief and regret washing over her. She was glad he was going, glad he'd agreed to allow her to figure out what she wanted, so why did she feel this way?

Lost? Abandoned?

But that didn't make sense. She wasn't being abandoned, and yet her eyes burned and her heart hurt. She blinked hard clearing away the tears. If only the world wasn't such a hard, confusing place!

Dinner that evening was challenging. Adriano was quite upset that his *zio* had left him without saying goodbye. Furthermore, why did his *zio* leave at all?

"Sweetheart, Uncle Rocco has his own home," she explained. "He has work, just like I do, and so he returned to Rome so he could get his work done, but we'll see him again, I promise you."

Adriano's chin jutted, his expression mutinous. "He should have said goodbye."

"That would have been better, yes."

"Why didn't he?"

"Well, that may have been my fault," she said carefully. "He knew I had a lot on my mind and I think he was trying to make it easy for me."

Adriano's hand gestured as only an Italian could gesture.

Clare just looked at her son, uncertain how to handle him like this. She'd never seen him so fierce and fiery and after a moment she began to eat again, hoping he was ready to move forward and let it go, but as the minutes passed, he continued to sit there, arms folded across his chest, his face that of a martyr.

Finally she set her fork down. "Adriano, why won't you finish your dinner?"

"I'm mad."

She suppressed her smile. "I know. I can tell."

He looked at her, dark eyes bright and indignant. "I finally have an uncle, Mama, and he leaves."

"He will be back you know."

"When?"

"A week? Two? I don't know, but it won't be that long—"

"Call him." Adriano pointed to her watch which he knew she sometimes took calls on.

She laughed even as tears burned the back of her eyes. "Can we finish dinner and then I'll let you call him?"

Adriano studied her for a moment than nodded. "Okay."

The moment dinner was over Adriano jumped up and

pulled her to her feet, leading her upstairs to where her phone was charging on her desk. Clare had a strict policy of no phones during family time and so when they entered her office Adriano ran to her desk and unplugged it, then handed it to her.

Clare was just about to tell him she had to find his uncle's number when she saw the business card in the middle of her desk. It was Rocco's card, with a number scrawled on the front.

Her heart fell a little, a swoosh that made her breathless.

"Call, Mama," Adriano urged her.

She smiled at him and then pushed the numbers and waited. The phone rang, and rang and rang. "I'm going to have to leave a message," she said to Adriano, anticipating getting Rocco's voice mail, but then at the last moment Rocco answered.

"Hello?"

"It's Clare," she answered, putting a hand to her chest, trying to slow the wild beating of her heart. "Adriano was disappointed you didn't say goodbye to him. Would you mind talking to him?"

There was silence at the other end of the line and then Rocco cleared his throat. "Of course. Put him on."

Clare handed the phone to her son. "He wants to talk to you," she told Adriano.

Adriano put the phone to his ear, but after glancing up at her, he gave her a look that made him look thirteen instead of almost three, and then walked away, the phone still pressed to his ear. "Zio Rocco?"

"*Sì*," Clare heard Rocco say before Adriano had moved far enough away so that she couldn't hear anymore.

A few minutes later Adriano walked back to her, holding the phone out, the call ended.

"Well?" she said to him.

"Zio is going to take me to the coliseum."

She took the phone and placed it on her desk. "Where?"

"In Roma!" Adriano frowned at her. "Don't you know?"

Laughing at his indignation she wrapped her arms around him and hugged him tight. "Come on, let's go get ready for your bath."

After getting him ready for bed, tucking him in and kissing him good-night, she returned to her office and checked her phone for the text notification that had come in earlier while she'd been with Adriano in the nursery.

Don't worry about anything, cara. Try to get some sleep.

Clare read the text a second time before closing out of text messages and turning off the phone and slipping it into her pocket.

What a crazy few days. Was it really only three days ago that Rocco's helicopter landed on the lawn, turning her world upside down? How could Adriano have become so attached in such a short period of time? It didn't make sense. But then, life rarely made sense.

Leaving her office, she switched off the light and then headed up another flight of stairs to the floor she shared with Adriano. Her suite was just off the stairs while Adriano's spacious nursery was at the back. Adriano would be sleeping now, or almost asleep, and she wasn't needed, not when Ava was there.

Feeling at loose ends Clare went into her suite and

closed her door, leaning against it. Easy for Rocco to say, try to get some sleep. She wasn't going to be able to sleep, not after a day like today, not when her emotions were all over the place.

She did go through the motions of getting ready for bed, though, a bath, pajamas, teeth brushed, but once between her covers, she couldn't even close her eyes.

Marry Rocco?

He'd been her enemy for years. He'd made her life so difficult. He'd made her relationship with Marius beyond challenging.

Marius hadn't understood the coldness between them. Rocco was Marius's hero. How could Clare dislike him? What could she dislike about him?

She couldn't articulate her dislike or mistrust, not to Marius, and so she and Marius had agreed it would be better to let Marius and Rocco meet without her. And Marius... Marius loved her so much he accepted this, spending time with Rocco when Clare was traveling for business. It was an arrangement that suited all of them. The brothers could enjoy each other without tension, and she could get her work done without feeling guilty that she'd deserted Marius.

Not that Marius needed constant companionship. He was far more extroverted than she was and had a large group of friends, fellow polo players and friends from his university days, even ex-girlfriends who had stayed on good terms with him despite the romance being over. Clare didn't worry about him being with any of them. Marius was true to her. Their bond strong, deep. They were family to each other. Family was respected, protected.

Indeed, their friendship and commitment to each other was so strong that it held primary importance in their relationship, making everything easy. Effortless. Perhaps their lovemaking hadn't been adventurous, but their connection had been deeply satisfying. He'd shown her more affection in their few years together than she'd known in her entire life. His hugs, the way his arms wrapped around her, the way he held her to his chest, and kissed her temple and said something sweet, his lips curving, a smile in his voice, had been everything. Truly. His hugs were the best thing she'd ever known. Those hugs meant more than the sexual act itself. An orgasm was fine when she had one, but what she craved was Marius's warmth, and Marius's affectionate nature.

Just remembering put a lump in her throat and a sting in her eyes. She missed him so much. She missed everything about him.

In life Marius radiated calm, acceptance, encouragement. His validation had changed the way she'd thought about herself. It had changed her. Love was so powerful, so transformative that she'd become graver, stronger, more hopeful because of Marius's love.

But Marius was gone. She didn't want to ever replace him. But what about Adriano? What about what he needed?

Two days passed since Rocco had left. Clare hadn't spoken to Rocco since Adriano had wanted to call him. There had been no more texts.

She was glad as she needed the distance, as well as some calm. Clare was exhausted—mentally, emotionally, physically. At night she couldn't quiet her thoughts enough to drift off and stay asleep. Instead she'd toss and turn and then finally fall asleep but would wake abruptly, heart pounding, mouth dry. She couldn't do this.

Rocco wasn't the right one for her. Rocco wasn't her person at all. And yet she could picture his face, and his pewter eyes, glowing with heat and life.

On the third night after he'd left, she left her bed in the middle of the night, turned off the security alarm at her French doors and stepped out onto her balcony and looked up into the sky as if she could read the stars...

What would Marius want?

She searched the sky in case Marius was trying to send her a message. What would he say to her now?

Would he approve of her marrying Rocco, or would it upset him? That was the real question. Part of her thought he would sanction it, as he, like Rocco, was fiercely devoted to family. He'd be glad Rocco was there...taking care of her and his son.

It took four days before Clare had an answer for Rocco. He'd left her, giving her space, but after she'd texted him to say she wanted to discuss things with him, he replied with a message that he'd be there that evening after work.

Hearing a car approach she left her desk and went to her office window overlooking the front drive. It was a car she'd seen before, a pre–World War II Alfa Romeo, classic and rare, the exterior the palest butter yellow, and the interior a warmer caramel leather. Marius had given his brother the car for Rocco's birthday—she couldn't remember which—and Rocco had at first refused the gift, saying it was too expensive, too much, too extravagant for a man about to become a family man. But Marius insisted, and Rocco gave in and kept it, and watching Rocco now park and climb out, dressed in a dark smartly cut blazer over a white shirt, the shirt unbuttoned at the collar, Clare was glad. She was glad he had the gift from Marius, glad that they'd loved each other so much. Two brothers united against the world...at least, until she appeared. She'd nearly driven a wedge between them. Thank goodness they'd found a way around it. The last thing she wanted was to create pain for either of them.

Clare leaned closer to the glass watching Rocco approach the villa's front door. Gio descended the steps, intercepting him. At the very same moment her watch buzzed with a security alert. She pressed the green clear, and Gio moved aside allowing Rocco to enter.

Clare left the window and walked into the marble bathroom adjacent to her office and smoothed her dark hair, combing it back behind her ears. She didn't look herself in the eyes, not wanting to see what might be there. Instead she slicked on some dark pink lipstick, and dabbed a bit of the color on her cheeks, trying to hide her paleness. She hadn't slept well in days. She hadn't been eating very much, either. Both responses were typical for her, a natural response to stress, but still, she didn't want to look like death as she met Rocco in the salon downstairs.

He was waiting for her on the terrace, his back to the doorway, facing the sea. The Cosentino brothers were both athletic, but Rocco's shoulders were broader, and his legs longer. Rocco's height coupled with the width of his shoulders made him imposing, even without looking into his cool silver eyes set in that very chiseled face.

Fortunately, he already had a glass of something amber. A neat shot to help ease into the evening. She was glad someone had already provided him with a drink, one less thing for her to worry about. Her staff was exceptional that way, and in every way. They were highly trained and very loyal, and paid well for their loyalty.

"Was there a lot of traffic leaving Rome?" she asked, stepping from the villa into the late afternoon sunshine, the golden rays stretching long across the stone terrace. She lifted a hand to shield her eyes. In a few minutes the sun would drop, but for now, the glare was almost blinding.

Rocco turned to look at her, his gaze studying her intently, the movement temporarily blocking the setting sun. "Nothing out of the ordinary. In fact, I made good time." His gaze now swept from the top of her head to her feet, and up again. "You look well."

Heat rushed to her cheeks, the surge of warmth making her light-headed. She shifted one of the chairs so she wouldn't be looking into the sun's long, piercing golden rays, and dropped into it, then crossed her legs affecting an air of calm. She didn't feel well in that moment. Her heart was racing and her stomach was somersaulting and she didn't even know how to begin the conversation they needed to have.

Roberto arrived with a glass of wine for Clare and she took it with a quiet thank-you. "Are you driving back tonight?" she asked, looking over at Rocco.

"I'd hoped to return tomorrow, after having breakfast with you and Adriano. If that met with your approval."

She nodded, fighting a bubble of panic. Could she do this? Could they?

"Good. I'm looking forward to seeing Adriano. How is he?"

"Well." She hesitated, before adding, "He's asked about you every day. You certainly made an impression on him."

"Has he already gone to bed?"

"Just before you arrived, yes. He'd wanted to stay up to see you, but I wasn't sure what time you'd get here."

"I'm sorry. I should have called and given you a time I'd be arriving. That was thoughtless of me."

The apology was nice, but it was hard to focus when Rocco was prowling around the terrace reminding her of a big cat pacing a cage. A gorgeous big cat. She'd never noticed before that Rocco was every bit as athletic as Marius, but with a different power. Marius was one with his horses, a perfect partnership, whereas Clare couldn't imagine Rocco on a horse. He needed his feet planted, the earth grounding him.

Rocco was walking toward her, but instead of joining her, he walked behind her. She felt him behind her, too, and she shivered, sensation streaking through her, skin tingling, breasts aching, her belly tightening. The awareness was unlike anything she'd ever felt before and she peeked over her shoulder watching Rocco reach the end of the terrace. He leaned over and picked up Adriano's favorite green ball. He tossed it up, once, twice, and then lightly tossed it so that it rolled past the sitting area and gently came to rest near one of the French doors.

"What's his favorite color?" Rocco asked, moving toward her.

"Green," she said, as he passed so close behind her that the hair on her nape rose and delicious prickles ran up and down her arms. He was an arm's length away, but she could feel him as strongly as if he'd reached out and touched her, his fingertips running across the back of her neck.

Clare drew a quick, unsteady breath, nerves taut, every fiber of her being awake. Alert. Aware of him. It was so intense, dizzying really.

What was he doing to her? Did he even know the impact he had on her?

Rocco retrieved his crystal tumbler with the splash of amber liquor. Instead of sitting down in a chair, he perched on the edge of the coffee table, hands clasped between his legs, forearms sinewy. His legs were so long his knees were nearly touching hers. She glanced at his strong hands, his fingers wrapped around the glass, and then to his hips and the fit of his trousers, fine black wool snug on muscular thighs, the black leather belt around his hips, and then below the buckle, the thickness, evidence of his masculinity.

She swallowed and looked away, blushing furiously. She wasn't a virgin and she shouldn't feel shy, but she did.

She felt emotions she couldn't understand. Emotions that made her realize just how hard the past three years had been. She didn't want to be sad, not anymore.

She didn't want to be grieving or alone. She wanted more. Rocco was offering more.

Wound tightly, she jerked and her knee bumped his. His eyes met hers and held for an impossibly long moment and time slowed. His eyes weren't cold, the silver irises with bits of bronze and gold. She dragged in a breath and his gaze fell, focusing on her mouth which had gone dry.

Parched, she touched the tip of her tongue to her upper lip. Her pulse was pounding so hard now, but her body felt treacherously weak, as if her bones had melted and she was just heat. She couldn't move if she wanted. There was no way to escape him and in that moment she didn't want to, the fire beneath her skin burning hotter and brighter chasing away the coldness she'd carried with her these years.

He leaned in, his broad shoulders close, filling her vision. "Are you okay, *cara*?" he asked.

His voice was so deep and it burrowed inside her chest, filling some of the emptiness. She nodded, her gaze focused on the faint shadow of a beard on his jaw and the firmness of his mouth. His mouth intrigued her. He smelled good, too, rather intoxicating, and she forced herself to nod, even manage a faint smile. "I'm getting by."

He put a finger beneath her chin, tipping her face up to his. "Just getting by?"

She didn't know why her eyes burned and a lump filled her throat. She was strong. She didn't just fall apart, but Rocco was unraveling something inside of her and she couldn't pull herself back together fast enough. "It's been a strange week."

"It has," he agreed, thumb stroking her cheek. "Scared?"

"If I say yes, nothing will ever be the same."

"Such is life, full of change. But not all change is bad. Change can be good."

She searched his eyes. "Is this good?"

"You tell me." With another caress to her cheek and jaw, he leaned in, and covered her lips with his.

The pressure of his mouth made her pulse leap, the jolt of electricity immediate, making her mouth soften and tingle. She made a soft whimpering sound and Rocco took advantage of her parted lips to deepen the kiss even as he drew her from the chair onto his lap. She couldn't resist, the sensations intense, her body melting into his.

It was a kiss unlike any she'd ever experienced. It was consuming and hot, so hot she trembled against him, helpless, mindless, wanting more of everything, wanting all he offered and as his hands touched her, shaping her, stirring nerve endings she'd forgotten even existed, she felt almost desperate. Nothing made sense. The world didn't make sense. But as long as Rocco kept kissing her and making her feel so sensitive and alive, she wouldn't complain.

It was impossible to know how much time passed. Minutes? Hours? But by the time Rocco's head lifted and he gazed down into her eyes, his silver eyes now smoky with desire, she felt almost drunk on sensation. She'd never been kissed like that, kissed so deeply that she'd forgotten who she was, or where she was.

"So," he said, his voice deep. "What do you think?"

"I think you know how to kiss."

"And the rest of it?"

Her gaze dropped to his lap, to the thickness of his shaft pressing against the wool fabric. "I don't know about the rest of it."

He laughed lowly. "I'm talking about the future. About Adriano. About us."

He might as well have dashed some cold water in her face as she blinked and returned to her senses.

She was on his lap. Her lips were tingling and throbbing. Her body was humming, too. She slid off his lap and returned to her chair, drawing her knees up as if to create a wall between them.

She needed a barrier, something to provide defense.

"You said you've given it thought," he added calmly, looking relaxed and perfectly in control. "When you called it sounded as if you'd made a decision."

"I had." She swallowed. "I have. I've thought about everything a great deal. As you know, I was an only child and I hated it. I used to pray for a younger brother or sister, someone to keep me company, someone to play with in the nursery. I don't want Adriano to know the loneliness I knew. I don't want him to be an only child." She frowned, her brows pulling. "But I need to take this slow. This is a huge change. It's scary."

He placed his hands on her knees and left them there. "Which part is scary?"

Her shoulders rose and fell. "All of it?"

"We have tomorrow, we have the day after, we have weeks and years ahead of us. We can take our time, get to know each other. There is no rush."

"Do you mean that?" she asked, hope rushing through her, easing some of her tension. She was someone who needed order and safety, and the idea of marriage, which represented a loss of control, filled her with overwhelming anxiety.

"I do. Why would I want you to feel nervous or unhappy? How is that good for anyone?"

It was a good question, and her shoulders relaxed and she managed a small smile. "Maybe we could talk some more in the morning?"

"The morning sounds good. We'll get some sleep and then discuss whatever it is you wish to discuss."

CHAPTER SIX

IN THE MORNING they had breakfast with Adriano on the terrace, and then while Clare handled a few business matters, Rocco played football on the lawn with Adriano. Adriano wanted to do something together, all of them like the day they visited the *castello*, but Rocco told the child that Rocco needed some time to discuss things with his mother.

Adriano reluctantly accepted this and Ava stepped in to play football with Adriano while Rocco went in search of Clare. Knowing she'd probably be in her office he went there first, and knocked on her closed door. She called for him to come in, and opening the door he stood on the threshold and watched her typing on her keyboard, fingers flying, brow furrowed in concentration.

She looked up at him after a moment and almost looked surprised to see him there. "Have you been waiting long?"

"Not that long."

"I was trying to find a diplomatic way to answer a less than diplomatic email."

"Did you?"

"I hope so. I hit Send." She wrinkled her nose as she smiled. "I don't tend to overthink those things. Just do it and be done with it. I can't stand a full inbox."

He liked looking at her, liked listening to her, too. She

was beautiful. Her dark hair was loose over her shoulders, and her short-sleeve blouse, a shade of cool mint, brought out the lavender-blue of her eyes. "Could you tear yourself away from your computer for an hour or two? I thought we might go for a drive. It's a beautiful day and I have my convertible."

She glanced at one of the windows and then back at him. "I'd like that. Let me just grab a light sweater and sunglasses."

"I'll be down at the car."

"I'll meet you soon."

She was quick, too, outside in less than five minutes with the sweater, sunglasses and a purse. She'd pulled her hair back into a ponytail and changed her shoes, now wearing pretty sandals that tied around her ankles.

"Where are we going?" she asked as he held the passenger door for her.

"I thought we'd go to Ostia Antica, and we can decide what we feel like once there. We can explore the ruins, have lunch or just enjoy a coffee."

"I've never been," she said. "But it's a place I thought Adriano would like to go."

"It's quite big, and there's so much to see that I propose we drive—"

"Do you think there will be a lot of tourists?" she asked.

"There will probably be buses for tourists coming in from Rome, yes."

"Could we maybe go somewhere else? Just drive north, or south? It will feel good just to have the sun on our faces and the wind in our hair."

"We shall go north then, maybe to Ladispoli?"

"Another castle in another seaport town."

"So you know it?" he asked.

"I do, but I haven't been in a couple of years and I'd love to see if my favorite bakery is there. They made the best bread and pastries."

"We can go find out."

It was a pleasure to be driving the Alfa Romeo, especially with Clare sitting beside him. Rocco didn't try to make conversation, and Clare seemed happy to just soak up the sun and let the world pass them by. It was a scenic drive too, small villages dotting the coastline, the water a sparkling blue.

He liked having her in his car, at his side. He was ready to move forward, making a life with her. Marriage. Intimacy. Family.

He hadn't thought he'd ever marry again.

But now she was here next to him, Rocco was amazed and alarmed. Had he wished for this? Had he craved her so much that he'd set in motion a series of terrible events? Part of him knew life didn't work that way. The rational part of his brain knew Marius's accident on the polo field had been just that, a terrible accident, but Rocco had spent his life taking care of his brother, protecting him, providing for him. But now, to be here, in this place, with this opportunity to have a family with Clare and Adriano, created the terrible tension within him.

Now he was the one who felt as if he didn't deserve her.

Now he struggled with guilt and self-loathing. He could marry her, become her husband, stepping into Marius's vacant position. But was it right? Was it fair to any of them?

If Clare knew the truth, if she understood that his coldness and reserve had been motivated by jealousy, she'd be appalled. As she should be. But that didn't make him want her less. It didn't make him drop the idea of marriage. If anything he was even more determined to have her, claim her. And he meant to claim her—heart, mind, body, soul. Desire hadn't faded. If anything, it had just grown stronger. When she was close, he felt alive, almost as if he was multidimensional, everything right and fierce, everything driven and focused.

He hadn't thought it was possible to feel this way about another person. He hadn't wanted anyone like this before, and even though he'd been married, he and his wife had been childhood sweethearts, growing up together and he'd loved his wife, but it had never been this fierce, consuming desire he felt for Clare.

Clare made him feel incomplete, as if she was the other half of his soul, and this certainty gave him patience. He'd wait for her, for as long as need be.

The sense of rightness—not morally, but physically, spiritually—helped his self-control. He didn't want to frighten her. He wanted her to feel safe with him, and to trust him. Trust took time. Trust was important so that when she was finally his, she'd give all of herself to him, not just the broken pieces, but all the pieces, all the hopes, all the pain, all the dreams.

That was his plan, and the goal. And he had to succeed, otherwise guilt and Marius would haunt him forever, and that would be a terrible outcome for him…for Clare…for all of them.

Clare had no idea of the heaviness of his thoughts as Rocco was outstanding company that day. A good driver, he put her at ease, and the warm air and sunlight made her relax and tip her head back, savoring all that was good.

She didn't unplug very often. She stayed busy to keep from thinking or feeling too much, as truth be told, she worried about things, worried about the future. She tried to do everything well, but it was impossible. There were always things that slipped through the cracks. She prayed Adriano would have all his needs met, but she was human and he would grow up and need more than her one day. He'd become a boy and require an education and he'd have to find his place in the world. She just prayed he'd find the world easier than she had.

Rocco glanced at her. "You were smiling a few moments ago. What happened? What are you thinking?"

She turned her head toward him and smiled faintly. "How can you read me so well?"

"I have always been aware of you," he said simply. "Even when I didn't seem sensitive."

"You mean, even when you were beastly?" she teased.

He grimaced. "Especially then."

"But why?" she asked, facing him more fully, or as fully as she could with the seat belt holding her secure. "I'm sure you know why. Can you try to explain?"

"You won't like it. I don't like it."

"Try me."

"I was jealous. Jealous that you and Marius had found so much happiness."

"Oh, Rocco! I'm sorry," she said, putting a hand on his arm. "That was never our intention."

"No, of course not. It was my problem, not yours."

"But no one likes to feel like a third wheel, especially when you and Marius had been so close."

They reached Ladispoli far more quickly than Clare liked. It had been wonderful being in the car, feeling free for the first time in ages, especially as a tour bus was parked at the *castello* and hordes of people wandered around with cameras.

They escaped the crowds by taking a walk along a seawall and it was there Clare brought up his proposal, which had been constantly on her mind. "*If* I agreed to marry you, Rocco, you misunderstand I am not ready for a physical relationship. You are essentially a stranger and I need time to get to know you. It might take a long time before I'm comfortable around you. Perhaps years. I don't know. You'd need to be patient with me, and patient with us becoming a family as it won't be natural or easy. Adriano will adapt relatively quickly, he's just a baby, but..." She swallowed hard. "I will need more time. The physical makes me uneasy. I know we kissed, but there's a big difference between a kiss and being naked."

Especially with you, she mentally added. Rocco was so intense and the sparks between them were overwhelming. She didn't want to be overwhelmed. She craved the safety she'd known with Marius.

"I am not marrying you because I can't find sexual partners elsewhere," Rocco said calmly. "I'm not marrying you to please to gratify some sexual need. I'm proposing marriage to provide permanence and stability for Adriano. I am marrying you so that he will have a father, not that he didn't have a father, but a father who will be present, a father who will love him, and be there to support him, always. You and I might not always see eye to eye, but I hope we can agree to put him first, and focus on doing what is best for him."

Clare leaned against the wall, stone rough but warmed by the sun. "I feel exactly the same way."

"Good. He doesn't need to be caught up in adult dramas. It's confusing for children and unfair to be pulled between two people who should be mature."

She glanced up at him, trying to see behind the sunglasses shielding his eyes. "You sound as if you speak from experience."

Rocco shrugged. "My parents—my father and Marius's mother—had some quarrels in the year before they succumbed to their illness. The quarrels were loud and carried. I was old enough to know that the storm would pass, but it was hard for my brother to hear the fighting and storming around."

Clare had heard plenty of yelling as a child, only it was her father who did the shouting, and her father who gave the commands. The women in his life never really stood a chance. It was one of the reasons she loved Marius so. He was easygoing and nonconfrontational. Marius hated conflict and they'd never really had a fight—neither of them wanted one, and so if things grew tense, they just moved forward. She wondered now how that would have worked if he'd lived. Was that the best way to handle problems in a marriage? "I've only had one significant other, and that was your brother. He was my first real boyfriend, and my only sexual partner." Clare stared out at the ocean as she shared this, embarrassed by the revelation but thinking it important Rocco know and understand. "I've been a late bloomer my whole life, and I hadn't wanted to be intimate with anyone until I met him. I can't even imagine intimacy with anyone else."

Much less you, she silently added.

The words were never spoken aloud, but they hung in the air between them.

He nodded after a long moment, his gaze sweeping over her, a slow scrutiny from head to toe. "When we marry, there will be no one else in my life, no other woman, just you. I think it's important you know that."

His scrutiny made her hot, and her skin prickly. "But maybe there should be," she said, flushing, "because if it is years until I am comfortable with you, I'd hate to think you're being denied...company."

"I'm a man, not a child. I can handle desire. I know how to manage needs. That should not be your worry—"

"It's not my worry," she interrupted tersely, pushing away from the wall. "I just don't need one more thing to feel guilty about."

Silence followed, the silence so long and heavy that Clare found herself squirming inwardly.

"What do you feel guilty about?" Rocco asked.

She lifted one shoulder. "It doesn't matter."

"But it does. It's important to understand how you're feeling, and not just about us, but for the future, and the past."

There was something about Rocco's presence that made her feel restless, that made her need to move, walk, put a little distance between them. She never felt that way about Marius. For her, Marius had been like a favorite blanket...a warm embrace. She'd melted in his arms, finding such comfort in his nearness. There was none of that with Rocco.

"I can't explain it so that you'd understand." Clare's voice sharpened. "I sometimes don't understand it, but I do feel guilty. I feel guilty that I'm alive and Marius is dead. I feel guilty that Marius died without knowing we'd made a child. I feel guilty that Adriano won't have the loving father he should have. I feel guilty for even having this conversation, considering a future where I'm replacing Marius—"

"You're not replacing Marius," Rocco growled. "Let's agree on that one point. He will never be replaced. He can't be replaced. Clare, we both know Marius is irreplaceable. So that's not what this is about. This is about making sure his son, someone incredibly important, has the best life possible, and I'm not so vain to think that there can't be other men to love him as a father, but I can assure you, that I will love him as a son. As my son. Because he is the closest thing to a son I'll ever have."

"You could have children of your own—"

"No. That's not in the cards." His features hardened, his jaw jutting like granite. Even his silver gaze looked like stone. "It is you, Clare, or it is no one."

His fierce tone felt like a blow to her chest and she took a step back, shocked. Marius avoided conflict but Rocco's words landed with a thump in her chest. His words shocked her, and she didn't know if she was flattered or horrified.

It is you, Clare, or it is no one.

The grim certainty in his voice forced her gaze up and she looked into his eyes, trying to see what it was that made him say such things. He didn't want to marry again, but he'd marry her. He didn't want to date again, but he'd been envious of her and Marius's happiness. It didn't make sense, but she did believe Rocco would take his role as a surrogate father to Adriano seriously, and with Adriano wanting Rocco in his life, she was the only thing standing in the way.

"When would we marry?" she asked, voice surprisingly steady.

"As soon as we could get the necessary paperwork. Two weeks? Ten days?"

So soon. She swallowed around the lump in her throat. "I imagine we will get married at a courthouse?"

"That is no wedding."

"I don't need a wedding."

"It's your first marriage, you should have a wedding. I'll have someone handle the details. Is there anything you'd like…anything you don't want?"

She was already second-guessing her decision. "Just simple, please. Simple and quick."

Back at the villa, with Rocco on his way to Rome, Clare locked herself in her bedroom and cried.

What had she done?

Why had she agreed to this?

It was foolish. She'd lost her mind, gotten caught up in the moment trying to make everyone happy. But marriage to Rocco wouldn't make her happy.

It wasn't just that Rocco was still virtually a stranger, but it felt like a betrayal to Marius's memory. How could she move on already? She'd loved him so dearly; she wasn't ready to replace him. She didn't think she could ever replace him. Rocco could say what he wanted, but she didn't really know him, not yet. Yes, they were building a new relationship, but the past weighed heavy. He hadn't been kind to her in the past. He'd been hard and brooding and what if that was the real Rocco?

Marriage was such a huge step and yes, she was doing it for Adriano, but that didn't ease all of her fears. In fact, the fears were so strong that she didn't know how to reconcile her heart and her head.

She needed time. She needed to think this through and not be rushed into a decision.

Clare had other homes, other properties she and Adriano would be safe at. She'd find someplace for them, someplace Rocco couldn't find them, at least not immediately, which would give her time to pull herself together.

Of course she'd send him a message—a text or an email, something. She'd try to explain. She owed him that much at least.

In the morning at breakfast she told Adriano that they were going to go on a trip, fly to the United States, and visit some of the properties she owned.

"To Florida?" he asked, aware that her father lived there.

"I was thinking we'd go to California. We have a big house and vineyard we've never been to. I thought maybe we would go see it and decide if we want to keep it or sell it. You could help me decide."

Adriano hesitated. "Is uncle coming?"

Clare froze, guilt washing through her. "No. I hadn't planned on it. California is far away."

"But he's my uncle."

"And we just spent several days with him. He has work and things he needs to take care of in Rome."

"Maybe we should go to Rome instead."

Her pulse thudded harder. "What would we do in Rome?"

Adriano answered promptly. "*Potremmo andare a vedere piu castelli e rovine.*" *We could go see more castles and ruins.*

"But if we go to California we could maybe go to Disneyland, see Mickey Mouse."

"Then *zio* should come."

"But wouldn't it be more fun if it was just us?" she asked, voice low.

"No. I like my uncle."

Adriano had never been so fixated on anyone or anything before and it was throwing Clare off balance. She could understand Adriano's enthusiasm to a point; their family was very small; it was just the two of them, so the addition of a new relative had to be exciting, but what about Rocco did Adriano like so much? "What is your favorite thing about *zio*?"

Adriano took the question very seriously, taking several long moments to think. Finally he answered. "*Zio* knows many things. He is Italian, and family. My family." His dark head tipped and his gaze met hers. "What do you like?"

Again her pulse felt jagged, beating fast, making her breathless. "That he is your uncle, your family."

"*Our* family." Adriano's small hand gestured from her to him, the gesture so very Latin and expressive.

She smiled and swallowed, trying to hold the tears back. He was such a beautiful bright boy. He deserved the sun and the moon and the stars, and she'd try to give him that and more, but a father wasn't in the picture. Marriage was not in the picture. She needed to break this off quickly, and if Rocco remained in Adriano's life, it would be as an uncle, and nothing more.

Rocco read the letter delivered by courier to him at his office and then set it aside. He walked out onto the penthouse terrace which looked out over the Roman Forum. He loved the columns and ruins, the remnants of older civilizations. Centuries passed and technology changed, but man didn't.

Clare wasn't going to marry him after all.

Rocco's lips twisted. Part of him was angry, but another part felt sympathetic, aware that Clare must be in turmoil. He didn't blame her. Death and grief were impossible things. Grief lingered on and on. Rocco felt as if he spent most of his life in mourning. He didn't even know what it was to not grieve. Grief was always with him. The loss of all of those he loved. So no, any anger he felt wasn't toward Clare, but toward fate, which had made life so difficult.

He understood her note quite well, but it wasn't that simple. He wasn't going to walk away from her, or abandon Adriano. He still wanted to give Adriano the family name. He still wanted Adriano to be raised as a Cosentino.

And then there was Clare. He still wanted Clare. After that kiss, after the fierce physical connection he wanted her more than ever. She was his. She was always meant to be his.

Rocco returned to his desk and after sitting down he made some calls, discovering she'd left the villa for the executive airport. He made another call and her flight plan had been filed, an international flight plan and she'd be taking off within the hour.

He made another call and his helicopter was on the way. He was heading to the business airport. Rocco was not going to let her go without a fight.

Clare couldn't believe it when Rocco boarded the jet. Her flight had been delayed due to a mechanical—at least that's what she'd been told—but as Rocco walked down the narrow aisle toward her she wondered if that was true.

"Zio!" Adriano cried, delighted to see his uncle.

Rocco put a hand on the top of the boy's head even as his gaze locked with Clare's. "Where are you heading?" he asked her lightly, conversationally.

"California," Adriano answered, tipping his head back to see Rocco better. "I wanted you to come, but Mama said you had to work."

"California?" Rocco said, sitting down in one of the leather chairs that formed a sitting area, two on one side facing two on the other. "What will you do there?"

"Maybe go to Disneyland," Adriano said, unbuckling his seat belt and sliding out of his seat. He went to Rocco and climbed on his lap. "Do you meet Mickey Mouse?"

Clare shifted uncomfortably, aware that Rocco was watching her, his gaze pinning her to her seat. She'd known he would look for her, and suspected he'd find her, but she hadn't expected him to find her so soon, before she'd even left the ground.

Her letter to him was supposed to arrive today, after she'd departed, not before. Clare put a hand to her head, feeling it throb. Nothing was working out the way she wanted. Why?

"Are you well?" Rocco asked, his voice low, his tone surprisingly gentle, but then, Adriano was snuggling on his lap as if they were lifelong friends.

"Are you furious?" She asked, answering his question with a question of her own. She didn't like anger. Her father had been prone to terrible outbursts, rages that made everyone around him cower. It had been a relief to move to Europe, away from the rage and outbursts from a man who enjoyed his own temper tantrums.

"Not furious, and not upset, just sorry you felt it necessary to run away from me. Rather than a note, I wish you would have talked to me. Wish you could have talked to me," he corrected.

Clare swallowed and glanced out the window to the tarmac. "I didn't know what to say." She looked back at him. "It seemed an easier thing to write, less emotion, less drama—"

"I'd argue that running away has a certain element of drama to it."

His tone was mild, and amused, and Clare blushed because there were other reasons she'd run away, reasons she couldn't admit. Rocco exerted such a strange power over her. She didn't want to be drawn to him, didn't want the attraction and curiosity, but when near him, her body overrode her head. She wanted to be strong, wanted to resist him and the only way she could do that was if there was distance between them.

If he didn't come for her.

If he didn't fight for her.

"Do you really want to go to California?" he asked, black eyebrow lifting.

"No," Adriano said firmly. He leaned forward and looked his mother in the eye. "We want to stay here with Zio Rocco."

CHAPTER SEVEN

EVERYTHING WAS HAPPENING quickly now, too quickly. Clare's head spun. She wanted to slow time down, wanted to slow Rocco down, but now that she'd agreed to marry him, he'd put the wheels in motion, and they were turning. Spinning.

The late September weather was perfect for a wedding, not that there would be guests who had to worry about traveling to attend a wedding. It would just be the family and the staff, but still, a wedding deserved a blue sky and sunshine.

The wedding was to be held in the Cosentino family's chapel at the family's ancestral home, a historic palazzo, in Rome. The chapel had been decorated with garlands of flowers, pale pink and dark pink roses with delicate orchids. Clare had left all of the wedding plans to Rocco's assistant, as she couldn't bring herself to plan another wedding, especially one which would see her become a Cosentino, just not the right wife to the right Cosentino. But for the sake of Adriano they'd agreed to make it picture-perfect, and so it was a grand wedding on a very intimate scale.

Her wedding gown was the palest pink. Just as she couldn't bring herself to plan another wedding, Clare couldn't bring herself to wear white, not after having a son, not after burying her love. Instead of a traditional white dress, she wore a stunning couture gown with a full chiffon skirt and a fitted bodice with the most delicate cap sleeves. In the soft pink gown she felt as if she were a butterfly about to fly away. If only she could fly away.

Even though the wedding ceremony was small, it was a proper ceremony, and long, at least to Clare it seemed long, and she felt faint at one point, the warmth in the chapel and the fragrant flowers making her dizzy.

She'd glanced at Adriano who stood next to Rocco, and sternly she reminded herself that this was for him. Adriano would be protected. He'd have two of them to watch out for him, and two of them to love him, and should life become difficult, two to fight for him.

But then her eyes met Rocco's silver gaze and she couldn't breathe. It was too much, too quickly. Her mouth dried and her lips parted and she wanted to run away, run—

Rocco reached out, putting a hand on her lower back. "Are you okay?"

She shook her head, tears filling her eyes.

He held up a hand to the priest, halting him midsentence, midservice. "You don't have to do this," Rocco said quietly, supporting her weight as her legs were trembling like mad. "We can stop this right now."

She couldn't look away from his eyes. She could see his concern, and feel it, too. "Do you mean that?" she answered huskily.

"Absolutely. I want to marry you; if it's what you want to do. But if it's not, we stop and just let it go."

Clare glanced down at Adriano waiting so patiently at Rocco's side. Clare might not love Rocco, but Adriano did. She couldn't disappoint her son, not when he was so happy to have found family. And truthfully, this wasn't even about love anymore. There were so many other emotions, so many other conflicting feelings…desire, fear, attraction and more.

She craved things she couldn't articulate, craved power and pressure, heat and sensation. She wanted to be wanted. She wanted to be touched. She wanted to be seduced. But it was also rather terrifying as she'd never felt these intense needs and wants with Marius. Marius never made her ache…or crave.

"It's just warm in here," she said, pushing away the thoughts, refusing to feel guilty for wanting something she'd never known, wanting heat to make her melt and burn. "I'm fine." Her voice shook and she added more firmly, "I'll be fine, I promise. Let's continue, please."

Twenty minutes later the ceremony was over and the photographer posed them, requesting they stand with the priest, then with the witnesses who were Ava and Gio, and then it was the three of them, Rocco, Clare and Adriano, and finally, it was just her and Rocco.

She swallowed around the lump in her throat as he faced her, both her hands in his, and looked down into her eyes. He didn't smile, even though the photographer kept trying to get a smile from them. But his gaze wasn't icy. She didn't know what was in his eyes, only there was no ice, and nothing cruel. Determination, yes. Pride, yes. Possession, possibly? It crossed her mind that he was glad she'd become his wife—

Adriano suddenly flung himself at Clare's legs, laughing as he escaped Ava's hand that had been trying to keep him in place.

Rocco laughed, too, and lifted Adriano up into his arms. "Let's go inside. We're having an early dinner tonight so we can all celebrate together."

They had dinner in a room painted silver and gold. Pink flowers with silver-and gold-painted leaves formed a centerpiece, and the china was white with gold, and the glasses were pink Venetian stemware. It was just the three of them eating in the formal dining room. Adriano was curious about everything and took in the new environment with admirable calm and confidence. The meal, five courses' worth, did drag on, far more food than Clare wanted or needed, but finally a wedding cake was served and Adriano, sleepy and yawning, tried to wake up enough to eat a slice.

He managed to eat three and a half bites before his eyes began to close again. Clare had taken her watch off for the wedding and couldn't alert Ava, but someone must have because it was just a few minutes later that Ava appeared, her gaze meeting Clare's.

Clare nodded, and Ava lifted him from his chair. He nestled his chest on her shoulder and closed his eyes.

"I'll be just down the hall," Clare whispered to Ava.

"I'll be in the nursery with him. Gio is here, too, don't worry."

As Ava passed by Rocco, Rocco reached out and smoothed Adriano's dark hair. The tender gesture made Clare's heart tighten and her eyes burn.

But she wasn't going to fall apart, she told herself. There would be no tears tonight. She'd made the decision to marry and she was now Rocco's wife, and there would be no more looking back, no more lamenting the past.

Rocco sat at the end of the table feeling Clare's emotion. He was always aware of her, but tonight he could see the shimmer of tears in her eyes and he remembered how she'd trembled in his arm in the chapel, exhausted, overwhelmed, uncertain of her decision. But then she'd found her resolve and she'd made it through the ceremony and they'd made it through the dinner, too.

This was not a happy wedding, this wasn't one of those events celebrated by a loving family and dozens of friends. They had no others. No one to celebrate with, no one who'd care that this wasn't a love match...at least on Clare's part.

Rocco had no regrets, though. This was what he'd wanted. He'd wanted her for so long, and he'd waited for her, not allowing another woman into his life, unwilling to even entertain the idea of another woman for him. He'd loved his wife, and he'd loved Clare and that was all. There would be no other loves, not for him.

But he hated seeing Clare with tears in her eyes, hated knowing she was struggling. He wasn't struggling. He had what he wanted. Clare as his woman, his wife. It might take weeks, maybe months, but one day she'd drop her guard and let him in. Not just tolerate him but love him. Which is why he could be patient. He'd waited this long for her...what was another six months, or a year?

He'd give her time, and seduce her so slowly she wouldn't even realize she was being wooed, and won.

They had separate bedrooms, a his and her layout with an enormous shared dressing room in the middle. Alone in her room Clare couldn't get out of her wedding gown, not without help and unlike at her villa, she had no staff here to call, no one available to help her with the hooks that lined the hidden seams of the dress. She could ask Ava to come to her, but that wasn't Ava's job, and Clare respected the nanny too much to ask her to leave her room just to help Clare undress. On her wedding night. It would look silly and possibly cause gossip that she didn't need.

Drawing a breath for courage, Clare went to the door between her and Rocco's room. She knocked once, firmly, and waited.

He opened the door after a few moments, so tall and broad shouldered that he filled the doorway, nearly blocking all the light shining behind him. He was in the process of undressing, and his white shirt was unbuttoned, but he was still wearing his black trousers. His chest, although scarred, was a wonder of hard muscle, planes and hollows and a dusting of black hair low on his abdomen, disappearing into his trousers. She jerked her head up and focused on his chin—so much safer than his hips, or even his eyes or mouth. "I'm afraid I need assistance with my dress. There are dozens of little hooks."

"I was wondering if you'd need help," he said. "But I didn't want to presume."

"These gowns are made for women with stylists and designers," she said, trying to sound casual when her pulse raced and her mouth felt dry.

"Or husbands," he said lightly, gesturing for her to step back. She did and he followed her into her room.

He took a seat in one of the armchairs in front of the

marble surround and reached a hand to her. "Come. Where are these hooks?"

She stood with her back to him. "They're tucked into those small seams. I warn you, there are many."

"I am prepared to do my duty," he said dryly, hands settling on her hips, his warmth steeling through her skirts into her skin.

She could feel his fingers on her back exploring the dress and the exquisite tailoring and held her breath as he slowed to inspect the long seam where the majority of the hooks were. With one hand on her lower back to keep her steady he unfastened the first hook, and then the next. Clare closed her eyes trying not to let her imagination run wild, but every time his knuckles brushed her spine, every time her gown opened a little more, shivers raced through her, little darts of sensation that made her mouth dry and heart race.

She'd never been undressed by anyone before. It was new and erotic and she didn't want it to be erotic. She wanted to think of Rocco as a partner, not a lover, but his touch stirred her senses and as her gown opened down the back, revealing bare skin she found herself wishing he'd touch her, slide a finger across her sensitive skin, caress the hollows of her lower back.

Her inner muscles clenched as he turned her sideways to work the last of the hooks that ran on the seam beneath the corset-like bodice. His fingers brushed the underside of her breast and she bit into her lip, feeling carnal and full of longing.

It had been so long since she'd been loved. It had been years since she'd been held and touched. If Rocco wanted to kiss her, she'd let him. If he wanted to take her to bed, she'd welcome the company. She hated feeling so much need, but standing half-naked in front of him had filled her with wants and needs that felt almost overwhelming.

The bodice of her gown slid down to her hips, and then Rocco's hands were at her hips helping to ease the gown over her bottom, sliding it down until the pale pink gown pooled at her feet.

She turned to face him, her hands covering her breasts, her eyes meeting his.

His gaze traveled over her, from her dark hair over her covered breasts to her rounded hips and the delicate pink scrap of satin that was her thong.

"You're beautiful," he said, his deep voice pitched low, the husky timber reverberating in her.

"I want you," he added, reaching out to capture a curled tendril that rested on her collarbone, the warmth of his fingers setting her skin on fire, "but I can't make love to you tonight, and I won't make love to you until you're comfortable being…mine."

"I am," she said faintly, face hot.

He put his hand on her waist, stroked her side, and her gently rounded hip. It was, oh, so delicious, she thought, and so seductive. Clare swayed a little as he plucked at the tiny thong, adjusting the pink fabric to better cover her. She sucked in a breath as her nerves screamed with pleasure. He was toying with her, she thought, and her body loved it. He ran his palm over her bottom, cupping the full cheek, caressing on one side, and then the other before taking his hand away.

"You're not," he said, looking up into her face. "You can hardly look at me. One day when you're ready, we will make love, but not until then."

Disappointment rushed through her as he rose and stepped around her. She felt silly and naked, and rather rejected. "Lots of people have sex on the first date. This isn't even a first date. We're married—"

"And I don't want to have sex with you. I want more than that. I want it, when we come together, to mean something." He tipped her chin up and looked deeply into her eyes. "Trust me, we will be glad we waited—"

"I doubt it," she interrupted, cheeks hot, knees locking, her innermost core clenching. "I think you just enjoy having all the control!"

He drew her into his arms and kissed her then, a hot fierce kiss of possession that stole her breath and fogged her brain. She couldn't think of anything but him, her senses overcome, her bare body pressed to his frame. He was so warm and his arms wrapped around her, drawing her closer, his hands cupping her butt, and lifting her up against him so that she felt the length of his erection through the trousers, his body hard against her pelvis. His body so much muscle and power.

By the time he let her go, she didn't know where she was, only that everything within her was hot and molten. She couldn't bear for him to leave her like this, couldn't bear to be left so full of unanswered desire.

But then he brushed her cheek, the pad of his thumb stroking her swollen lower lip before heading to the door where he quietly wished her a good night and disappeared into the connecting dressing room, his door closing behind him.

Rocco took the longest, coldest shower of his life, and he emerged still hard, still throbbing, still so hungry for her.

She was beautiful, truly beautiful and the shape of her, and the softness of her skin, and the tiny little moans she made while he touched her nearly drove him mad. All he wanted was to be in her body, feeling her warmth and softness, giving her the pleasure and release they both knew she wanted. That he wanted, too, but his needs came second to hers. And he'd been waiting five years for her and now that she was his wife, he didn't just want her body, he wanted her heart.

Clare didn't understand this new marriage, or her new husband, who was as handsome and charming and de-voted as a new husband could be…except that he avoided touching her, and kept kisses to a minimum, mostly a light kiss good-night before they retired to their own rooms.

They didn't sleep together once that first week.

Rocco was attentive during the day, spending time with her and Adriano. He planned excursions for them, making the honeymoon feel like a holiday, one that fo-cused on Adriano, which she appreciated, but Clare wanted Rocco to focus on her.

Instead they enjoyed a private tour of the coliseum, Rocco arranging for them to enter an hour before it opened to the public so their tour was truly private, fo-cused on the interests of a young child, featuring tales of brave gladiators and wild beasts, a moveable stage, and how it would have looked filled with all the people.

Another day they visited the Trevi Fountain and the Spanish Stairs, this done under a very tight, discreet, security detail. There was also a trip to the mountains, where they did an easy hike in the regional park of the

Monti Simbruini, walking amongst the birch trees, keeping their eyes open for wildlife. Adriano was thrilled to spot a peregrine falcon, although he'd called it a hawk, and Rocco saw a fox peeking between ferns and rocks while Clare mostly saw gophers. They enjoyed a lunch at a guesthouse that had been booked for them. The service was attentive, and the meal was delicious. Clare had no reason to complain. Not with the guesthouse anyway.

Now, Rocco...he wasn't just puzzling, he was infuriating.

He was charming during the day, but he wasn't oblivious to her. She knew he watched her, and his focus was intense; his focus made her feel naked, breathless. He wanted her. She could feel how he desired her. But why then at night did he stay away?

Why kiss her good-night and then disappear, leaving her to go to bed alone?

She'd been alone for years now. She shouldn't mind, but she did.

Another day passed. Another day of a devoted husband being attentive to his new family. Another night where he slipped away from her after a sweet, chaste kiss and a pleasant good-night.

The chaste kiss made her rage, and she knew he felt her impatience. Annoyance. She knew because the energy between them just kept building, the energy humming strongly, the awareness so hot and sharp the air practically crackled with desire. And still Rocco left her.

Two weeks of marriage with no intimacy. No husband in her bed. No touch, no friction, no satisfaction.

Clare was beyond frustrated. She was ready for more from her husband, certainly more than conversation and little pecks good-night. The next time he kissed her good-night, she wouldn't let him walk away from her. She'd demand more. He owed her more. They were married, weren't they?

The next time was that very evening, after dinner, after drinks in his gorgeous library that also served as a media room with an enormous TV screen that came down, hiding a long wall of books. The surround sound system had been built into the antique shelves giving the old room new life and purpose. After Adriano had gone to bed they'd curled up on the leather sofa and watched a thriller, and it had been quite intense in places, resulting in Clare sitting ever closer to Rocco.

Even though they were both watching the film, and she was trying to concentrate on the plot, she was more aware of Rocco, and his arm behind her shoulder, his other hand on her thigh.

At first the hand on her thigh was nothing, but gradually his palm felt warmer, and she grew hotter, and she didn't know if she shifted, or his hand moved up, but his fingers were on the inside of her thigh and he wasn't doing anything, but the weight of his hand and the pressure made her wish he'd do something.

The movie finally ended and Rocco turned off the TV with a remote, and then pushed another button on the remote and the screen disappeared.

"Did you enjoy that?" he asked, turning to look at her.

"I did."

His hand, still between her thighs, moved up several inches. "You seemed distracted."

She met his silver gaze and it wasn't innocent. A knowing heat glowed in his eyes and his hand inched higher again, his fingers so close to the juncture of her thighs.

"It's hard to concentrate when your husband's hand is making you melt."

"You do feel hot," he agreed, his hand now against the seam of her leggings, right where she wanted him.

"I think you should kiss me," she said huskily.

"I've been thinking the same thing." Rocco lifted her up and settled her on his lap so that she was facing him. His lap was warm, and hard, and she could feel him through her thin leggings. She shuddered a little at the erotic pressure of his body against her.

His hands were on her hips, holding her firmly, fingers grazing her hipbones making her gasp at how sensitive he made her feel. His touch lit fire everywhere beneath her skin, and she tried not to wiggle because every little movement made his shaft rub her there where she had a million nerve endings. But then when his hands cupped her butt, holding her in such a way that she felt open, Clare whimpered. "I thought you were going to kiss me."

"Don't worry, I am. I just want to feel you first. You have such a beautiful shape, all curves and softness. I could sink into your softness."

"I wish you would," she answered.

He clasped her face, his mouth covering hers and he kissed her then, a deep, fierce, intoxicating kiss, a kiss of barely leashed hunger, a kiss that promised endless pleasure. She wanted endless pleasure. She wanted him with her and in her, wanted to be as close as possible. He held her hips to his, and as he kissed her, she could feel him grow harder, and harder, until they were both throbbing with need.

She wrapped her arms around his neck, pressing her breasts to his chest, craving friction and satisfaction.

When he broke off the kiss she was certain he was going to suggest going to his room, or hers and she wanted it, was ready for it, but instead he gazed down into her eyes. "I shouldn't have let this happen. I got carried away. I'm sorry."

She stiffened, caught off guard, the apology a blow to her chest, making her heart seize up and the air bottle in her lungs. She hated the apology, and found herself—unreasonably, perhaps—hating him.

How could he say such a thing when her mouth was still tender, the lower lip tingling, her body filled with shivery sensation? How could he apologize for any of it? "It was just a kiss," she said lowly, climbing off his lap and tugging on her tunic, covering her hips and bottom, adjusting the sleeves. "Nothing to apologize for," she added, looking anywhere but at him. "And certainly nothing to feel guilty about."

"I don't feel guilty. You're my wife." He reached for her hand, tugged her back so that she had to face him. His gaze was like molten silver, hot, so hot, but his expression as fierce, determined. "You're the one I'm trying to protect. I don't want *you* to feel guilty...later."

She tried to shake him off, but he wouldn't let go. "And you think I would."

"I know you would. You love him. Not me."

Clare flinched, stunned. So that's what this was about. Oh, wow. She hadn't expected that, but maybe she should have. Ironically, Clare certainly hadn't been thinking of Marius. She thought of him less and less lately, but she'd thought maybe it was a good thing, maybe it meant she was ready to move forward and live again.

"I married you," she said, hating the lump in her throat. "I chose to say yes. I chose to start a life with you."

"I worry I've rushed you."

Clare didn't love him, if that's what he wanted. She didn't know if she'd ever love him, but she was attracted to him and desired him. These past few nights she'd touched herself trying to be patient, but it was him she wanted, and the pleasure his powerful body promised. She wanted all of it—the discovery, the release, the comfort. "Many people fall in bed on the first date. We've been married for two weeks now and there have only been these little kisses, and that's fine for children, but we're adults, and married. Is there a reason I can't desire you?" she asked, chin lifting defiantly. "You are my husband. You are now mine."

The corner of his mouth tilted up slightly even as her words made his expression fiercer. He pulled her down onto the leather sofa and stretched out over her, his body trapping her on the couch. He kissed her deeply, possessively, his tongue tasting her, teasing her, a hand beneath her bottom, holding her to him.

This is what she'd wanted, this fire, this burn, hot wine in her veins, heat and need between her legs.

She thought she'd go mad with need. And in that moment, with him close, but not close enough, Clare thought she'd do—give—anything to have him in her, filling her, making her feel complete. Because she'd been empty and lonely, and she'd had enough. Enough chivalry.

Enough safety. Enough being smart and careful and good.

"I want you," she breathed against his mouth. "It's not him. It's you, only you."

His gaze locked with hers. Her heart pounded, thudding painfully in her chest.

"When you kiss me," she continued, "I know it's you kissing me. When you touch me, I know it's you touching me. I am not pretending you are someone else. I am not fantasizing about anyone else. I am with you, and only you."

He captured her hands and lifted them over her head, holding them captive in one hand even as he slid a thigh between hers, his knee where she was hot and wet. "When I see you," he rasped, his head bending to press a light kiss beneath her ear to the side of her neck. "I only see you. I only desire you."

He transferred her hands to one of his and allowed the other hand to slide down her body, from her breasts over her flat stomach to the hem of her tunic. He reached beneath the tunic to stroke up one thigh, and then down her thigh and then back up again, his touch slow, building the pleasure but also the torment. Finally he was at the elastic waistband of her leggings and he tugged it down on her hips, low, lower. With her tunic pushed up, and her leggings down, she was exposed, the only thing between her and his eyes her orange silk thong, which offered little coverage and even less protection.

He pressed his palm to the orange silk covering her mound, and when she shuddered, he lowered his head and kissed her there, through the damp silk.

She gasped, legs trembling. He was touching her now beneath the silk, ever so gently, fingers slipping through her curls to her very tender skin, and she nearly cried at the exquisite sensation. "You're wet," he said.

"You're a very good kisser."

"That's all from a kiss?"

"Do you want a medal, Rocco?"

He laughed softly, amused, and aroused. She heard it in the huskiness of his voice, and the gleam in his eyes. He was still lightly stroking, exploring, watching her face and she tried not to squirm, so difficult when she ached for him.

With his mouth on her, blowing on her through the silk, his hand was between her thighs, circling the tender inner lips, outlining the shape of her, making her gasp and tilt her hips trying to capture more. He gave her more, thrusting a finger inside her and she rocked against his hand to feel more pleasure.

The tip of his tongue was against her nub and his finger found a spot within her that craved pressure and friction. She panted as he plunged another finger into her, taking her, filling her, then retreating to do it again, slow and deep, while he sucked on her silk-covered clit, pleasure building, pressure everywhere, his mouth and tongue and teeth driving her over the edge. She wrestled her hands free and one hand pushed hard against his shoulder while the other tangled in his hair. Clare cried his name as she shattered, the intensity of the orgasm rippling through her, again and then again.

When she'd finally begun to recover and pull what was left of her blown mind together, she looked at Rocco who was watching her, and waiting for her to return to the present.

"That was...uh...um...amazing," she said, cheeks still hot and flushed.

"That was just the *cicchetti*," he murmured, cicchetti meaning small snack. "Wait until I give you everything."

Upstairs Rocco took her to his room, and she slept with him there, safe in the circle of his muscular arm, his broad chest against her back.

He woke her up in the night and made love to her slowly, thoroughly, and Clare didn't think she'd ever understood the power of sex until then. Of making love. It was so deeply satisfying that it wasn't just a physical act, but emotional, almost spiritual. With him in her, she felt whole, and at peace. Grateful, she wrapped her arms around his shoulders and held him tightly, loving the press of his hard chest to her breasts, his hips against hers, legs tangled. They'd become one, and she didn't want it to end. She wanted to feel this connected forever, and kissing him back, she gave herself up to him, and in doing so, Clare felt a shift within her, as though a lock had been turned and her chest opened, her heart freed.

For the first time since the wedding she thought—knew—she could be happy with him. That they could be happy together.

Maybe, maybe this was what was meant to be.

The next morning they breakfasted with Adriano and over breakfast Rocco asked Adriano what his favorite beach was.

Adriano thought and then answered. "I only know the beach at our villa." He thought for another moment. "But Castello di Palo has a beach, too."

"What about a beach with palm trees? And water so

warm you never want to get out of it?" Rocco's eyebrow rose. "And sand so soft it's like touching velvet?"

Adriano's eyes grew wide and he glanced at his mom, who was looking at Rocco with a little amusement and puzzlement. Where was Rocco going with this?

Rocco looked at her, creases at his eyes, the smile lines making him even more attractive. "Should we go somewhere? Have a proper honeymoon—taking Adriano, of course."

Clare hadn't felt deprived in any way. Going on a honeymoon hadn't even crossed her mind, not when they'd married for the sake of Adriano, but also, taking a holiday, going somewhere tropical and exotic...exposing Adriano to someplace new. Her pulse jumped. Excitement flooded her. "I'd love that," she answered. "When could we go?"

"How soon can you be ready?"

"An hour. Maybe two so I won't feel frantic."

"Take your time, but remember, you won't need too much. It's an island and we'll be living in swimsuits much of the time."

They left from the private executive airport outside Rome, traveling in one of Rocco's private jets which would be able to land on a shorter runway, which was the only runway on the island. Ava and Gio were coming, too, which made Clare feel better as she knew little about where they were going, but was also excited to just be surprised. For years she'd been in charge of everything, having to think of everything, responsible for every detail, worried that she might make a potentially tragic mistake. But Clare trusted Rocco. She knew he'd protect them and take care of them and she could let go and just breathe. And be.

They landed on a tiny island in the middle of turquoise water. Clare had held her breath as the pilots made the most of the short runway, coming to a quick but smooth stop. Beyond the window were palm trees and the sparkling ocean. Rocco had been holding Adriano on his lap for the descent and Adriano's gaze was fixed on the view. "Are we here, Zio?" he asked.

"We are here," Rocco said. "And it's going to be so warm outside. You'll think it's a little bit like heaven."

It was more than a little like heaven, Clare thought, as they transferred into little golf carts with Rocco at the wheel of one, and Gio and Ava and the luggage in the other. The drive was lined with trees and blooming shrubs, flowers she recognized from growing up in southern Florida—hibiscus, plumeria, orchids, jasmine and ginger. Close to the house tangerine cannas with dark green and purple leaves competed for attention with purple and pink bougainvillea. The house itself was a sprawling compound of cool white stucco walls and enormous glass windows and doors that could be opened all the way so that living flowed seamlessly between inside the house and outside.

Adriano ran through the house, all built on one level, and every room with breathtaking views. Furniture was low and welcoming, the fabric all neutrals so nothing competed with the vivid colors of paradise.

Rocco walked Adriano and Clare through the garden, on paths, and off, explaining to Adriano that he was not to go near a pool or fountain without an adult, and that if he wanted to go for a swim, he only had to ask and he'd be taken to the beach or the pool. He crouched down in front of the boy, hands on his shoulders. "Your mama loves you and we must not make her worry. When we love people, we take care of them, yes?"

Adriano nodded somberly. "*Sì*."

"Good." Rocco kissed his forehead then added, "Remember, family always takes care of each other, and you are a Cosentino."

Adriano looked even more serious and nodded again.

Rocco rose and they finished their tour of the gardens but Clare found herself replaying Rocco's words. *Family always takes care of each other.*

And they were family. Rocco and Clare and Adriano.

She'd become a Cosentino at last, even though it hadn't been the way any of them had expected, but Marius would approve. He'd be glad that Rocco was there with them, for them, glad that Rocco had stepped up when Clare and Adriano were on their own.

Making love with Rocco was better than good. It answered a need that she hadn't even known existed, healing the broken pieces of her. Rocco's body, crisscrossed with scars, echoed the scars she carried on her heart, scars she'd had since a child whose world had been upended when her parents had gone through a terrible divorce, and then her mother's death, followed by an exile to Europe where she wouldn't be in the way anymore. Rocco made love to her as if she were perfect and beautiful, and in his arms, she became almost perfect and beautiful. The hollow aching sensation in her was filling and fading. She slept better, she ate better, she felt better about everything, including the future.

Especially the future.

Before they made love, Clare had thought it would take them weeks to become comfortable with each other, that intimacy might feel awkward at times, and that they'd probably leave the heat of the bedroom in the bedroom and function like colleagues out of it.

She was wrong. Rocco was sensual and sexual night and day. She felt him even when they weren't in the same room and the connection was intense, and constant, the desire always there.

It was almost like being born again, born into this different body, born into this new life. Clare had never cared that much about sex. She'd enjoyed it, but it hadn't been earth-shattering, not in the way making love with Rocco was shattering. With Rocco it was such a fierce, physical coupling that afterward she felt raw and naked and, oh, so very vulnerable. But Rocco always held her, and reassured her that she was the most glorious thing in the world, and he made her believe it. Made her believe she was safe. She'd hired Gio to keep her and her son safe, but he was hired, he was paid to protect. Rocco vowed to protect her with his life.

And she knew he would.

In a matter of weeks she'd come to trust him in a way she'd never trusted anyone.

With Rocco she felt safe to explore her boundaries, safe to feel everything, and when something was too much, she could tell him and he never questioned her, or pressured her, or made her doubt herself in any way.

It was amazing how they'd married for Adriano and yet the marriage was proving to be her salvation. She would have never dreamed that Rocco could be so patient and good with her, or so loving and devoted to her. Time and again he went out of his way to please her, and pleasure her, and also give her space to process emotion her way.

With time, she could be happy with him. Very happy. As happy and content as if it had been a love match.

Everything on the island was easy; life was easy, the days relaxed. Neither Clare nor Rocco were at computers or taking phone calls. They'd both agreed to unplug from the world and put business on hold. It was a much-needed break, one that Rocco was grateful for as it gave him time to just relax and be with Clare and Adriano. Being with them, both of them, felt right, and normal. The three of them were a family, his family.

Rocco could see Marius in Adriano, but he could also see Clare. Adriano was very smart, as well as perceptive, and Rocco looked forward to their morning walk each day, going out after breakfast just the two of them to walk on the beach and see if they could find shells and look for fish swimming in the shallow water near the beach.

It was during this time that Rocco would tell Adriano about his father, Marius, and how good and loving he'd been, a friend to many, and a wonderful much loved younger brother. One day on their walk, as they bent over to look at a little crab digging down into the sand, Adriano asked if he would be a brother.

"Do you want to be a brother?" Rocco asked him.

"Yes," Adriano answered. "A brother like you. The big brother."

Rocco's chest squeezed, too aware that he had failed

his brother, that Adriano should aspire to more. Rocco knew he was no hero. "You want to be like your papa," Rocco said. "Your papa was the best man I knew."

Adriano began walking again. "But I want to be like you," he said after a minute. "My new papa." He glanced up at Rocco, eyes squinting against the sun. "Papa Rocco."

Nothing more was said, but later during dinner, Adriano called Rocco Papa during the meal and he heard Clare inhale, and saw her expression. She was surprised, but didn't seem angry. Curious more than anything.

"I am your *zio*," Rocco gently corrected.

"And my papa." Adriano gestured across the table. "Papa and Mama."

Rocco opened his mouth to protest, but Clare put a hand on his arm. "It's okay," she said softly. "You are his father now. It's why we married."

"I don't want him to forget his real father," Rocco answered as quietly, deeply conflicted because he loved Adriano and he'd raise Adriano as his son, but at the same time, the only reason Rocco was here was because Marius was gone.

Clare's gaze met his and held. "You are his real father now. No matter what happens, you have made a commitment to him. A commitment to us." Her hand was still on his arm, and she slid her fingers over the back of his wrist, to take his hand in hers. "I've searched my heart and I truly believe Marius wouldn't mind."

That evening as Clare lay in the circle of Rocco's arm, she thought about the conversation at dinner, both Rocco's reluctance to take Marius's place, as well as Adriano's eagerness to have his own papa. It was complicated but not, as they were all so comfortable and happy together.

Clare loved to watch Rocco and Adriano together. If they were walking a great distance, Rocco would swing Adriano onto his shoulders and carry him. Other times he'd walk holding Adriano's small hand. At the end of the day when Adriano was tired, Rocco would carry the child and Adriano would slump against Rocco's chest, sleepy and safe.

They looked like father and son, but of course she never forgot Marius, and she'd talk to him sometimes and thank him. She'd tell him they were doing well and that Adriano was happier than she'd ever known him.

Ever since Adriano's birth, she'd tried to be both mother and father to Adriano, and there were times she thought she was succeeding, but whenever she saw Rocco hug Adriano, or crouch down to talk to him, or help him with something whether it was big or small, she felt Adriano's gratitude, and could see how his big brown eyes would shine.

Adriano's happiness gave her peace. She'd struggled making the decision to marry, but she was glad she'd chosen to give Adriano a father, and not just any father, but Rocco Cosentino, a man of integrity and strength. Rocco was a family man and he'd spent his life putting others first, including Marius. Could there be a better role model for her young son?

They had one more week on the island and then they'd return to Italy. Clare and Rocco spent several evenings discussing which home should be the family home. Rocco suggested the seaside villa because it was outside the city and there was little noise and traffic, but Clare knew Rocco had an office, a large office, and unlike her, he went to the office daily whereas she worked remotely, meeting with staff when necessary, preferring to hold most meetings online.

"Don't you want to raise Adriano in the Cosentino family home? It's where you were raised, and where you raised Marius after your parents died." Clare curled her legs under her, very comfortable in the chair in the living room, the sliding glass doors open so they could enjoy the warm night.

"But it's not really a home," Rocco said after a moment, "not the way you think of a home. It's huge, and so formal. It's easy to feel lost in such a place. It's why I've taken up residence in just one small part of the palazzo. That way I don't have to deal with the rest of it."

"It is a palazzo, but it is also where generations of Cosentinos have lived. I think it's important for Adriano to know his past."

Rocco shrugged uneasily. "Sometimes we can live too much in the past. Sometimes what we need is a break with the past—"

"Rocco! What are you saying?" She turned to look at him more closely. "Your past has made you who you are. You should be proud of your family. You come from a very close, loving family. I envy those family ties, and that commitment to each other. I've never had that. It was one of the things that drew me to Marius. His love of family. His love for you."

Rocco's brow creased. "Sometimes I worry that you've put me on a pedestal. You shouldn't. Don't forget that I once was cold and harsh—"

She laughed, interrupting him, and left her chair to settle into his lap. She put an arm around his shoulder and kissed him lightly, but the moment their lips touched, it was fire, the kiss becoming hot and explosive. Rocco's hand slid under her blouse, under her lace bra to cup her breast, her nipple hardening against his palm. She gasped as he rubbed the tender nipple, her body instantly growing hot, her core tightening, body aching, wanting him, always wanting him.

"I don't recognize that man," she whispered against his mouth as Rocco caressed her, turning her on. He was always turning her on and then giving her pleasure.

Making her feel good, making her happy.

She couldn't imagine being happier.

He carried her into the bedroom and stripping her clothes off, he licked and sucked between her legs until she was panting and squirming, drawing out the pleasure as long as he could, and she felt like clay in Rocco's hands, she was his to love, his to pleasure, and he gave her such pleasure, bringing her to a climax so intense she cried out, shattering in the stars, becoming nothing more than diamond dust.

Later they made love slowly, and it was extraordinary the connection between them. If Clare hadn't known better she would have thought they were made for each other. They came together so well, and satisfied each other so completely, that she felt gratitude and love—

Love.

Clare froze, startled by the realization that yes, she was falling in love with him and no, this wasn't just a physical thing. She enjoyed making love with Rocco, but their relationship had become important to her; he'd become important. Rocco had found his way into her heart, and he'd taken up residence there.

She didn't know how he'd done it. Initially she hadn't wanted him, or needed him, but with time and patience and endless affection he'd melted her reserve and made her care. He'd made her love *him*.

CHAPTER EIGHT

THEY WERE BACK in Italy and they'd come to a compromise on where they'd live. During the week they'd be at the Cosentino palazzo and on weekends they'd go to her villa where they could relax.

It was a good compromise, Clare thought, and she was the one who'd thought of it. Rocco had been gratified that she'd want to move into his home, and to help her ease the transition, he'd had a suite prepared for her, one that would be fresh and bright with the latest in technology so she could accomplish everything she needed, or wanted, to do while at the palazzo.

The children's nursery was on one of the upper levels of the palazzo, far from the wing where Rocco and Clare were most comfortable, and without even needing to discuss it, Rocco created a comfortable bedroom and playroom for Adriano—airy, colorful rooms sandwiched between the master bedroom suite and Clare's new office suite.

Under Gio's direction, Rocco had also upgraded palazzo security, adding in cameras and sensors, as well as other essential changes Gio thought necessary. All in all, life in their small portion of the palazzo was comfortable, provided they weren't wandering through the rest of the enormous palazzo itself which had over thirty rooms all shrouded with sheets and covers to protect furniture, a vast ballroom with six Venetian chandeliers, and four hundred years of antiques and family portraits and mementos.

Rocco's personal style favored a clean, modern design so Clare understood why he found the palazzo repressive, but at the same time, she was fascinated by the Cosentinos' history, a history that wove together families and industries, making the Cosentinos powerful for hundreds of years.

Rocco rarely referenced the past, or any of his ancestors, focusing instead on the present and creating new memories for them. He was incredibly thoughtful, always trying to think of activities Adriano would enjoy, as well as romantic moments for just the two of them.

When Clare thought back to her first impressions of him, that he was hard and cold and unfeeling, she smiled, amused, because Rocco was warmth and passion, loyalty and devotion, and it amazed her now that she'd ever thought him so icy and harsh. And maybe Rocco could still be hard with the rest of the world, but he was impossibly gentle with her. He was nothing but thoughtful and patient, and kind. So kind. She and Adriano were lucky to have such a good man in their lives after all the grief and loss. She counted her blessings, aware that Rocco was a gift, a gift that she and Adriano loved without reservation.

Clare told him that night, in between slow, hot, intoxicating kisses. Adriano had been in bed for hours and she and Rocco had made love and then left their bed to get a snack from the kitchen, and they sat with their cheese and chocolate talking and talking and then he leaned

over and kissed her, and they returned to the bedroom
to continue there.

She didn't want to make love again without him knowing. She didn't want the pleasure to be just a physical
thing. He should know how she felt in her heart, in her
mind, in her body and soul. "I love you," she whispered,
lightly stroking his cheekbone, where he was scarred,
where he'd once hurt so much. "You are our knight in
shining armor, our hero and our heart."

He looked at her in the dim light of the bedroom and
his jaw worked. "I don't deserve that," he said unsteadily,
his deep voice a rumble.

"But you do," she said, kissing his lips, and then again.
"You have made us all so very happy. I am beyond grateful. I am yours forever."

I am yours forever.

The words stayed with Rocco, echoing in his head long
after Clare had fallen asleep in his arms. They were there
as he slept, mocking him in his dreams. They were there
as he woke, exhausted and tortured by guilt.

He wasn't who she thought he was.

He wasn't the hero or a knight in shining armor.

And because of the guilt, he couldn't tell her he loved
her, not because he didn't love her—my God, she was
his world—but because he knew he didn't deserve her.
He didn't deserve this perfect little family of his.

For the next week he was in a fog, tormented by the
truth and the realization that he'd deceived Clare in the
worst sort of way.

Every day he determined to come clean, but then at
night, when it was just them, he couldn't bring him-

self to speak, instead he just wanted her, to be with her, no words, just touch. He let his body tell her what he couldn't—that she was everything to him, and that he'd never loved anyone the way he loved her. He hadn't believed in love at first sight, but from the moment he laid eyes on her, he wanted her, needed her, loved her.

At night he made love to her as if it was their last night, a desperation filling him, as he filled her. He wanted to escape and forget, and as they made love, he could almost forget, but in the morning it all came back.

She didn't know the truth. He should have told her the truth before marrying her.

"What's wrong?" Clare asked at breakfast the next morning. She'd been watching him with a troubled expression for days and he knew she was concerned, but how did he tell her?

What did he say?

"It's nothing," he said, finishing his coffee and rising. He leaned over and kissed her. "I'll see you tonight."

She caught his hand, held it tightly. "You can talk to me, Rocco."

He squeezed her hand in his. "I know."

But as he drove to work he tried to figure out how he'd tell her what weighed so heavily on his conscience. How to tell her something that would hurt her, and potentially tear them apart?

Again that night, after dinner, while lying in bed, Clare stroked his arm lightly, gently. "I can feel your worry," she whispered, her own voice filled with dread. "If there is something you must tell me, please, just tell me. I hate to see you so troubled."

Rocco closed his eyes, his arms closing protectively

around her. He didn't want to hurt her. He didn't want to ruin what they had. They were all so happy together, the three of them, it was a good marriage, a deeply satisfying marriage.

But he'd married her under false pretenses.

He'd married her not for Adriano or even for her needs. He'd married her for himself.

Clare eventually slept, but he couldn't, his mind at war with himself. The easy thing would be to let the entire issue go. To pretend he'd been completely honorable in his intentions. To continue on as if he were a good, true, altruistic man. That would be an easy thing, and it would allow them to move forward happily, no bumps, no anger, no drama. But Rocco hated the guilt, and how it made his love feel mean and small.

How it took the beautiful world they'd created and made it dirty. Shameful.

The guilt was eating him alive, and the guilt threatened to destroy the future.

But how did he tell Clare that he'd had ulterior motives in marrying her? How did he say he'd been selfish and determined to make her his? That he'd always wanted her, even when she was engaged to Marius?

He couldn't do that. Only a fool would tell her such a thing. But he must be a fool because he was considering confronting Clare with the truth, all of it. Not because he believed it would make things better, but because he couldn't live with himself like this. He couldn't hide the truth from her. He wanted her. He'd always wanted her. And he couldn't imagine a time when he wouldn't want her, but if there were to be more children, those children should be conceived in love, and truth, and raised in truth, love and honesty. Integrity. Which is how a Cosentino was supposed to be.

Rocco resolved that after dinner, after Adriano was in bed, he'd tell her all of it, and he prayed she would be able to forgive him.

Clare sat at one end of the leather sofa in the library trying to process what Rocco was saying. She finally put a hand up to stop him. "You're not making sense. Please say that last part again."

Rocco's jaw tightened, his silver gaze shuttered. "Which part?" he gritted.

"The part where you said you struggled with Marius's and my relationship because you had feelings for me." She knotted her hands in her lap, her heart thudding hard. "At least, that's what it sounded like you said."

"That's exactly what I said."

"And you were cold to me because you were trying to remain indifferent to me?"

He nodded once.

Clare's heart hammered and she tried to remain calm, but she was shocked by his admission, shocked that he'd had such strong feelings for her all those years ago. "So the real reason you didn't want Marius to marry me wasn't that you didn't like me," she said after a moment, nails digging into her palms. "It was because you were jealous of him. You wanted me for...yourself."

Rocco's dark head inclined and, horrified, she felt her heart plummet.

What was happening? How could this be real? And if it was true, why was he telling her now? His honesty wasn't to be admired, the truth coming too late. It was all a lie. It was all a big game. She struggled to take it all in, but couldn't, her mind shying away from the facts he'd so calmly laid out, like playing cards onto a table.

"So this was never about Adriano," she whispered, feeling physically ill. "This wasn't about Adriano in any way. It was just your weird possessive need to have me."

Rocco didn't speak and Clare felt her heart break. This couldn't be happening. This couldn't be real.

"I trusted you," she whispered, unable to look at him, unable to let him see how much he'd hurt her, crushing her dreams, smashing her love and faith in him. Their relationship was still so new, but it had been beautiful, and so full of light and warmth, happiness and hope, and now it was all gone.

"I beg your forgiveness. I am determined to earn your trust again," he said.

"No." She rose and, shaking her head, looked at him and then away, too stunned, too much in pain. "No more words. No more anything. I need to be alone. I can't think with you here."

Clare fled to a distant wing of the palazzo, pacing the long sculpture gallery where the walls were lined with framed canvases by centuries of Italy's greatest artists. It was cold in the gallery, but she walked quickly, feeling trapped and panicked. Her pulse was racing and her hands were shaking and she felt on the verge of losing the last shred of control.

She'd come to the gallery because she couldn't go to her bedroom, not when she shared it with Rocco. She couldn't go anywhere close to the nursery because she couldn't let Ava see her, and certainly not Adriano. She had to protect him from the upheaval. He was so young and so trusting. He needed protection, protection from people—men—who lied and deceived, men who had to win at all costs.

She knew about those men. She'd been raised by one. Her father always had to win, and he'd do whatever it took to have the upper hand.

And to think she'd married one!

Legs trembling, Clare turned at the end of the long gallery and passed pedestals with marble busts, walking between tall marble statues. She was chilled through, and yet fire raged within her, fire burning her heart while on the outside she shivered, teeth chattering.

He'd betrayed her. He'd used Adriano to get to her. Rocco used a child, *her* child—

"Whatever you're doing, whatever you're thinking isn't helping." Rocco's low hard voice came from the end of the gallery. "Stop, please. You're making it worse."

"I'm making this worse?" she choked, anger lashing through her as she spun to face him. "How dare you? How dare you turn this around! My anger isn't about what I did. This is about you, and what you did."

"I didn't want to love you. I didn't want to want you—"

"You were a man, not a prepubescent boy."

"Agreed. *Cara*, I was confounded by my attraction. I am a disciplined man and you were not mine. I shouldn't have been drawn to you. I shouldn't have wanted you, but I did. Don't think I liked feeling that way about you. I tried to create a wall so that I could be detached, but in creating a wall, and creating detachment, Marius took offense. He didn't understand why I couldn't be near you, he couldn't understand why I wasn't more receptive of you, and I couldn't tell him that I was jealous. That I

wanted his woman. What kind of brother is so disloyal?
I hated myself, and in trying to contain my feelings—"

"You hated me."

"No," Rocco's voice dropped, low, full of pain. "I never
hated you. It was Marius I was upset with, Marius for
being so lucky to have not just a woman like you, but you."

"That's even worse. Marius was so loving and accepting. He thought you were the greatest man alive. Did he
know how you felt about me?"

"No."

"Thank God," she choked. "At least he never knew the
truth about you. At least he died thinking you were still
the wonderful Rocco Cosentino."

"I loved my brother, and I would have protected him
with my life—"

"You're sure you didn't spook the horse that day? Or
perhaps you wished him dead?"

"Never." Rocco nearly roared the word. "Never, ever.
I loved him his entire life, and protected him with my
life, and his death made me hate myself."

"Good."

Her voice was pitched low, but she knew Rocco heard
her. His head lifted and his silver gaze met hers. Clare
knew she was being cruel, but in that moment she didn't
care. Everything she'd believed was a lie. Everything
she'd come to love was false.

Clare sank onto a small upholstered bench, legs no
longer able to support her.

"I married you out of love," Rocco said, walking toward her.

She turned her face away from him. "And Adriano?
What of him? Or does he not factor in any of this?"

"I love him as my son."

"I don't believe you," she said under her breath, pain and grief washing through her in unrelenting waves.

"I am his father now—"

"No!" She jumped up to stand in front of him, eyes blazing and hands fisted. "You are not his father. Marius was his father. You are…you are…nothing to us."

Rocco gave her the bedroom since she didn't want him there. He slept in the library and spent much of the night watching the fire burn down to a soft red glow. The library grew cold and all was quiet, but there would be no sleeping tonight, not when he felt as if someone had just died. He couldn't lose Clare. She was his world, his heart—

The library door opened and she was there, in a robe, and a blanket over that. "I'm so mad at you," she said from the doorway. "I'm so sad, too. You've ruined everything. It will never be the same."

"Clare, please, come sit down."

"I can't. I can't be near you."

"*Cara*, I know you're hurt—"

"Hurt? Rocco, this isn't hurt. You've destroyed us. You've taken our lives and destroyed us."

"That wasn't my intention."

"What did you expect to happen?" She took a step into the room, her body swallowed by the shadows.

"I don't know," he admitted.

She was shivering as she walked toward him again. "Why tell me in the first place? What did you want from me? Forgiveness? Absolution? But I'm not someone who can absolve you of your sins! I'm not saintly and pious.

I'm not going to just shrug and not care, because I'm livid, Rocco. I'm disgusted and filled with so much resentment, and regret. You are not the man I thought I married."

It hurt to breathe. It hurt to hear the pain in her voice. He'd broken her trust and that was a terrible thing to do. "I understand," he said.

"Do you?" she whispered, voice cracking.

He didn't answer immediately. "Yes. I do."

She said nothing, but he heard her exhale. She was crying.

"I'm sorry, Clare."

"You're sorry?" Her voice rose, high and thin. "Is that all you have to say?"

"I don't want to make excuses, Clare. I can't pretend to be the hero anymore. I'm not a hero—"

"So true. You're the antithesis of the hero. You're a pretender. Fake, false, manipulative. You coerced me into marriage. You played the family card, the let's-do-the-best-thing-for-Marius's-son card, knowing I didn't want to marry you, knowing I'd never marry you—"

"You wanted me, too."

"Not like this! Never like this."

Her voice cracked again. She was falling apart, sobbing, broken. He'd done this to her. He'd created this pain and he'd do anything to take it away, make things better. Make things right. "Forgive me, Clare."

"I can't."

"Maybe not now—"

"Never." She was crying so hard she hiccupped. "Did you think I would?"

"I'd hoped."

"Then you're a fool!"

He said nothing and his silence pushed her over the edge.

"Why?" she cried, leaning against a bookcase. "Why couldn't you let me be happy?"

"I wanted you to know the truth—"

"We were doing well. We were happy. Rocco, for God's sake, I was so happy with you. I loved being your wife. I thought finally it's my turn for love and security, and now this? I can't believe you had to do this. I can't believe you felt it necessary to tell me this terrible history between you and your brother."

He didn't know what to say. He wished he had a good answer. He wished he understood himself. Because she was asking all the right questions. But they were questions he didn't have an answer for. Why did he have to do this? Why when she was happy?

And just like that he knew.

Because he didn't trust happiness. And he didn't trust himself.

He didn't feel like a good person and he needed her to love him for who he was, complex and complicated, lonely and confused, hopeful and afraid. He needed her love, and needed her to love him despite the stupid, selfish things he'd done.

Standing there, facing her, he realized that his hope was irrational. One didn't just vomit out one's sins—the crimes committed—and expect forgiveness. As she'd said, she wasn't a priest, she couldn't absolve him. And yet somehow he thought, hoped, she could forgive him. And still love him.

He needed her love.

He needed her.

He needed someone to know him, and accept him,

flaws and all. Someone who'd say, *You're not a monster, Rocco.*

But obviously he was. She was horrified and her disgust made him feel such shame.

He didn't want to be a monster. He didn't want to be the bad brother anymore. He loved her, and he loved Adriano, and he wanted to be a husband and father more than he'd ever wanted anything.

In his desire to have complete honesty, he broke her trust. In his desire to build a strong relationship, he'd destroyed the one they'd had.

He'd messed it all up. He destroyed her love. The truth had destroyed the love.

"I am sorry," he said quietly, so quietly because if he'd spoken any louder his voice would crack and his pain would seep out, and he couldn't embarrass himself further. He'd laid himself bare and he'd failed her...and Adriano. Adriano did not deserve any of this, either.

Clare leaned against the bookshelf, head bowed, and the heavy silence filled the dark library, weighting it. After long, painful minutes she exhaled. "I am, too," she whispered, before walking out of the room.

Clare was in a hell of her own making. She'd agreed to marry Rocco for her son's sake. That was why she'd married him. That had been the chief motivating factor. Otherwise, she wouldn't have married. She had no need to marry, but once married to Rocco, she'd discovered how much she liked being married. How much she liked being his wife. How much she craved his touch.

She had enjoyed everything about their marriage—the companionship, the conversations, the meals together, the time spent with Adriano, and of course, the lovemaking. The lovemaking was unlike anything she'd known, and it made her feel young and alive, beautiful and vital. She'd been happy, so happy with him. But everything she thought was a lie built on a lie.

He'd married her under false pretenses.

He had not married her with Adriano's best interests at heart. He'd married her to have her, as if she was a possession to be won. Claimed.

The betrayal was sickening. The betrayal changed everything. How could she look at Rocco and see him as she'd seen him before? He wasn't the same person now. He wasn't honest. He wasn't a man she could admire, much less a man she trusted around her child.

There was no way to move forward with Rocco. She couldn't imagine ever looking at him without seeing his selfishness. The ugliness. The absolute lack of morals and character.

There could be no future.

Rocco wasn't the right person. Not for her, and not for him. He wasn't who she'd thought he was. He'd deceived them all, but it was over. She was done.

Rocco woke early, but not early enough. Clare and Adriano were gone. He'd known she'd want him to leave, or maybe even ask him to leave, but he hadn't thought it would happen in the middle of the night. He'd thought there would be more time. He'd thought there might be another conversation. He was wrong, so wrong about so many things.

His staff treated him as they always did—with respect and formality. There was no unnecessary conversation.

He was presented with his coffee and his newspaper. He had a second espresso later with a roll. He didn't touch either.

He didn't ask his staff for information about when Clare left, or why no one had alerted him because it served no point. The fact was, she'd gone and they knew. But did they know it was his fault? Did they know he'd brought the destruction on himself?

A brief email arrived in his inbox when he was at work.

I will be initiating a legal separation until we can begin the divorce. You are to stay away from us. I do not wish to hear from you, and you are not to contact me, or Adriano. I have instructed Gio to enforce no communication—no mail, no calls, no appearances. If you ever cared for me, you will respect my wishes. Clare

The weeks passed, and then a month, and another without another word from Clare. There was no communication, not at Christmas, or in the new year.

Christmas in the palazzo was so miserable that he realized he was done with the mausoleum of a place, and done with Rome, too. Not just temporarily, but permanently. He had grown up in this huge, sprawling marble edifice and he'd done his best to make it comfortable for Marius, but there was no reason to try to be comfortable, or happy there any longer. He was tired of taking care of it, tired of being trapped by it.

As he returned to the house from his office it crossed his mind that there was no reason to keep it. He didn't have to. So what if it had been in the family for centuries? So what if he was its custodian? He didn't like being responsible for a place that he didn't enjoy. Which led to another question—what did he enjoy? Where did he enjoy being? Because if Rome wasn't to be his home anymore, where did he want to be?

Where could he go when he didn't feel as if he belonged anywhere anymore?

CHAPTER NINE

As the months passed Clare grew even more unhappy. She was miserable. Beyond miserable.

She could barely drag herself from bed to her desk at her villa. She faked it, of course, for Adriano's sake, who didn't understand what was happening but was young enough to believe it was all temporary, and in his mind Papa Rocco was just "traveling."

But Clare leaned on Ava more than ever, needing Ava to keep Adriano busy. From her office window Clare could see them on the lawn playing soccer. Gio even joined in a game now and then. Clare was glad Adriano was protected from the pain she was feeling, because Clare struggled to function. Dressing was a chore, eating was the most unpleasant activity she could do. She lived on coffee and now and then a bite of something, but every time she tried to chew, food stuck in her throat and it was painful to swallow.

She'd cried so much she despised herself, and the sadness was all-pervasive. Her body ached, her chest so tight and heavy that it was as if she'd swallowed an enormous stone. The grief she'd felt when Marius died was one thing, but this was different, this was, this was a pain she had not asked for or needed, a pain that stemmed from betrayal and heartbreak. Marius's funeral had brought a terrible closure to their life and relationship, a devastating end to all those dreams they'd shared with each other. But now, Clare felt utterly lost, her heart and body no longer her own because Rocco wasn't dead, he was just somewhere else, and that…that seemed unforgiveable. She didn't want anything bad to happen to him— she did care for him, even if she wished she didn't—but he was too alive in her mind, too present in her heart. If she closed her eyes she could picture Rocco at the lake villa, could see him in his car, could imagine him at work, and in every image he was so alive, while she was here, hurting. Suffering.

She'd grown to hope they'd have a long life together, a good life, one filled with warmth and happiness. She thought she'd finally found happiness again. She thought, she thought… Oh, everything she thought was wrong.

It wasn't fair! None of this was fair. If only she hadn't given him a chance, if only she'd refused his proposal. If only she didn't miss him so much.

Tidying her desk one day she uncovered a creased slip of paper with a scrawl of words:

I will love you to the end of time. R

Clare froze, feeling as if she'd been dropped in a volcano, consumed by lava. She flashed back to the weekend following their honeymoon when he'd presented her with the gift of a delicate pink diamond bracelet, and in the bottom of the jeweler's box was this note on a scrap of paper.

I will love you to the end of time.

Trembling, Clare crumpled the letter and threw it in the fire, and then sobbed as it burned.

She cried for the future they weren't going to have. She cried for the weeks of happiness she'd known. She cried for Adriano who would never know his family because she was done with Rocco, done with all Cosentinos, done with Italy.

Clare owned a small island in Greece, it was tiny and rocky with a little cove for a boat, and a few gnarled olive trees at the back. She took Adriano there, along with her immediate staff. Adriano had never been to the island and he wasn't sure he wanted to be there. It was still winter, early February and bitterly cold and windy. The stone house felt chilly even with the furnace on, and the wind rattled the old glass windows night and day despite the wood shutters.

Adriano begged to return to the villa and the lawn where he could play soccer. He wanted to go to Roma and see Papa Rocco. He was so angry that Papa Rocco had forgotten them. Clare bit her tongue, holding back the truth. Adriano was too young, he was sweet and bright and full of light and love. He didn't need to know how manipulative men could be.

By mid-March Clare was desperate to return to Italy, too. She knew why she'd never spent much time on her little Greek island. It was only an oasis in summer, and in the peak of summer it felt too hot.

No, the island was not idyllic and not a good place to recover from a broken heart.

Clare wished she hadn't burned the note Rocco had given her with the bracelet. The note where he said he loved her. She knew she couldn't trust him, but the note was one of the few things with his writing, and she wished she had something of his to keep. Just a memory.

And yet keeping love notes wouldn't help her get over him. Because she wasn't over him yet.

But she would be, eventually. She had to remain firm. His words were pretty, but his idea of love wasn't hers. Love wasn't manipulative, love wasn't dishonest, love didn't deceive.

The wind in April was even stronger than the March wind. The wind blew through the old house, rattling and whistling, and while it wasn't as cold as it had been in February, it was far from cozy and the wind kept knocking out the electricity, and it was one thing to go without internet for a few days, but another to have no power at all.

Easter week they left Greece and returned to their villa in Italy. Adriano was overjoyed, and after arriving at the estate, he rolled on the lawn, and then dashed down the stairs to the beach, running through the waves, the saltwater soaking his rolled-up jeans.

Clare stood on the beach watching her son, a fist pressed to her mouth, feeling her worlds collide. He looked like his father, but also his uncle, with his dark hair and eyes, and his sturdy athletic little frame. He wasn't a shy child, and he handled change as well as anyone, but he was smart, sweet and so loving.

He hadn't stopped asking for Rocco, either.

But one day he would. It would just take time.

Adriano was sure Rocco would return for his third birthday. Clare tried to discourage Adriano for believing such a thing because there had been no contact, no calls, nothing at all. As an only child with no cousins and no friends, it was hard to have a proper party, but Clare organized for a colorful tent to be set up in the yard, and a pony for pony rides. She hired a magician and a man with lizards and snakes—so many snakes—and she shuddered as the snakes were brought out, one by one, but Adriano wasn't afraid and wanted to handle them. She watched, heart in her mouth, as a boa wrapped around him, coil after coil, and nodded at Gio when she couldn't bear it any longer.

The chef made Adriano's favorite pasta and pizza, and there was cake and gelato for dessert. Clare had gifts for him, his first bike along with a new football. Some of the staff had small gifts, as well. Adriano seemed happy and as Clare tucked him into bed that night he gave her a fierce hug and thanked her for his birthday party.

"You are so welcome, my love," she answered, leaning over to kiss his forehead and then the tip of his nose. "How is it you are three already?"

He nodded somberly. "I know. I'm old now."

She laughed and then tears started to her eyes. She couldn't bear to admit it, but she'd also half expected Rocco to show today. The fact that he didn't come hurt nearly as bad as the day she left him. She knew she'd told him to stay away, but surely he might have come just to wish Adriano happy birthday?

The fact that he hadn't come, the fact that he'd given them up, the fact that he hadn't fought for them spoke volumes.

She'd hoped...needed—no, she couldn't keep wishing. It was over. The past was over. It was time to move forward with the divorce.

She'd held off from filing for divorce for reasons she couldn't explain, but it was time. Rocco had been gone for months. She'd felt numb for months. Where had all the happiness gone? What had happened to all those beautiful dreams?

She kissed Adriano again and then left him snug in his bed. She was fighting tears as she exited his room, and gave Ava a watery smile as she passed her. Clare didn't want to cry. Crying solved nothing.

In her bedroom she lay down on her bed and pressed her pillow to her cheek. Tears streaked down her face and worn out, she let them fall.

Marius's death was a freak accident, but Rocco wasn't dead. Rocco was alive and doing his thing, living his best life in Rome. So why didn't he make an appearance today for Adriano's birthday? Why didn't he call? Why abandon Adriano?

And then the littlest voice whispered inside her head, *Why abandon me?*

For the first time since that terrible day at the palazzo, Clare hated that they weren't raising Adriano together, and wondered why they couldn't raise him together.

Why couldn't they have managed to be mature adults and do what was best for Adriano? It's why they'd married—to take care of him. But they were failing him. They weren't doing their best for him, or by him.

For the first time in months, Clare didn't block out Rocco. She didn't want to pretend he was gone. Dead. He wasn't dead.

She was so tired of feeling heartsick, so tired of the anger and pain, the grief and disbelief. Why couldn't they come together on special occasions and celebrate Adriano's milestones? Why couldn't they try to be good parents...a loving family?

Clare suddenly wanted to speak with him. Worse, she

missed him. She missed his scars and his broken parts, his fierceness and his passionate heart. Rocco wasn't perfect, but he loved her…and she wasn't over him, and she didn't know if she could ever forgive him, but at the same time, she couldn't forget him.

It was so confusing, so consuming. She didn't want to love him anymore, but she did. She wanted to let go of the anger and be civil with him, have a civil relationship for Adriano's sake. If it was possible. Could it be possible?

Perhaps seeing Rocco would give her answers. Maybe a conversation would provide some closure, at least romantically. There had been no closure with Marius. One moment he was there, and the next he was gone. But Rocco…she should talk to him and try to come to an understanding which would allow Adriano to be loved by both of them instead of being in the middle. He shouldn't be in the middle.

Clare pushed the notification on her phone, alerting Gio she needed him. It wasn't the panic alert, but the alert requesting his presence.

Gio was at her door in minutes. Clare welcomed him into her living room. "I need your help," she said. "Can you find out something for me?"

"Of course."

"I want you to drive me to the city tomorrow, but I'm not sure if Rocco will be at his office or at his home. Could you find out where he'll be and take me to him, please?"

Gio hesitated. "He's not in Rome. He closed his offices in Rome months ago."

She frowned. "And the house? The palazzo?"

"Apparently he sold it. Close to two months ago."

She dropped onto the edge of her couch. "The Cosentino home?"

"Yes. I heard about it through one of our staff. I checked into the story, wondering about the facts, and it seems they are true. The house was quietly sold to a private investor. Work is being done on the palazzo now. Some think it's to be turned into a luxury hotel."

Clare shuddered. She'd bought private homes that had been turned into resorts, but she'd never taken a private historic home and created a commercial property from it. "I don't understand why he would sell his home. It doesn't make sense. It was one day going to belong to Adriano. He said Adriano was the heir, and he was to inherit."

"I believe, if I am correct, you told him to set you and Adriano free. I believe by selling the Cosentino palazzo he was doing just this—releasing you and Adriano from your ties and responsibilities to the Cosentino family." Gio looked at her and waited, and after a minute had passed and there was only her silence, he excused himself.

Clare heard the door shut behind him, but she couldn't make herself move. She was shocked, and horrified. Rocco had let the palazzo go? He'd left Rome entirely?

What in God's name had Rocco done?

The week dragged by and May turned into June. Clare was tired of work, tired of the long nights, tired of trying to pretend she wasn't missing Rocco, because she was missing him, even more if such a thing was possible.

During the day she could stay busy and distract herself with calls and meetings, discussing possible acquisitions, and then there was time with Adriano, and that was by far her favorite part of the day. She'd begun to let him stay up a little later just so they had more time together. But of course he eventually went to bed and it was during the long, quiet nights that Clare couldn't escape herself, or her heartache.

Where had Rocco gone? What was he doing now? Did he ever think of her...of them?

One evening, exhausted, she wept into her pillow, the gorgeous pink diamond bracelet clutched tightly in her fist.

It took her a moment to realize Adriano was with her. "Mama, why are you crying?"

Clare sat up quickly, and setting the bracelet on the nightstand scrubbed her face dry. "I'm not," she said, forcing a watery smile. "What are you doing out of bed?"

"I couldn't sleep. I'm hungry."

"Didn't you eat enough dinner?" she asked, holding a hand out to him.

He climbed up onto her bed and settled into the crook of her arm. "I didn't like it. I don't like fish when it's all mushy."

"I didn't think it was mushy," she said, remembering that she'd had dinner at her desk tonight because of a late night meeting with the vineyard staff in California. "But it is a soft fish."

"No more fish."

"Fish is good for us."

"Pizza is good for us," he answered.

She laughed, and kissed his head. "You like other foods besides pizza. Gnocchi. Ravioli. Spaghetti."

"Gelato. I love gelato."

She felt some of the heaviness in her chest ease. "I like gelato, too."

Adriano snuggled against her, his hand finding hers, fingers lacing tightly. For several minutes they just sat together comforting each other. "Mama?"

"Yes, my love?"

"Where's Papa Rocco?"

The pain returned with a vengeance, so sharp it felt like a knife between her ribs. "He's traveling—"

"Still?"

"He works a lot. He owns many businesses and they all need to see him and speak to him."

"Like you have to do?"

"Yes," she answered, "but I don't travel as much. I prefer working from here. That way I can be with you every day."

Adriano thought about this. "He should do that, too. Work here, so he could see us."

She said nothing. What could she say?

"Or does he not want to see us?" he asked, turning to look up at her, shadows in his beautiful brown eyes. "Does he not want us anymore?"

"He will always love you," she said, hoping the answer would appease him.

Adriano fidgeted. "We should go see him. Go to the palazzo. Maybe he forgot about us. Maybe—"

"He's not in Rome anymore."

"No?"

Clare shook her head. "I'm not sure where he is, maybe Argentina, to take care of your father—" she broke off, bit her lip. "The grapes and the house in Mendoza. You have land and beautiful estates waiting for you there, and vineyards and horses. Remember, you are not just Italian, you are also Argentinian."

"And American," he said. "You are American, remember?"

Clare smiled even as her eyes burned, gritty with tears. Her clever, beautiful boy. "How could I forget?"

She'd found him.

Or more correctly, Gio had found him, and Clare had been wrong. Rocco was not in Argentina but in the Caribbean, on his island.

She made arrangements to travel the next day, leaving Adriano with Ava and Gio at the villa, knowing he'd be safe with them.

Clare packed lightly, and slept poorly, ready to go. She didn't know what she'd say to him once she saw him, but figured those words would come. For now, she just needed to get there.

The ten-hour flight felt endless. She struggled to relax, and when she couldn't nap, watched a movie on the plane's individual movie screen and when that and dinner were over, tried to work. She went through paperwork checking numbers and dates, and then did some reading on her laptop, but she couldn't stay focused, the words dancing around on the screen.

Would Rocco be glad to see her?

What would they say to each other?

It turned out to be easy, once she was in front of him. Anger filled her, anger that he'd promised to care for Adriano and then he'd so quickly abandoned him. "You missed Adriano's birthday," Clare said, voice low. "He turned three just a few weeks ago. May fourteenth—"

"I know. I was there. I came to the villa but was turned away."

She looked at him, astonished. "No one said anything to me."

"Your security is very good and very efficient. I'd hoped Gio would speak to you, but apparently your word is law."

She flinched, hating the sound of that, thinking it made her sound like her father, and he was the last person she wanted to be like. "I wish I'd known. He'd wanted to see you. Adriano asked about you all week and then—" she broke off swallowed, terribly remorseful. "He was disappointed, and I tried to make light of it, but I was wrong. It was a mistake. I've always sworn that I would put him first and I haven't put him first. I had married you so he could have a father, but then I pushed you away."

There was only silence and the silence was heavy and uncomfortable. After a long time Rocco spoke, "But if it is better for him…if Adriano is doing better without me—"

"He's not." Clare swallowed, deeply ashamed. "He has missed you and I thought by now the missing would have eased, that he might have stopped speaking of you so often but it hasn't happened."

She turned and looked across the room, at the place where they had been so happy back in October. The island had been such a lovely getaway for all of them. There had been few distractions, but they hadn't needed distractions. They had been happy just being together. "I've been selfish. Heady. It was one thing for me to tell you to go away, but it was another for me to make that decision so abruptly for Adriano. I'm not sure how to fix it, but I think something has to be done. Perhaps he could come here and see you, spend some time with you—"

"Without you?" Rocco asked.

Her forehead creased, pain splintering through her heart. "I don't know how to make this work. I don't know how to move forward. I don't know how to navigate this next part."

"You don't think you could forgive?"

His voice, those words, made her heart knot and ache. She was creating pain for him, and the fact that she was determined to stay angry at him baffled her. She didn't consider herself an angry person. She didn't like holding grudges. So why was she?

And then she remembered how he'd sold the Cosentino palazzo and had left Rome, and her anger burned again. "I understand you've sold the palazzo. Why?"

He said nothing and she took several steps toward him. "How could you, Rocco? Why would you? It was Adriano's heritage. It was the Cosentino family home. You could have at least discussed it with me not because I wanted it or needed it, but Adriano is the heir."

"How could I discuss anything with you?" he said quietly. "There has been no contact. Anything I've sent to you has been returned. Any call blocked."

She dropped onto a chair, stressed and exhausted and so confused. "Would you have talked to me about it?"

"Of course. You're my wife."

Not, you were my wife, but you are my wife.

Her eyes burned. "Why did you sell it then?"

"I don't think he should have to inherit a place, and be forced to care for it. The palazzo is huge and expensive, it's a constant financial drain, and it traps him to a place, it traps him to a history he might not want. I did this to protect him, to protect his future. Adriano deserves to choose his future. He should be able to have the life he wants, not the life he must inherit. The problem of being an heir, whether it's to a title, an estate or a legacy, is that you are locked into choices made long before you were ever conceived, choices that can be an unbearable burden."

"You found being a Cosentino a burden?"

"When Marius was alive, it wasn't a burden. The palazzo was expensive, there were always plumbing and electrical issues, there were ongoing repairs, and big gardens require tremendous care. But I didn't mind then because it was for Marius, because we shared a legacy, and we shared the past. Once he was gone…it was an anchor, and not a good one. I was a caretaker for these immense estates, a conservator for wealth that I'd never spend, and there was no purpose for it—"

"Adriano."

"I didn't know he existed then. I didn't realize there was another generation."

"But you do now, and you've sold the Cosentino palazzo!"

"One's life shouldn't be spent caring for things." He hesitated before adding, "It should be spent caring for people."

His words made her heart ache. She had never been included in her father's circle, she knew little about the people—or things—important to him.

For her, her legacy would be her son, and yes, Rocco was right. Adriano should have freedom to choose his path without being burdened with the relics of a past long gone.

Rocco had done Adriano a favor. She just hadn't understood it at the time.

"What if he should want it in the future?" she asked. "What if he should want that responsibility?"

"Then he will have an opportunity to have it back. The palazzo isn't exactly sold. It's only been leased, albeit, a twenty-year lease to the Italian government. They plan to use it as a museum to house art collections by Italy's twentieth-century artists. The gardens will be open to the public as well, so nothing will be destroyed, everything will be taken care of so should Adriano choose, at the age of twenty-three, to keep his home, the palazzo will be his. And should he want to sell it to the government, they have indicated they would like to own it. But it's up to him. The palazzo is his, held in the Cosentino trust, of which he is the beneficiary."

She didn't know what to say. She hadn't expected any of this. "So you didn't sell his birthright."

"It's not mine to dispose of. He is the future, but that means he chooses his future."

She studied his face, seeing the fatigue there. "You never had that choice, did you?"

He shrugged. "He is Marius's son. But I love him as if he were my own."

Clare blinked back tears, aware that for a time, Adriano was his. She rose, and paced, running a hand across her face, drying her eyes. "I've been so angry with you," she said, pacing back toward him, "for months now. I'm tired of it. I'm tired of feeling this way about someone I once loved."

She saw how he flinched at that and she hated that her words hurt him. She hadn't meant to inflict more pain now. It was time for change. Clare was tired of being angry, tired of grieving; life was too short for all this unhappiness.

"How are you?" she asked him. "Really?"

"Now that you are here, I am better," he answered. "And you? How are you, *cara*?"

She searched his lovely silver eyes so full of sorrow and shadows. "I am better," she whispered, "now that I am here."

"You haven't changed," he said after a moment, lips quirked. "You wouldn't come because you needed me, but you've come because Adriano did."

Clare bit into her lower lip, struggling with her answer. "We both need you," she said unsteadily. "And we both miss you."

Her eyes began to fill with tears and Rocco drew her down onto the white couch, and wrapped his arm around her, holding her close to his chest, and for a moment Clare was afraid to breathe, afraid to move in case this was a dream, but no, she could hear the steady beating of his heart, and the warmth of his skin, and the hard muscle of his chest.

This was real. He was real.

Gradually she relaxed, his warmth soothing her, his arm holding her secure and she wasn't going to think, or let her brain take over. For now, she would just savor being here with him.

It had been so long since she'd felt like things might be okay, and while she didn't know the future, in this moment, right now, in Rocco's arms, her cheek above his heart, she felt peace. She felt as if she was home. Rocco was home.

Her eyes stung and she blinked hard to hold in the emotion.

Love, she loved him, and it had been so hard to be away from him. And it came to her—how did one forgive? You forgave because you loved.

You forgave because you wanted more.

Clare desperately wanted more, not less. She desperately wanted to feel like she belonged somewhere and with someone. Rocco would always be home. Why had she taken so long to see it? Believe it?

Rocco kissed the top of her head. "Don't cry." His voice was low, husky, comforting.

She felt like Adriano when he came to her room late at night, unable to sleep, wanting to feel safe. Everyone needed love, everyone craved family and security. Everyone needed second chances and hope. Good God, she needed hope. The tears she'd been struggling to hold back fell.

"I don't want to lose you, too." Clare said thickly, finding it so hard to talk and breathe while crying. "I don't understand any of this, but I know we should at least talk. Try to have a conversation."

"I agree." He pulled her onto his lap so that both arms could hold her more firmly. "But I think we should have a conversation later when you're done with the tears. So cry now, and I promise you, we'll talk when you're ready."

They did talk later. They talked for hours; they talked and went for a walk, then talked again and kissed.

The kiss had surprised him because she'd been the one to reach out to him. She'd caught his face in her hands and studied it, looking deep into his eyes before whispering, "I do love you. And if you still love me, is there a future for us?"

"Yes." He kissed her, once and then again. "You are my future. You, and Adriano, are everything to me. But since you are here, let me show you just how much I've missed you and want you."

"I think that's a very good idea," she murmured, shivering as his lips brushed across her neck, and then lower, light kisses along her collarbone and then lower still.

He did show her how much he loved her. He showed her all night long.

Love is patient.

And true love forgives.

EPILOGUE

THE BEST MONTHS to visit the Caribbean were in the fall, between October and December, and as Rocco wanted the children to grow up with an American Thanksgiving, they began to go to their island late November, where they'd remain until mid-December, when they'd return to the seaside villa outside Rome.

Adriano was always thrilled to return to the island. Fortunately, so were his younger brothers and sister as each arrived, growing from infants to toddlers and from toddlers to proper playmates. Adriano was always very careful to teach them about the dangers of the ocean, as well as all the different fountains and pools.

One early December when Adriano was nine years old, Clare emerged from the house with arms filled with towels as they were all going to the pool for a swim. The children were waiting for her on the patio, but she could hear Adriano speaking quite sternly to his five-year-old brother, four-year-old sister and the two-year-old baby, Jaco, whom Adriano was holding by the hand.

"See this," Adriano said gesturing to the infinity pool that overlooked the ocean, "this is dangerous. You can drown, Jaco. If you fell in you'd die. So never, *ever* go near the pool or touch the water unless Mama and Papa are with you."

Hidden by the shadow of a potted tree, Clare bit her lip, fighting her smile, proud of her very responsible oldest son. Adriano was more like Rocco than any of the younger ones. Five-year-old Marcus was the wild one, constantly on the go. Four-year-old Daniela was a little timid but terribly loyal and sweet. While two-year-old Jaco was in awe of the older siblings.

Adriano wasn't just a good brother, but a good son, always aware of the dangers, and determined to protect his family. He didn't like risk. He thought carefully about potential problems, and never believed that one nanny should watch all the kids because something could still happen.

"But I can swim," Marcus said exasperated, annoyed that Adriano was once again giving a lecture. "I swim even better than you, Adriano."

Daniela made a gasping sound. "Adriano is a great swimmer. He is the best, Marcus, and he's the oldest."

Rocco emerged then from the house, joining Clare in the shadows of the tree. He saw her watching the children, and whispered, "Who are we spying on, and why?"

She looked up at him, smiling into his eyes, thinking he was far more gorgeous now than when they'd married. "We're spying on the children as Adriano is teaching about the dangers of the ocean…as well as all the pools and fountains."

Rocco arched a brow. "Again?"

She smothered a laugh. "But this time there's Jaco, and he must be taught, too. Adriano takes his job as the big brother very seriously."

"Very seriously," Rocco agreed, wrapping his arms around Clare, and holding her against him. "We're lucky."

"So lucky," she agreed, sighing softly as he kissed the side of her neck, and sighing again as his hands caressed the length of her before sliding up to cup her breasts. "This is how we end up pregnant," she said, a little breathless. "Don't you think four little Cosentinos might be enough?"

"Probably," he murmured, one of his hands slipping beneath her bikini top, palming her bare breast and the pert nipple. "But it's good to practice, just in case."

She was melting, just as she always did, and as his teeth scraped the side of her neck, Clare pressed her bottom against his hard body, loving him, loving the feel of him, loving the life they'd made together.

"We can practice tonight," she said, trying very hard to be quiet when he was setting her body on fire.

"Or maybe during nap time?"

"Or maybe both if you're good."

He pinched her nipple just hard enough for her to whimper and wiggle against him. "Oh, *cara*, my love, I am always good."

She laughed even as she sighed. "So true."

* * * * *

COMING SOON!

We really hope you enjoyed reading this book.
If you're looking for more romance
be sure to head to the shops when
new books are available on

Thursday 7th December

To see which titles are coming soon, please visit
millsandboon.co.uk/nextmonth

MILLS & BOON

MILLS & BOON®

Coming next month

AN HEIR MADE IN HAWAII
Emmy Grayson

A dull roaring drowned out the sounds around her. Each beat of her heart felt magnified, thundering inside her body as Anika stared at him.

'What?' she finally managed to gasp.

'You want me. I want you.'

'I never said I wanted you,' she sputtered.

Nicholas watched her, his fingers pressing more firmly against her back, his eyes glowing with that same predatory light she'd glimpsed on the catamaran.

'You also never said you didn't. So tell me now, Anika. Tell me you haven't thought about me kissing you. Tell me,' he continued, his husky voice washing over her and sending sinful shivers racing over her body, 'you didn't think about how we'd be together when you were in my arms on the boat. That you didn't imagine me tracing my fingers, my lips, over every inch of your incredible body.'

Say something!

But she couldn't. Not when her imagination was conjuring up carnal images of her and Nicholas entwined, arms wrapped around each other as he trailed his lips over her neck, her breasts, his hips pressing against hers without any barriers between them.

'Ah.' His smile deepened. 'So you have thought about it.'

Continue reading
AN HEIR MADE IN HAWAII
Emmy Grayson

Available next month
www.millsandboon.co.uk

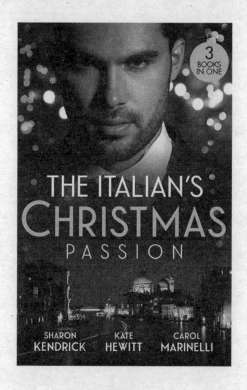

LET'S TALK

Romance

For exclusive extracts, competitions and special offers, find us online:

f MillsandBoon

🐦 @MillsandBoon

📷 @MillsandBoonUK

♪ @MillsandBoonUK

Get in touch on 01413 063 232

For all the latest titles coming soon, visit
millsandboon.co.uk/nextmonth